Jonathan Kellerman is one of the world's most popular authors. He has brought his expertise as a child psychologist to numerous bestselling tales of suspense (which have been translated into two dozen languages), including sixteen previous Alex Delaware novels; *The Butcher's Theatre*, a story of serial killing in Jerusalem; and *Billy Straight*, featuring Hollywood homicide detective Petra Connor. His most recent novel is *Flesh and Blood*. He is also the author of numerous essays, short stories, and scientific articles, two children's books, and three volumes of psychology, including *Savage Spawn: Reflections on Violent Children*. Kellerman has won the Samuel Goldwyn, Edgar Allan Poe and Anthony Boucher awards and has been nominated for a Shamus award. He and his wife, the novelist Faye Kellerman, have four children.

the murder book

jonathan kellerman

headline

First published in 2002
by HEADLINE BOOK PUBLISHING

First published in paperback in 2003
by HEADLINE BOOK PUBLISHING

A HEADLINE paperback

10 9 8 7 6 5 4 3 2 1

ISBN 0 7472 6501 1

Typeset in Plantin by
Letterpart Limited, Reigate, Surrey

Printed and bound in Great Britain by
Mackays of Chatham plc, Chatham, Kent

HEADLINE BOOK PUBLISHING
A division of Hodder Headline
338 Euston Road
London NW1 3BH

www.headline.co.uk
www.hodderheadline.com

To Faye

one

The day I got the murder book, I was still thinking about Paris. Red wine, bare trees, gray river, city of love. Everything that happened there. Now, this.

Robin and I flew in to Charles de Gaulle airport on a murky Monday in January. The trip had been my idea of a surprise. I'd pulled it together in one manic night, booking tickets on Air France and a room at a small hotel on the outskirts of the Eighth *arrondissement*, packing a suitcase for two, speeding the 125 freeway miles to San Diego. Showing up at Robin's room at the Del Coronado just before midnight with a dozen coral roses and a *voilà!* grin.

She came to the door wearing a white T-shirt and a hip-riding red sarong, auburn curls loose, chocolate eyes tired, no makeup. We embraced, then she pulled away and looked down at the suitcase. When I showed her the tickets, she turned her back and shielded me from her tears. Outside her window the night-black ocean rolled, but this was no holiday on the beach. She'd left L.A. because I'd lied to her and put myself in danger. Listening to her cry now, I wondered if the damage was irreparable.

1

I asked what was wrong. As if I had nothing to do with it.

She said, 'I'm just . . . surprised.'

We ordered room-service sandwiches, she closed the drapes, we made love.

'Paris,' she said, slipping into a hotel bathrobe. 'I can't believe you did all this.' She sat down, brushed her hair, then stood. Approached the bed, stood over me, touched me. She let the robe slither from her body, straddled me, shut her eyes, lowered a breast to my mouth. When she came the second time, she rolled away, went silent.

I played with her hair and, as she fell asleep, the corners of her mouth lifted. Mona Lisa smile. In a couple of days, we'd be queuing up as robotically as any other tourists, straining for a glimpse of the real thing.

She'd fled to San Diego because a high school chum lived there – a thrice-married oral surgeon named Debra Dyer, whose current love interest was a banker from Mexico City. ('So many white teeth, Alex!') Francisco had suggested a day of shlock-shopping in Tijuana followed by an indeterminate stay at a leased beach house in Cabo San Lucas. Robin, feeling like a fifth wheel, had begged off, and called me, asking if I'd join her.

She'd been nervous about it. Apologizing for abandoning me. I didn't see it that way, at all. Figured her for the injured party.

I'd gotten myself in a bad situation because of poor planning. Blood had spilled and someone had died. Rationalizing the whole thing wasn't that tough: innocent lives had been at stake, the good guys had won, I'd ended up on my feet. But as Robin roared away in her truck, I faced the truth:

2

My misadventures had little to do with noble intentions, lots to do with a personality flaw.

A long time ago, I'd chosen clinical psychology, the most sedentary of professions, telling myself that healing emotional wounds was how I wanted to spend the rest of my life. But it had been years since I'd conducted any long-term therapy. Not because, as I'd once let myself believe, I'd burned out on human misery. I had no problem with misery. My other life force-fed me *gobs* of misery.

The truth was cold: once upon a time I *had* been drawn to the humanity and the challenge of the talking cure, but sitting in the office, dividing hour after hour by three quarters, ingesting other people's problems, had come to *bore* me.

In a sense, becoming a therapist had been a strange choice. I'd been a wild boy – poor sleeper, restless, overactive, high pain threshold, inclined to risk-taking and injuries. I quieted down a bit when I discovered books but found the classroom a jail and raced through school in order to escape. After graduating high school at sixteen, I bought an old car with summer-job cash, ignored my mother's tears and my father's scowling vote of no-confidence, and left the plains of Missouri. Ostensibly for college, but really for the threat and promise of California.

Molting like a snake. Needing something *new*.

Novelty had always been my drug. I craved insomnia and menace punctuated by long stretches of solitude, puzzles that hurt my head, infusions of bad company and the delicious repellence of meeting up with the slimy things that coiled under psychic rocks. A racing heart jolted me happy. The kick start of adrenaline punching my chest made me feel alive.

When life slowed down for too long, I grew hollow.

But for circumstance, I might've dealt with it by jumping out of airplanes or scaling bare rocks. Or worse.

Years ago, I'd met a homicide detective and that changed everything.

Robin had put up with it for a long time. Now she'd had enough and, sooner rather than later, I'd have to make some kind of decision.

She loved me. I know she did.

Maybe that's why she made it easy for me.

two

In Paris, clichés are just fine.

You leave your hotel, step out into the winter drizzle, walk aimlessly until you find yourself at a café near the Jardin des Tuileries where you order overpriced baguettes and grainy, French-press coffee, then move on to the Louvre, where even during the off-season the lines prove daunting. So you cross the Seine on the Pont Royal, ignoring the motor din that washes the bridge, study the murk of the water below, try the Musée d'Orsay and murder your feet for a couple of hours, sucking in the fruits of genius. Then, deeper into the grubby side streets of the Left Bank, where you press yourself into the all-in-black throng, and laugh inwardly at an imagined wheezy accordion soundtrack overpowering the burping motor scooters and the whining Renaults.

It was early afternoon, near a shop in St Germain, when it happened.

Robin and I had stepped into a dark, narrow men's haberdashery with a window full of aggressive neckties and slouching mannequins with pickpocket eyes. The rain had been coming in fitful bursts all day. The umbrella we'd cadged from the hotel concierge wasn't generous enough to shelter both of us and we each ended

5

up more than half-wet. Robin didn't seem to mind. Her curls were beaded with droplets and her cheeks were flushed. She'd been quiet since we'd boarded the plane in L.A., sleeping for most of the flight, refusing dinner. This morning, we'd woken up late and barely talked. During the walk across the river, she seemed distracted – staring off at nothing in particular, holding my hand, then dropping it, then grabbing again and squeezing hard, as if scrambling to cover for some infraction. I put it down to jet lag.

The St Germain stroll led us past a private school where beautiful, chittering adolescents spilled out onto the sidewalk, then a bookstore where I'd intended to browse until Robin pulled me into the clothing store, saying, 'These are good silks, Alex. You could use something new.'

The store peddled menswear, but smelled like a nail salon. The shop girl was a skinny thing with hacked-up hair the color of eggplant rind and the anxiety of a new hire. Robin took a while thumbing through the goods, finally found me a very blue shirt and an extravagant red-and-gold tie of heavy weave, got my nod, asked the girl to wrap it up. Aubergine Tresses scurried to a back room and returned with a stout, cardiganed woman in her sixties who sized me up, took the shirt, and returned moments later brandishing a steaming iron in one hand and the garment in the other – newly pressed, on a hanger, shielded by a clear plastic bag.

'Talk about service,' I said, as we returned to the street. 'Hungry?'

'No, not yet.'

'You didn't touch breakfast.'

Shrug.

6

The stout woman had followed us out and was standing in the doorway of the shop. She looked up at the sky dubiously. Checked her watch. Seconds later, thunder clapped. Flashing us a satisfied smile, she went back inside.

The rain was harder, colder. I tried to draw Robin under the umbrella but she resisted, remained out in the open, raised her face and caught the spray full force. A man scrambling for cover turned to stare.

I reached for her again. She continued to balk, licked moisture from her lips. Smiled faintly, as if enjoying a private joke. For a moment I thought she'd share it. Instead, she pointed to a brasserie two doors up the street and ran in ahead of me.

'Bonnie Raitt,' I repeated.

We were at a tiny table tucked in a corner of the clammy brasserie. The restaurant floor was a grubby mesh of white tile and the walls were cloudy mirrors and oft-painted brown woodwork. A clinically depressed waiter brought us our salads and wine as if service was harsh penance. Rain washed the front window and turned the city to gelatin.

'Bonnie,' she said. 'Jackson Brown, Bruce Hornsby, Shawn Colvin, maybe others.'

'Three-month tour.'

'At least three months,' she said, still avoiding my eyes. 'If it goes international, it could stretch longer.'

'World hunger,' I said. 'Good cause.'

'Famine and child welfare,' she said.

'Nothing nobler.'

She turned to me. Her eyes were dry and defiant.

'So,' I said. 'You're an equipment manager, now. No more guitar-making?'

'There'll be luthiery involved. I'll be overseeing and repairing all the gear.'

I'll, not *I'd*. One-vote election, nothing tentative.

'When exactly did you get the offer?' I said.

'Two weeks ago.'

'I see.'

'I know I should've said something. It wasn't – it dropped in my lap. Remember when I was at Gold-Tone Studios and they needed those vintage archtops for that retro Elvis video? The tour manager happened to be in the next booth, watching some mixing, and ended up talking.'

'Sociable fellow.'

'Sociable woman,' she said. 'She had her dog with her – an English bulldog, a female. Spike started playing with her and we started talking.'

'Animal magnetism,' I said. 'Is the tour dog-friendly, or do I keep Spike?'

'I'd like to take him along.'

'I'm sure that'll thrill him no end. When do you leave?'

'In a week.'

'A week.' My eyes hurt. 'Lots of packing ahead.'

She lifted her fork and pronged dead lettuce leaves. 'I can call it off—'

'No,' I said.

'I wouldn't have even considered it, Alex, not for the money—'

'Good money?'

She named the figure.

'Very good money,' I said.

'Listen to what I'm saying, Alex: that doesn't matter. If you're going to hate me, it can be undone.'

'I don't hate you, and you don't want it undone.

8

Maybe you accepted the offer because I made you unhappy, but now that you've committed yourself, you're seeing all kinds of positives.'

I craved argument but she didn't answer. The restaurant was filling, drenched Parisians seeking shelter from the downpour.

'Two weeks ago,' I said, 'I was running around with Milo on Lauren Teague's murder. Hiding what I was doing from you. I was stupid to think this trip would make a difference.'

She pushed salad around. The room had grown hotter, smaller; scowling people crowded tiny tables, others stood huddled at the doorway. The waiter began to approach. Robin repelled him with a glare.

She said, 'I've felt so alone. For a while. You were gone all the time. Putting yourself in *situations*. I didn't bring up the tour, because I knew you couldn't – shouldn't be distracted.'

She rolled the side of a small fist along the table rim. 'I guess I've always felt that what you do is important and that what I do is . . . just craft.' I started to speak but she shook her head. 'But this last time, Alex. Meeting with that woman, seducing her. Planning a damned *date* in order to – your intentions were good, but it still came down to seduction. Using yourself as a . . .'

'Whore?' I said. Thinking suddenly about Lauren Teague. A girl I'd known a long time ago, from my quiet job. She'd sold her body, ended up head-shot and dumped in an alley . . .

'I was going to say "lure." Despite all we've had together – this supposed enlightened *relationship* we've got, you go about your own business . . . Alex, basically you've built this whole other life from which I'm

9

excluded. From which I *want* to be excluded.'

She reached for her wineglass, sipped, made a face.

'Bad vintage?'

'Fine vintage. I'm sorry, baby, I guess it just comes down to timing. Getting the offer exactly when I was so down.' She grabbed my hand, squeezed hard. 'You love me, but you left me, Alex. It made me realize how alone I'd been for so long. We both were. The difference is, you enjoy going it alone – you get high on solitude and danger. So when Trish and I started talking and she told me she'd heard about my work – my reputation – and all of a sudden I realized I *had* a reputation, and here was someone offering me great money and the chance for something of my own, I said yes. Just blurted it out. And then driving home, I panicked, and said, *What did you just* do? And told myself I'd have to renege and wondered how I'd do it without looking like an idiot. But then I got home and the house was empty and all of a sudden I didn't *want* to renege. I went out to my studio and cried. I still might've changed my mind. I probably *would've*. But then you arranged that date with that tramp and . . . it felt completely right. It still does.'

She looked out the rain-clouded window. 'Such a beautiful city. I never want to see it again.'

The weather remained gray and wet and we kept to our room. Being together was agonizing: suppressed tears, edgy silences, too-polite chit-chat, listening to the rain tormenting the dormer windows. When Robin suggested we return early to L.A., I told her I'd try to change her ticket but I'd be staying for a while. That hurt her but it also relieved her and the next day when the cab showed up to take her to the airport, I carried her bags, held her elbow as she got into the taxi, paid the driver in advance.

'How long will you be staying?' she said.

'Don't know.' My teeth ached.

'Will you be back before I leave?'

'Sure.'

'Please be, Alex.'

'I will.'

Then: the kiss, the smile, trembling hands concealed.

As the taxi drove away I strained for a look at the back of her head – a tremor, a slump, any sign of conflict, regret, grief.

Impossible to tell.

Everything moved too fast.

three

The break came on a Sunday – some young smiley-faced, ponytailed guy I wanted to punch, arriving with a large van and two paunchy roadies wearing black *Kill Famine Tour* T-shirts. Ponytail had a Milk-Bone for Spike, high fives for me. Spike ate out of his hand. How had the bastard known to bring the treat?

'Hi, I'm Sheridan,' he said. 'The tour coordinator.' He wore a white shirt, blue jeans, brown boots, had a narrow body and a clean, smooth face full of optimism.

'Thought that was Trish.'

'Trish is the overall tour manager. My boss.' He glanced at the house. 'Must be nice, living up here.'

'Uh-huh.'

'So you're a psychologist.'

'Uh-huh.'

'I was a psych major in college. Studied psycho-acoustics at UC Davis. Used to be a sound engineer.'

How nice for you. 'Hmm.'

'Robin's going to be part of something important.'

'Hey,' I said.

Robin came down the front stairs with Spike on a leash. She wore a pink T-shirt and faded jeans and tennis shoes and big hoop earrings, began directing the roadies as they loaded her valises and her toolboxes into the van. Spike looked stoned. Like most dogs, his emotional barometer is finely tuned and for the last few days he'd been uncommonly compliant. I went over and stooped to pat his knobby French bulldog head, then I kissed Robin, and recited, 'Have fun,' and turned my back and trudged up to the house.

She stood there, alongside Sheridan. Waved.

Standing at the door, I pretended not to notice, then decided to wave.

Sheridan got behind the wheel of the van and everyone piled in behind him.

They rumbled away.

Finally.

Now, for the hard part.

I started off determined to maintain my dignity. That lasted about an hour and for the next three days I turned off the phone, didn't check with my service or open the curtains or shave or collect the mail. I did read the paper because news coverage is heavily biased toward the hopeless. But other people's misfortunes failed to cheer me and the words danced by, as foreign as hieroglyphics. The little I ate, I didn't taste. I'm no problem drinker but Chivas became a friend. Dehydration took its toll; my hair got dry and my eyes creaked and my joints stiffened. The house, always too big, expanded to monstrous proportions. The air curdled.

On Wednesday, I went down to the pond and fed the koi because why should they suffer? That got me into a scut-work frenzy, scouring and dusting and sweeping and straightening. On Thursday I finally collected my messages. Robin had called every day, left numbers in Santa

Barbara and Oakland. By Tuesday, she sounded anxious, by Wednesday, confused and annoyed and talking fast: the bus was headed for Portland. Everything was fine, Spike was fine, she was working hard, people were being great. *Iloveyouhopeyou'reokay.*

She called twice on Thursday, wondered out loud if I'd gone off on a trip of my own. Left a cell-phone number. I punched buttons. Got: *Your call cannot be completed.*

Just after 1 P.M. I put on shorts and a workout shirt and sneakers, began stomping up Beverly Glen facing the traffic, easing into a clumsy jog when I felt loose enough, ending up running harder and faster and more punishingly than I'd done for years.

When I got home, my body burned and I could barely breathe. The mailbox down at the bridle path that leads up to the front gate was stuffed with paper and the postman had left several packages on the ground. I scooped it all up, dumped the batch on the dining-room table, thought about more Scotch, drank a half-gallon of water instead, returned to the mail and began sorting listlessly.

Bills, ads, solicitations from real estate brokers, a few worthy causes, lots of dubious ones. The packages were a psychology book I'd ordered a while back, a free sample of toothpaste guaranteed to heal my gums and feed my smile, and an eight-by-twelve rectangle wrapped in coarse blue paper with DR A. DELAWARE and my address typed on a white label.

No return information. Downtown postmark, no stamps, just a meter. The blue paper, a heavy linen rag so substantial it felt like cloth, had been folded neatly and sealed tightly with clear tape. Slitting the folds revealed another snug layer of wrapping – pink butcher paper that I peeled away.

Inside was a three-ring binder. Blue, pebble-grain leather – substantial morocco, thumbed, grayed and glossy in spots.

Stick-on gold letters were centered precisely on the front cover.

THE MURDER BOOK

I flipped the cover to a blank, black frontispiece. The next page was also black paper, encased in a stiff plastic jacket.

But not blank. Mounted with black, adhesive corner pockets was a photograph: sepia-toned, faded, with margins the color of too-whitened coffee.

Medium shot of a man's body lying on a metal table. Glass-doored cabinets in the background.

Both feet were severed at the ankles, placed just under ragged tibial stumps, like a puzzle in partial reassembly. No left arm on the corpse. The right was a mangled lump. Same for the torso above the nipples. The head was wrapped in cloth.

A typed caption on the bottom margin read: **East L.A., nr Alameda Blvd. Pushed under a train by common-law wife.**

The facing page featured a shot of similar vintage: two sprawled gape-mouthed bodies – men – lying on a wooden plank floor, angled at forty degrees from each other. Dark stains spread beneath the corpses, tinted deep brown by age. Both victims wore baggy pants with generous cuffs, plaid shirts, lace-up work boots. Extravagant holes dotted the soles of the man on the left. A shot glass lay on its side near the elbow of the second, clear liquid pooling near the rim.

Hollywood, Vermont Ave. Both shot by 'friend' in dispute over money.

I turned the page to a photo that appeared less antique – black-and-white images on glossy paper, close-up of a couple in a car. The woman's position concealed her face: stretched across the man's chest and sheathed by a mass of platinum blond curls. Polka-dot dress, short sleeves, soft arms. Her companion's head rested against the top of the car seat, stared up at the dome light. A black blood-stream trickled from his mouth, separated into rivulets when it reached his lapel, dribbled down his necktie. Skinny necktie, dark with a pattern of tumbling dice. That and the width of the lapel said the fifties.

Silver Lake, near the reservoir, adulterers, he shot her, then put the gun in his mouth.

Page 4: pale, naked flesh atop the rumpled covers of a Murphy bed. The thin mattress took up most of the floor space of a dim, wretched closet of a room. Undergarments lay crumpled at the foot. A young face stiffened by rigor, lividity pools at the shins, black-thatched crotch advertised by splayed legs, panty hose gathered to midcalf. I knew sexual positioning when I saw it so the caption was no surprise.

Wilshire, Kenmore St. Rape-murder. Seventeen-year-old Mexican girl, strangled by boyfriend.

Page 5: **Central, Pico near Grand, 89 y.o. lady crossing street, purse snatch turned to head-injury homicide.**

Page 6: **Southwest, Slauson Ave. Negro gambler beaten to death over craps game.**

The first color photo showed up on page ten: red blood on sand-colored linoleum, the green-gray pallor that marked escape of the soul. A fat, middle-aged man sat slumped amid piles of cigarettes and candy, his sky-blue shirt smeared purple. Propped near his left hand was a sawed-off baseball bat with a leather thong threaded through the handle.

Wilshire, Washington Blvd near La Brea, liquor store owner shot in holdup. Tried to fight back.

I flipped faster.

Venice, Ozone Avenue, woman artist attacked by neighbor's dog. Three years of arguments.

. . . Bank robbery, Jefferson and Figueroa. Teller resisted, shot six times.

. . . Strong-arm street robbery, Broadway and Fifth. One bullet to the head. Suspect stuck around, discovered still going through victim's pockets.

. . . Echo Park, woman stabbed by husband in kitchen. Bad soup.

Page after page of the same cruel artistry and matter-of-fact prose.

Why had this been sent to me?

That brought to mind an old cartoon: *Why not?*

I thumbed through the rest of the album, not focusing on the images, just searching for some personal message.

Finding only the inert flesh of strangers.

Forty-three deaths, in all.

At the rear, a black end page with another centered legend, similar stick-on gold letters:

THE END

four

I hadn't talked to my best friend in a while, and that was fine with me.

After giving the DA my statement on Lauren Teague's murder, I'd had my fill of the criminal justice system, was happy to stay out of the loop until trial time. A wealthy defendant and a squadron of paid dissemblers meant that would be years away, not months. Milo had remained chained to the details, so I had a good excuse for keeping my distance: the guy was swamped, give him space.

The real reason was, I didn't feel like talking to him, or anyone. For years, I'd preached the benefits of self-expression but *my* tonic since childhood had been isolation. The pattern had been set early by all those bowel-churning nights huddled in the basement, hands over ears, humming 'Yankee Doodle' in order to block out the paternal rage thundering from above.

When things got rough, I curled like a mollusk into a gray pocket of solitary confinement.

Now I had forty-three death shots on my dining-room table. Death was Milo's raw material.

I called the West L.A. detectives' room.

'Sturgis.'

'Delaware.'

'Alex. What's up?'

'I got something I thought you should see. Photo album full of what look like crime-scene photos.'

'Photos or copies?'

'Photos.'

'How many?'

'Forty-three.'

'You actually counted,' he said. 'Forty-three from the same case?'

'Forty-three different cases. They look to be arranged chronologically.'

'You "got" them? How?'

'Courtesy the US Postal Service, first-class, downtown cancellation.'

'No idea who might've favored you with this.'

'I must have a secret admirer.'

'Crime-scene shots,' he said.

'Or someone takes very nasty vacations and decided to keep a scrapbook.' The call-waiting signal clicked. Usually I ignore the intrusion, but maybe it was Robin from Portland. 'Hold for a sec.'

Click.

'*Hello*, sir,' said a cheerful female voice. 'Are you the person who pays the phone bill in the house?'

'No, I'm the sex toy,' I said, and reconnected to Milo. Dial tone. Maybe he'd gotten an emergency call. I punched his desk number, got the West L.A. civilian receptionist, didn't bother to leave a message.

The doorbell rang twenty minutes later. I hadn't changed out of my running clothes, hadn't made coffee or checked the fridge – the first place Milo heads. Looking at portraits of violent death would make most people lose their appetites, but he's been doing his job for a long time, takes comfort food to a whole new level.

I opened the door, and said, 'That was quick.'

'It was lunchtime, anyway.' He walked past me to where the blue leather binder sat in full view, but made no move to pick it up, just stood there, thumbs hooked in his belt loops, big belly heaving from the run up to the terrace.

Green eyes shifted from the book to me. 'You sick or something?'

I shook my head.

'So what's this, a new look?' A sausage finger aimed at my stubbled face.

'Maintaining a leisurely shaving schedule,' I said.

He sniffed, took in the room. 'No one chewing at my cuffs. El Poocho out back with Robin?'

'Nope.'

'She's here, right?' he said. 'Her truck's out front.'

'You must be a detective,' I said. 'Unfortunately, false leads abound. She's out.' I pointed to the book. 'Check that out while I forage in the larder. If I can find anything that hasn't petrified, I'll fix you a sandwich—'

'No thanks.'

'Something to drink?'

'Nothing.' He didn't budge.

'What's the problem?' I said.

'How do I put this delicately,' he said. 'Okay: you look like shit, this place smells like an old-age home, Robin's truck is here but she isn't and my bringing her up makes your eyes drop to the floor like a suspect. What the hell's going on, Alex?'

'I look like shit?'

20

'To euphemize.'

'Oh, well,' I said. 'Better cancel the photo shoot with *In Style*. And speaking of photography . . .' I held the book out to him.

'Changing the subject,' he said, squinting down at me from his six-three vantage. 'What do they call that in psychologist school?'

'Changing the subject.'

He shook his head, kept his expression mild, folded his arms across his chest. But for spring-loaded tension around the eyes and mouth, he looked at peace. Pallid, acne-pitted face a bit leaner than usual, beer gut light-years from flat but definitely less bulge.

Dieting? On the wagon, yet again?

He'd dressed with uncommon color harmony: cheap but clean navy blazer, cotton khakis, white shirt with just a touch of fray at the neckline, navy tie, brand-new beige desert boots with pink rubber soles that squeaked as he shifted his weight and continued to study me. Brand-new haircut, too. The usual motif – clipped fuzzy at the sides and back, the top left long and shaggy, multiple cowlicks sprouting at the crown. A black forelock hooked over his pockmarked forehead. The hair from his temples to the bottoms of too-long sideburns had denatured to snow-white. The contrast with the black hair on top was unseemly – Mr Skunk, he'd taken to calling himself.

'Spiffed and freshly barbered,' I said. 'Is this some new-leaf thing? Should I not attempt to feed you? Either way, take the damn book.'

'Robin—'

'Later.' I thrust the blue album at him.

He kept his arms folded. 'Just put it back down on the table.' Pulling out a pair of surgical gloves from the sets, he encased his hands in latex, studied the blue leather cover, opened the book, read the frontispiece, moved on to the first photo.

'Old,' he murmured. 'The tint and the clothes. Probably someone's creepy collection from the attic.'

'Department shots?'

'Probably.'

'A home collection pilfered from the evidence room?'

'Cases get filed away, someone gets itchy-fingered, who's gonna notice if one shot per file gets lifted.'

'A cop?'

'A cop or a civilian ghoul. Lots of people have access, Alex. Some of them like the job because they dig blood.'

' "The murder book," ' I said. 'Same title as an official case file.'

'Same color, too. Whoever sent this knows procedure.'

'Evoking procedure . . . why send it to me?'

He didn't answer.

I said, 'It's not all antique. Keep going.'

He studied several more photos, flipped back to the initial shot, then forward to where he'd left off. Resuming his inspection, picking up speed and skimming the horror, just as I had. Then he stopped. Stared at a photo toward the back of the book. Chunky knuckles swelled the gloves as he gripped the album.

'When exactly did you get this?'

'Today's mail.'

He reached for the wrapping paper, took in the address, verified the postmark. Turned back to the album.

'What is it?' I said.

He placed the book on the table, open to the page that had stopped him. Resting his palms on either side of the album, he sat there. Ground his teeth. Laughed. The sound could have paralyzed prey.

Photograph Number 40.

A body in a ditch, muddy water pooled in the trough. Rusty blood on beige dirt. Off to the right side of the frame, dry weeds bristled. White-ink arrows were aimed at the subject, but the subject was obvious.

A young woman, maybe a teenager. Very thin – concave belly, washboard ribcage, fragile shoulders, spindly arms and legs. Slash and puncture wounds meshed her abdomen and neck. Curious black polka dots, too. Both breasts were gone, replaced by purplish discs the shape of marquis diamonds. Her angular face had been posed in profile, gazing to the right. Above her brow, where the hair should have been, floated a ruby cloud.

Purple ligature marks banded both wrists and ankles. More black dots speckled both legs – punctuation marks ringed with rosy haloes – inflammation.

Cigarette burns.

Long white legs had been drawn up in a parody of sexual welcome.

I'd skimmed right past this one.

Central, Beaudry Ave, body dump above 101 freeway on-ramp. Sex murder, scalped and strangled and slashed and burned. NS.

' "NS," ' I said. 'No Solve?'

Milo said, 'There was nothing else besides the book and wrapping? No note?'

'Nope. Just this.'

He checked the blue wrapping again, did the same for the pink butcher paper, returned to the brutalized girl. Sat there for a long time until, finally, he freed one hand and rubbed his face as if washing without water. Old nervous habit. Sometimes it helps cue me in to his mood, sometimes I barely notice it.

He repeated the gesture. Squeezed the bridge of his nose. Rubbed yet again. Twisted his mouth and didn't relax it and stared some more.

'My, my,' he said.

Several moments later: 'Yeah, that would be my guess. No Solve.'

' "NS" wasn't appended to any of the other photos,' I said.

No answer.

'Meaning this is what we're supposed to look at?' I said.

No answer.

'Who was she?' I said.

His lips slackened and he looked up at me and showed me some teeth. Not a smile, not even close to a smile. This was the expression a bear might take on when it spots a free meal.

He picked up the blue book. It vibrated. Shaking hands. I'd never seen that happen before. Emitting another terrible laugh, he repositioned the binder flat on the table. Squared the corners. Got up and walked into the living room. Facing the fireplace, he lifted a poker and tapped the granite hearth very softly.

I took a closer look at the mutilated girl.

His head shook violently. 'What do you wanna fill your head with that for?'

'What about *your* head?' I said.

'Mine's already polluted.'

Mine, too. 'Who was she, Milo?'

He put the poker back. Paced the room.

'Who was she?' he said. 'Someone turned into nothing.'

five

The first seven killings weren't as bad as he'd thought.
Not bad at all, compared to what he'd seen in Vietnam.

The department had assigned him to Central Division, not far – geographically or culturally – from Rampart, where he'd paid a year of uniform dues, followed by eight months with Newton Bunco.

Managing to talk his way out of the initial Newton assignment: Vice. Wouldn't *that* have been a yuk-fest. Ha ha ha. The sound of one voice laughing.

He was twenty-seven years old, already fighting the battle of the bulge, brand-new to Homicide and not sure if he had the stomach for it. For any kind of police work. But, at this point – after Southeast Asia, what else was there?

A freshly minted Detective One, managing to hold on to his secret, though he knew there'd been talk.

No one confronting him directly, but he had ears.

Something different about him – like he thinks he's better than anyone.

Drinks, but doesn't talk.

Doesn't shoot the shit.

Came to Hank Swangle's bachelor party but when they

25

brought the groupie in and the gang bang started, where the fuck was he?

Free blow job and he splits.

Doesn't chase pussy, period.

Weird.

His test scores and solve-rates and persistence got him to Central Homicide, where they paired him with a rail-thin forty-eight-year-old D-II named Pierce Schwinn, who looked sixty and fancied himself a philosopher. Mostly, he and Schwinn worked nights, because Schwinn thrived in the dark: bright lights gave the guy migraines, and he complained of chronic insomnia. No big mystery there, the guy popped decongestants like candy for a perpetually stuffed nose and downed a dozen cups of coffee per shift.

Schwinn loved driving around, spent very little time at his desk, which was a pleasant switch from the butt-numbing routine Milo had experienced at Bunco. But the downside was Schwinn had no attention span for white-collar work, couldn't wait to shove all the paperwork at his new junior partner.

Milo spent hours being a goddamned secretary, figured the best thing was to keep his mouth shut and listen, Schwinn had been around, must have something to offer. In the car, Schwinn alternated between taciturn and gabby. When he did talk, his tone got hyper and preachy – always making a *point*. Guy reminded him of one of his grad school professors at Indiana U. Herbert Milrad, inherited wealth, specialist on Byron. Lockjaw elocution, obese pear of a physique, violent mood swings. Milrad had figured Milo out by the middle of the first semester and tried to take advantage of it. Milo, still far from clear about his sexuality, had declined with tact. Also, he found

Milrad physically repugnant.

Not a pretty scene, the Grand Rejection, and Milo knew Milrad would torment him. He was finished with academia, any idea of a PhD. He finished the goddamned MA thesis by flogging the life out of poor Walt Whitman's words, escaped with a bare pass. Bored to tears, anyway, by the bullshit that passed for literary analysis, he left IU, lost his student deferment, answered a want ad at the campus student employment center, and took a job as a groundsman at the Muscatatuck National Wildlife Refuge, waiting for Selective Service to call. Five weeks later, the letter arrived.

By year's end, he was a medic wading through rice paddies, cradling young boys' heads and watching the departure of the barely formed souls, cupping steaming viscera in his hands – intestines were the big challenge, the way they slipped through his fingers like raw sausage. Blood browning and swirling as it hit the muddy water.

He made it home alive, found civilian life and his parents and brothers unbearable, struck out on a road trip, spent a while in San Francisco, learned a few things about his sexuality. Found SF claustrophobic and self-consciously hip, bought an old Fiat, and drove down the coast to L.A., where he stayed because the smog and the ugliness were reassuring. He knocked around for a while on temp jobs, before deciding police work might be interesting and why the hell not?

Then there he was, three years later. Seven P.M. call, as he and Schwinn sat in the unmarked in the parking lot of a Taco Tio on Temple Street, eating green chili burritos, Schwinn in one of his quiet moods, eyes jumpy as he gorged himself with no apparent pleasure.

When the radio squawked, Milo talked to the dispatcher,

took down the details, said, 'Guess we'd better shove off.'

Schwinn said, 'Let's eat first. No one's coming back to life.'

Homicide number eight.

The first seven had been no big deal, gross-out-wise. Nothing whodunit about them, either. Like nearly every Central case, the victims were all black or Mexican and the same for the victimizers. When he and Pierce showed, the only other white faces at the scene would be uniforms and techs.

Black/brown cases meant tragedy that never hit the papers, charges that mostly got filed and plea-bargained, or, if the bad guy ended up with a really stupid public defender, a long stay in county lockup, then a quick trial and sentencing to the max allowable.

The first two calls had been your basic bar shootings, juicehead perpetrators drunk enough to stick around when the uniforms arrived – literally holding the smoking guns, putting up no resistance.

Milo watched Schwinn deal with fools, caught on to what would turn out to be Schwinn's routine: first, he'd mumbled an unintelligible Miranda to an uncomprehending perp. Then he'd pressured the idiot for a confession right there at the scene. Making sure Milo had his pen and his pad out, was getting everything down.

'Good boy,' he'd say afterward to the suspect, as if the asshole had passed a test. Over-the-shoulder aside to Milo: 'How's your typing?'

Then back to the station, where Milo would pound the keys and Schwinn would disappear.

Cases Three, Four, and Five had been domestics. Dangerous for the responding blues, but laid out neatly for the Ds. Three low-impulse husbands, two shootings, one stabbing. Talk to the family and the neighbors, find out where the bad guys were 'hiding' – usually within walking distance – call for backup, pick 'em up, Schwinn mumbles Miranda . . .

Killing Six was a two-man holdup at one of the discount jewelry outlets on Broadway – cheap silver chains and dirty diamond chips in cheesy ten-karat settings. The robbery had been premeditated, but the 187 was a fluke that went down when one of the stickup morons' guns went off by accident, the bullet zipping straight into the forehead of the store clerk's eighteen-year-old son. Big, handsome kid named Kyle Rodriguez, star football player at El Monte High, just happened to be visiting Dad, bringing the good news of an athletic scholarship to Arizona State.

Schwinn seemed bored with that one, too, but he did show his stuff. In a manner of speaking. Telling Milo to check out former employees, ten to one that's the way it would shake out. Dropping Milo off at the station and heading off for a doctor appointment, then calling in sick for the rest of the week. Milo did three days of legwork, assembled a list, zeroed in on a janitor who'd been fired from the jewelry store a month ago for suspected pilferage. Turned the guy up in an SRO hotel on Central, still rooming with the brother-in-law who'd been his partner in crime. Both bad guys were incarcerated and Pierce Schwinn showed up looking pink and healthy, and saying, 'Yeah, there was no other possibility – did you finish the report?'

That one stuck in Milo's head for a while: Kyle Rodriguez's beefy bronze corpse slumped over the jewelry case. The image kept him up for more than a few nights. Nothing philosophical or theological, just general edginess. He'd seen plenty of young, healthy guys die a lot more painfully than Kyle, had long ago given up on making sense out of things.

He spent his insomnia driving around in the old Fiat. Up and down Sunset from Western to La Cienega, then back again. Finally veering south onto Santa Monica Boulevard.

As if that hadn't been his intention all along.

Playing a game with himself, like a dieter circling a piece of cake.

He'd never been much for willpower.

For three consecutive nights, he cruised Boystown. Showered and shaved and cologned, wearing a clean white T-shirt and military-pressed jeans and white tennies. Wishing he was cuter and thinner, but figuring he wasn't that bad if he squinted and kept his gut sucked in and kept his nerves under control by rubbing his face. The first night, a sheriff's patrol car nosed into the traffic at Fairfax and stayed two car lengths behind his Fiat, setting off paranoia alarms. He obeyed all the traffic rules, drove back to his crappy little apartment on Alexandria, drank beer until he felt ready to burst, watched bad TV, and made do with imagination. The second night, no sheriffs, but he just lacked the energy to bond and ended up driving all the way to the beach and back, nearly falling asleep at the wheel.

Night three, he found himself a stool in a bar near Larabee, sweating too damn much, knowing he was even tenser than he felt because his neck hurt like hell and his teeth throbbed like they were going to crumble. Finally, just before 4 A.M., before sunlight would be cruel to his complexion, he picked up a guy, a young black guy, around his own age. Well-dressed, well-spoken, education

30

grad student at UCLA. Just about the same place as Milo, sexual-honesty wise.

The two of them were jumpy and awkward in the guy's own crappy little grad student studio apartment on Selma south of Hollywood. The guy attending UCLA but living with junkies and hippies east of Vine because he couldn't afford the Westside. Polite chitchat, then . . . it was over in seconds. Both of them knowing there would be no repeat performance. The guy telling Milo his name was Steve Jackson but when he went into the bathroom, Milo spotted a date book embossed WES, found an address sticker inside the front cover. Wesley E. Smith, the Selma address.

Intimacy.

A sad case, Kyle Rodriguez, but he got over it by the time Case Seven rolled around.

A street slashing, good old Central Avenue, again. Knife fight, lots of blood all over the sidewalk, but only one db, a thirtyish Mexican guy in work clothes, with the homemade haircut and cheap shoes of a recently arrived illegal. Two dozen witnesses in a nearby *cantina* spoke no English and claimed blindness. This one wasn't even detective work. Solved courtesy of the blues – patrol car spotted a lurching perp ten blocks away, bleeding profusely from his own wounds. The uniforms cuffed him as he howled in agony, sat him down on the curb, called Schwinn and Milo, *then* phoned for the ambulance that transported the wretch to the jail ward at County Hospital.

By the time the detectives got there, the idiot was being loaded onto a gurney, had lost so much blood it was touch-and-go. He ended up surviving but gave up most of his colon and a bedside statement, pled guilty from a wheelchair, got sent back to the jail ward till someone figured out what to do with him.

Now, Number Eight. Schwinn just kept munching the burrito.

Finally, he wiped his mouth. 'Beaudry, top of the freeway, huh? Wanna drive?' Getting out and heading for the passenger side before Milo could answer.

Milo said, 'Either way,' just to hear the sound of his own voice.

Even away from the wheel, Schwinn went through his jumpy predrive ritual. Ratcheting the seat back noisily, then returning it to where it had been. Checking the knot of his tie in the rearview, poking around at the corner of his lipless mouth. Making sure no cherry-colored residue of decongestant syrup remained.

Forty-eight years old but his hair was dead white and skimpy, thinning to skin at the crown. Five-ten and Milo figured him for no more than 140, most of it gristle. He had a lantern jaw, that stingy little paper cut of a mouth, deep seams scoring his rawboned face, and heavy bags under intelligent, suspicious eyes. The package shouted dust bowl. Schwinn had been born in Tulsa, labeled himself Ultra-Okie to Milo minutes after they'd met.

Then he'd paused and looked the young detective in the eye. Expecting Milo to say something about his own heritage.

How about Black Irish Indiana Fag?

Milo said, 'Like the Steinbeck book.'

'Yeah,' said Schwinn, disappointed. '*Grapes of Wrath.* Ever read it?'

'Sure.'

32

'I didn't.' Defiant tone. 'Why the fuck should I? Everything in there I already learned from my daddy's stories.' Schwinn's mouth formed a poor excuse for a smile. 'I hate books. Hate TV and stupid-ass radio, too.' Pausing, as if laying down a gauntlet.

Milo kept quiet.

Schwinn frowned. 'Hate sports, too – what's the point of all that?'

'Yeah, it can get excessive.'

'You've got the size. Play sports in college?'

'High school football,' said Milo.

'Not good enough for college?'

'Not nearly.'

'You read much?'

'A bit,' said Milo. Why did that sound confessional?

'Me too.' Schwinn put his palms together. Aimed those accusatory eyes at Milo. Leaving Milo no choice.

'You hate books but you read.'

'Magazines,' said Schwinn, triumphantly. 'Magazines cut to the chase – take your *Reader's Digest*, collects all the bullshit and condenses it to where you don't need a shave by the time you finish. The other one I like is *Smithsonian*.'

Now there was a surprise.

'*Smithsonian*,' said Milo.

'Never heard of it?' said Schwinn, as if relishing a secret. 'The museum, in Washington, they put out a magazine. My wife went and subscribed to it and I was ready to kick her butt – just what we needed, more paper cluttering up the house. But it's not half-bad. They've got all sorts of stuff in there. I feel educated when I close the covers, know what I mean?'

'Sure.'

33

'Now *you*,' said Schwinn, 'they tell me you *are* educated.' Making it sound like a criminal charge. 'Got yourself a master's degree, is that right?'

Milo nodded.

'From where?'

'Indiana U. But school isn't necessarily education.'

'Yeah, but sometimes it is – what'd you study at Indiana *Yoo*o?'

'English.'

Schwinn laughed. 'God loves me, sent me a partner who can spell. Anyway, give me magazines and burn all the books as far as I'm concerned. I like science. Sometimes when I'm at the morgue I look at medical books – forensic medicine, abnormal psychology, even anthropology 'cause they're learning to do stuff with bones.' His own bony finger wagged. 'Let me tell you something, boy-o: one day, science is gonna be a big damn deal in our business. One day, to be doing our job a guy's gonna have to be a scientist – show up at a crime scene, scrape the db, carry a little microscope, learn the biochemical makeup of every damn scrote the vic hung out with for the last ten years.'

'Transfer evidence?' Milo said. 'You think it'll get that good?'

'Sure, yeah,' Schwinn said, impatiently. 'Right now transfer evidence is for the most part useless bullshit, but wait and see.'

They had been driving around Central on their first day as partners. Aimlessly, Milo thought. He kept waiting for Schwinn to point out known felons, hot spots, whatever, but the guy seemed unaware of his surroundings, all he wanted to do was talk. Later, Milo would learn that Schwinn had plenty to offer. Solid detective logic and basic advice. ('Carry your own camera, gloves, and fingerprint powder. Take care of your own self, don't depend on anyone.') But right now, this first day, riding around – everything – seemed pointless.

'Transfer,' said Schwinn. 'All we can transfer now is ABO blood type. What a crock. Big deal, a million scrotes are type O, most of the rest are A, so what does *that* do? That and hair, sometimes they take hair, put it in little plastic envelopes, but what the fuck can they do with it, you always get some Hebe lawyer proving hair don't mean shit. No, I'm talking serious science, something nuclear, like the way they date fossils. Carbon dating. One day, we'll be anthropologists. Too bad you don't have a master's degree in anthropology . . . can you type okay?'

A few miles later. Milo was taking in the neighborhood on his own, studying faces, places, when Schwinn proclaimed: 'English won't do you a damn bit of good, boy-o, 'cause our customers don't talkie mucho *English*. Not the Mexes, not the niggers, either – not unless you want to call that jive they give you English.'

Milo kept his mouth shut.

'Screw English,' said Schwinn. '*Fuck* English in the ass with a hydrochloric acid dildo. The wave of the future is science.'

They hadn't been told much about the Beaudry call. Female Caucasian db, discovered by a trash-picker sifting through the brush that crested the freeway on-ramp.

Rain had fallen the previous night and the dirt upon which the corpse had been placed was poor-drainage clay that retained an inch of grimy water in the ruts.

Despite a nice soft muddy area, no tire tracks, no

footprints. The ragpicker was an old black guy named Elmer Jacquette, tall, emaciated, stooped, with Parkinsonian tremors in his hands that fit with his agitation as he retold the story to anyone who'd listen.

'And there it was, right out there, Lord Jesus . . .'

No one was listening anymore. Uniforms and crimescene personnel and the coroner's man were busy doing their jobs. Lots of other people stood around, making small talk. Flashing vehicles blocked Beaudry all the way back to Temple as a bored-looking patrolman detoured would-be freeway speeders.

Not too many cars out: 9 P.M. Well past rush hour. Rigor had come and gone, as had the beginnings of putrefaction. The coroner was guestimating a half day to a day since death, but no way to know how long the body had been lying there or what temperature it had been stored at. The logical guess was that the killer had driven up last night, after dark, placed the corpse, zipped right onto the 101, and sped off happy.

No passing motorist had seen it, because when you were in a hurry, why would you study the dirt above the on-ramp? You never get to know a city unless you walk. Which is why so few people know L.A., thought Milo. After living here for two years, he still felt like a stranger.

Elmer Jacquette walked all the time, because he had no car. Covered the area from his East Hollywood flop to the western borders of downtown, poking around for cans, bottles, discards he tried to peddle to thrift shops in return for soup kitchen vouchers. One time, he'd found a working watch – gold, he thought, turned out to be plated but he got ten bucks for it, anyway, at a pawnshop on South Vermont.

He'd seen the body right away – how could you not

from up close, all pale in the moonlight, the sour smell, the way the poor girl's legs had been bent and spread – and his gorge had risen immediately and soon his franks-and-beans dinner was coming back the wrong way.

Jacquette had the good sense to run a good fifteen feet from the body before vomiting. When the uniforms arrived, he pointed out the emetic mound, apologizing. Not wanting to annoy anyone. He was sixty-eight years old, hadn't served state time since fifteen years ago, wasn't going to annoy the police, no way.

Yessir, nossir.

They'd kept him around, waiting for the detectives to arrive. Now, the men in suits were finally here and Jacquette stood over by one of the police cars as someone pointed him out and they approached him, stepping into the glare of those harsh lights the cops had put all over the place.

Two suits. A skinny white-haired redneck type in an old-fashioned gray sharkskin suit and a dark-haired, pasty-faced heavyset kid whose green jacket and brown pants and ugly red-brown tie made Elmer wonder if nowadays *cops* were shopping at thrift shops.

They stopped at the body first. The old one took one look, wrinkled his nose, got an annoyed look on his face. Like he'd been interrupted in the middle of doing something important.

The fat kid was something else. Barely glanced at the body before whipping his head away. Bad skin, that one, and he'd gone white as a sheet, started rubbing his face with one hand, over and over.

Tightening up that big heavy body of his like *he* was ready to lose his lunch.

Elmer wondered how long the kid had been on the job, if he'd actually blow chunks. If the kid did heave, would he be smart enough to avoid the body, like Elmer had? 'Cause this kid didn't look like no veteran.

six

This was worse than Asia.

No matter how brutal it got, war was impersonal, human chess pieces moving around the board, you fired at shadows, strafed huts you pretended were empty, lived every day hoping you wouldn't be the pawn that flipped. Reduce someone to The Enemy, and you could blow off his legs or slice open his belly or napalm his kids without knowing his name. As bad as war got, there was always the chance for making nice sometime in the future – look at Germany and the rest of Europe. To his father, an Omaha Beach alumnus, buddying up to the krauts was an abomination. Dad curled his lip every time he saw a 'hippie-faggot in one of those Hitler beetle-cars.' But Milo knew enough history to understand that peace was as inevitable as war and that as unlikely as it seemed, one day Americans might be vacationing in Hanoi.

War wounds had a chance of healing *because* they weren't personal. Not that the memory of guts slipping through his hands would fade, but maybe, somewhere off in the future . . .

But *this*. This was nothing *but* personal. Reduction of human form to meat and juice and refuse. Creating the antiperson.

He took a deep breath and buttoned his jacket and managed another look at the corpse. How old could she be, seventeen, eighteen? The hands, about the only parts of her not bloody, were smooth, pale, free of blemish. Long, tapering fingers, pink-polished nails. From what he could tell – and it was hard to tell anything because of the damage – she'd had delicate features, might've been pretty.

No blood on the hands. No defense wounds . . .

The girl was frozen in time, a heap of ruin. Aborted – like a shiny little wristwatch, stomped on, the crystal shattered.

Manipulated after death, too. The killer spreading her legs, tenting them, pointing the feet at a slight outward angle.

Leaving her out in the open, horrible statuary.

Overkill, the assistant coroner had pronounced, as if you needed a medical degree for *that.*

Schwinn had told Milo to count wounds, but the task wasn't that simple. The slashes and cuts were straight-forward, but did he count the ligature burns around both wrists and ankles as wounds? And what about the deep, angry red trench around her neck? Schwinn had gone off to get his Instamatic – always a shutterbug – and Milo didn't want to ask him – loathed coming across uncertain, the rookie he was.

He decided to include the ligatures in a separate column, continued making hash marks. Reviewed his count of the knife wounds. Both premortem and after death, the coroner was guessing. One, two, three, four . . . he confirmed fifty-six, began his tally of the cigarette burns.

Inflammation around the singed circles said the burns

had been inflicted before death.

Very little spent blood at the scene. She'd been killed somewhere else, left here.

But lots of dried blood atop the head, forming a blackening cap that kept attracting the flies.

The finishing touch: scalping her. Should that be counted as one giant wound, or did he need to peer under the blood, see how many times the killer had hacked away the skin?

A cloud of night gnats circled above the body, and Milo scatted it away, noted 'removal of cranial skin,' as a separate item. Drawing the body and topping it with the cap, his lousy rendering making the blood look like a beanie, so inadequately offensive. He frowned, closed his pad, stepped back. Studied the body from a new perspective. Fought back yet another wave of nausea.

The old black guy who'd found her had heaved his cookies. From the moment Milo had seen the girl, he'd struggled not to do the same. Tightening his bowels and his gut, trying to come up with a mantra that would do the trick.

You're no virgin, you've seen worse.

Thinking of the worst: *melon-sized holes in chests, hearts bursting – that kid, that Indian kid from New Mexico – Bradley Two Wolves – who'd stepped on a mine and lost everything below the navel but was still talking as Milo pretended to do something for him. Looking up at Milo with soft brown eyes – alive eyes, dear God – talking calmly, having a goddamn conversation with nothing left and everything leaking out. That was worse, right? Having to talk back to the upper half of Bradley Two Wolves, chitchatting about Bradley's pretty little girlfriend in Galisteo, Bradley's dreams – once he got back to the States, he was gonna marry Tina, get a*

41

job with Tina's dad putting up adobe fences, have a bunch of kids. Kids. With nothing below the— Milo smiled down at Bradley and Bradley smiled back and died.

That had been worse. And back then Milo had managed to keep his cool, keep the conversation going. Cleaning up afterward, loading half-of-Bradley in a body bag that was much too roomy. Writing out Bradley's death tag for the flight surgeon to sign. For the next few weeks, Milo had smoked a lot of dope, sniffed some heroin, done an R and R in Bangkok, where he tried some opium. He'd even hazarded an attempt at a skinny Bangkok whore. That hadn't gone so great, but bottom line: he'd *maintained.*

You can handle this, stupid.

Breathe slowly, don't give Schwinn something else to lecture about—

Schwinn was back now, clicking away with his Instamatic. The LAPD photographer had spotted the little black plastic box, caressed his Nikon, smirked. Schwinn was oblivious to the contempt, in his own little world, crouching on all sides of the body. Getting close to the body, closer than Milo had hazarded, not even bothering to shoo the gnats swarming his white hair.

'So what do you think, boy-o?'

'About . . . ?' said Milo.

Click click click. 'The bad guy – what's your gut telling you about him?'

'Maniac.'

'Think so?' Schwinn said, almost absently. 'Howling-lunatic-drooling-crazyman?' He moved away from Milo, kneeled right next to the flayed skull. Close enough to kiss the mangled flesh. Smiled. 'Look at this – just bone and a few blood vessels, sliced at the back . . . a few tears, some serrations . . . real sharp blade.' *Click click.* 'A maniac . . . some shout-at-the-moon Apache warrior? *You,* naughty squaw, *me* scalpum?'

Milo battled another abdominal heave.

Schwinn got to his feet, dangled the camera from its little black string, fiddled with his tie. His Oakie hatchet face bore a satisfied look. Cool as ice. How often had *he* seen this? How often did this kind of thing come up in Homicide? The first seven – even Kyle Rodriguez – had been tolerable compared to this . . .

Schwinn pointed at the girl's propped-up legs. 'See the way he posed her? He's talking to us, boy-o. Talking through her, putting words in her mouth. What's he want her to say, boy-o?'

Milo shook his head.

Schwinn sighed. 'He wants her to say, "Fuck me." To the whole world – "C'mon over, whole damn world, and fuck me silly, anyone wants to do anything to me, they can 'cause I got no power." He's using her like . . . a puppet – you know how kids move puppets around, get puppets to say things they're too scared to say for themselves? This guy's like that, only he likes big puppets.'

'He's scared?' said Milo doubtfully.

'What the fuck do *you* think?' said Schwinn. 'We're talking about a coward, can't talk to women, get laid in any normal way. Which isn't to say he's a wimpy type. He could be macho. He's sure nervy enough, taking the time for that.' Backward glance at the legs. 'Posing her right out in the open, risking being seen. I mean, think about it: you had your fun with the body, needed to get rid of the body, you're carrying it around in your car, want to dump it, where would you go?'

'Somewhere remote.'

'Yeah, 'cause you're not a nervy killer, to you it would just be dumping. Not our boy. On the one hand, he's smart. Doing it right by the freeway – once he's finished, he can get back on, no one's conspicuous on the 101. He does it after dark, checks to make sure no one's watching, pulls over, arranges her, then zoom zoom zoom. It's a decent plan. It could work nice, especially this late, rush hour's over. But taking the time to *stop* is still a risk, just to play puppet. So this wasn't about dumping. This was showing off – having his cake and eating it twice. He ain't stupid or crazy.'

'Playing a game,' said Milo, because that sounded agreeable. Thinking about chess, but unable to really reconcile this with any game.

' *"Look at me,"* ' said Schwinn. 'That's what he's telling us. "Look what I can do." It's not enough he over-powered her and fucked the hell out of her – hundred to one we'll find a mess of semen up her twat, her ass. What he wants now is to share her with the world. I control her, everyone hop on board.'

'Gang bang,' said Milo, hoarsely, flashing back to Hank Swangle's party at Newton Division. The Newton groupie, a heavy, blonde bank clerk, prim and upright during the day, a whole other life when it came to cops. Pillowy, drunk, and glazed when collegial hands had shoved Milo into the room with her. The groupie reach-ing out to Milo, lipstick smeared, mouthing, 'Next.' Like a take-a-number line in a bakery. He'd muttered some excuse, hurried out . . . why the hell was he thinking of that, now? And now the nausea was returning – his hands throbbed, he was clenching them.

Schwinn was staring at him.

He forced himself to release the fingers, kept his voice level. 'So he's more rational than a maniac. But we are talking someone mentally abnormal, right? Someone normal wouldn't do this.' Hearing the stupidity of each word as it tumbled out.

Schwinn smiled again. 'Normal. Whatever the hell that means.' He turned his back on Milo, walked away without a word, swinging his camera. Stood off by himself next to the coroner's van, leaving Milo with his bad sketches and compulsive hash marks.

Whatever the hell that means.

A knowing smile. Loose talk about Milo's sexuality wafting from Rampart and Newton to Central? Was that why the guy was so hostile?

Milo's hands were clenching again. He'd started to think of himself as maybe fitting in, handling the first seven 187s okay, getting into the 187 groove and thinking he might stick with Homicide, murder would turn out to be something he could finally live with.

Now he cursed the world, got close to the girl. Closer even than Schwinn. Taking in the sights, the smell, every wound – drinking in the horror, telling himself *shut up, idiot, who the hell are you to complain, look at her.*

But the rage intensified, flowed over him, and suddenly he felt hard, cruel, vengeful, analytic.

Seized by a rush of *appetite.*

Trying to make sense of this. Needing to.

He smelled the girl's rot. Wanted, suddenly, to enter her hell.

It was nearly eleven by the time he and Schwinn were back in the unmarked.

'You drive again,' said Schwinn. No sign of any

45

hostility, no more possible doubles entendres, and Milo started to think he'd been paranoid about the normalcy comment. Just Schwinn flapping his lips, because the guy was like that.

He started up the engine. 'Where to?'

'Anywhere. Tell you what, take the freeway for a couple exits, then turn around, go back downtown. I need to think.'

Milo complied. Cruising down the ramp, as the killer had done. Schwinn stretched and yawned, sniffed and produced his bottle of decongestant and took a long red swallow. Then he leaned over and switched off the radio, closed his eyes, fooled with the corners of his lips. This was going to be one of those silent stretches.

It lasted until Milo was back on city streets, driving up Temple, passing the Music Center and the dirt lots that surrounded it. Lots of empty space as the rich folk planned additional shrines to culture. Talking urban renewal – pretending anyone would ever bother with this poor excuse for a downtown, pretending it wasn't a cement grid of government buildings where bureaucrats worked the day shift and couldn't wait to get the hell out of there and everything got cold and black at night.

'So what's next?' said Schwinn. 'On the girl. What do you think?'

'Find out who she was?'

'Shouldn't be too hard, those smooth nails, nice straight teeth. If she was a street slut, her comedown was recent. Someone'll miss her.'

'Should we start with Missing Persons?' said Milo.

'*You'll* start with Missing Persons. Start calling tomorrow morning 'cause MP doesn't staff heavy at night, good luck trying to get those guys off their asses at this hour.'

'But if she was reported missing, getting the info tonight would give us a head start—'

'On what? This is no race, boy-o. If our bad boy's out of town, he's long gone, anyway. If not, a few hours won't make a damn bit of difference.'

'Still, her parents have got to be worried—'

'Fine, amigo,' said Schwinn. 'Be a social worker. I'm going home.'

No anger, just that know-it-all smugness.

'Want me to head back to the station?' said Milo.

'Yeah, yeah. No, forget that. Pull over – *now*, boy-o. Over *there*, yeah yeah yeah stop next to that *bus* bench.'

The bench was a few yards up, on the north side of Temple. Milo was in the left-hand lane and had to turn sharply not to overshoot. He edged to the curb, looked around to see what had changed Schwinn's mind.

Dark, empty block, no one around – no, there *was* someone. A figure emerging from the shadows. Walking west. Walking quickly.

'A source?' said Milo, as the shape took form. Female form.

Schwinn tightened his tie knot. 'Stay put and keep the engine going.' He got out of the car, quickly, got to the sidewalk just in time to meet the woman. Her arrival was heralded by spike heels snapping on the pavement.

A tall woman – black, Milo saw, as she shifted into the streetlight. Tall and busty. Maybe forty. Wearing a blue leather mini and a baby blue halter top. Jumbo pile of henna-colored waves atop her head, what looked to be ten pounds of hair.

Schwinn, standing facing her, looking even skinnier than usual. Legs slightly spread. Smiling.

The woman smiled back. Offered both cheeks to

Schwinn. One of those Italian movie greetings.

A few moments of conversation, too low for Milo to make out, then both of them got in the backseat of the unmarked.

'This is Tonya,' said Schwinn. 'She's a good pal of the department. Tonya, meet my brand-new partner, Milo. He's got a master's degree.'

'Ooh,' said Tonya. 'Are you masterful, honey?'

'Nice to meet you, ma'am.'

Tonya laughed.

'Start driving,' said Schwinn.

'Master's degree,' said Tonya, as they pulled away.

At Fifth Street, Schwinn said, 'Turn left. Drive into the alley behind those buildings.'

'Masturbator's degree?' said Tonya.

'Speaking of which,' said Schwinn. 'My darling dear.'

'Ooh, I love when you talk that way, Mr S.'

Milo reduced his speed.

Schwinn said, 'Don't do that, just drive regular – turn again and make a right – go east. Alameda, where the factories are.'

'Industrial revolution,' said Tonya, and Milo heard something else: the rustle of clothing, the *sprick* of a zipper undone. He hazarded one look in the rearview, saw Schwinn's head, resting against the back of the seat. Eyes closed. Peaceful smile. Ten pounds of henna bobbing.

A moment later: 'Oh, yes, Miss T. I missed you, did you know that?'

'Did you, baby? Aw, you're just saying that.'

'Oh, no, it's true.'

'*Is* it, baby?'

48

'You bet. Miss me, too?'

'You know I do, Mr S.'

'Every day, Miss T?'

'Every day, Mr S – c'mon, baby, move a little, help me with this.'

'Happy to help,' said Schwinn. 'Protect and serve.'

Milo forced his eyes straight ahead.

No sound in the car but heavy breathing.

'Yeah, yeah,' Schwinn was saying now. His voice weak. Milo thought: This is what it takes to knock off the asshole's smugness.

'Oh yeah, just like that, my darling . . . dear. Oh, yes, you're . . . a . . . specialist. A . . . scientist, yes, yes.'

seven

Schwinn told Milo to drop Tonya off on Eighth near Witmer, down the block from the Ranch Depot Steak House.

'Get yourself a hunk of beef, darling.' Slipping her some bills. 'Get yourself a lovely T-bone with one of those giant baked potatoes.'

'Mr S,' came the protest. 'I can't go in there dressed like this, they won't serve me.'

'With this they will.' Another handful of paper pressed into her hand. 'You show this to Calvin up front, tell him I sent you – you have any problem, you let me know.'

'You're sure?'

'You know I am.'

The rear door opened, and Tonya got out. The smell of sex hung in the car. Now the night filtered in, cool, fossil-fuel bitter.

'Thank you, Mr S.' She extended her hand. Schwinn held on to it.

'One more thing, darling. Hear of any rough johns working the Temple-Beaudry area?'

'How rough?'

'Ropes, knives, cigarette burns.'

'Ooh,' said the hooker, with pain in her voice. 'No, Mr

50

S, there's always lowlife, but I heard nothing like that.'

Pecks on cheeks. Tonya clicked her way toward the restaurant, and Schwinn got back in front. 'Back to the station, boy-o.'

Closing his eyes. Self-satisfied. At Olive Street, he said: 'That's a very intelligent nigger, boy-o. Given the opportunity a free, white woman woulda had, she woulda made something of herself. What's that about?'

'What do you mean?'

'The way we treat niggers. Make sense to you?'

'No,' said Milo. Thinking: What the hell is this *lunatic* about?

Then: Why hadn't Schwinn offered the hooker to *him*?

Because Schwinn and Tonya had something special? Or because he *knew*?

'What it says,' offered Schwinn. 'The way we treat niggers, is that sometimes smart doesn't count.'

Milo dropped him off at the Central Division parking lot, watched him get into his Ford Fairlane and drive off to Simi Valley, to the wife who liked books.

Alone, at last.

For the first time since the Beaudry call, he was breathing normally.

He entered the station, climbed the stairs, hurried to the scarred metal desk they'd shoved into a corner of the Homicide room for him. The next three hours were spent phoning Missing Persons bureaus at every station and when that didn't pay off, he extended the search to various sheriffs' substations and departments of neighboring cities. Every office kept its own files, no one coordinated, each folder had to be pulled by hand, and MP skeleton crews were reluctant to extend themselves, even on a 187. Even when he pressed, emphasized the whodunit aspect, the ugliness, he got resistance. Finally, he hit upon something that pried cooperation and curses on the other end: the likelihood of news coverage. Cops were afraid of bad press. By 3 A.M., he'd come up with seven white girls in the right age range.

So what did he do, now? Get on the horn and wake up worried parents?

Pardon me, Mrs Jones, but did your daughter Amy ever show up? Because we've still got her listing as missing and are wondering if a sackful of tissue and viscera cooling off in a coroner's drawer just might be her?

The only way to do it was preliminary phone contact followed by face-to-face interviews. Tomorrow, at a decent hour. Unless Schwinn had other ideas. Something else to correct him about.

He transcribed all the data from his pad onto report sheets, filled out the right forms, redrew the outline of the girl's body, summarized the MP calls, created a neat little pile of effort. Striding across the room to a bank of file cabinets, he opened a top drawer and pulled out one of several blue binders stored in a loose heap. Recycled binders: when cases were closed, the pages were removed and stapled, placed in a manila folder, and shipped over to the evidence room at Parker Center.

This particular blue book had seen better times: frayed around the edges with a brown stain on the front cover vaguely reminiscent of a wilting rose – some D's greasy lunch. Milo affixed a stickummed label to the cover.

Wrote nothing. Nothing to write.

He sat there thinking about the mutilated girl. Wondered what her name was and couldn't bring himself to substitute *Jane Doe*.

First thing tomorrow, he'd check out those seven girls, maybe get lucky and end up with a name.

A title for a brand-new murder book.

Bad dreams kept him up all night, and he was back at his desk by 6:45 A.M., the only detective in the room, which was just fine; he didn't even mind getting the coffee going.

By 7:20, he was calling families. MP number one was Sarah Jane Causlett, female cauc, eighteen, five-six, 121, last seen in Hollywood, buying dinner at the Oki-burger at Hollywood and Selma.

Ring, ring ring. 'Mrs Causlett? Good morning, hope I'm not calling too early . . .'

By 9 A.M., he was finished. Three of the seven girls had returned home, and two others weren't missing at all, just players in divorce dramas who'd escaped to be with noncustodial parents. That left two sets of distraught parents, Mr and Mrs Estes in Mar Vista, Mr and Mrs Jacobs in Mid-City. Lots of anxiety, Milo withheld facts, steeled himself for the face-to-face.

By 9:30 a few detectives had arrived, but not Schwinn, so Milo placed a scrawled note on Schwinn's desk, left the station.

By 1 P.M., he was back where he started. A recent picture of Misty Estes showed her to be substantially obese with short curly hair. West L.A. Missing Persons had misrecorded her stats: 107 pounds instead of 187. Oops, sorry. Milo left the tearful mother and hypertensive father standing in the doorway of their GI Bill bungalow.

Jessica Jacobs was approximately the right size, but definitely not the girl on Beaudry: she had the lightest of blue eyes, and the victim's had been deep brown.

53

Another clerical screwup, no one bothering to note eye color in the Wilshire Division MP file.

He left the Jacobs house sweating and tired, found a pay phone outside a liquor store at Third and Wilton, got Schwinn on the line, and gave a lack-of-progress report.

'Morning, boy-o,' said Schwinn. 'Haul yourself over here, there might be something.'

'What?'

'Come on back.'

When he got to the Homicide room, half the desks were full, and Schwinn was balancing on two legs of his chair, wearing a nice-looking navy suit, shiny white-on-white shirt, gold tie, gold tie tack shaped like a tiny fist. Leaning back precariously as he chomped a burrito the size of a newborn baby.

'Welcome home, prodigious son.'

'Yeah.'

'You look like shit.'

'Thanks.'

'Don't mention it.' Schwinn gave one of his corkscrew smiles. 'So you learned about our excellent record-keeping. Cops are the worst, boy-o. Hate to write and always make a mess out of it. We're talking barely literate.'

Milo wondered about the extent of Schwinn's own education. The topic had never come up. The whole time they'd worked together, Schwinn had parceled out very few personal details.

'Clerical screwups are the fucking rule, boy-o. MP files are the worst, because MP knows it's a penny ante outfit, most of the time the kid comes home, no one bothers to let them know.'

'File it, forget it,' said Milo, hoping agreement would shut him up.

'File it, *fuck* it. That's why I was in no big hurry to chase MP.'

'You know best,' said Milo.

Schwinn's eyes got hard. Milo said, 'So what's interesting?'

'*Maybe* interesting,' Schwinn corrected. 'A source of mine picked up some rumors. Party on the Westside two days before the murder. Friday night, Upper Stone Canyon – Bel Air.'

'Rich kids.'

'Filthy rich kids, probably using Daddy and Mommy's house. My source says there were kids from all over showing up, getting stoned, making noise. The source also knows a guy, has a daughter, went out with her friends, spent some time at the party, and never came home.'

Maybe interesting.

Schwinn grinned and bit off a wad of burrito. Milo had figured the guy for a late-sleeping pension-sniffing gold-brick and turned out the sonofabitch had been working overtime, doing a solo act, and *producing*. The two of them were partners in name only.

He said, 'The father didn't report it to MP?'

Schwinn shrugged. 'The father's a little bit . . . marginal.'

'Lowlife?'

'Marginal,' Schwinn repeated. Irritated, as if Milo was a poor student, kept getting it wrong. 'Also, the girl's done this before – goes out partying, doesn't come home for a few days.'

'If the girl's done it before, why would this be different?'

'Maybe it's not. But the girl fits stat-wise: sixteen, around five-seven, skinny, with dark hair, brown eyes, nice tight little body.'

An appreciative tone had crept into Schwinn's voice. Milo pictured him with the source – some street lech, the source laying it on lasciviously. Hookers, pimps, perverts, Schwinn probably had a whole stable of lowlifes he could count on for info. And Milo had a master's degree . . .

'She's supposed to be cute,' Schwinn went on. 'No virgin, a wild kid. Also, at least one time before, she got herself in trouble. Hitchhiking on Sunset, got picked up by some scrote who raped her, tied her up, left her in an alley downtown. A juicehead found her, lucky for her he was just a bum, not a perve fixing to get himself some sloppy seconds. The girl never reported it officially, just told a friend, and the story made the rounds on the street.'

'Sixteen years old, tied and raped and she doesn't report it?'

'Like I said, no virgin.' Schwinn's hatchet jaw pulsed, and his Okie squint aimed at the ceiling. Milo knew he was holding back something.

'Is the source reliable?'

'Usually.'

'Who?'

Schwinn's headshake was peevish. 'Let's concentrate on the main thing: we got a girl who fits our vic's stats.'

'Sixteen,' said Milo, bothered.

Schwinn shrugged. 'From what I've read – psychology articles – the human rope gets kinked up pretty early.' He leaned back and took another big bite of burrito, wiped salsa verde from his mouth with the back of his hand, then gave the hand a lick. 'You think that's true, boy-o?

56

Think maybe she didn't report it 'cause she liked it?'

Milo covered his anger with a shrug of his own. 'So what's next? Talk to the father?'

Schwinn righted his chair, swabbed his chin, this time with a paper napkin, stood abruptly, and walked out of the room, leaving Milo to follow.

Partners.

Outside, near the unmarked, Schwinn turned to him, smiling. 'So tell me, how'd you sleep last night?'

Schwinn recited the address on Edgemont, and Milo started up the car.

'Hollywood, boy-o. A real-life Hollywood girl.'

Over the course of the twenty-minute ride, he laid out a few more details for Milo: the girl's name was Janie Ingalls. A sophomore at Hollywood High, living with her father in a third-floor walk-up in a long-faded neighborhood, just north of Santa Monica Boulevard. Bowie Ingalls was a drunk who might or might not be home. Society was going to hell in a handbasket; even white folk were living like pigs.

The building was a clumsy pink thing with undersized windows and lumpy stucco. Twelve units was Milo's guess: four flats to a floor, probably divided by a narrow central corridor.

He parked, but Schwinn made no attempt to get out, so the two of them just sat there, the engine running.

'Turn it off,' said Schwinn.

Milo twisted the key and listened to street sounds. Distant traffic from Santa Monica, a few bird trills, someone unseen playing a power mower. The street was poorly kept, litter sludging the gutters. He said, 'Besides being a juicehead, how's the father marginal?'

JONATHAN KELLERMAN

'One of those walking-around guys,' said Schwinn. 'Name of Bowie Ingalls, does a little of this, little of that. Rumor has it he ran slips for a nigger bookie downtown – how's that for a white man's career? A few years ago, he was working as a messenger at Paramount Studios, telling people he was in the movie biz. He plays the horses, has a chicken-shit sheet, mostly drunk and disorderly, unpaid traffic tickets. Two years ago he got pulled in for receiving stolen property but never got charged. Small-time, all around.'

Details. Schwinn had found the time to pull Bowie Ingalls's record.

'Guy like that, and he's raising a kid,' said Milo.

'Yeah, it's a cruel world, isn't it? Janie's mother was a stripper and a hype, ran off with some hippie musician when the kid was a baby, overdosed in Frisco.'

'Sounds like you've learned a lot.'

'That what you think?' Schwinn's voice got flinty, and his eyes were hard, again. Figuring Milo was being sarcastic? Milo wasn't sure he hadn't *meant* to be sarcastic.

'I've got a lot to learn,' he said. 'Wasting my time with those MP clowns. Meanwhile you're getting all this—'

'Don't lick my ass, son,' said Schwinn, and suddenly the hatchet face was inches from Milo's and Milo could smell the Aqua Velva and the salsa verde. 'I didn't *do* dick, and I don't *know* dick. And you did way *less* than dick.'

'Hey, sorry if—'

'*Fuck* sorry, pal. You think this is some *game*? Like getting a master's degree, hand in your homework, and lick the teacher's ass and get your little ass-licking *grade*? You think *that's* what this is about?'

58

Talking way too fast for normal. What the hell had set him off?

Milo kept silent. Schwinn laughed bitterly, moved away, sat back so heavily against the seat that Milo's heavy body rocked. 'Let me tell you, boy-o, that other shit we've been shoveling since I let you ride with me – niggers and pachucos offing each other and waiting around for us to pick 'em up and if we don't, no one gives a shit – you think that's what the 187 universe is all about?'

Milo's face was hot from jawline to scalp. He kept his mouth shut.

'This . . .' said Schwinn, pulling a letter-sized, baby blue envelope from an inside suit pocket and removing a stack of color photos. Twenty-four-hour photo lab logo. The Instamatic shots he'd snapped at Beaudry.

He fanned them out on his skinny lap, face up, like fortune-teller's cards. Close-ups of the dead girl's bloody, scalped head. Intimate portraits of the lifeless face, splayed legs . . .

'*This*,' he said, 'is why we get paid. The other stuff *clerks* could handle.'

The first seven murders had gotten Milo to think of himself as a clerk with a badge. He didn't dare agree. Agreement seemed to infuriate the sonofa—

'You thought you were gonna get some fun for yourself when you signed up to be a Big Bad Homicide Hero,' said Schwinn. 'Right?' Talking even faster, but managing to snap off each word. 'Or maybe you heard that bullshit about Homicide being for intellectuals and you've got that master's degree and you thought hey, that's me! So tell me, this look *intellectual* to you?' Tapping a photo. 'You think this can be figured out using brains?'

Shaking his head and looking as if he'd tasted something putrid, Schwinn hooked a fingernail under a corner of a photo and flicked.

Plink, plink.

Milo said, 'Look, I'm just—'

'Do you have any idea how often something like this actually gets closed? Those clowns in the Academy probably told you Homicide has a seventy, eighty percent solve rate, right? Well, that's *horseshit*. That's the stupid stuff – which should be a hundred percent it's so stupid, so big fucking deal, eighty percent. *Shit.*' He turned and spit out the window. Shifted back to Milo. 'With *this*' – *plink, plink* – 'you're lucky to close four outta ten. Meaning most of the time you lose and the guy gets to do it again and he's saying "Fuck you" to *you* just like he is to *her.*'

Schwinn freed his fingernail and began tapping the snapshot, blunt-edged index finger landing repetitively on the dead girl's crotch.

Milo realized he was holding his breath, had been doing it since Schwinn launched the tirade. His skin remained saturated with heat, and he wiped his face with one hand.

Schwinn smiled. 'I'm pissing you off. Or maybe I'm scaring you. You do that – with the hand – when you're pissed off or scared.'

'What's the point, Pierce?'

'The point is you said I learned a lot, and I didn't learn dick.'

'I was just—'

'Don't *just* anything,' said Schwinn. 'There's no room for just, there's no room for bullshit. I don't need the brass sending me some . . . fly-by-night master's deg—'

60

'Fuck that,' said Milo, letting out breath and rage. 'I've been—'

'You've been watching me, checking me out, from the minute you started—'

'I've been hoping to learn something.'

'For what?' said Schwinn. 'So you can add up the brownie points, then move on to an ass-warming job with the brass. Boy-o, I know what you're about—'

Milo felt himself using his bulk. Moving closer to Schwinn, looming over the skinny man, his index finger pointing like a gun. 'You don't know shi—'

Schwinn didn't yield. 'I know assholes with master's degrees don't stick with *this*.' *Tap tap.* 'I *know* I don't wanna waste my time working a whodunit with a suck-up intellectual who all he wants to do is climb the ladder. You got ambition, find yourself some suck-up job like Daryl Gates did, driving Chief Parker's car, one day that clown'll probably end up chief.' *Taptaptap.* '*This* ain't career-building, muchacho. This is a *whodunit*. Get it? *This* likes to munch on your insides, then shit you out in pellets.'

'You're wrong,' said Milo. 'About me.'

'Am I?' Knowing smile.

Ah, thought Milo. *Here it comes. The crux.*

But Schwinn just sat there, grinning, tapping the photo.

Long silence. Then suddenly, as if someone had pulled the plug on him, the guy slumped heavily, looking defeated. 'You have no *idea* what you're up against.' He slipped the photos back in the envelope.

Milo thought: *If you hate the job, retire, asshole. Grab your pension two years early and waste the rest of your life growing tomatoes in some loser trailer park.*

Long, turgid moments passed.

Milo said, 'Big whodunit, and we're sitting here?'

'What's the alternative, Sherlock?' said Schwinn, hooking a thumb at the pink building. 'We go in there and talk to this asshole and maybe his daughter's the one who got turned into shit, or she's not. One way, we've crawled an inch on a hundred-mile hike, the other way, we haven't even started. Either way we got nothing to be proud of.'

eight

Just as quickly as his moods had shifted, Schwinn bounded out of the car.

The guy was unstable, no question about it, Milo thought as he followed.

The front door was unlocked. Twelve mailboxes to the right. The layout was precisely as Milo had envisioned.

Screw you, expert.

Box Eleven was labeled *Ingalls* in smudged red ballpoint. They climbed the stairs, and Schwinn was out of breath by the time they reached the third floor. Tightening his tie knot, he pounded the door, and it opened a few seconds later.

The man who answered was bleary-eyed and skinny-fat.

All sharp bones and stick limbs and saggy sallow skin but with a melon gut. He wore a dirty yellow tank top and blue swim shorts. No hips or butt, and the shorts bagged under the swell of his pot. Not an ounce of extra flesh anywhere but his belly. But what he carried there was grotesque and Milo thought, *Pregnant.*

'Bowie Ingalls?' said Schwinn.

Two-second delay, then a small, squirrelly nod. Beery sweat poured out of the guy, and the sour smell wafted into the hallway.

Schwinn hadn't recited any physical stats on Ingalls – hadn't said anything at all by way of preparation. To Milo, Ingalls appeared in his midforties, with thick, wavy coarse black hair worn past his shoulders – too long and luxuriant for a guy his age – and five days of gray stubble that did nothing to mask his weak features. Where his eyes weren't pink they were jaundiced and unfocused. Deep brown irises, just like those of the dead girl.

Ingalls studied their badges. The guy's timing was off, like a clock with damaged works. He flinched, then grinned, said, 'Whus up?' The words wheezed out on a cloud of hops and malt that mixed with the odors already saturated into the building's walls: mold and kerosene, the incongruous blessing of savory home cooking.

'Can we come in?' said Schwinn.

Ingalls had opened the door halfway. Behind him was dirt-colored furniture, heaps of rumpled clothes, takeout Chinese cartons, Bud empties.

Lots of empties, some crushed, some intact. Even at a good clip, the number of cans added up to more than one day of serious drinking.

A multiday bender. Unless the guy had company. Even *with* company, a focused juice-a-thon.

Guy's daughter goes missing for four days, he doesn't report it, holes up instead, sucking suds. Milo found himself entertaining the worst-case scenario: Daddy did it. Began scanning Ingalls's sallow face for anxiety, guilt, scratches, maybe that explained the delays . . .

But all he saw was confusion. Ingalls stood there, caught up in a booze-flummox.

'Sir,' said Schwinn, using the word as an insult, the way only cops can, 'can we come in?'

'Uh – yeah, sure – whu for?'

'Whu *for* your daughter.'

Ingalls's eyes drooped. Not anxiety. Resignation. As in, *here we go again*. Preparing himself for a lecture on child-rearing.

'Whu, she cut school again? They call in the cops for that now?' Schwinn smiled and moved to enter the apartment and Ingalls stepped aside, nearly stumbling. When the three of them were on the other side of the door, Schwinn closed it. He and Milo began the instinctive visual scan.

Off-white walls, brown deepening to black in the cracks and the corners. The entire front space was maybe fifteen feet square, a living room–dining area–kitchen combo, the kitchen counters crowded with more takeout boxes, used paper plates, empty soup cans. Two miserly windows on the facing wall were shuttered by yellow plastic blinds. A scabrous brown-gray sofa and a red plastic chair were both heaped with unwashed clothes and crumpled paper. Next to the chair, a stack of records tilted precariously. The Mothers of Invention's *Freak Out* on top, a fifteen-year-old LP. Nearby was a cheap phonograph half-covered by a snot green bathrobe. An open doorway led to a dead-end wall.

A full view of the front room revealed even more beer cans.

'Where does Janie go to school, sir?' said Schwinn.

'Hollywood High. What kinda hassle she get herself into now?' Bowie Ingalls scratched an armpit and drew himself up to his full height. Trying to produce some fatherly indignation.

'When's the last time you saw her, sir?'

'Um . . . she was – she slept over a friend's.'

'When, sir?' said Schwinn, still taking in the room.

Cool, all business. No one watching him do the detective thing would've imagined his lunatic tirade five minutes ago.

Milo stood to the side, worked on his cool. His mind wanted to work, but his body wasn't giving up the anger planted by Schwinn's outburst; heart still racing, face still hot. Despite the importance of the task at hand, he kept entertaining himself with images of Schwinn falling on his ass – hoist on his own petard, the self-righteous fucker – busted *in flagrante* with Tonya or some other 'source.' That brought a smile to Milo's brain. Then a question arose: if Schwinn didn't trust him, why had he risked doing Tonya right in front of him? Maybe the guy was just nuts . . . he shook all that off and returned to Bowie Ingalls's face. Still no fear, just maddening dullness.

'Um . . . Friday night,' Ingalls said, as if guessing. 'You can sit down if you want.'

There was only one place to sit in the damned sty. A man-sized clearing among the garbage on the couch. Ingalls's dozing spot. Appetizing.

'No, thanks,' said Schwinn. He had his pad out now. Milo waited a few moments before producing his. Not wanting to be part of some Ike-and-Mike vaudeville routine. 'So Janie slept at a friend's Friday night.'

'Yeah. Friday.'

'Four days ago.' Schwinn's gold Parker ballpoint was out, and he scrawled.

'Yeah. She does it all the time.'

'Sleeps over at friends'?'

'She's sixteen,' said Ingalls, whining a bit.

'What's the friend's name? The one from Friday night.'

Ingalls's tongue rolled around his left cheek. 'Linda . . . no – *Me*linda.'

66

'Last name?'

Blank stare.

'You don't know Melinda's last name?'

'Don't like the little slut,' said Ingalls. 'Bad influence. Don't like her coming around.'

'Melinda's a bad influence on Janie?'

'Yeah. You know.'

'Gets Janie in trouble,' said Schwinn.

'You know,' said Ingalls. 'Kids. Doing stuff.'

Milo wondered what could possibly offend a scrote like Ingalls.

Schwinn said, 'Stuff.'

'Yeah.'

'Such as?'

'You know,' Ingalls insisted. 'Cutting school, running around.'

'Dope?'

'I dunno about that.'

'Hmm,' said Schwinn, writing. 'So Melinda's a bad influence on Janie but you let Janie sleep over Melinda's house.'

'*Let?*' said Ingalls, coughing. 'You got kids?'

'Haven't been blessed.'

'Figures you ask me that. Nowadays, kids don't get *let* anything. They do whatever the hell they want to. Can't even get her to tell me where she's going. Or to stay in school. I tried dropping her off, personally, but she just went in, waited till I was gone, and left. That's why I figured this was about school. What is it about, anyway? She in trouble?'

'You've had trouble with Janie before?'

'No,' said Ingalls. 'Not really. Like I said, just school and running around. Being gone for a few days. But she always comes back. Let me tell you, man, you can't control 'em. Once the hippies got in and took over the city, forget it. Her mother was a hippie back in the hippie days. Hippie junkie slut, ran out on us, left me with Janie.'

'Janie into drugs?'

'Not around here,' said Ingalls. 'She knows better than that.' He blinked several times, grimaced, trying to clear his head and not succeeding. 'What's this about? What'd she do?'

Ignoring the question, Schwinn kept writing. Then: 'Hollywood High . . . what year's she in?'

'Second year.'

'Sophomore.'

Another delayed-reaction nod from Ingalls. How many of the cans had been consumed this morning?

'Sophomore.' Schwinn copied that down. 'When's her birthday?'

'Um . . . March,' said Ingalls. 'March . . . um . . . ten.'

'She was sixteen last March ten.'

'Yeah.'

Sixteen-and-a-half-year-old sophomore, thought Milo. A year behind. Borderline intelligence? Some kind of learning problem? Yet another factor that had propelled her toward victimhood? If she was the one . . .

He glanced at Schwinn but Schwinn was still writing and Milo hazarded a question of his own: 'School's hard for Janie, huh?'

Schwinn's eyebrows rose for a second, but he kept making notes.

'She hates it,' said Ingalls. 'Can barely read. That's why she hated to—' The bloodshot eyes filled with fear. 'What's going on? What'd she do?'

Focused on Milo, now. Looking to Milo for an answer,

but that was one ad lib Milo wasn't going to risk, and Ingalls shifted his attention back to Schwinn. 'C'mon, what's going on, man? What'd she do?'

'Maybe nothing,' said Schwinn, producing the blue envelope. 'Maybe something was done to her.'

He fanned out the snaps again, stretching his arm and offering Ingalls the display.

'Huh?' said Ingalls, not moving. Then: 'No.'

Calmly, no inflection. Milo thought: Okay, it wasn't her, false lead, good for him, bad for us, they'd accomplished nothing, Schwinn was right. As usual. The pompous bastard, he'd be gloating, the remainder of the shift would be unbearable—

But Schwinn continued to hold the pictures steady, and Bowie Ingalls continued to stare at them.

'No,' Ingalls repeated. He made a grab for the pictures, not a serious attempt, just a pathetic stab. Schwinn held firm, and Ingalls stepped away from the horror, pressing his hands to the sides of his head. Stamping his foot hard enough to make the floor quake.

Suddenly, he grabbed his melon-belly, bent over as if seized by cramps. Stamped again, howled, '*No!*'

Kept howling.

Schwinn let him rant for a while, then eased him over to the clearing on the couch, and told Milo, 'Get him some fortification.'

Milo found an unopened Bud, popped the top, held it to Ingalls's lips, but Ingalls shook his head. 'No, no, no. Get that the fuck away from me.'

The guy lives in a booze-haze but won't medicate himself when he sinks to the bottom. Milo supposed that passed for dignity.

He and Schwinn stood there for what seemed to be an eternity. Schwinn serene – used to this. Enjoying it?

Finally, Ingalls looked up. 'Where?' he said. 'Who?'

Schwinn gave him the basic details, talking quietly. Ingalls moaned through the entire recitation.

'Janie, Janie—'

'What can you tell us that would help us?' said Schwinn.

'Nothing. What could I tell . . . ?' Ingalls shuddered. Shivered. Crossed skinny arms over his chest. 'That – who would – oh, God . . . *Janie* . . .'

'Tell us something,' pressed Schwinn. 'Anything. Help us.'

'What . . . I don't know . . . She didn't – since she was fourteen, she's basically been gone, using this place as a crash pad but always gone, telling me to fuck off, mind my own business. Half the time, she ain't here, see what I'm sayin'?'

'Sleeping at friends' houses,' said Schwinn. 'Melinda, other friends.'

'Whatever . . . oh God, I can't believe this . . .' Tears filled Ingalls's eyes, and Schwinn was there with a snow-white hankie. PS monogram in gold thread on a corner. The guy talked despair and pessimism, but offered his own starched linen to a drunk, for the sake of the job.

'Help me,' he whispered to Ingalls. 'For Janie.'

'I would . . . I don't know – she . . . I . . . we didn't talk. Not since . . . she used to be my kid, but then she didn't want to be my kid, telling me to fuck off all the time. I'm not saying I was any big deal as a daddy, but still, without me, Janie would've . . . she turned thirteen and all of a sudden she didn't appreciate anything. Started going out all hours, the school didn't give a shit.

Janie never went, no one from the school ever called me, not one time.'

'You call them?'

Ingalls shook his head. 'What's the point? Talking to people who don't give a shit. I'da called, they'da probably sent cops over and busted me for something, child neglect, whatever. I was busy, man. Working – I used to work at Paramount Studios.'

'Oh, yeah?' said Schwinn.

'Yeah. Publicity department. Information transfer.'

'Janie interested in the movies?'

'Nah,' said Ingalls. 'Anything I was into she *wasn't* into.'

'What was she into?'

'Nothing. Running around.'

'This friend, Melinda. If Janie never told you where she was going, how do you know she was with Melinda Friday night?'

'Because I seen her with Melinda on Friday.'

'What time?'

'Around six. I was sleeping, and Janie busts in to get some clothes, I wake up, by the time I'm sitting up, she's heading out the door, and I look out there.' He jabbed a thumb at the shuttered windows. 'I seen her walking away with Melinda.'

'Walking which way?'

'That way.' Hooking his finger north. Toward Sunset, maybe Hollywood Boulevard, if the girls had kept going.

'Anyone else with them?'

'No, just the two of them.'

'Walking, not driving,' said Schwinn.

'Janie didn't have no license. I got one car, and it barely drives. No way was I gonna – she didn't care, anyway. Got around by hitching. I told her about that – I used to

hitch, back when you could do it, but now, with all the –
you think that's what happened? She hitched and
some . . . oh, God . . .'

Unaware of Janie's downtown rape? If so, the guy was
being truthful about one thing: Janie had been lost to him
for a long time.

'Some what?' said Schwinn.

'Some – you know,' moaned Ingalls. 'Getting picked up
– some stranger.'

The death snaps were back in the envelope, but
Schwinn had kept the envelope in full view. Now he
waved it inches from Ingalls's face. 'I'd say, sir, that only a
stranger would do something like this. Unless you have
some other idea?'

'Me? No,' said Ingalls. 'She was like her mother. Didn't
talk – gimme that beer.'

When the can was empty, Schwinn waved the envelope
again. 'Let's get back to Friday. Janie came home to get
clothes. What was she wearing?'

Ingalls thought. 'Jeans and a T-shirt – red T-shirt . . .
and those crazy black shoes with those heels – platform
heels. She was *carrying* her party clothes.'

'Party clothes.'

'When I woke up and saw her going out the door, I
could see part of what she had in the bag.'

'What kind of bag?'

'Shopping bag. White – Zody's, probably, 'cause that's
where she shops. She always stuffed her party stuff inside
shopping bags.'

'What did you see in the bag?'

'Red halter the size of a Band-Aid. I always told her it
was hooker shit, she should throw it out, used to threaten
her I'd throw it out.'

'But you didn't.'

'No,' said Ingalls. 'What woulda been the point?'

'A red halter,' said Schwinn. 'What else?'

'That's all I saw. Probably a skirt, one of those micro-minis, that's all she buys. The shoes she already had on.'

'Black with big heels.'

'Shiny black,' said Ingalls. 'Patent leather. Those crazy heels, I kept telling her she'd fall and break her neck.'

'Party outfit,' said Schwinn, copying.

Red-and-black party outfit, thought Milo. Remembering something that had gone round in high school, boys sitting around pontificating, pointing with glee: red and black on Fridays meant a girl put out all the way. Him, laughing along, pretending to care . . .

Bowie Ingalls said, 'Except for the jeans and T-shirts, that's all she buys. Party stuff.'

'Speaking of which,' said Schwinn, 'let's take a look at her closet.'

The rest of the apartment was two cell-sized bedrooms separated by a windowless bathroom stale with flatulence.

Schwinn and Milo glanced into Bowie Ingalls's sleep chamber as they passed. A queen-size mattress took up most of the floor. Unwashed sheets were pulled half-off, and they puddled on cheap carpeting. A tiny TV threatened to topple from a pressed-wood bureau. More Bud empties.

Janie's room was even smaller, with barely enough space for a single mattress and a nightstand of the same synthetic wood. Cutouts from teen magazines were taped to the walls, mounted at careless angles. A single, muddy-looking stuffed koala slumped on the nightstand, next to a soft pack of Kents and a half-empty box of Luden's cough drops. The room was so cramped that the mattress prevented the closet door from opening all the way, and Schwinn had to contort to get a look inside.

He winced, stepped out, and told Milo, 'You do it.'

Milo's size made the task excruciating, but he obeyed.

Zody's was a cut-rate barn. Even at their prices, Janie Ingalls hadn't assembled much of a wardrobe. On the dusty floor sat one pair of tennis shoes, size 8, next to red Thom McAn platform sandals and white plastic boots with see-through plastic soles. Two pairs of size S jeans were carelessly hung in the closet, one faded denim with holes that could've been genuine wear or contrivance, the other denim patchwork, both made in Taiwan. Four ribbed, snug-fit T-shirts with bias-cut sleeves, a floral cotton blouse with moth wounds pocking the breast pocket, three shiny, polyester halter tops not much bigger than the hankie Schwinn had offered to Ingalls – peacock blue, black, pearlescent white. A red sweatshirt emblazoned *Hollywood* in puffy gold letters, a black plastic shortie jacket pretending to be leather, cracking like an old lady's face.

On the top shelf were bikini underpants, bras, panty hose, more dust. Everything stank of tobacco. Only a few pockets to search. Other than grit and lint and a Double-mint wrapper, Milo found nothing. Such a *blank* existence – not unlike his own apartment, he hadn't bothered to furnish much since arriving in L.A., had never been sure he'd be staying.

He searched the rest of the room. The magazine posters were the closest thing to personal possessions. No diary or date book or photographs of friends. If Janie had ever called this dump home, she'd changed her mind some time ago. He wondered if she had some other place of refuge – a crash pad, a sanctuary, somewhere she *kept* stuff.

He checked under the bed, found dirt. When he extricated himself, his neck hurt and his shoulders throbbed.

Schwinn and Ingalls were back in the front room, and Milo stopped to check out the bathroom, compressing his nostrils to block out the stench, examining the medicine cabinet. All over-the-counter stuff – painkillers, laxatives, diarrhea remedies, antacids – a host of antacids. Something eating at Bowie Ingalls's gut? Guilt or just alcohol?

Milo found himself craving a drink.

When he joined Schwinn and Ingalls, Ingalls was slumped on the couch, looking disoriented, saying, 'What do I do now?'

Schwinn stood away from the guy, detached. No more use for Ingalls. 'There'll be some procedures to go through – identification, filling out forms. Identification can wait till after the autopsy. We may have more questions for you.'

Ingalls looked up. 'About what?'

Schwinn handed Ingalls his card. 'If you think of anything, give a call.'

'I already told you everything.'

Milo said, 'Was there anywhere else Janie mighta crashed?'

'Like what?'

'Like a crash pad. Somewhere kids go.'

'I dunno where kids go. Dunno where my own kid goes, so how would I know?'

'Okay, thanks. Sorry for your loss, Mr Ingalls.'

Schwinn motioned Milo to the door, but when they got

there, he turned back to Ingalls. 'One more thing: what does Melinda look like?'

Basic question, thought Milo, but he hadn't thought to ask it. Schwinn had, but he orchestrated it, timed everything. The guy was nuts but miles ahead of him.

'Short, big tits – built big – kinda fat. Blond hair, real long, straight.'

'Voluptuous,' said Schwinn, enjoying the word.

'Whatever.'

'And she's Janie's age?'

'Maybe a little older,' said Ingalls.

'A sophomore, too?'

'I dunno what she is.'

'Bad influence,' said Schwinn.

'Yeah.'

'Do you have a picture of Janie? Something we could show around?'

'I'd have to have one, wouldn't I?' said Bowie, making it sound like the answer to an oral exam. Pulling himself to his feet, he stumbled to his bedroom, returned moments later with a three-by-five snap.

A dark-haired child around ten years old, wearing a sleeveless dress and staring at a five-foot-tall Mickey Mouse. Mickey giving that idiot grin, the kid unimpressed – scared, actually. No way to connect this child to the outrage on Beaudry.

'Disneyland,' said Ingalls.

'You took Janie there?' said Milo, trying to imagine that.

'Nah, it was a school trip. They got a group discount.'

Schwinn returned the photo to Ingalls. 'I was thinking in terms of something more recent.'

'I should have something,' said Ingalls, 'but hell if I can

76

find anything – if I do, I'll call you.'

'I noticed,' said Milo, 'that there was no diary in Janie's room.'

'You say so.'

'You never saw a diary or a date book – a photo album?'

Ingalls shook his head. 'I stayed out of Janie's stuff, but she wouldn't have any of that. Janie didn't like to write. Writing was hard for her. Her mother was like that, too: never really learned to read. I tried to teach Janie. The school didn't do shit.'

Papa Juicehead huddled with Janie, tutoring. Hard to picture.

Schwinn frowned – he'd lost patience with Milo's line of questioning and gave the doorknob a sharp twist. 'Afternoon, Mr Ingalls.'

As the door closed, Ingalls cried out: 'She was my kid.'

'What a stupid asshole,' said Schwinn, as they headed to Hollywood High. 'Stupid parents, stupid kid. Genes. That's what you were getting at, right, with those questions about school?'

'I was thinking learning problems coulda made her an easier victim,' said Milo.

Schwinn grumbled, 'Anyone can be a victim.'

The school was an ugly pile of gray-brown stucco that filled a block on the north side of Sunset just west of Highland. As impersonal as an airport, and Milo felt the curse of futility the moment his feet touched down on the campus. He and Schwinn walked past what seemed to be thousands of kids – every one of them bored, spaced, surly. Smiles and laughter were aberrations, and any eye contact directed at the detectives was hostile.

They asked directions of a teacher, got the same icy reception, not much better at the principal's office. As Schwinn talked to a secretary, Milo studied girls walking through the sweaty corridor. Tight or minimal clothes and hooker makeup seemed to be the mode, all those freshly developed bodies promising something they might not be able to deliver, and he wondered how many potential Janies were out there.

The principal was at a meeting downtown, and the secretary routed them to the vice principal for operations, who sent them farther down the line to the guidance office. The counselor they spoke to was a pretty young woman named Ellen Sato, tiny, Eurasian, with long, side-winged, blond-tipped hair. The news of Janie's murder made her face crumple, and Schwinn took advantage of it by pressing her with questions.

Useless. She'd never heard of Janie, finally admitted she'd been on the job for less than a month. Schwinn kept pushing and she disappeared for a while, then returned with bad news: no *Ingalls, J.* files on record for any guidance sessions or disciplinary actions.

The girl was a habitual truant, but hadn't entered the system. Bowie Ingalls had been right about one thing: no one cared.

The poor kid had never had any moorings, thought Milo, remembering his own brush with truancy: back when his family still lived in Gary and his father was working steel, making good money, feeling like a bread-winner. Milo was nine, had been plagued by terrible dreams since the summer – visions of men. One dreary Monday, he got off the school bus and instead of entering the school grounds just kept walking aimlessly, placing one foot in front of the other. Ending up at a park, where he sat on a bench like a tired old man. All day. A friend of his mother spotted him, reported him. Mom had been perplexed; Dad, always action-oriented, knew just what to do. Out came the strap. Ten pounds of oily iron-worker's belt. Milo hadn't sat comfortably for a long, long time.

Yet another reason to hate the old man. Still, he'd never repeated the offense, ended up graduating with good grades. Despite the dreams. And all that followed. Certain his father would've killed him if he knew what was *really* going on.

So he made plans at age nine: *You need to get away from these people.*

Now he mused: *Maybe I was the lucky one.*

'Okay,' Schwinn was telling Ellen Sato, 'so you people don't know much about her—'

The young woman was on the verge of tears. 'I'm sorry, sir, but as I said, I just . . . what happened to her?'

'Someone killed her,' said Schwinn. 'We're looking for a friend of hers, probably a student here, also. Melinda, sixteen or seventeen. Long blond hair. Vo*lup*tuous.' Cupping his hands in front of his own, scrawny chest.

Sato's ivory skin pinkened. 'Melinda's a common name—'

'How about a look at your student roster?'

'The roster . . .' Sato's graceful hands fluttered. 'I could find a yearbook for you.'

'You have no student roster?'

'I – I know we have class lists, but they're over in V.P. Sullivan's office and there are forms to be filled out. Okay, sure, I'll go look. In the meantime, I know where the yearbooks are. Right here.' Pointing to a closet.

79

'Great,' said Schwinn, without graciousness.

'Poor Janie,' said Sato. 'Who would do such a thing?'

'Someone *evil*, ma'am. Anyone come to mind?'

'Oh, heavens no – I wasn't . . . let me go get that list.'

The two detectives sat on a bench in the counseling office waiting room, flipping through the yearbooks, ignoring the scornful eyes of the students who came and went. Copying down the names of every Caucasian Melinda, freshmen included, because who knew how accurate Bowie Ingalls was about age. Not limiting the count to blondes, either, because hair dye was a teenage-girl staple.

Milo said, 'What about light-skinned Mexicans?'

'Nah,' said Schwinn. 'If she was a greaser, Ingalls would've mentioned it.'

'Why?'

'Because he doesn't like her, would've loved to add another bad point to the list.'

Milo returned to checking out young white faces.

The end product: eighteen possibles.

Schwinn regarded the list and scowled. 'Names but no numbers. We'll still need a fucking roster to track her down.'

Talking low but his tone was unmistakable and the receptionist a few feet away looked over and frowned.

'Howdy,' said Schwinn, raising his voice and grinning at the woman furiously. She flinched and returned to her typewriter.

Milo looked up Janie Ingalls's freshman photo. No list of extracurricular activities. Huge, dark hair teased with abandon over a pretty oval face turned ghostly by slathers of makeup and ghoulish eye shadow. The image before him was neither the ten-year-old hanging with Mickey nor the corpse atop the freeway ramp. So many identities for a sixteen-year-old kid. He asked the receptionist to make a photocopy, and she agreed, grudgingly. Staring first at the picture.

'Know her, ma'am?' Milo asked her as pleasantly as possible.

'No. Here you go. It didn't come out too good. Our machine needs adjusting.'

Ellen Sato returned, freshly made-up, weak-eyed, forcing a smile. 'How'd we do?'

Schwinn bounded up quickly, was in her face, bullying her with body language, beaming that same hostile grin. 'Oh, just great, ma'am.' He brandished the list of eighteen names. 'Now how about introducing us to these lovely ladies?'

Rounding up the Melindas took another forty minutes. Twelve out of eighteen girls were in attendance that day, and they marched in looking supremely bored. Only a couple were vaguely aware of Janie Ingalls's existence, none admitted to being a close friend or knowing anyone who was, none seemed to be holding back.

Not much curiosity, either, about why they'd been called in to talk to cops. As if a police presence was the usual thing at Hollywood High. Or they just didn't care.

One thing *was* clear: Janie hadn't made her mark on campus. The girl who was the most forthcoming ended up in Milo's queue. Barely blond, not-at-all voluptuous Melinda Kantor. 'Oh yeah, her. She's a stoner, right?'

'Is she?' he said.

The girl shrugged. She had a long, pretty face, a bit equine. Two-inch nails glossed aqua, no bra.

81

Milo said, 'Does she hang around with other stoners?'

'Uh-uh, she's not a social stoner – more like a loner stoner.'

'A loner stoner.'

'Yeah.'

'Which means . . .'

The girl shot him a *you-are-a-prime-lame-o* look. 'She run away or something?'

'Something like that.'

'Well,' said Melinda Kantor, 'maybe she's over on the Boulevard.'

'Hollywood Boulevard?'

The resultant smirk said, *Another stupid question,* and Milo knew he was losing her. 'The boulevard's where the loner stoners go.'

Now Melinda Kantor was regarding him as if he were brain-dead. 'I was just making a *suggestion*. What'd she do?'

'Maybe nothing.'

'Yeah, right,' said the girl. 'Weird.'

'What is?'

'Usually they send over narcs who are young and cute.'

Ellen Sato produced addresses and phone numbers for the six absent Melindas, and Milo and Schwinn spent the rest of the day paying house calls.

The first four girls lived in smallish but tidy single homes on Hollywood's border with the Los Feliz district and were out sick. Melindas Adams, Greenberg, Jordan were in bed with the flu, Melinda Hohlmeister had been felled by an asthma attack. All four mothers were in attendance, all were freaked out by the drop-in, but each allowed the detectives access. The previous generation

82

still respected – or feared – authority.

Melinda Adams was a tiny, platinum-haired, fourteen-year-old freshman who looked eleven and had a little kid's demeanor to match. Melinda Jordan was a skinny fifteen-year-old brunette with a frighteningly runny nose and vengeful acne. Greenberg was blond and long-haired and somewhat chesty. Both she and her mother had thick, almost impenetrable accents – recent immigrants from Israel. Science and math books were spread over her bed. When the detectives had stepped in, she'd been underlining text in yellow marker, had no idea who Janie Ingalls was. Melinda Hohlmeister was a shy, chubby, stuttering, homely kid with short, corn-colored ringlets, a straight A average, and an audible wheeze.

No response to Janie's name from any of them.

No answer at Melinda Van Epps's big white contemporary house up in the hills. A woman next door picking flowers volunteered that the family was in Europe, had been gone for two weeks. The father was an executive with Standard Oil, the Van Eppses took all five kids out of school all the time for travel, provided tutors, lovely people.

No reply, either, at Melinda Waters's shabby bungalow on North Gower. Schwinn knocked hard because the bell was taped over and labeled 'Broken.'

'Okay, leave a note,' he told Milo. 'It'll probably be bullshit, too.' Just as Milo was slipping the *please-call-us* memo and his card through the mail slot, the door swung open.

The woman who stood there could have been Bowie Ingalls's spiritual sister. Fortyish, thin but flabby, wearing a faded brown housedress. She had a mustard complexion, wore her peroxided hair pinned back carelessly.

Confused blue eyes, no makeup, cracked lips. That furtive look.

'Mrs Waters?' said Milo.

'I'm Eileen.' Cigarette voice. 'What is it?'

Schwinn showed her the badge. 'We'd like to talk to Melinda.'

Eileen Waters's head retracted, as if he'd slapped her. 'About what?'

'Her friend, Janie Ingalls.'

'Oh. Her,' said Waters. 'What'd she do?'

'Someone killed her,' said Schwinn. 'Did a right sloppy job of it. Where's Melinda?'

Eileen Waters's parched lips parted, revealing uneven teeth coated with yellow scum. She'd relied upon suspiciousness as a substitute for dignity and now, losing both, she slumped against the doorjamb. 'Oh my God.'

'Where's Melinda?' demanded Schwinn.

Waters shook her head, lowered it. 'Oh God, oh God.'

Schwinn took her arm. His voice remained firm. 'Where's Melinda?'

More headshakes, and when Eileen Waters spoke again her voice was that of another woman: timid, chastened. Reduced.

She began crying. Finally stopped. 'Melinda never came home, I haven't seen her since *Friday*.'

nine

The Waters household was a step up from Bowie Ingalls's flop, furnished with old, ungainly furniture that might've been hand-me-downs from some upright Midwestern homestead. Browning doilies on the arms of overstuffed chairs said someone had once cared. Ashtrays were everywhere, filled with gray dust and butts, and the air felt sooty. No beer empties, but Milo noticed a quarter-full bottle of Dewars on a kitchen counter next to a jam jar packed with something purple. Every drape was drawn, plunging the house into perpetual evening. The sun could be punishing when your body subsisted on ethanol.

Either Schwinn had developed an instant dislike for Eileen Waters or his bad mood had intensified or he had a genuine reason for riding her hard. He sat her down on a sofa, and began peppering her with questions.

She did nothing to defend herself other than chain-smoke Parliaments, was easy with the confessions:

Melinda was wild, had been wild for a long time, had fought off any attempts at discipline. Yes, she used drugs – marijuana, for sure. Eileen had found roaches in her pockets, wasn't sure about anything harder, but wasn't denying the possibility.

'What about Janie Ingalls?' asked Schwinn.

'You kidding? She's probably the one introduced Melinda to dope.'

'Why's that?'

'That kid was stoned all the time.'

'How old's Melinda?'

'Seventeen.'

'What year in school?'

'Eleventh grade – I know Janie's in tenth but just because Melinda's older doesn't mean she was the instigator. Janie was street-smart. I'm sure Janie's the one got Melinda into grass . . . Lord, where could she *be*?'

Milo thought back to his search of Janie's room: no evidence of dope, not even rolling paper or a pipe.

'Melinda and Janie were a perfect pair,' Waters was saying. 'Neither of them gave a damn about school, they cut all the time.'

'What'd you do about it?'

The woman laughed. 'Right.' Then the fear came back. 'Melinda will come back, she always does.'

'In what way was Janie streetwise?' said Schwinn.

'You know,' said Waters. 'You can just tell. Like she'd been around.'

'Sexually?'

'I assume. Melinda was basically a good girl.'

'Janie spend much time here?'

'No. Mostly she'd pick up Melinda, and they'd be off.'

'That the case last Friday?'

'Dunno.'

'What do you mean?'

'I was out shopping. Came home, and Melinda was gone. I could tell she'd been here because she left her underwear on the floor and some food out in the kitchen.'

'Food for one?'

Waters thought. 'One Popsicle wrapper and a Pepsi can – I guess.'

'So the last time you saw Melinda was Friday morning, but you don't know if Janie came by to pick her up.'

Waters nodded. 'She claimed she was going to school, but I don't think so. She had a bag full of clothes, and when I said, "What's all that?" she said she was going to some party that night, might not be coming home. We got into a hassle about that, but what could I do? I wanted to know where the party was but all she told me was it was fancy, on the Westside.'

'Where on the Westside?'

'I just told you, she wouldn't say.' The woman's face twitched. 'Fancy party. Rich kids. She said that a bunch of times. Told me I had nothing to worry about.'

She looked to Schwinn, then Milo, for reassurance, got two stone faces.

'Fancy Westside party,' said Schwinn. 'So maybe Beverly Hills – or Bel Air.'

'I guess . . . I asked her how she was getting all the way over there, she said she'd find a way. I told her not to hitch, and she said she wouldn't.'

'You don't like her hitching.'

'Would you? Standing there on Sunset, thumbing, any kind of pervert . . .' She stopped, went rigid. 'Where was – where'd you find Janie?'

'Near downtown.'

Waters relaxed. 'So there you go, the complete opposite direction. Melinda wasn't with her. Melinda was over on the Westside.'

Schwinn's slit eyes made the merest turn toward Milo. Bowie Ingalls had seen Melinda pick up Janie on Friday,

87

watched the two girls walking north toward Thumb Alley. But no reason to get into that, now.

'Melinda'll come back,' said Waters. 'Sometimes she does that. Stays away. She always comes back.'

'Sometimes,' said Schwinn. 'Like once a week?'

'No, nothing like that – just once in a while.'

'And how long does she stay away?'

'A night,' said Waters, sagging and trying to calm herself with a twenty-second pull on her cigarette. Her hand shook. Confronting the fact that this was Melinda's longest absence.

Then she perked up. 'One time she stayed away two days. Went up to see her father. He's in the Navy, used to live in Oxnard.'

'Where's he live now?'

'Turkey. He's at a naval base there. Shipped out two months ago.'

'How'd Melinda get to Oxnard?'

Eileen Waters chewed her lip. 'Hitched. I'm not going to tell him. Even if I could reach him in Turkey, he'd just start in with the accusations . . . and that bitch of his.'

'Second wife?' said Schwinn.

'His whore,' spat Waters. 'Melinda hated her. Melinda will come home.'

Further questioning was futile. The woman knew nothing more about the 'fancy Westside party,' kept harping on the downtown murder site as clear proof Melinda hadn't been with Janie. They pried a photo of Melinda out of her. Unlike Bowie Ingalls, she'd maintained an album, and though Melinda's teen years were given short shrift, the detectives had a page of snaps from which to choose.

Bowie Ingalls hadn't been fair to Melinda Waters.

Nothing chubby about the girl's figure, she was beautifully curvy with high, round breasts and a tiny waist. Straight blond hair hung to her rear. Kiss-me lips formed a heartbreaking smile.

'Looks like Marilyn, doesn't she?' said her mother. 'Maybe one day she'll be a movie star.'

Driving back to the station, Milo said, 'How long before her body shows up?'

'Who the fuck knows?' said Schwinn, studying Melinda's picture. 'From the looks of this, maybe Janie was the appetizer and this one was the main dish. Look at those tits. That'd give him something to play with for a while. Yeah, I can see him holding on to this one for a while.'

He pocketed the photo.

Milo envisioned a torture chamber. The blond girl nude, shackled . . . 'So what do we do about finding her?'

'Nothing,' said Schwinn. 'If she's already dead, we have to wait till she shows up. If he's still got her, he's not gonna tell us.'

'What about that Westside party?'

'What about it?'

'We could put the word out with West L.A., the sheriffs, Beverly Hills PD. Sometimes parties get wild, the blues go out on a nuisance call.'

'So what?' said Schwinn. 'We show up at some rich asshole's door, say, "Excuse me, are you cutting up this kid?" ' He sniffed, coughed, produced his bottle of decongestant, and swigged. 'Shit, Waters's dump was dusty. All-American mom, another poor excuse for an adult. Who knows if there even *was* a party.'

'Why wouldn't there be?'

'Because kids lie to their parents.' Schwinn swiveled

toward Milo. 'What's with all these fucking questions? You thinking of going to law school?'

Milo held his tongue, and the rest of the ride was their usual joyfest. A block from the station, Schwinn said, 'You wanna go snooping for Westside nuisance calls, be my guest, but I think Blondie was lying to Mommy like she always did because a fancy Westside party was exactly the kind of thing that would calm the old lady down. Hundred to one Blondie and Janie were fixing to thumb the Strip, score some dope, maybe trade blow jobs for it, or whatever. They got into the wrong set of wheels and ended up downtown. Janie was too stupid to learn from her past experience – or like I said, maybe she liked being tied up. She was a stoner. Both of them probably were.'

'Your source mentioned a Westside party.'

'Street talk's like watermelon, you got to pick around the seeds. The main thing is Janie was *found* downtown. And chances are Melinda's somewhere around there, too, if a scrote got her and finished with her. For all we know, he kept her in the trunk while he was setting up Janie on Beaudry. Got back on the freeway, he could be in Nevada by now.'

He shook his head. 'Stupid kids. Two of them thought they had the world in their sweet little hands, and the world upped and bit 'em.'

Back at the station, Schwinn collected his things from his desk and walked off without a word to Milo. Not even bothering to sign out. No one noticed: none of the detectives paid much attention to Schwinn, period.

An outcast, Milo realized. *Did they stick me with him by coincidence?*

Pushing all that aside, he played phone poker until

well after dark. Contacting every police entity west of Hollywood Division in search of 415 party calls. Throwing in rent-a-cop outfits, too: The Bel Air Patrol, and other private firms that covered Beverlywood, Cheviot Hills, Pacific Palisades. The privates turned out to be the worst to deal with – no one was willing to talk without supervisory clearance and Milo had to leave his name and badge number, wait for callbacks that probably wouldn't happen.

He kept going, casting his net to Santa Monica and beyond, even including the southern edge of Ventura County, because Melinda Waters had once hitched the Pacific Coast Highway to Oxnard to see her father. And kids flocked to the beach for parties – he'd spent many a sleepless night driving up and down the coast highway, spotting bonfires that sparked the tide, the faint silhouettes of couples. Wondering what it would be like to have someone.

Four hours of work resulted in two measly hits – either L.A. had turned sleepy, or no one was complaining about noise anymore.

Two big zeros: an eye surgeon's fiftieth birthday party on Roxbury Drive in Beverly Hills had evoked a Friday midnight complaint from a cranky neighbor.

'Kids? No, don't think so,' laughed the BH desk officer. 'We're talking black tie, all that good stuff. Lester Lanin's orchestra playing swing and still someone bitched. There's always some killjoy, right?'

The second call was a Santa Monica item: a bar mitzvah on Fifth Street north of Montana had been closed down just after 2 A.M., after rambunctious thirteen-year-olds began setting off firecrackers.

Milo put the phone down and stretched. His ears

burned and his neck felt like dry ice. Schwinn's voice was an obnoxious mantra in his head as he left the station just before 1 A.M.

Told you so, asshole. Told you so, asshole.

He drove to a bar – a straight one on Eighth Street, not far from the Ambassador Hotel. He'd passed it several times, a shabby-looking place on the ground floor of an old brick apartment building that had seen better days. The few patrons drinking this late were past their prime, too, and his entrance lowered the median age by a few decades. Mel Tormé on tape loop, scary-looking tooth-picked shrimp and bowls full of cracker medley decorated the cloudy bar top. Milo downed a few shots and beers, kept his head down, left, and drove north to Santa Monica Boulevard, cruising Boystown for a while, but didn't even wrestle with temptation: tonight the male hookers looked predatory, and he realized he wanted to be with no one, not even himself. When he reached his apartment, images of Melinda Waters's torment had returned to plague him, and he pulled down a bottle of Jim Beam from a kitchenette cupboard. Tired but wired. Removing his clothes was an ordeal, and the sight of his pitiful, white body made him close his eyes.

He lay in bed, wishing the darkness was more complete. Wishing for a brain valve that would choke off the pictures. Alcohol lullabies finally eased him, stumbling, to sleep.

The next morning, he drove to a newsstand and picked up the morning's *Times* and *Herald-Examiner*. No reporter had called him or Schwinn on the Ingalls murder, but something that ugly was sure to be covered.

But it wasn't, not a line of print.

That made no sense. Reporters were tuned in to the

police band, covered the morgue, too.

He sped to the station, checked his own box and Schwinn's for journalistic queries. Found only a single phone slip with his name at the top. Officer Del Monte from the Bel Air Patrol, no message. He dialed the number, talked to a few flat, bored voices before finally reaching Del Monte.

'Oh, yeah. You're the one called about parties.' The guy had a crisp, clipped voice, and Milo knew he was talking to an ex–military man. Middle-aged voice. Korea, not VN.

'That's right. Thanks for calling back. What've you got?'

'Two on Friday, both times kids being jerks. The first was a sweet sixteen on Stradella, all-girls' sleepover that some punks tried to crash. Not local boys. Black kids and Mexicans. The girls' parents called us, and we ejected them.'

'Where were the crashers from?'

'They claimed Beverly Hills.' Del Monte laughed. 'Right.'

'They give you any trouble?'

'Not up front. They made like they were leaving Bel Air – we followed them to Sunset, then hung back and watched. Idiots crossed over near UCLA, then tried to come back a few minutes later and head over to the other party.' Del Monte chuckled, again. 'No luck, Pachuco. Our people were already there on a neighbor complaint. We ejected them before they even got out of the car.'

'Where was the second party?'

'That was the live one, big-time noise. Upper Stone Canyon Drive way above the hotel.'

93

The locale Schwinn's source had mentioned. 'Whose house?'

'Empty house,' said Del Monte. 'The family bought a bigger one but didn't get around to selling the first one and the parents took a vacation, left the kiddies behind and, big surprise, the kiddies decided to use the empty house for fun 'n' games, invited the entire damn city. Must've been two, three hundred kids all over the place, cars – Porsches and other good wheels, and plenty of outside wheels. By the time we showed up, it was a scene. It's a big property, coupla acres, no real close-by neighbors, but by now the closest neighbors were fed up.'

'By now?' said Milo. 'This wasn't the first time?'

Silence. 'We've had a few other calls there. Tried to contact the parents, no luck, they're always out of town.'

'Spoiled brats.'

Del Monte laughed. 'You didn't hear that from me. Anyway, what's up with all this?'

'Tracing a 187 victim's whereabouts.'

Silence. 'Homicide? Nah, no way. This was just kids partying and playing music too loud.'

'I'm sure you're right,' said Milo. 'But I've got rumors that my db might've attended a party on the Westside, so I've gotta ask. What's the name of the family that owns the house?'

Longer silence. 'Listen,' said Del Monte. 'These people – you do me wrong, I could be parking cars. And believe me, no one saw anything worse than drinking and screwing around – a few joints, big deal, right? Anyway, we closed it down.'

'I'm just going through the routine, Officer,' said Milo. 'Your name won't come up. But if I don't check it out, *I'll* be parking cars. Who owns the house and what's the address?'

'A rumor?' said Del Monte. 'There had to be tons of parties Friday night.'

'Any party we hear about, we look into. That's why yours won't stick out.'

'Okay . . . the family's named Cossack.' Del Monte uttered it weightily, as if that was supposed to mean something.

'Cossack,' said Milo, keeping his tone ambiguous.

'As in office buildings, shopping malls – Garvey Cossack. Big downtown developer, part of that bunch wanted to bring another football team to L.A.'

'Yeah, sure,' lied Milo. His interest in sports had peaked with Pop Warner baseball. 'Cossack on Stone Canyon. What's the address?'

Del Monte sighed and read off the numbers.

'How many kids in the family?' said Milo.

'Three – two boys and a girl. Didn't see the daughter there, but she could've been.'

'You know the kids personally?'

'Nah, just by sight.'

'So the boys threw the party,' said Milo. 'Names?'

'The big one's Garvey Junior and the younger one's Bob but they call him Bobo.'

'How old?'

'Junior's probably twenty-one, twenty-two, Bobo's maybe a year younger.'

More than kids, thought Milo.

'They gave us no trouble,' said Del Monte. 'They're just a couple guys like to have fun.'

'And the girl?'

'Her I didn't see.'

Milo thought he picked up something new in Del Monte's voice. 'Name?'

'Caroline.'

'Age?'

'Younger – maybe seventeen. It was really no big deal, everyone dispersed. My message said you're Central. Where was your db found?'

Milo told him.

'There you go,' said Del Monte. 'Fifteen miles from Bel Air. You're wasting your time.'

'Probably. Three hundred partying kids just caved when you showed up?'

'We've got experience with that kind of thing.'

'What's the technique?' said Milo.

'Use sensitivity,' said the rent-a-cop. 'Don't treat 'em like you would a punk from Watts or East L.A. 'cause these kids are accustomed to a certain style.'

'Which is?'

'Being treated like they're important. If that doesn't work, threaten to call the parents.'

'And if that doesn't work?'

'That usually works. Gotta go, nice talking to you.'

'I appreciate the time, Officer. Listen, if I came by and showed a photo around, would there be a chance anyone would recognize a face?'

'Whose face?'

'The vic's.'

'No way. Like I said, it was a swarm. After a while they all start to look alike.'

'Rich kids?'

'Any kids.'

It was nearly 10 A.M., and Schwinn still hadn't shown up.

Figuring sooner rather than later was the best time to spring Janie's photo on Del Monte and his patrol buddies, Milo threw on his jacket and left the station.

Del Monte had been decent enough to call and look where it got him.

No good deed goes unpunished.

It took nearly forty minutes to reach Bel Air. The patrol office was a white, tile-roofed bungalow tucked behind the west gate. Lots of architectural detail inside and out – Milo would've been happy to make it his house. He'd heard that the gates and the private-cop scrutiny had been instituted by Howard Hughes when he lived in Bel Air because the billionaire didn't trust LAPD.

The rich taking care of their own. Just like the party on Stone Canyon: ticked-off neighbors, but everything kept private, no nuisance call had reached the West L.A. station.

Del Monte was at the front desk, and when Milo came in, his dark, round face turned sour. Milo apologized and whipped out a crime-scene snap he'd taken from the pile Schwinn had left in his desk. The least horrifying of the collection – side view of Janie's face, just the hint of ligature ring around the neck. Del Monte's response was a cursory head flick. Two other guards were drinking coffee, and they gave the picture more careful study, then shook their heads. Milo would have liked to show Melinda Waters's photo, but Schwinn had pocketed it.

He left the patrol office and drove to the party house on Stone Canyon Drive. Huge, redbrick, three-story, six-column colonial. Black double doors, black shutters, mullioned windows, multiple gables. Milo's guess was twenty, twenty-five rooms.

The Cossack family had moved to something more generous.

A huge dry lawn and flaking paint on some of the shutters said the maintenance schedule had slackened since the house had emptied. Shredded hedges and scraps of paper confettiing the brick walkway were the only evidence of revelry gone too far. Milo parked, got out, picked up one of the shreds, hoping for some writing, but it was soft and absorbent and blank – heavy-duty paper towel. The gate to the backyard was bolted and opaque. He peered over, saw a big blue egg of a pool, rolling greenery, lots of brick patio, blue jays pecking. Behind one of the hedges, the glint of glass – cans and bottles.

The nearest neighbor was to the south, well separated from the colonial by the broad lawns of both houses. A much smaller, meticulously maintained one-story ranch emblazoned with flower beds and fronted by dwarf junipers trimmed Japanese-style. The northern border of the Cossack property was marked by a ten-foot stone wall that went on for a good thousand feet up Stone Canyon. Probably some multiacre estate, a humongous chateau pushed back too far from the street to be visible.

Milo walked across the dry lawn and the colonial's empty driveway, up to the ranch house's front door. Teak door, with a shiny brass knocker shaped like a swan. Off to the right a small cement Shinto shrine presided over a tiny, babbling stream.

A very tall woman in her late sixties answered his ring. Stout and regal with puffy, rouged cheeks, she wore her silver hair tied back in a bun so tight it looked painful, had sheathed her impressive frame in a cream kimono hand-painted with herons and butterflies. In one liver-spotted hand was an ivory-handled brush with pointed bristles tipped with black ink. Even in black satin flat slippers she was nearly eye level with Milo. Heels would have made her a giantess.

'Ye-es?' Watchful eyes, deliberate contralto.

Out came the badge. 'Detective Sturgis, Mrs . . .'

'Schwartzman. What brings a detective to Bel Air?'

'Well, ma'am, last Friday your neighbors had a party—'

'A party,' she said, as if the description was absurd. She aimed the brush at the empty colonial. 'More like rooting at the trough. The aptly named Cossacks.'

'Aptly named?'

'Barbarians,' said Mrs Schwartzman. 'A scourge.'

'You've had problems with them before.'

'They lived there for less than two years, let the place go to seed. That's their pattern, apparently. Move in, degrade, move out.'

'To something bigger.'

'But of *course*. Bigger is better, right? They're vulgarians. No surprise, given what the father does.'

'What does he do?'

'He destroys period architecture and substitutes grotesquerie. Packing cartons pretending to be office buildings, those drive-in monstrosities – strip malls. And *she* . . . desperately blonde, the sweaty anxiety of an *arriviste*. Both of them gone all the time. No supervision for those brats.'

'Mrs Schwart—'

'If you'd care to be precise, it's Dr Schwartzman.'

'Pardon me, Doctor—'

'I'm an endocrinologist – retired. My husband is Professor Arnold Schwartzman, the orthopedic surgeon.

We've lived here twenty-eight years, had wonderful neighbors for twenty-six – the Cantwells, he was in metals, she was the loveliest person. The two of them passed on within months of one another. The house went into probate, and *they* bought it.'

'Who lives on the other side?' said Milo, indicating the stone walls.

'Officially, Gerhard Loetz.'

Milo shot her a puzzled look.

'German industrialist.' As if everyone should know. 'Baron Loetz has homes all over the world. Palaces, I've been told. He's rarely here. Which is fine with me, keeps the neighborhood quiet. Baron Loetz's property extends to the mountains, the deer come down to graze. We get all sorts of wildlife in the canyon. We love it. Everything was perfect until *they* moved in. Why are you asking all these questions?'

'A girl went missing,' said Milo. 'There's a rumor she attended a party on the Westside Friday night.'

Dr Schwartzman shook her head. 'Well, I wouldn't know about that. Didn't get a close look at those hood-lums, didn't want to. Never left the house. Afraid to, if you'd like to know. I was alone, Professor Schwartzman was in Chicago, lecturing. Usually, that doesn't bother me, we have an alarm, used to have an Akita.' The hand around the brush tightened. Man-sized knuckles bulged. 'But Friday night was alarming. So *many* of them, running in and out, screaming like banshees. As usual, I called the patrol, had them stay until the last barbarian left. Even so, I was nervous. What if they came back?'

'But they didn't.'

'No.'

'So you never got close enough to see any of the kids.'

'That's correct.'

Milo considered showing her the death photo anyway. Decided against it. Maybe the story hadn't hit the papers because someone upstairs wanted it that way. Dr Schwartzman's hostility to the Cossacks might very well fuel another rumor. Working alone like this, he didn't want to screw up big-time.

'The patrol,' he said, 'not the police— '

'That's what we do in Bel Air, Detective. We pay the patrol, so they respond. Your department, on the other hand – there seems to be a belief among law enforcement types that the problems of the . . . fortunate are trivial. I learned that the hard way, when Sumi – my doggie – was murdered.'

'When was this?'

'Last summer. Someone poisoned him. I found him right there.' Indicating the front lawn. 'They unlatched the gate and fed him meat laced with rat poison. That time, I did call your department, and they finally sent someone out. A detective. Allegedly.'

'Do you remember his name?'

Dr Schwartzman gave a violent headshake. 'Why would I? He barely gave me the time of day, clearly didn't take me seriously. Didn't even bother to go over there, just referred it to Animal Control, and all *they* offered to do was dispose of Sumi's body, thank you very much for nothing.'

'They?' said Milo.

Schwartzman's brush pointed at the party house.

'You suspect one of the Cossacks poisoned Sumi?'

'I don't suspect, I know,' said Schwartzman. 'But I can't prove it. The daughter. She's mad, quite definitely. Walks around talking to herself, a bizarre look in her eyes, all hunched over. Wears the same clothes for days on end. And she brings black boys home – clearly not right. Sumi despised her. Dogs have a nose for madness. Anytime that crazy girl walked by, poor Sumi would fly into a rage, throw himself against the gate, it was all I could do to calm him down. And let me tell you, Detective, the only time he responded that way was to stranger intrusion. Protective, Akitas are, that's the whole point of an Akita. But sweet and smart – he loved the Cantwells, even grew accustomed to the gardeners and the mailman. But never to that girl. He knew when someone was wrong. Simply despised her. I'm sure she poisoned him. The day I found his poor body, I spied her. Watching me through a second-story window. That pair of mad eyes. Staring. I stared right back and waved my fist, and you'd better believe that drapery snapped back into place. *She* knew that *I* knew. But soon after, she came out and walked past me – right past me, staring. She's a frightening thing, that girl. Hopefully that party was the last time we'll see them around here.'

'She was at the party?' said Milo.

Dr Schwartzman crossed her arms across her bosom. 'Have you been listening to me, young man? I told you, I didn't get close enough to check.'

'Sorry,' said Milo. 'How old is she?'

'Seventeen or eighteen.'

'Younger than her brothers.'

'*Those* two,' said Schwartzman. 'So *arrogant*.'

'Ever have any problems with the brothers other than parties?'

'All the time. Their attitude.'

'Attitude?'

'Entitled,' said Schwartzman. 'Smug. Just thinking

about them makes me angry, and anger is bad for my health, so I'm going to resume my calligraphy. Good day.'

Before Milo could utter another syllable, the door slammed shut and he was staring at teak. No sense pushing it; *Frau Doktor* Schwartzman could probably beat him in an arm wrestle. He returned to the car, sat there wondering if anything she'd said mattered.

The Cossack brothers had a bad attitude. Like every other rich kid in L.A.

The sister, on the other hand, sounded anything but typical – if Schwartzman could be believed. And if Schwartzman's suspicion about her dog was right, Sister Cossack's quirkiness was something to worry about.

Seventeen years old made Caroline Cossack an age peer of Janie Ingalls and Melinda Waters. A rich girl with a wild side and access to the right toys might very well have attracted two street kids.

Taking black boys home. Racism aside, that spelled rebel. Someone willing to push the envelope.

Dope, a couple of party girls venturing from Hollywood into uncharted territory . . . still, it came down to nothing more than rumor, and he had nowhere to take it.

He stared at the empty party house, took in Bel Air silence, shabby grace, a lifestyle he'd never attain. Feeling out of his element, every inch the ignorant rookie.

And now he had to report back to Schwinn.

This is a whodunit. This likes to munch on your insides, then shit you out in pellets . . .

The bastard's reproachful voice had crept into his head and camped there, obnoxious but authoritative.

While Milo'd spun his wheels, Schwinn had come up with the single useful lead on the Ingalls case: the tip that had led them straight to Janie's father.

A source he wouldn't identify. Not even bothering to be coy, coming right out and accusing Milo of spying for the brass.

Because he knew he was under suspicion? Maybe *that's* why the other Ds seemed to shun the guy. Whatever was going on, Milo'd been shoved square in the middle of it . . . he had to push all that aside and concentrate on the *job*. But the job – going nowhere – made him feel inadequate.

Poor Janie. And Melinda Waters – what was the chance *she* was alive? What would *she* look like when they finally found her?

It was nearly noon and he couldn't remember the last time he'd eaten. But he could find no reason to stop for grease. Had no appetite for anything.

ten

e arrived back at the station wondering if Schwinn
had returned and hoping he hadn't. Before he made
it to the stairwell, the desk sergeant said, 'Someone's
waiting for you,' without looking up.

'Who?'

'Go see for yourself. Interview Five.'

Something in the guy's voice pinged Milo's gut. 'Interview Five?'

'Uh-huh.' The blue kept his head down, busy with
paperwork.

An interrogation room. Someone being questioned – a
suspect for Ingalls in custody so soon? Had Schwinn
pulled off another solo end run?

'I wouldn't keep them waiting,' said the sergeant,
writing something down, still avoiding eye contact.

Milo peered over the counter, saw a crossword puzzle
book. 'Them.'

No answer.

Milo hurried down the too-bright corridor that housed
the interview rooms and knocked on Five. A voice, not
Schwinn's, said, 'Come in.'

He opened the door and came face to face with two tall
men in their thirties. Both were broad-shouldered and

good-looking, in well-cut charcoal suits, starched white shirts, and blue silk ties.

Corporate Bobbsey twins – except one guy was white – Swedish pink, actually, with a crew cut the color of cornflakes – and the other was black as the night.

Together they nearly spanned the width of the tiny, stale room, a two-man offensive line. Black had opened the door. He had a smooth, round head topped by a razor-trimmed cap of ebony fuzz and glowing, hairless, blue-tinged skin. The clear, hard eyes of a drill instructor. His unsmiling mouth was a fissure in a tar pit.

Pinkie hung toward the rear of the tiny room, but he was the first to speak.

'Detective Sturgis. Have a seat.' Reedy voice, Northern inflection – Wisconsin or Minnesota. He pointed to the room's solitary chair, a folding metal affair on the near side of the interrogation table, facing the one-way mirror. The mirror, not even close to subterfuge, every suspect knew he was being observed, the only question was by whom? And now Milo was wondering the same thing.

'Detective,' said the black man. Offering him the *suspect* chair.

On the table was a big, ugly Satchell-Carlson reel-to-reel tape recorder, the same gray as the twins' suits. Everything color-coordinated – like some psychology experiment and guess who was the guinea pig . . .

'What's going on?' he said, remaining in the doorway.

'Come in and we'll tell you,' said Pinkie.

'How about a proper introduction?' said Milo. 'As in who are you and what's this all about?' Surprising himself with his assertiveness.

The suits weren't surprised. Both looked pleased, as if Milo had confirmed their expectation.

'Please come in,' said Black, putting some steel into 'please.' He came closer, stepped within inches of Milo's nose, and Milo caught a whiff of expensive aftershave, something with citrus in it. The guy was taller than Milo – six-four or -five – and Pinkie looked every bit as big. Size was one of the few advantages Milo figured God had given him; for the most part, he'd used it to avoid confrontation. But between these guys and the Wagnerian Dr Schwartzman it had been a bad day for exploiting body type.

'Detective,' said Black. His face was strangely inani- mate – an African war mask. And those eyes. The guy had presence; he was used to being in charge. That was curious. Since the Watts riots, there'd been some race progress in the department, but for the most part it was lip service. Blacks and Mexicans were despised by the brass, shunted to dead-end patrol jobs in the highest- crime segments of Newton, Southwest, and Central, with scant chance for advancement. But this guy – his suit looked like mohair blend, the stitching on the lapels hand-sewn – what kind of dues had he paid and who the hell was he?

He stepped aside and, as Milo entered the room, nodded approvingly. 'In terms of an introduction, I'm Detective Broussard and this is Detective Poulsenn.'

'Internal Affairs,' said Poulsenn.

Broussard smiled. 'In terms of why we want you here, it would be better if you sat down.'

Milo settled on the folding chair.

Poulsenn remained in the far corner of the interroga- tion room, but cramped quarters placed him close enough for Milo to count the pores in his nose. If he'd had any. Like Broussard, his complexion glowed like a poster for clean living. Broussard positioned himself to Milo's right, angled so Milo had to crane to see his lips move.

'How do you like Central Division, Detective?'

'I like it fine.' Milo chose not to strain to meet Broussard's eyes, kept his attention on Poulsenn but stayed inert and silent.

'Enjoying homicide work?' said Broussard.

'Yes, sir.'

'What about homicide work do you like, specifically?'

'Solving problems,' said Milo. 'Righting wrongs.'

'Righting wrongs,' said Broussard, as if impressed by the originality of the response. 'So homicide can be righted.'

'Not in the strict sense.' This was starting to feel like one of those stupid grad school seminars. Professor Milrad taking out his frustration on hapless students.

Poulsenn checked his fingernails. Broussard said, 'Are you saying you enjoy trying to achieve justice?'

'Exactly—'

'Justice,' said Poulsenn, 'is the point of all police work.'

'Yes, it is,' said Broussard. 'Sometimes, though, justice gets lost in the shuffle.'

Slipping a question mark into the last few words. Milo didn't bite, and Broussard went on: 'A shame when that happens, isn't it, Detective Sturgis?'

Poulsenn inched closer. Both IA men stared down at Milo.

He said, 'I'm not getting the point of—'

'You were in Vietnam,' said Broussard.

'Yes—'

'You were a medic, saw lots of action.'

'Yes.'

108

'And before that you earned a master's degree.'

'Yes.'

'Indiana University. American literature.'

'Correct. Is there some—'

'Your partner, Detective Schwinn, never went to college,' said Broussard. 'In fact, he never finished high school, got grandfathered in back when that was acceptable. Did you know that?'

'No—'

'Nor did Detective Schwinn serve in any branch of the military. Too young for Korea, too old for 'Nam. Have you found that a problem?'

'A problem?'

'In terms of commonality. Developing rapport with Detective Schwinn.'

'No, I . . .' Milo shut his mouth.

'You . . . ?' said Broussard.

'Nothing.'

'You were about to say something, Detective.'

'Not really.'

'Oh, yes you were,' said Broussard, suddenly cheerful. Milo craned, involuntarily. Saw his purplish, bowed lips hooked up at the corners. But Broussard's mouth locked shut, no teeth. 'You were definitely going to say something, Detective.'

'I . . .'

'Let's recap, Detective, to refresh your memory. I asked you if Detective Schwinn's lack of higher education and military service had posed a problem for you in terms of rapport and you said, "No, I . . .". It was fairly obvious that you changed your mind about saying what you were going to say.'

'There's no problem between Detective Schwinn and

myself. That's all I was going to say. We get along fine.'

'Do you?' said Poulsenn.

'Yes.'

Broussard said, 'So Detective Schwinn agrees with your point of view.'

'About what?'

'About justice.'

'I – you'd have to ask him.'

'You've never discussed weighty issues with Detective Schwinn?'

'No, as a matter of fact, we concentrate on our cases—'

'You're telling us that Detective Schwinn has never verbalized any feelings about the job to you? About righting wrongs? Achieving justice? His attitude toward police work?'

'Well,' said Milo, 'I can't really pinpoint—'

Poulsenn stepped forward and pushed the RECORD button on the Satchell-Carlson. Kept going and ended up inches from Milo's left side. Now both IA men were flanking him. Boxing him in.

Broussard, 'Are you aware of any improper behavior on the part of Detective Schwinn?'

'No—'

'Consider your words before you speak, Detective Sturgis. This is an official department inquiry.'

'Into Detective Schwinn's behavior or mine?'

'Is there a reason to look into *your* behavior, Detective Sturgis?'

'No, but I didn't know there was any reason to look into Detective Schwinn's behavior.'

'You didn't?' said Poulsenn. To Broussard: 'His position seems to be that he's unaware.'

Broussard clicked his tongue. Switched off the

recorder, pulled something out of a jacket pocket. A sheaf of papers that he waved. Milo was craning hard now, saw the front sheet, the familiar layout of a photocopied mug shot.

Female arrestee, dead-eyed and dark-skinned. Mexican or a light-skinned black. Numbers hanging on her chest.

Broussard peeled off the sheet, held it in front of Milo's eyes.

Darla Washington, DOB 5-14-54, HT 5-06 WT 134.

Instinctively, Milo's eyes dropped to the penal code violation: **653.2**

Loitering for the purpose of prostitution . . .

'Have you ever met this woman?' said Broussard.

'Never.'

'Not in the company of Detective Schwinn or anyone else?'

'Never.'

'It wouldn't be in the company of anyone else,' said Poulsenn, cheerfully.

Nothing happened for a full minute. The IA men letting that last bit of dialogue sink in. Letting Milo know that they knew he was the least likely man in the room to engage a female hooker?

Or was *he* being paranoid? This was about Schwinn, not him. *Right?*

He said, 'Never saw her anywhere.'

Broussard placed Darla Washington's sheet at the bottom of the stack, flashed the next page.

LaTawna Hodgkins.

P.C. 653.2.

'What about this woman?'

'Never saw her.'

This time, Broussard didn't push, just moved to the

next page. The game went on for a while, a collection of bored/stoned/sad-eyed streetwalkers, all black. Donna Lee Bumpers, Royanne Chambers, Quitha Martha Masterson, DeShawna Devine Smith.

Broussard shuffled the 653.2 deck like a Vegas pro. Poulsenn smiled and watched. Milo kept outwardly cool but his bowels were churning. Knowing exactly where this was going.

She was the eighth card dealt.

Different hair than last night's red extravagance – a bleached blond mushroom cloud that made her look ridiculous. But the face was the same.

Schwinn's backseat tumble.

Tonya Marie Stumpf. The Teutonic surname seemed incongruous, where had *that* come from—

The mug shot danced in front of him for a long time, and he realized he hadn't responded to Broussard's, 'And this woman?'

Broussard said, 'Detective Sturgis?'

Milo's throat tightened and his face burned and he had trouble breathing. Like one of those anaphylactic reactions he'd seen as a medic. Perfectly healthy guys surviving firefights only to keel over from eating peanuts.

He felt as if *he'd* been force-fed something toxic . . .

'Detective Sturgis,' Broussard repeated, nothing friendly in his tone.

'Yes, sir?'

'This woman. Have you seen her before?'

They'd been watching the unmarked, surveilling Schwinn and *him* – for how long? Had they been spying the Beaudry murder site? Snooped during the entire time he and Schwinn had been riding together?

So Schwinn's paranoia *had* been well justified. And yet,

he'd picked up Tonya Stumpf and had her do him in the backseat, the stupid, no-impulse-control sonofa—

'Detective Sturgis,' Broussard demanded. 'We need an answer.'

A whir from the table distracted Milo. Tape reels, revolving slowly. When had the machine been switched on again?

Milo broke out in a full-body sweat. Recalling Schwinn's tirade in front of Bowie Ingalls's building, the sudden, vicious distrust, convinced Milo was a plant, and now . . .

Told you so.

'Detective,' said Broussard. 'Answer the question. *Now.*'

'Yes,' said Milo.

'Yes, what?'

'I've seen her.'

'Yes, you have, son,' said Broussard, crouching low, exuding citrus and success.

Son. The asshole was only a few years older than Milo, but it was clear who had the power.

'You definitely *have* seen her.'

They kept him in there for another hour and a half, taping his statement then replaying it, over and over. Explaining that they wanted to make sure everything had copied accurately, but Milo knew the real reason: wanting him to hear the fear and evasiveness in his own voice in order to instill self-loathing, soften him up for whatever they had in store.

He copped only to the basic details of Tonya's pickup – stuff they knew already – and resisted the pressure to elaborate. The room grew hot and rancid with fear as they changed the subject from Tonya to Schwinn's comportment, in general. Picking at him like gnats, wanting to hear about Schwinn's political views, racial attitudes, his opinions about law enforcement. Prodding, pushing, cajoling, threatening Milo subtly and not so subtly, until he felt as alive as chuck steak.

They returned to probing sexual details. He maintained his denial of witnessing any actual sexual encounters between Schwinn and Tonya or anyone else. Which was technically correct, he'd kept his eyes on the road, had harbored no desire to rearview-peep the blow job.

When they asked about the conversation between Schwinn and Tonya, he gave them some bullshit story about not hearing because it had all been whispers.

'Whispers,' said Broussard. 'You didn't think that was unusual? Detective Schwinn whispering to a known prostitute in the backseat of your department-issue vehicle?'

'I figured it for work talk. She was an informant, and Schwinn was pressing her for info.'

Waiting for the obvious next question: 'Info on what?' But it never came.

No questions at all about Janie Ingalls's murder or any other case he and Schwinn had worked.

'You thought she was an informant,' said Poulsenn.

'That's what Detective Schwinn said.'

'Then why the whispering?' said Broussard. 'You're Detective Schwinn's alleged partner. Why would he keep secrets from you?'

Because he knew this would happen, asshole. Milo shrugged. 'Maybe there was nothing to tell.'

'Nothing to tell?'

114

'Not every snitch has something to offer,' said Milo.

Broussard waved that off. 'How long were Schwinn and Tonya Stumpf in the backseat of the car as *you* drove?'

'Not long – maybe a few minutes.'

'Quantify that.'

Knowing the car had probably been observed, Milo kept it close to the truth. 'Ten, maybe fifteen minutes.'

'After which Tonya Stumpf was dropped off.'

'Correct.'

'Where?'

'Eighth Street near Witmer.'

'After she left the unmarked, where did she go?'

He named the Ranch Depot Steak House, but didn't mention Schwinn's funding of Tonya's dinner.

'Did money exchange hands?' said Poulsenn.

Not knowing how much they'd seen, he chanced a lie. 'No.'

Long silence.

'During the entire time,' Broussard finally said, 'you were driving.'

'Correct.'

'When Detective Schwinn asked you to stop to pick up Tonya Stumpf, you weren't at all concerned about being an accessory to prostitution?'

'I never saw any evidence of prosti—'

Broussard's hand slashed air. 'Did Tonya Stumpf's mouth make contact with Detective Schwinn's penis?'

'Not that I—'

'If you were driving, never looked back, as you claim, how can you be so sure?'

'You asked me if I saw something. I didn't.'

'I asked you if oral-genital contact occurred.'

115

'Not that I saw.'

'So Tonya Stumpf's mouth might have made contact with Detective Schwinn's penis without your seeing it?'

'All I can say is what I saw.'

'Did Detective Schwinn's penis make contact with Tonya Stumpf's vagina or Tonya Stumpf's *anus*?'

'I never saw that.' Was the bastard emphasizing *anus* because . . . ?

'Did Tonya Stumpf engage in physical intimacy of any sort with Detective Schwinn?'

'I never saw that,' Milo repeated, wondering if they'd used some sort of night scope, had everything on film and he was burnt toast—

'Mouth on penis,' said Poulsenn. 'Yes or no?'

'No.'

'Penis on or in vagina.'

'No.'

'Penis on or in *anus*.'

Same emphasis. Definitely not coincidence. 'No,' said Milo, 'and I think I'd better talk to a Protective League representative.'

'Do you?' said Broussard.

'Yes, this is obviously—'

'You could do that, Detective Sturgis. If you think you really need representation. But why would you think that?'

Milo didn't answer.

'Do you have something to worry about, Detective?' said Broussard.

'I didn't until you guys hauled me in—'

'We didn't haul you, we invited you.'

'Oh,' said Milo. 'My mistake.'

Broussard touched the tape recorder, as if threatening

to switch it on again. Leaned in so close Milo could count the stitches on his lapel. No pores. Not a single damn pore, the bastard was carved of ebony. 'Detective Sturgis, you're not implying coercion, are you?'

'No—'

'Tell us about your relationship with Detective Schwinn.'

Milo said, 'We're partners, not buddies. Our time together is spent on work. We've cleared seven homicides in three months – one hundred percent of our calls. Recently, we picked up an eighth one, a serious whodunit that's gonna require—'

'Detective,' said Broussard. Louder. Cutting off that avenue of conversation. 'Have you ever witnessed Detective Schwinn receiving money from anyone during work hours?'

No desire to talk about Janie Ingalls.

Caught up in his headhunter ritual, one that wouldn't – couldn't – be stopped – until it played itself out. Or something else: an *active* disinterest in Janie Ingalls?

Milo said, 'No.'

'Not with Tonya Stumpf?'

'No.'

'Or anyone else?' barked Broussard.

'No,' said Milo. 'Never, not once.'

Broussard lowered his face and stared into Milo's eyes. Milo felt his breath, warm, steady, minty – now suddenly sour, as if bile had surged up his gullet. So the guy had body processes after all.

'Not once,' he repeated.

They let him go as abruptly as they'd hauled him in, no parting words, both IA men turning their backs on him.

117

He left the station directly, didn't go upstairs to his desk or bother to check his messages.

The next morning a departmental notice appeared in his home mailbox. Plain white envelope, no postmark, hand-delivered.

Immediate transfer to the West L.A. station, some gobbledygook about manpower allocation. A typed addendum said he'd already been assigned a locker there and listed the number. The contents of his desk and his personal effects had been moved from Central.

His outstanding cases had been transferred to other detectives.

He phoned Central, tried to find out who'd caught Janie Ingalls's murder, got a lot of runaround, finally learned that the case had left the station and gone to Metro Homicide – Parker Center's high-profile boys.

Kicked upstairs.

Metro loved publicity, and Milo figured finally Janie would hit the news.

But she didn't.

He phoned Metro, left half a dozen messages, wanting to give them the information he hadn't had time to chart in the Ingalls murder book. The Cossack party, Melinda Waters's disappearance, Dr Schwartzman's suspicions about Caroline Cossack.

No one returned his calls.

At West L.A., his new lieutenant was piggish and hostile, and Milo's assignment to a partner was delayed – more department gibberish. A huge pile of stale 187s and a few new ones – idiot cases, luckily – landed on his desk. He rode alone, walked through the job like a robot, disoriented by his new surroundings. West L.A. had the lowest crime stats in the city, and he found himself missing the rhythm of the bloody streets.

He made no effort to make friends, avoided socializing after hours. Not that invitations came his way. The Westside's Ds were even colder than his Central colleagues, and he wondered how much of it could be blamed on his pairing with Schwinn, maybe picking up a snitch jacket. Or had the rumors followed him here, too?

Fag cop. Fag *snitch* cop? A few weeks in, a cop named Wes Baker tried to be social – telling Milo he'd heard Milo had a master's, it was about time someone with brains went into police work. Baker figured himself for an intellectual, played chess, lived in an apartment full of books and used big words when small ones would've sufficed. Milo saw him as a pretentious jerk, but allowed Baker to rope him in on double dates with his girlfriend and her stewardess pals. Then one night Baker drove by and spotted him standing on a West Hollywood street corner, waiting for the light to change. The only men out walking were seeking other men, and Baker's silent stare told Milo plenty.

Shortly after, someone broke into Milo's locker and left a stash of sadomasochistic gay porn.

A week after that, Delano Hardy – the station's only black D – was assigned to be his partner. The first few weeks of their rides were tight-lipped, worse than with Schwinn, almost unbearably tense. Del was a religious Baptist who'd run afoul of the brass by criticizing the department's racial policies, but he had no use for sexual nonconformity. News of the porn stash had gotten round; ice-eyes seemed to follow Milo around.

Then things eased. Del turned out to be psychologically flexible – a meticulous straight-arrow with good instincts and an obsession with doing the job. The two of them began working as a team, solved case after case, forged a bond based on success and the avoidance of certain topics. Within six months, they were in the groove, putting away bad guys with no sweat. *Neither* of them invited to station house barbecues, bar crawls. Cop-groupie gang bangs.

When the work day was over, Del returned to a Leimert Park tract home and his upright, uptight wife who still didn't know about Milo, and Milo skulked back to his lonely-guy pad. But for the Ingalls case, he had a near-perfect solve rate.

But for the Ingalls case . . .

He never saw Pierce Schwinn again, heard a rumor the guy had taken early retirement. A few months later he called Parker Center Personnel, lied, managed to learn that Schwinn had left with no record of disciplinary action.

So maybe it had nothing to do with Schwinn, after all, and everything to do with Janie Ingalls. Emboldened, he phoned Metro again, fishing for news on the case. Again, no callback. He tried Records, just in case someone had closed it, was informed they had no listing of the case as solved, no sighting of Melinda Waters.

One hot July morning, he woke up dreaming about Janie's corpse, drove over to Hollywood, and cruised by Bowie Ingalls's flop on Edgemont. The pink building was gone, razed to the dirt, the soil chewed out for a subterranean parking lot, the beginnings of framework set in place. The skeleton of a much larger apartment building.

He drove to Gower and headed a mile north. Eileen Waters's shabby little house was still standing but Waters was gone and two slender, effeminate young men –

antiques dealers – were living there. Within moments, both were flirting outrageously with Milo, and that scared him. He'd put on all the cop macho, and still they could tell . . .

The pretty-boys were renting, the house had been vacant when they'd moved in, neither had any idea where the previous tenant had gone.

'I'll tell you one thing,' said one of the lads. 'She was a smoker. The place reeked.'

'Disgusting,' agreed his roomie. 'We cleaned up everything, went neo-Biedermeier. You wouldn't recognize it.' Grinning conspiratorially. 'So tell us. What did she *do*?'

eleven

Milo finished the story and walked into my kitchen.
    The beeline to the fridge, finally.

I watched him open the freezer compartment where the bottle of Stolichnaya sat. The vodka had been a gift from him to Robin and me, though I rarely touched anything other than Scotch or beer and Robin drank wine.

Robin . . .

I watched him fill half a glass, splash in some grapefruit juice for color. He drained the glass, poured a refill, returned to the dining-room table.

'That's it,' he said.

I said, 'A black detective named Broussard. As in . . .'

'Yup.'

'Ah.'

Tossing back the second vodka, he returned to the kitchen, fixed a third glass, more booze, no juice. I thought of saying something – sometimes he wants me to play that role. Remembered how much Chivas I'd downed since Robin's departure and held my tongue.

This time, when he returned, he sat down heavily, wrapped thick hands around the glass, and swirled, creating a tiny vodka whirlpool.

'John G. Broussard,' I said.

'None other.'

'The way he and the other guy leaned on you. Sounds Kafkaesque.'

He smiled. 'Today I woke up as a cockroach? Yeah, good old John G. had a knack for that kind of thing from way back. Served the lad well, hasn't it?'

John Gerald Broussard had been L.A.'s chief of police for a little over two years. Handpicked by the outgoing mayor, in what many claimed was an obvious pander aimed at neutralizing critics of LAPD's racial problems, Broussard had a military bearing and a staggeringly imperious personality. The City Council distrusted him, and most of his own officers – even black cops – despised him because of his headhunter background. Broussard's open disdain for anyone who questioned his decisions, his apparent disinterest in the details of street policing, and his obsession with interdepartmental discipline helped complete the picture. Broussard seemed to revel in his lack of popularity. At his swearing-in ceremony, decked out as usual in full dress uniform and a chestful of ribbon candy, the new chief laid out his number one priority: zero tolerance for any infractions by police officers. The following day, Broussard dissolved a beloved system of community-police liaison outposts in high-crime neighborhoods, claiming they did nothing to reduce felonies and that excessive fraternization with citizens 'deprofessionalized' the department.

'Spotless John Broussard,' I said. 'And maybe he helped bury the Ingalls case. Any idea why?'

He didn't answer, drank some more, glanced again at the murder book.

'Looks like it was really sent to you,' I said.

Still no reply. I let a few more moments pass. 'Did anything ever develop on Ingalls?'

He shook his head.

'Melinda Waters never showed up?'

'I wouldn't know if she did,' he said. 'Once I got to West L.A., I didn't pursue it. For all I know, she got married, had kids, is living in a nice little house with a big-screen TV.'

Talking too fast, too loud. I knew confession when I heard it.

He ran a finger under his collar. His forehead was shiny, and the stress cracks around his mouth and eyes had deepened.

He finished the third vodka, stood, and aimed his bulk back at the kitchen.

'Thirsty,' I said.

He froze, wheeled. Glared. 'Look who's talking. Your eyes. You gonna tell me you've been dry?'

'This morning I have been,' I said.

'Congratulations. Where's Robin?' he demanded. 'What the hell's going on with you two?'

'Well,' I said, 'my mail's been interesting.'

'Yeah, yeah. Where is she, Alex?'

Words filled my head but logjammed somewhere in my throat. My breath got short. We stared at each other.

He laughed first. 'Show you mine if you show me yours?'

I told him the basics.

'So it was an opportunity for her,' he said. 'She'll get it out of her system, and come back.'

'Maybe,' I said.

'It happened before, Alex.'

124

Thanks for the memory, pal. I said, 'This time I can't help thinking it's more. She kept the offer from me for two weeks.'

'You were busy,' he said.

'I don't think that's it. The way she looked at me in Paris. The way she left. The fault line might have shifted too much.'

'C'mon,' he said, 'how about some optimism? You're always preaching to me about that.'

'I don't preach. I suggest.'

'Then I *suggest* you shave and scrape the crud from your eyes and get into clean clothes, stop ignoring her calls, and try to work things out, for God's sake. You guys are like . . .'

'Like what?'

'I was gonna say an old married couple.'

'But we're not,' I said. 'Married. All these years together and neither of us took the initiative to make it legal. What does that say?'

'You didn't need the paperwork. Believe me, I know all about that.'

He and Rick had been together even longer than Robin and I.

'Would you if you could?' I said.

'Probably,' he said. 'Maybe. What's the big issue between you guys, anyway?'

'It's complicated,' I said. 'And I haven't been avoiding her. We just keep missing each other.'

'Try harder.'

'She's on the road, Milo.'

'Try harder, anyway, goddammit.'

'What's *with* you?' I said.

'Acute *disillusionment.* On top of all the chronic

disillusionment the job deals me.' He clapped a hand on my shoulder. 'I need some things in my life to be constant, pal. As in you guys. I want Robin and you to be okay for *my* peace of mind, okay? Is that too much to ask? Yeah, yeah, it's self-centered, but tough shit.'

What can you say to that?

I sat there, and he swiped at his brow. More sweat leaked through. He looked thoroughly miserable. Crazily enough, I felt guilty.

'We'll work it out,' I heard myself saying. 'Now tell me why you looked like death when you saw Janie Ingalls's photo?'

'Low blood sugar,' he said. 'No time for breakfast.'

'Ah,' I said. 'Hence the vodka.'

He shrugged. 'I thought it was out of my head, but maybe I figure I should've pursued it.'

'Maybe "NS" means someone else thinks you should pursue it now. Do any of the other photos in the book mean anything to you?'

'Nope.'

I looked at the gloves he'd discarded. 'Going to run prints?'

'Maybe,' he said. Then he grimaced.

'What?'

'Ghost of failures past.'

He poured a fourth glass, mostly juice, maybe an ounce of vodka.

I said, 'Any guesses who sent it?'

'Sounds like you've got one.'

'Your ex-partner, Schwinn. He had a fondness for photography. And access to old police files.'

'Why the hell would he be contacting me now? He

126

couldn't stand me. Didn't give a damn about the Ingalls case or any other.'

'Maybe time has mellowed him. He worked Homicide for twenty years before you came on. Meaning he'd have been on the job during much of the period covered by the photos. The ones that preceded his watch, he swiped. He bent the rules, so lifting a few crime-scene photos wouldn't have been much of an ethical stretch. The book could be part of a collection he assembled over the years. He called it the murder book and bound it in blue, to be cute.'

'But why send it to me *via* you? Why now? What's his damn point?'

'Is Janie's picture one Schwinn could've snapped himself?'

Peeling on a new pair of gloves, he flipped back to the death shot.

'Nah, this is professionally developed, better quality than what he'd have gotten with that Instamatic.'

'Maybe he had the film reprocessed. Or if he's still a photography bug, he's got himself a home darkroom.'

'Schwinn,' he said. 'Screw all this hypothesizing, Alex. The guy didn't trust me when we worked together. Why would he be contacting me?'

'What if he learned something twenty years ago that he's finally ready to share? Such as the source that directed him to Bowie Ingalls and the party. Maybe he feels guilty about holding back, has the urge to come clean. By now, he'd be close to seventy, could be sick or dying. Or just introspective – age can do that. He knows *he's* in no position to do anything about the case but figures you might be.'

He thought about that. Degloved again, stood, stared

at the fridge but didn't move. 'We can spin theories all day, but the book could've been sent by anyone.'

'Could it?' I said. 'Janie's murder never hit the news, so it had to be someone with inside information. And Schwinn's belief in science becoming a major investigative tool might play into it. That day has arrived, right? DNA testing, all that other good stuff. If semen and blood samples were saved—'

'I don't even know if there *was* any semen in her, Alex. Schwinn figured it for a sex thing, but neither of us ever saw the autopsy results. Once they closed us down, I never saw a scrap of official paper.' A big fist slammed the table, and the murder book jumped. 'This is total bullshit.'

I kept my mouth shut.

He began pacing the dining room. 'Bastard – I have a good mind to go face to face with him. If it was him – so why was it sent to you?'

'Covering tracks,' I said. 'Schwinn knew we worked together – another indication of an interest in police affairs.'

'Or just someone who reads the paper, Alex. Our names were paired on the Teague case.'

'And you came out of that one smelling sweet, big solve. Schwinn may not have liked you or respected or trusted you, but maybe he's followed your career and changed his mind.'

'Give me a break.' He picked up his glass. A thread of vodka had settled on the bottom, an icy ribbon of alcohol. 'All this hypothesizing, my head feels like it's gonna split open. Sometimes I wonder what exactly it is that forms the basis for our friendship.'

'That's easy,' I said. 'Common pathology.'

'What pathology?'

'Mutual inability to let go. Schwinn – or whoever sent the murder book – knows it.'

'Yeah, well screw him. I'm not biting.'

'Your decision.'

'Damn right.'

'Ah,' I said.

'I hate when you do that,' he said.

'Do what?'

'Say "Ah." Like a fucking dentist.'

'Ah.'

His arm drew back and a big-fisted hand shot toward my jaw. He tapped gently, mouthed, 'Pow.'

I hooked a thumb at the blue album. 'So what do you want me to do, toss it?'

'Don't do anything.' He got to his feet. 'I'm feeling a little . . . gonna take a nap. The spare bedroom fixed up?'

'As always. Pleasant dreams.'

'Thank you, Norman Bates.' He stomped toward the rear of the house, was gone for maybe ten minutes before returning tieless, shirt untucked. Looking as if he'd crammed a night's worth of nightmares into six hundred seconds.

'What I'm gonna do—' he said. '—all I'm gonna do, is make a basic attempt to find Schwinn. As in make a call. If I find him and it turns out he did send the book, he and I will have a little chat, believe me. If it wasn't him, we forget the whole thing.'

'Sounds like a plan.'

'What? You don't like it?'

'It's fine with me,' I said.

'Good. 'Cause that's it.'

'Great.'

Regloving, he picked up the murder book, headed for the front door, said, 'Sayonara. It's almost been fun.' As he stepped outside, he said: 'Be there for Robin's call. Deal with it, Alex.'

'Sure.'

'I don't like when you get agreeable.'

'Then screw you.'

He grinned. 'Ah.'

I sat there a long time, feeling low. Wondering if Robin would call from Eugene. Figuring if she didn't within a couple of hours, I'd go somewhere, anywhere.

I fell asleep at the dining-room table. The phone woke me two hours later.

'Alex.'

'Hi.'

'I finally got you,' she said. 'I've tried so many times.'

'Been out. Sorry.'

'Out of town?'

'Just errands. How's it going?'

'Fine. Great – the tour. We've been getting excellent publicity. Sellout crowds.'

'How's Oregon?'

'Green, pretty. Mostly I've seen soundstages.'

'How's Spike?'

'He's good . . . adapting . . . I miss you.'

'Miss you, too.'

'Alex?'

'Uh-huh?'

'What's – are you okay?'

'Sure . . . so tell me, are sex, drugs, and rock 'n' roll what they're cracked up to be?'

'It's not like that,' she said.

'Which part? The sex or the drugs?'

Silence. 'I'm working really hard,' she said. 'Everyone is. The logistics are incredible, putting everything together.'

'Exciting.'

'It's satisfying.'

'I'd hope so,' I said.

Longer silence. 'I feel,' she said, 'that you're very far away from me. And please don't be literal.'

'As opposed to metaphorical?'

'You're angry.'

'I'm not, I love you.'

'I really *do* miss you, Alex.'

'Nothing's stopping you from coming home anytime,' I said.

'It's not that simple.'

'Why not?' I said. 'What, it's turned into a heavy metal tour, shackles and chains?'

'Please don't be like this, Alex.'

'Like what?'

'Sarcastic – veiled. I know you're mad at me, and that's probably the real reason you didn't call me back right away, but—'

'You leave, and I'm the bad guy?' I said. 'Yes, the real reason we missed each other was I was in no shape to talk to anyone. Not anger, I just got . . . hollow. After that I did try to call but like you said, you're busy. I'm not angry, I'm . . . do what you need to do.'

'Do you want me to quit?'

'No, you'd never forgive me for that.'

'I want to stay.'

'Then stay.'

'Oh, Alex . . .'

'I'll try to be Mr Cheerful,' I said.

'No, I don't want that.'

'Probably couldn't pull it off anyway. Never been much of a performer – guess I wouldn't fit in with your new buddies.'

'Alex, please . . . oh, *damn* – hold on! They're calling me, some sort of crisis – dammit, I don't want to sign off like this—'

'Do what you need to do,' I said.

'I'll call you later – I love you, Alex.'

'Love you too.'

Click.

Good work, Delaware. For this we sent you to therapist school?

I shut my eyes, struggled to empty my head, then filled it with mental snapshots.

Finally, I found the image I wanted and wedged it behind my eyes.

Janie Ingalls's brutalized body.

A dead girl, granting me momentary grace, as I lost myself in her imagined agony.

twelve

One thing about sensory deprivation: it does tend to freshen up your perceptions. And a plan – any plan – opens the door to self-importance.

When I left the house, the sun kissed me like a lover, and the trees were greener under a benevolent sun that reminded me why people kept moving to California. I collected the day's mail – junk junk junk – then walked around to the rear garden and stopped at the pond. The koi were a sinuous brocade, hyperactive, clamoring at the rock border, brought to the surface by my footsteps.

Ten very hungry fish. I made them happy. Then I drove to school.

I used my crosstown med school faculty card to get a parking spot on the U's north campus, walked to the Research Library, sat myself down in front of a computer, began with the in-house data banks, then logged onto the Internet and made my way through half a dozen search engines.

Janie or *Jane Ingalls* pulled up the Ingalls-Dudenhoffer family tree website from Hannibal, Missouri. Great-great-great-grandmother Jane Martha Ingalls would be 237 years old next week.

Bowie Ingalls connected me to a David Bowie fan club in Manchester, England, and to a University of Oklahoma history professor's site on Jim Bowie.

Several *Melinda Waters* hits popped up but none seemed remotely relevant: a physicist by that name worked at Lawrence Livermore Laboratory, nineteen-year-old Melinda Sue Waters was hawking nude pictures of herself from a small town in Arkansas, and Melinda Waters, Attorney-at-Law (*'Specializing in Bankruptcy and Evictions!'*) advertised her services on a legal bulletin board out of Santa Fe, New Mexico.

No crime stories or death notices on either girl. Perhaps Janie's friend had indeed surfaced, as Milo had suggested, and slipped back into society unnoticed.

I tried her mother's name – Eileen – with no success.

Next search: Tonya Marie Stumpf. Nothing on Pierce Schwinn's back-seat playmate. No surprise there, I hadn't expected an aging hooker to have her own website.

No data on Pierce Schwinn, either. His surname pulled up several Schwinn bicycle items and one news piece that caught my eye because it was relatively local: a Ventura weekly's account of a horse show last year. One of the winners was a woman named Marge Schwinn, who raised Arabians in a place called Oak View. I looked up the town. Seventy miles north of L.A., near Ojai. Exactly the kind of semirural escape that might attract an ex-cop. I wrote down her name.

Logging the activities of the Cossack family kept me busy for a long time, as I caught dozens of articles in the *L.A. Times* and the *Daily News* that stretched back to the sixties.

The boys' father, Garvey Cossack, Senior had received

intermittent coverage for tearing down buildings and putting up shopping centers, working the zoning board for variances, mixing with politicians at fundraisers. Cossack Development had contributed to the United Way and to all the right diseases, but I found no records of donations to the Police Benevolent Society or any links to John G. Broussard or the LAPD.

A twenty-five-year-old social-page picture showed Cossack Senior to be a short, bald, rotund man, with huge black-framed eyeglasses, a tiny dyspeptic mouth, and a fondness for oversize pocket squares. His wife, Ilse, was taller than he by half a head, with dishwater hair worn too long for her middle-aged face, hollow cheeks, tense hands, and barbiturate eyes. Other than chairmanship of a Wilshire Country Club charity debutante ball, she'd stayed out of the limelight. I checked the list of young women presented at the ball. No mention of Caroline Cossack, the girl who never changed her clothes and might've poisoned a dog.

Garvey, Jr and Bob Cossack began making the papers by their midtwenties – just a few years after the Ingalls murder. Senior had keeled over on the seventh hole of the Wilshire Country Club golf course, and the reins of Cossack Development passed to the sons. They'd diversified almost immediately, continuing ongoing construction projects but also bankrolling a slew of independent foreign films, none of which made money.

Calendar shots showed the Cossack brothers attending premieres, sunning in Cannes, venturing to Park City for the Sundance Festival, eating hip-for-a-nanosecond cuisine, hanging out with starlets and fashion photographers, addicted heirs, people famous for being famous, the usual assortment of Hollywood leeches.

Garvey Cossack, Jr seemed to love the camera – his face was always closest to the lens. But if he thought himself photogenic, that was more than a bit of delusion. The visage he flaunted was squat, porcine, topped by thinning, curly, light brown hair and anchored by a squishy dinner roll of a neck that propped up the sphere of cranium like an adipose brace. Younger brother Bob ('Bobo' because as a kid he'd loved the wrestler Bobo Brazil) was also coarse-featured, but thinner than his brother, with long, dark hair combed straight back from a low, square brow and a Frank Zappa mustache that diminished his chin. Both brothers favored the black suit-and-T-shirt combo, but it came across as costumery. Nothing fit Garvey right, and Bobo looked as if he'd shoplifted his threads. These countenances were meant for the back room, not the klieg lights.

The Cossack brothers' big-screen adventures appeared to last for three years, then they shifted gears and began making noises about bringing a football team to the Coliseum. Resurrecting one of their father's unfulfilled dreams. Assembling a 'consortium' of financial types, the brothers submitted a proposal to the city council that ended up being denounced by the more populist members as a scheme to lock in taxpayer financing of their for-profit plan.

The sports venture fizzled as had the movie game, and for a couple years, the Cossacks were out of print. Then Garvey Cossack resurfaced with plans for a federally funded community redevelopment project in the San Fernando Valley, and Bobo garnered attention for attempting to demolish a Hollywood bowling alley that the locals wanted preserved as a landmark in order to put up a giant strip mall.

Their mother's obituary was dated three years ago. Ilse Cossack had died '. . . *after a long battle with Alzheimer's disease . . . private services, in lieu of flowers, donations to. . .* '

Still no mention of Sister Caroline.

I began scanning the Web and the periodicals files for accounts of sexual homicides taking place within five years of Janie Ingalls's murder, found nothing dramatically similar. Interesting, because sexual sadists don't quit voluntarily, so maybe Janie's murderer was dead or imprisoned. If so, would Milo ever get the answers he wanted?

I went downstairs to the Public Affairs Room, got my hands on every back issue of the *FBI Law Enforcement Journal* I could find, along with stacks of forensic magazines and crime periodicals. Because the savagery of what had been done to Janie was notable and perhaps the wound pattern – scalping in particular – had repeated itself.

But if it had, I couldn't find the evidence. The FBI magazine had veered away from VICAP alerts and detailed crime studies to bland cop-speak articles geared for public relations, and the only case report involving removal of cranial skin cropped up in a wire service piece on crime in Brazil: a German-born doctor, son of a Nazi immigrant, had murdered several prostitutes and kept their scalps as trophies. The man was in his late twenties – a toddler at the time of the Ingalls case. Everyone starts off as a cute little baby.

Maybe Janie's murderer had continued to pursue his grisly interests without leaving any bodies behind.

But that didn't make sense. He'd flaunted Janie's corpse twenty years ago and was likely to get more, not less, brazen.

When I got home, my message machine registered zero calls. I phoned Milo's house and Rick Silverman answered, sounding sleepy. He's an ER surgeon. No matter when I call, I seem to be waking him up.

'Alex. How's it going?' He sounded casual. So Milo hadn't told him about Robin.

'Fine, and with you?'

'I'm working, they're paying me, I'm not complaining.'

'You're the only doctor who isn't.'

He laughed. 'Actually, I'm bitching plenty, but too much of that and you get bored with yourself. I keep telling myself it's a good thing I'm salaried, don't have to deal with the HMOs directly. Maybe one day Milo'll pay all the bills.'

'That'll be the year he heads to Paris for the big couture shows.'

He laughed again but I was thinking: *Paris? Where did that come from, Professor Freud?*

'So you're busy,' I said.

'Just came off an eighteen-hour fun-fest. Multicar collision. Daddy and Mommy having a spat in front, two kids in the back, three and five, no car seats, no belts. Daddy and Mommy survived. She may even walk again – enough of this or I'll have to pay you. The big guy's not in. Breezed by for dinner, then left.'

'He say where he was going?'

'Nope. We had Chinese takeout and I nearly fell asleep

in my moo goo. When I woke, he'd tucked me in and left a note saying he might be busy for a while. He did seem a little edgy. Is there something I should know about? You two into something new?'

'No,' I said. 'Everything's old.'

I tried reading, watching TV, listening to music, meditating – what a joke *that* was, all I could focus on was bad stuff. By 10 P.M. I was ready to claw the plaster from the walls and wondering when Robin would call again.

At this hour, the Eugene concert would be in full force and she'd be backstage, wonderfully harried. *Needed.* All those guitar-strumming, save-the-world sonofabitch—

Rrrrring.

My 'hello' was breathless. 'What, you in the middle of working out?' said Milo.

'I'm in the middle of nothing. What's up?'

'I can't locate Schwinn, but I might've found his old lady.'

'First name Marge? Mecca Ranch in Oak View?' I said.

His exhalation was a protracted hiss. 'Well, well, well, someone's been a busy worker bee.'

'More like a drone. How'd you find her?'

'Exemplary detective work,' he said. 'I got hold of Schwinn's retirement file – a naughty thing, so this stays between you and me.'

'His pension checks went to the ranch?'

'For the first fifteen years after he left, they went to an address in Simi Valley. Then he switched to a post-office box in Oxnard for two years, *then* the ranch. He's not listed in any DMV files, but the address cross-referenced

139

to Marge Schwinn. I just called her, got a machine, left a message.'

'No DMV listing for him,' I said. 'Think he's dead?'

'Or he doesn't drive anymore.'

'An ex-cop who doesn't drive?'

'Yeah,' he said. 'True.'

'Suburban life in Simi followed by a two-year POB interlude before the ranch. That could be divorce, intervening lonely bachelorhood, remarriage.'

'Or widowhood. His first wife was named Dorothy and she stopped being a beneficiary when he moved to Oxnard. Two years later, Marge came on.' He paused. 'Dorothy . . . I think he mentioned her name. It's getting hard to tell what I remember and what's wishful thinking. Anyway, that's it, for now.'

I recounted my time in the library, what I'd learned about the Cossacks.

'Rich kids stay rich,' he said. 'Big surprise. I also looked for Melinda Waters. She's on no state files, and neither is her mother, Eileen. That may not mean much if she got married and/or Mom got remarried and they both changed their names. I wish I knew the name of Melinda's Navy dad, but I never learned it. The guy had shipped out to Turkey, good luck tracing that. I did locate Bowie Ingalls, and he's definitely dead. Nineteen years dead.'

'A year after Janie,' I said. 'What happened?'

'Single-motorist vehicular accident up in the hills. Ingalls plowed into a tree and went through the windshield. Blood alcohol four times the legal limit, dozen Bud empties in the car.'

'Up in the hills where?'

'Bel Air. Near the reservoir. Why?'

'Not that far from the party house.'

'So maybe he was reminiscing,' he said. 'The facts still say drunk driver. The whole Cossack angle was pure supposition. For all I know, Janie and Melinda went to a whole other party. Or Schwinn was right and there was no Westside link at all, they got picked up by a psychopath and slaughtered nearer to the dump site. I'm tired, Alex. Gonna head home.'

'What's the plan with Marge Schwinn?'

'She's got my message.'

'And if she doesn't return it?'

'I'll try again.'

'If Schwinn is dead, maybe Marge sent the murder book,' I said. 'She could've come across it in his effects, along with a reference to you and me—'

'Anything's possible, my friend.'

'If you do reach her, mind if I tag along?'

'Who says I'm visiting her?'

I didn't answer. He said, 'What, you've got nothing better to do?'

'Not a thing.'

He humphed.

'Robin called,' I said. 'We talked.'

'Good,' he said, putting a question mark on the end of it.

I swerved back into safe territory: 'By the way, did you have time to run the prints on the murder book?'

'Just one set that I can see.'

'Mine.'

'Well,' he said, 'I'm no ace powder man, but I *have* printed you, and those whorls look familiar.'

'So whoever sent it wiped it clean,' I said. 'Interesting. Either way.'

He knew exactly what I meant: a careful cop, or a fastidious, taunting killer.

'Whatever,' he said. 'Nighty-night.'

'Have some sweet dreams, yourself.'

'Oh, sure. Here come the sugarplum fairies.'

thirteen

I didn't expect to hear from him anytime soon, but the following morning at eleven, he showed up at my front door, wearing a navy windbreaker over a plaid shirt and baggy jeans. Below the jacket, his gun bulged his waistline, but otherwise he looked like a guy with a day off. I was still in my robe. No call, so far, from Robin.

'Ready for fresh air?' he said. 'Horse manure? All of the above?'

'The second Mrs Schwinn got back to you.'

'The second Mrs Schwinn didn't, but I figured what the hell, Ojai's pretty this time of year.'

A reflexive 'Ah' rose in my throat and stuck there. 'I'll get dressed.'

'That would be best.'

He said, 'The Seville's nice on long drives,' and I obliged. The moment I started the engine, he threw back his head, shut his eyes, covered them with a handkerchief, let his mouth drop open. For the next hour, he dozed in the passenger seat, opening his eyes periodically to gaze out the window and appraise the world with distrust and wonder, the way kids and cops do.

I didn't feel conversational, either, and I played music

for company. Some old Oscar Aleman cuts from the Buenos Aires days, Aleman wailing away on a diamond-bright, nickel-silver National guitar. The route to Oak View was north on the 405, transfer to the 101 toward Ventura, then an exit on Highway 33. Ten more miles on two lanes that sliced through pink-gray mountains but rose barely above sea level took us toward Ojai. Ocean moisture hung in the air and the sky was cottony white above the horizon, then slate-colored strata where the sun should have been. The stifled light brought out the greens, turned the world nuclear-blast emerald.

It had been a few years since I'd been here – chasing down a psychopath bent on revenge and meeting up with an impressive man named Wilbert Harrison. I had no idea if Harrison still lived in Ojai. A psychiatrist and a philosopher, he'd taken a reflective view of life, and given the violence I'd introduced him to, I could see him moving on.

The first few miles of Highway 33 were insulted by slag fields, oil rigs, rows of metallic coils that crowned the cable-and-pylon salad of an electrical plant like so much oversize *fusilli*. Soon after that everything turned woodsy and Ojai-heterogenous: cute little cabins graced by meticulous stone walls and shadowed by live oaks and pines, cute little shops selling homemade candles and fragrances. Massage clinics, yoga institutes, schools that would teach you how to draw, paint, sculpt, find inner peace, if only you'd let them into your consciousness. Mixed in with all that was the other side of small-town life: rusty mobile homes behind barbed-wire fencing, bait-and-tackle sheds, trucks on blocks, dusty home-steads with one or two hollow-bellied horses nosing the dirt, crude placards advertising beef jerky and homemade chili, boarding stables, modest shrines to the conventional God. And everywhere the hawks, huge, relaxed, confident, circling in lazy predatory arcs.

Mecca Ranch was on the west side of 33, announced by nailed-on iron letters in a pine slab, the sign bordered by cactus and some sort of wild grass. A left turn up a barely paved road lined with scraggly birds of paradise in poor flower, took us five hundred yards into low, gentle hills that topped off at a couple of acres of gravel-colored mesa. Off to the right was a corral fashioned from iron posts and wooden crossbeams, more than big enough for the five brown horses grazing. Sleek, well-nourished steeds. They paid us no attention. Directly behind the enclosure were several unhitched horse trailers and a bunk of paddocks. Up at road's end, the birds of paradise were planted more closely together and better tended, and the orange-and-blue blossoms led the eye to a small, flat-roofed salmon-colored house with teal green wood trim. Parked in front were a ten-year-old brown Jeep Wagoneer and a Dodge pickup of the same color and vintage. A transitory shadow washed over the corral – a hawk orbiting so low I could see the surgical curve of its beak.

I turned off the engine, got out, filled my nose with the bite of pine and that curious maple-syrup-and-rot tang of dried equine dung. Dead silence. I could see Pierce Schwinn thinking this would be heaven. But if he was like Milo and so many other people hooked on noise and evil, how long would that have lasted?

Milo slammed the passenger door hard, as if offering fair warning. But no one came out to greet us, and no face appeared in the house's undraped front windows.

We walked to the front door. Milo's bell-push set off

fifteen seconds of chimes – some tune I couldn't identify, but it brought back memories of Missouri department store elevators.

Now, sound from the corral: one horse whinnying. Still no human response. The hawk had flown off.

I studied the animals. Well-muscled mahogany creatures, two stallions, three mares, manes glossy and combed. Over the corral arced a semicircle of iron soldered with vaguely Moorish lettering. *Mecca.* A triangle of blue had broken through the cottony sky. The foothills ringing the ranch were green-topped, gentle, a nurturant border. It was hard to imagine the murder book emanating from this quiet place.

Milo rang again, and a female voice called out, 'One minute!' Moments later the door opened.

The woman who stood there was petite and strong-shouldered, anywhere from fifty to sixty. She wore a royal blue and yellow checked shirt tucked into tight jeans that showed off a flat tummy, tight waist, boyish hips. Creased but clean work boots peeked out from under the jeans. White hair that retained some of its blond origins was tied back in a short ponytail – a merest upward twist of free locks. Her features were strong in a way that made them attractive in later life, but as a girl she'd probably been plain. Her eyes were a mottle of green and brown, lacking too much of the former to be called hazel. She'd plucked her eyebrows into spidery commas but wore no makeup. Her skin was testament to everything the sun could do to skin: puckered, cracked, corrugated, coarse to the point of woodiness. A few scary-looking dark patches danced under the eyes and crowned her chin. When she smiled, her teeth were the milky white pearls of a healthy virgin.

'Mrs Schwinn?' said Milo, reaching for the badge.

Before he got it out of his pocket, the woman said, 'I'm Marge, and I know who you are, Detective. I got your messages.' No apology for not returning the calls. Once the smile faded, not much in the way of any emotion, and I wondered if that contributed to even-tempered horses.

'I know the cop look,' she explained.

'What look is that, ma'am?'

'Fear mixed with anger. Always expecting the worst. Sometimes, Pierce and I would be riding, and there'd be a sound, a scurrying in the brush, and he'd get the look. So . . . you were his last partner. He talked about you.' She glanced at me. The past tense hung heavy.

She bit her lip. 'Pierce is dead. Died last year.'

'I'm sorry.'

'So am I. I miss him terribly.'

'When did—'

'He fell off a horse seven months ago. One of my tamest, Akhbar. Pierce was no cowboy, he never rode until he met me. That's why I gave him Akhbar as a regular mount, and they bonded. But something must've spooked Akhbar. I found him down near Lake Casitas, on his side, with two broken legs. Pierce was a few yards away, head split on a rock, no pulse. Akhbar had to be put down.'

'I'm so sorry, ma'am.'

'Yeah. I'm dealing with it okay. It's the goneness that hits you. One day someone's here and then . . .' Marge Schwinn snapped her fingers, looked Milo up and down. 'Basically, you're what I expected, given the passage of time. You're not here to tell me something bad about Pierce, are you?'

'No, ma'am, why would I—'

147

'Call me Marge. Pierce loved being a detective, but he had bitter feelings about the department. Said they'd been out to get him for years because he was an individualist. I've got his pension coming in, don't want funny business, don't want to have to hire a lawyer. That's why I didn't call you back. I wasn't sure what you were up to.'

Her expression said she still wondered.

Milo said, 'It's absolutely nothing about Pierce's pension, and I'm not here as a representative of the department. Just working a case.'

'A case you worked with Pierce?'

'A case I was supposed to work with Pierce, till he retired.'

'Retired,' said Marge. 'That's one way to put it . . . well, that's nice. Pierce would've liked that, you seeking his opinion after all these years. He said you were smart. Come in, coffee's still warm. Tell me about your days with Pierce. Tell me good things.'

The house was spare and low-ceilinged, walls alternating between rough pine paneling and sand-colored grass cloth, a series of tight, dim rooms furnished with well-worn, severe, tweedy fifties furniture for which some twenty-year-old starlet would gladly overpay at the latest La Brea junktique.

The living room opened to a rear kitchen, and we sat down opposite a blond, kidney-shaped coffee table as Marge Schwinn filled mugs with chicory-scented coffee. Western prints hung on the grass cloth, along with equestrian portraits. A corner trophy hutch was full of gold and silk. In the opposite corner was an old Magnavox console TV with Bakelite dials and a bulging, greenish screen. Atop the set was a single framed photo – a man and a woman, too far away to make out the details. The kitchen window framed a panoramic mountain view but the rest of the place was oriented toward the corral. The horses hadn't moved much.

Marge finished pouring and sat in a straight-backed chair that conformed to her perfect posture. Young body, old face. The tops of her hands were a giant freckle interrupted by spots of unblemished dermis, callused, wormed with veins.

'Pierce thought a lot of you,' she told Milo.

Milo got rid of the surprised look almost immediately, but she saw it and smiled.

'Yes, I know. He told me he gave you all sorts of grief. His last years on the force were a rough time in Pierce's life, Detective Sturgis.' She lowered her eyes for a moment. No more smile. 'Did you know that when you rode with Pierce he was a drug addict?'

Milo blinked. Crossed his legs. 'I remember that he used to take cold remedies – decongestants.'

'That's right,' said Marge. 'But not for his sinuses, for the high. The decongestants were what he did openly. On the sly, he was fooling around with amphetamines – speed. He started doing it to stay awake on the job, to be able to get back home to Simi Valley without falling asleep at the wheel. That's where he lived with his first wife. He got hooked bad. Did you know Dorothy?'

Milo shook his head.

'Nice woman, according to Pierce. She's dead, too. Heart attack soon after Pierce retired. She was a chain smoker and very overweight. That's how Pierce first got his hands on speed – Dorothy had lots of prescriptions for diet pills, and he started borrowing. It got the better of him, the way it always does. He told me he'd turned really nasty, suspicious, had mood swings, couldn't sleep. Said he took it out on his partners, especially you. He felt bad about that, said you were a smart kid. He figured you'd go far . . .'

She trailed off.

Milo tugged at the zipper of his windbreaker. 'Did Pierce talk much about his work, ma'am?'

'He didn't talk about specific cases, if that's what you mean. Just how rotten the department was. *I* think his work poisoned him as much as the speed. When I met him, he'd touched bottom. It was right after Dorothy's death, and Pierce had stopped paying rent on the Simi house – they never bought, just rented. He was living in a filthy motel in Oxnard and earning minimum wage sweeping the floors at Randall's Western Wear. That's where I first saw him. I was doing a show in Ventura, came in to Randall's to look at boots, collided with Pierce when he took out the trash. He knocked me on my rear, we both ended up laughing about it. I liked his laugh. And he made me curious. Someone that age, doing that job. Usually it's young Mexicans. Next time I came in, we talked some more. There was something about him – strong, no wasted words. I'm a gabby type, as you can see. Comes from living alone most of my life, talking to the horses. Talking to myself so as not to go nuts. This land was my grandfather's. I inherited it from my parents. I was the youngest, stayed home to take care of Mom and Dad, never strayed very far. The horses pretend they're listening to me. That's what I liked about Pierce, he was a good listener. Soon, I was making up reasons to drive down to Oxnard.' She smiled. 'Bought a lot of boots and jeans. And he never knocked me down again.'

She reached for her coffee. 'We knew each other a full

year before we finally agreed to get married. We did it because we're old-fashioned, no way would either of us live together without paper. But most of what we had was friendship. He was my best friend.'

Milo nodded. 'When did Pierce get off speed?'

'He was already getting off when I met him. That's why he moved into that fleabag. Punishing himself. He had some savings and his pension, but was living like he was a broke bum. Because that's how he thought of himself. By the time we started going out, he was off dope completely. But he was sure it did damage to him. "Swiss-cheese brain," he used to call it. Said if they ever x-rayed his head, they'd find holes big enough to stick a finger through. Mostly, it was his balance and his memory – he had to write things down or they were gone. I told him that was just age, but he wasn't convinced. When he told me he wanted to learn how to ride, I worried. Here he was, not a young man, no experience, not the best balance. But Pierce managed to stay in the saddle until . . . The horses loved him, he had a calming influence on them. Maybe because of all he'd been through, getting himself clean. Maybe he ended up at a higher level than if he hadn't suffered. You'll probably find this hard to believe, Detective Sturgis, but during his time with me, Pierce was a blessedly serene man.'

She got up, retrieved the picture atop the TV, held it out to us. Snapshot of Schwinn and her, leaning against the posts of the corral out front. I had only Milo's rawbone Oakie description to fuel my expectation of the former detective and had expected a grizzled old cop. The *look*. The man in the photo had long, white hair that snaked past his shoulders and a snowy beard that reached nearly to his navel. He wore a peanut-butter-colored buckskin jacket, denim shirt, blue jeans, a turquoise bracelet, one turquoise earring.

Old-time trapper or geriatric hippie, hand in hand with a sun-punished woman who barely reached his shoulder. I saw Milo's eyes widen.

'He was my Flower Power Grandpa,' said Marge. 'Different from when you knew him, huh?'

'A bit,' said Milo.

She placed the picture in her lap. 'So what kind of advice did you hope to get from him on this case of yours?'

'I was just wondering if Pierce had any general recollections.'

'Something that old and now you're working it again? Who got killed?'

'A girl named Janie Ingalls. Pierce ever mention that name?'

'No,' she said. 'Like I said, he didn't talk about his work.'

'Did Pierce leave any papers behind?'

'What kind of papers?'

'Anything to do with his work – newspaper clippings, photos, police mementos?'

'No,' she said. 'When he moved out of his Simi house, he got rid of everything. Didn't even own a car. When we went out, I had to pick *him* up.'

'Back when I knew him,' said Milo, 'he was a photography buff. He ever get back into that?'

'Yes, he did, as a matter of fact. He enjoyed taking walks in the hills and capturing nature, bought himself a cheap little camera. When I saw how much he liked it, I bought him a Nikon for his sixty-eighth birthday. His pictures were pretty. Want to see them?'

★ ★ ★

She took us to the house's single bedroom, a tidy, pine-paneled space filled by a queen bed covered with a batik spread and flanked by two mismatched nightstands. Framed photos blanketed the walls. Hills, valleys, trees, arroyos dry and flowing, sunrises, sunsets, the kiss of winter snow. Crisp colors, good composition. But nothing higher than vegetable on the evolutionary scale, not even a bird in the sky.

'Nice,' said Milo. 'Did Pierce have his own darkroom?'

'We converted a half bath. Wasn't he talented?'

'He was, ma'am. When I knew Pierce, he liked to read about science.'

'Did he? Well, I never saw that. Mostly he'd turned meditative. Could just sit in the living room and stare out at the view for hours. Except for the times when he got the cop look or had those dreams, he was at peace. Ninety-nine percent of the time he was at peace.'

'During the one percent,' I said, 'did he ever say what was bothering him?'

'No, sir.'

'During the last month or so before his accident, how was his mood?'

'Fine,' she said. Her face clouded. 'Oh no, don't go thinking *that*. It was an accident. Pierce wasn't a strong rider, and he was sixty-eight years old. I shouldn't have let him ride that long by himself, even on Akhbar.'

'That long?' said Milo.

'He was gone half a day. Usually, he only rode for an hour or so. He had his Nikon with him, said he wanted to catch some afternoon sun.'

'Taking pictures.'

'He never got to. The roll inside his camera was blank.

153

He must've fallen right at the beginning and lain there for a while. I should've gone looking sooner. The doctor assured me that kind of head wound would have taken him right away. At least he didn't suffer.'

'Hit his head on a rock,' said Milo.

She shook her head. 'I don't want to talk about this anymore.'

'Sorry, ma'am.' Milo stepped closer to the photos on the wall. 'These really *are* good, ma'am. Did Pierce keep any albums of his slides or proofs?'

Marge stepped around the bed to the left-hand night-stand. Atop the table were a woman's watch and an empty glass. Sliding open a drawer, she removed two albums and placed them on the bed.

A pair of blue leather books. Fine morocco, a size and style I recognized.

No labeling. Marge opened one, began turning pages. Photographs encased in stiff plastic jackets, held in place by black adhesive corner pockets.

Green grass, gray rock, brown dirt, blue sky. Pages of Pierce Schwinn's fantasy of an inanimate world.

Milo and I made admiring noises. The second book held more of the same. He ran a finger down its spine. 'Nice leather.'

'I bought them for him.'

'Where?' said Milo. 'Love to have one for myself.'

'O'Neill & Chapin, right down the road – over by the Celestial Café. They cater to artists, carry quality things. These are originally from England, but they're discontinued. I bought the last three.'

'Where's the third?'

'Pierce never got to it – you know, why don't I give it to you? I have no need for it and just thinking about Pierce's unfinished business makes me want to cry. And Pierce would've liked that – your having it. He thought a lot of you.'

'Really, ma'am—'

'No, I insist,' said Marge. Crossing the room and stepping into a walk-in closet, she emerged a moment later, empty-handed. 'I could swear I saw it up here, but that was a while back. Maybe it's somewhere else . . . maybe Pierce took it over to the darkroom. Let's check.'

The converted bathroom was at the end of the hall, five-by-five, windowless, acrid with chemicals, a narrow, wooden file cabinet next to the sink. Marge slid open drawers, revealed boxes of photographic paper, assorted bottles, but no blue leather album. No slides or proofs, either.

I said, 'Looks like Pierce mounted everything he had.'

'I guess,' she said. 'But that third book – so expensive, it's a shame to let it go to waste . . . it's got to be here, somewhere. Tell you what, if it shows up, I'll send it to you. What's your address?'

Milo handed her a card.

'Homicide,' she said. 'That word just jumps out at you. I never thought much about Pierce's life before me. Didn't want to picture him spending so much time with the dead – no offense.'

'It's not a job for everyone, ma'am.'

'Pierce – he was outwardly strong, but inside, he was sensitive. Had a need for beauty.'

'Looks like he found it,' said Milo. 'Looks like he found real happiness.'

Marge's eyes moistened. 'You're nice to say so. Well, it's been good meeting you. Coupla good listeners.' She smiled. 'Must be a cop thing.'

We followed her to the front door, where Milo said, 'Did Pierce ever have any visitors?'

'Not a one, Detective. The two of us hardly ever left the ranch, except to buy provisions, and that was maybe once a month for bulk shopping in Oxnard or Ventura. Once in a while we'd go into Santa Barbara for a movie or to a play at the Ojai Theater, but we never socialized. Tell the truth, we were both darned *anti*social. Evenings we'd sit and look up at the sky. That was more than enough for us.'

The three of us walked to the Seville. Marge looked toward the horses, and said, 'Hold on, guys, groom time's coming.'

Milo said, 'Thanks for your time, Mrs Schwinn.'

'Mrs Schwinn,' said Marge. 'Never thought I'd be Mrs Anybody, but I do like the sound of that. I guess I can be Mrs Schwinn forever, can't I?'

When we got in, she leaned into the passenger window. 'You would've liked the Pierce I knew, Detective. He didn't judge anyone.'

Touching Milo's hand briefly, she turned on her heel and hurried toward the corral.

fourteen

Back on Highway 33, I said, 'So now we know where the book came from.'

Milo said, 'Guy pierces his ear, turns into Mr Serene.'

'It's California.'

' "He didn't judge." You know what she meant by that, don't you? Schwinn decided my being gay was acceptable. Gee, I feel so validated.'

'When you rode together, was he homophobic?'

'Nothing overt, just general nastiness. But what man of that generation likes queers? I was always on edge with him. With everyone.'

'Fun times,' I said.

'Oh yeah, whoopsie-doo. I always felt he didn't trust me. Finally, he came out and said so but wouldn't explain why. Knowing what we know now, maybe it was speed-paranoia, but I don't think so.'

'Think the department knew about his addiction?'

'They didn't bring it up when they interrogated me, just concentrated on his whoring.'

'What I find interesting is that they eased him out with full pension rather than bring him up on charges,' I said. 'Maybe because going public about a doping, whoring cop might have brought other doping, whoring cops to

157

light. Or, it had something to do with handling the Ingalls case.'

Several miles passed before he spoke again. 'A speed freak. Asshole was a jumpy insomniac, skinny as a razor, gulped coffee and cough syrup like a vampire chugs blood. Add paranoia and the sudden mood swings, and it's Narco 101, I shoulda seen it.'

'You were concentrating on the job, not his bad habits. Anyway, turns out whatever personal feelings he had toward you, he respected your skills. That's why he had someone send you the book.'

'*Someone,*' he snarled. 'He dies seven months ago, and the book arrives now. Think that someone could be good old Marge?'

'She seemed to be dealing straight with us, but who knows? She's lived alone for most of her life, could've developed some survival instincts.'

'If it was her, what are we dealing with? Schwinn's last wish to wifey-poo? And that doesn't explain why you were the go-between.'

'Same reason,' I said. 'Schwinn covering his tracks. He pierced his ear but held on to a cop's survival instinct.'

'Paranoid to the end.'

'Paranoia can be useful,' I said. 'Schwinn had built a new life for himself, finally had something to lose.'

He thought about that. 'Okay, put aside who sent the damn thing and shift to the big question: Why? Schwinn held something back about Janie for twenty years and started feeling guilty all of a sudden?'

'For most of those twenty years, he had other things on his mind. Bitterness toward the department, widowhood, serious addiction. Sinking to the bottom, like Marge said. He got old, kicked his habit, and bought himself a bunch of new distractions: remarriage, easing into a new life. Learning to sit still and stare at the stars. Finally had time to introspect. I had a patient once, a dutiful daughter taking care of her terminally ill mother. A week before the mother passed on, she motioned the daughter over and confessed to stabbing the woman's father with a butcher knife as he lay sleeping. My patient had been nine at the time, all these years, she and the rest of the family had been living with the myth of the bogeyman – some nocturnal slasher. Her life had been a mass of fear and now she learned the truth from an eighty-four-year-old murderer.'

'What, Schwinn knew he was gonna die? The guy fell off a horse.'

'All I'm saying is old age and introspection can be an interesting combination. Maybe Schwinn started reflecting about unfinished business. Decided to communicate with you about Janie, but still wanted to hedge his bets. So he used me as a conduit. If I didn't pass the book on to you, he'd have fulfilled his moral obligation. If I gave it to you and you traced it to him, he'd deal with that. But if you threatened him in any way, he could always deny.'

'He puts together a whole bloody scrapbook just to remind me about Janie?'

'The book probably started out as a twisted hobby – exorcising his demons. It's no coincidence his later photos had no people in them. He'd seen people at the worst.'

We rode in silence.

'He sounds like a complicated man,' I said.

'He was a freak, Alex. Pilfered death shots from the evidence room and cataloged them for personal enjoyment. For all I know he got a sexual kick out of the book, then he grew old and couldn't get it up anymore and decided to share.' He frowned. 'I don't think Marge knew about the murder book. He wouldn'ta wanted her to think of him as a freak. That means someone else sent it to you, Alex. She made like the two of them had built this little domestic cocoon, but I think she was *real* wrong.'

'Another woman,' I said.

'Why not? Someone he visited when he wanted out from hilltop nirvana. This is a guy who tumbled with whores in the backseat while on duty. I don't have that much faith in transformation.'

'If there was another woman,' I said, 'she might live far from Ojai. This is a small town, too hard to be discreet. That would explain the L.A. postmark.'

'Bastard.' He cursed under his breath. 'I never liked the guy, and now he's yanking my chain from the grave. Let's say he did have some big moral epiphany about Janie. What does the book communicate? Where am I supposed to take it? Screw this, I don't have to play this game.'

We didn't talk until I was back on the freeway. At Camarillo, I shifted to the fast lane, pushed the Seville to eighty. He mumbled, 'Pedal to the metal . . . bastard starts feeling righteous, and I've got to jump like a trained flea.'

'You don't have to do anything,' I said.

'Damn right, I'm an *Amurrican*. Entitled to life, liberty and the pursuit of unhappiness.'

We crossed the L.A. county line by midafternoon, stopped at a coffee shop in Tarzana for burgers, got back on Ventura Boulevard, hooked a right at the newsstand at Van Nuys, continued to Valley Vista, and on to Beverly Glen. Along the way, I had Milo call my service on his cell-phone. Robin hadn't called.

When we reached my house, Milo was still in no mood to talk, but I said, 'Caroline Cossack sticks in my mind.'

'Why?'

'A girl poisoning a dog is more than a prank. Her brothers are all over the papers, but she doesn't get a word of newsprint. Her mother ran a debutante ball, but Caroline wasn't listed as one of the debs. She wasn't even included in her mother's funeral. If you hadn't told me the poisoning story, I'd never know she existed. It's as if the family spit her out. Maybe for good reason.'

'The neighbor – that cranky old lady doc, Schwartzman – might've been overly imaginative. She had no use for any of the Cossacks.'

'But her most serious suspicions were of Caroline.'

He made no move to exit the car. I said, 'A girl using poison makes sense. Poisoning doesn't require physical confrontation, so a disproportionate number of poisoners are female. I don't have to tell you psychopathic killers often start with animals, but they're usually males who dig blood. For a girl that young to act out so violently would be a serious red flag. I'm wondering if Caroline's been confined all these years. Maybe because of something a lot worse than killing a dog.'

'Or she died.'

'Find the death certificate.'

He knuckled his eyes, looked up at my house. 'Poison's sneaky. What was done to Janie was blatant – the way the body was dumped in an open spot. No way did a girl do that.'

'I'm not saying Caroline murdered Janie by herself, but she might've been part of it – might've served as a lure for whoever did the cutting. Plenty of killers have used young women as bait – Paul Bernardo, Charlie Manson, Gerald

161

Gallegos, Christopher Wilding. Caroline would've been the perfect lure for Janie and Melinda – a girl their age, outwardly inoffensive. And rich. Caroline could've stood by and watched as someone else did the wet work or participated the way the Manson girls did. Maybe it was a group thing, just like the Mansons, party scene gone bad. Females are affiliative – even female killers. Group settings lower their inhibitions.'

'Sugar and spice,' he said. 'And the family found out, put the screws on with the department to hush up the case, locked Crazy Caroline away somewhere . . . the ghoul in the attic.'

'Big family money can furnish a really nice attic.'

He accompanied me inside, where I went through the mail and he got on the phone with County Records and Social Security. No death certificate on Caroline Cossack; nor had she received a social security number or a driver's license.

Melinda Waters had received a card at age fifteen, but she'd never driven in California or worked or contributed payroll tax. Which made sense if she'd died young. But no certificate on her, either.

'Disappeared,' I said. 'Melinda probably died the same night Janie did, and Caroline's either very well hidden or she expired, too, and the family hushed it up.'

'Hidden as in hospitalized?'

'Or just watched carefully. Rich kid like that, she'd have a trust fund, could be living in some Mediterranean villa with twenty-four-hour supervision.'

He began pacing. 'Little Miss Nowhere . . . but at some point, when she was a kid, she had to have an identity. Be interesting to pinpoint when exactly she lost it.'

'School records,' I said. 'Living in Bel Air would've meant Palisades or University High if the Cossacks chose public school. Beverly, if they played fast and loose with residency forms. On the private side, there'd be Harvard-Westlake – which was Westlake School for Girls, back then – or Marlborough, Buckley, John Thomas Dye, Crossroads.'

He flipped open his pad, scrawled notes.

'Or,' I added, 'a school for troubled kids.'

'Any particular place come to mind?'

'I was in practice back then, can recall three very high-priced spreads. One was in West L.A., the others were in Santa Monica and the Valley – North Hollywood.'

'Names?'

I recited, and he got back on the phone. Santa Monica Prep was defunct, but Achievement House in Cheviot Hills and Valley Educational Academy in North Hollywood were still in business. He reached both schools but hung up frowning.

'No one'll give me the time of day. Confidentiality and all that.'

'Schools don't enjoy confidentiality privileges,' I said.

'You ever deal with either of the places, professionally?'

'I visited Achievement House, once,' I said. 'The parents of a boy I was seeing kept holding the place over the kid's head as a threat. "If you don't shape up, we'll send you to Achievement House." That seemed to scare him, so I dropped by to see what spooked him. Talked to a social worker, got the five-minute tour. Converted apartment building near Motor and Palms. What stuck in my mind was how small it was – maybe twenty-five, thirty kids boarding in, meaning it had to cost a fortune. No snake pit that I could see. Later, I talked to my patient and turns out what he was worried about was stigmatization. Being thought of as a "weirdo-geek-loser." '

'Achievement House had a bad reputation?'

'In his mind, any special placement had a bad reputation.'

'Did he get sent there?'

'No, he ran away, wasn't seen for years.'

'Oh,' he said.

I smiled. 'Don't you mean "*Ah*"?'

He laughed. Got himself grapefruit juice, opened the freezer and stared at the vodka bottle but changed his mind. 'Ran away. Your version of loose ends.'

'Loose ends were a big part of my life, back then,' I said. 'The price of an interesting job. As it turns out, this particular kid made it okay.'

'He stayed in touch?'

'He called after his second child was born. Ostensibly to ask about how to handle sibling jealousy. He ended up apologizing for being a surly teen. I told him he had nothing to be sorry about. Because I'd finally learned the whole story from his mother. His older brother had been molesting him since he was five.'

His face got hard. 'Family values.' He paced some more, finished his juice, washed the glass, got back on the phone. Contacting Palisades and University and Beverly Hills High Schools, then the private institutions. Putting on the charm, claiming to be conducting an alumnus search for *Who's Who*.

No one had Caroline Cossack on their files. 'Little Miss Nowhere.' He'd talked about washing his hands of the Ingalls case, but his face was flushed, and hunter's tension bunched his shoulders.

'I didn't tell you,' he said, 'but yesterday I went over to

Parker Center and searched for Janie's case file. Disappeared. Nothing at the Metro office or in evidence or the coroner's, not even a cold-case classification or a notice that the file had been moved somewhere else. There is absolutely no paper *anywhere* that says the case was ever opened in the first place. I know it was because I *opened* it. Schwinn used to shove all the paperwork at me. I filled out the right forms, transcribed my street notes, created the murder book.'

'No coroner's records, so much for science,' I said. 'When's the last time you saw the file?'

'The morning before my interrogation by Broussard and that Swede. After they worked me over, I was so shaken up I didn't return to my desk, just split the station. The next day, the transfer notice was in my box, and my desk had been cleared.'

He tilted back in his chair, stretched his legs, seemed suddenly relaxed. 'You know, my friend, I've been working too damn hard. Maybe *that's* what I can learn from old Mr Serene. Stop and sniff the manure.'

A smile, abrupt and broad, did something unsettling to his mouth. He rotated his head for several turns, as if working kinks out of his neck. Brushed black strands of hair out of his face. Sprang to his feet.

'See you. Thanks for your time.'

'Where are you headed?' I said.

'Into a life of meditative leisure. Got lots of vacation time stored up. Seems a good time to cash in.'

fifteen

Leisure was the last thing I needed. The moment the door closed, I reached for the phone.

Larry Daschoff and I have known each other since grad school. After our internships, I took a professorship at the med school crosstown and worked the cancer wards at Western Pediatric Medical Center, and he went straight into private practice. I stayed single and he married his high school sweetheart, sired six kids, made a good living, converted his square-meal-in-a-round-can defensive-guard physique to middle-aged fat, watched his wife go back to law school, took up golf. Now, he was a young grandfather, living on investment income, wintering in Palm Desert.

I reached him at his condo there. It had been some time since we'd spoken, and I asked him about the wife and kids.

'Everyone's great.'

'Especially the Ultimate Grandchild.'

'Well, as long as you asked, yes, Samuel Jason Daschoff is clearly the messenger of the Second Coming – another Jewish savior. Little guy just turned two and has evolved from sweetness and light to age-appropriate obnoxiousness. Let me tell you, Alex, there's no revenge sweeter than watching your own kids contend with the crap they shoveled at you.'

'I'll bet,' I said, wondering if I'd ever know.

'So,' said Larry, 'how've you been doing?'

'Keeping busy. I'm actually calling you about a case.'

'I figured as much.'

'Oh?'

'You were always task-oriented, Alex.'

'You're saying I can't be purely sociable?'

'Like I can be purely skinny. What kind of case, therapy or the bad stuff you do with the constabulary?'

'The bad stuff.'

'Still subjecting yourself to that.'

'Still.'

'I guess I can understand the motivation,' he said. 'It's a helluva lot more exciting than breathing in angst all day, and you were never one to sit still. So how can I help you?'

I described Caroline Cossack, without mentioning names. Asked him to guess where a teen that troubled might've been schooled twenty years back.

'Dosing Rover with cyanide?' he said. 'Impolite. How come she didn't end up in trouble?'

'Maybe family connections,' I said, as I realized incarceration would be an excellent reason not to have a social security card, and neither Milo nor I had thought of checking prison records. Both of us thrown off kilter.

'A *rich*, not-nice kid,' said Larry. 'Well, back then there was no real place for a run-of-the-mill dangerous delinquent other than the state hospital system – Camarillo. But I suppose a rich family could've placed her somewhere cushy.'

'I was thinking Achievement House or Valley Educational, or their out-of-state counterparts.'

'Definitely not Valley Educational, Alex. I consulted there, and they stayed away from delinquents, concentrated on learning probs. Even back then they were getting fifteen-grand tuition, had a two-year waiting list, so they could afford to be picky. Unless the family covered up the extent of the girl's pathology, but that kind of violent tendency would be hard to suppress for very long. As far as Achievement House, I never had any direct experience with them, but I know someone who did. Right around that time period, too, now that I think about it – nineteen, twenty years ago. Not a pretty situation.'

'For the students?'

'For the someone I know. Remember when I used to do mentoring for the department – undergrads considering psych as a career? One of my mentorees was a freshman girl, precocious, barely seventeen. She got herself a volunteer placement at Achievement House.'

'What problems did she have there?'

'The director got . . . overtly Freudian with her.'

'Sexual harassment?'

'Back then it was just called mashing and groping. Despite her age, the girl was a clearheaded feminist way ahead of her time, complained to the board of directors, who promptly gave her the boot. She talked to me about pursuing it – she was really traumatized – and I offered to back her up if she wanted to take it further, but in the end she decided not to. She knew it was his word against hers, he was the respected health administrator, and she was a good-looking teenager who wore her skirts too short. I supported the decision. What would she have gained other than a mess?'

'Was there ever any suggestion the director was molesting students?'

'Not that I heard.'

'Remember his name?'

'Alex, I really don't want my mentoree drawn into it.'

'I promise she won't be.'

'Larner. Michael Larner.'

'Psychologist or psychiatrist?'

'Business type – administrator.'

'Are you still in touch with the mentoree?'

'Occasionally. Mostly for cross-referrals. She stayed on track, graduated summa, got her PhD at Penn, did a fellowship at Michigan, moved back here. She's got a nice Westside practice.'

'Is there any way to ask her if she'd talk to me?'

Silence. 'You think this is important.'

'Honestly, I don't know, Larry. If asking her will put you in a difficult position, forget it.'

'Let me think about it,' he said. 'I'll let you know.'

'That would be great.'

'Great?' he said.

'Extremely helpful.'

'You know,' he said, 'right as we speak, I've got my feet up and my belt loosened and I'm looking out at miles of clean white sand. Just finished a plate of *chile rellenos con mucha cerveza*. Just let out a sonic-boom belch and no one's around to give me a funny look. To me, *that's* great.'

I heard from him an hour later. 'Her name's Allison Gwynn, and you can call her. But she definitely doesn't want to get involved in any police business.'

'No problem,' I said.

'So,' he said. 'How's everything else?'

'Everything's fine.'

'We should get together for dinner. With the women. Next time we come into town.'

'Good idea,' I said. 'Call me, Larry. Thanks.'

'Everything's really okay?'

'Sure. Why do you ask?'

'Don't know . . . you sound a bit . . . tentative. But maybe it's just that I haven't talked to you in a while.'

I called Dr Allison Gwynn at her Santa Monica exchange.

A *you-have-reached-the-office* tape answered, but when I mentioned my name, a soft-around-the-edges female voice broke in.

'This is Allison. It's funny, Larry calling out of the blue and asking if I'd talk to you. I've been reading some articles on pain control, and a couple were yours. I do some work at St Agnes Hospice.'

'Those articles are ancient history.'

'Not really,' she said. 'People and their pain don't change that much, most of what you said still holds true. Anyway, Larry says you want to know about Achievement House. It's been a long time – nearly twenty years – since I had anything to do with that place.'

'That's exactly the time period I'm interested in.'

'What do you need to know?'

I gave her the same anonymous description of Caroline Cossack.

'I see,' she said. 'Larry assures me you'll be discreet.'

'Absolutely.'

'That's essential, Dr Delaware. Look, I can't talk now,

have a patient in two minutes and after that I'm running a group at the hospice. This evening, I'll be teaching, but in between I will be eating dinner – fiveish, or so. If you want to stop by, that's fine. I usually go to Café Maurice on Broadway near Sixth, because it's close to St Agnes.'

'I'll be there,' I said. 'I really appreciate it.'

'No problem,' she said. 'I hope.'

I endured the afternoon by running too fast for too long. Trudged up my front steps winded and dehydrated and checked the phone machine. Two hang-ups and a canned solicitation for discount home loans. I pressed *69 and traced the hang-ups to a harried woman in East L.A. who spoke only Spanish and had dialed a very wrong number, and a Montana Avenue boutique wondering if Robin Castagna would be interested in some new silk fashions from India.

'I guess I should've left a message,' said the nasal girl on the other end, 'but the owner likes us to make personal contact. So do you think Robin might be interested? According to our records, she bought a bunch of cool stuff last year.'

'When I talk to her, I'll ask her.'

'Oh, okay . . . you could come in yourself, you know. Do like a *gift* thing? If she doesn't like it, we'll give her full store credit on return. Women love to be surprised.'

'Do they?'

'Oh, sure. Totally.'

'I'll bear that in mind.'

'You really should. Women *love* it when guys like surprise them.'

'Like a trip to Paris,' I said.

'Paris?' She laughed. 'You can surprise *me* with that –

don't tell Robin I said that, okay?'

At 4 P.M., I stepped out the kitchen door to the rear patio, crossed the garden to Robin's studio, unlocked the cool vaulted room, and walked around smelling wood dust and lacquer and Chanel No. 19 and listening to the echos of my footsteps. She'd swept the floor clean, packed her tools, put everything in its place.

Afternoon sun streamed through the windows. Beautiful space in perfect order. It felt like a crypt.

I returned to the house and skimmed the morning paper. The world hadn't changed much; why did I feel so altered? At four-thirty, I showered, got dressed in a blue blazer, white shirt, clean blue jeans, brown suede loafers. At ten after five, I walked into Café Maurice.

The restaurant was compact and dark, with a copper-topped bar and a half-dozen tables set with white linen. The walls were raised walnut panels, the ceiling repoussé tin. Inoffensive music on low volume competed with low conversation among three white-aproned waiters old enough to be my father. I couldn't help but think of the Left Bank bistro where Robin had told me of her plans.

I buttoned my jacket and allowed my eyes to acclimate. The sole patron was a dark-haired woman at a center table peering into a glass of burgundy. She wore a form-fitted, whiskey-colored tweed jacket over a cream silk blouse, a long, oatmeal-colored skirt with a slit up the side, beige calfskin boots with substantial heels. A big leather bag sat on the chair next to her. She looked up as I approached and gave a tentative smile.

'Dr Gwynn? Alex Delaware.'

'Allison.' She placed her bag on the floor and held out a slender white hand. We shook, and I sat.

She was a long-stemmed beauty out of John Singer

Sargent. Ivory face, soft but assertive cheekbones high-lighted with blush, a wide strong mouth shaded coral. Huge, judiciously lined deep blue eyes under strong, arching brows studied me. Warm scrutiny, no intrusiveness; her patients would appreciate that. Her hair was a sheet of true black that hung midway down her back. Circling one wrist was a diamond tennis bracelet; the other sported a gold watch. Baroque pearls dotted each earlobe, and a gold link cameo necklace rested on her breastbone.

Her hand returned to her wineglass. Good manicure, French-tipped nails left just long enough to avoid frivolousness. I knew she was thirty-six or -seven but despite the tailored clothes, the baubles, the cosmetics, she looked ten years younger.

'Thanks for your time,' I said.

'I wasn't sure if you were a punctual person,' she said, 'so I ordered for myself. I only have an hour till class.' Same gentle voice as over the phone. She waved, and one of the ancient waiters tore himself away from the staff confab, brought a menu, and hovered.

'What do you recommend?' I asked.

'The *entrecôte* is great. I like it rare and bloody, but they've got a pretty good selection of more virtuous stuff if you're not into red meat.'

The waiter tapped his foot. 'What're you drinking, sir? We've got a good selection of microbrews.' I'd expected a Gallic accent, but his drawl was pure California – surfer boy grown old – and I found myself musing about a future where grandmothers would be named Amber and Heather and Tawny and Misty.

'Grolsch,' I said. 'And I'll have the *entrecôte*, medium rare.'

He left and Allison Gwynn smoothed already-smooth hair and twirled her wineglass. She avoided my eyes.

'What kind of work do you do at St Agnes?' I said.

'You know the place.'

'I know of it.'

'Just some volunteer work,' she said. 'Mostly helping the staff cope. Do you still work in oncology?'

'No, not for a while.'

She nodded. 'It can be tough.' She drank some wine.

'Where do you teach?' I said.

'The U, adult extension. This quarter I'm doing Personality Theory and Human Relations.'

'All that and a practice. Sounds like a busy schedule,' I said.

'I'm a workaholic,' she said, with sudden cheer. 'Hyperactivity channeled in a socially appropriate manner.'

My beer arrived. We both drank. I was about to get down to substance when she said, 'The girl you described. Would that be Caroline Cossack?'

I put down my mug. 'You knew Caroline?'

'So it *was* her.'

'How did you know?'

'From your description.'

'She stood out?'

'Oh, yes.'

'What can you tell me about her?'

'Not much, I'm afraid. She stood out because of how they labeled her. There was a pink tab on her chart, the only one I'd seen. And I'd seen most of the charts, was a gofer that summer, running errands, picking up and delivering files. They used a color-coding system to alert the staff if a kid had a medical problem. Yellow for juvenile diabetes, blue for asthma, that kind of thing.

Caroline Cossack's tab was pink and when I asked someone what that meant, they said it was a behavioral warning. High risk for acting out. That and your saying it might be a police case helped me put it together.'

'So Caroline was high risk for violence.'

'Someone thought so, back then.'

'What specifically were they worried about?' I said.

'I don't know. She never did anything wrong during the month I was there.'

'But she was the only one labeled like that.'

'Yes,' she said. 'There weren't a lot of kids, period. Maybe thirty. Back then Achievement House was exactly what it is today: a repository for rich kids who fail to perform to their parents' expectations. Chronically truant, drug-abusing, noncompliant, children of the dream.'

I thought: Take away the dream and you had Janie and Melinda.

'But,' she went on, 'they were basically harmless kids. Other than the obvious sneaky doping and drinking, nothing seriously antisocial went on that I saw.'

'Harmless kids locked up,' I said.

'It wasn't that draconian,' she said. 'More carrot than stick. High-priced baby-sitting. They locked the doors at night, but it didn't feel like a prison.'

'What else can you tell me about Caroline?'

'She didn't seem scary, at all. I recall her as quiet and passive. That's why the behavioral warning surprised me.'

She licked her lips, moved her wineglass aside. 'That's really all I can tell you. I was a student volunteer, fresh out of high school, didn't ask questions.' Her face tilted to the left. The enormous blue eyes didn't blink. 'Bringing up that place is . . . not the most fun thing I've done all week. Larry told you about my experience there with Larner.'

I nodded.

'If the same thing happened today,' she said, 'you can bet I'd be a lot more proactive. Probably page Gloria Allred, close that place down, and walk away with a settlement. But I'm not blaming myself for how I handled it. So . . . have you worked with the police for a while?'

'A few years.'

'Do you find it difficult?'

'Difficult in what way?' I said.

'All the authoritarian personalities, for starts.'

'Mostly, I deal with one detective,' I said. 'He's a good friend.'

'Oh,' she said. 'So you find it fulfilling.'

'It can be.'

'What aspect?'

'Trying to explain the unexplainable.'

One of her hands covered the other. Jewelry everywhere else, but no rings on her fingers. Why had I noticed that?

I said, 'If you don't mind, I have a few more questions about Caroline.'

She grinned. 'Go ahead.'

'Did you have much personal contact with her?'

'Nothing direct, but I was allowed to sit in on some therapy groups, and she was in one of them. General purpose rap session. The leader tried to draw her out, but Caroline never talked, would just stare at the floor and pretend not to hear. I could tell she was taking it in, though. When she got upset, her facial muscles twitched.'

'What upset her?'

'Any personal probing.'

176

'What was she like physically?' I said.

'All this interest twenty years later?' she said. 'You can't tell me what she did?'

'She may have done nothing,' I said. 'Sorry to be evasive, but this is all very preliminary.' Unofficial, too. 'A lot of my work is random archaeology.'

Both her hands cupped her wineglass. 'No gory details? Aw, shucks.' She laughed, showed perfect teeth. 'I'm not sure I'd really want to know, anyway. Okay, Caroline, physically . . . this is all through the perspective of my seventeen-year-old eyes. She was short, kind of mousy . . . a little chubby – unkempt. Stringy hair . . . mousy brown, she wore it to here.' She leveled a hand at her own shoulder. 'It always looked unwashed. She had acne . . . what else? She had a defeated posture, as if something heavy sat on her shoulders. The kids were allowed to dress any way they wanted, but Caroline always wore the same shapeless dresses – old lady's housedresses. I wonder where she found them.'

'Dressing down,' I said. 'She sounds depressed.'

'Definitely.'

'Did she hang around with the other kids?'

'No, she was a loner. Shleppy, withdrawn. I guess today I'd look at her and be thinking schizoid.'

'But they saw her as potentially aggressive.'

'They did.'

'How'd she spend her time?'

'Mostly she sat in her room by herself, dragged herself to meals, returned alone. When I'd pass her in the hall, I'd smile and say hello. But I kept my distance because of the pink tab. A couple of times I think she nodded back, but mostly she shuffled on, keeping her eyes down.'

'Was she medicated?'

'I never read her chart. Now that I think about it, it's possible.'

'The group leader who tried to draw her out. Do you remember a name?'

'Jody Lavery,' she said. 'She was a clinical social worker – very nice to me when I had my problem with Larner. Years later I ran into her at a convention, and we ended up becoming friends, did some cross-referring. But forget about talking to her. She died two years ago. And she and I never talked about Caroline. Caroline was more of a nonentity than an entity. If not for the pink tab, I probably wouldn't have paid her any attention at all. In fact, the only—'

'Sir, madam,' said the waiter. Our dishes were set in place, and we cut into our steaks.

'Excellent,' I said, after the first bite.

'Glad you like it.' She speared a french fry.

'You were about to say something.'

'Was I?'

'You were talking about Caroline not being memorable. Then you said "In fact, the only—" '

'Hmm – oh yes, I was saying the only person I ever saw her talk to was one of the maintenance men. Willie something . . . a black guy . . . Willie Burns. I remember his name because it was the same as Robert Burns and I recall thinking there was nothing Scottish about him.'

'He paid special attention to Caroline?'

'I suppose you could say that. Once or twice I came across him and Caroline chatting in the hall, and they moved apart very quickly and Willie resumed working. And one time I did see Willie coming out of Caroline's room, carrying a mop and broom. When he saw me, he said she'd been sick, he was cleaning up. Volunteering an explanation. It was kind of furtive. Whatever the situation, Burns didn't stick around long. One week, he was there, then he was gone and Caroline went back to being alone.'

'A week,' I said.

'It seemed like a short period.'

'Do you remember what month this was?'

'Had to be August. I was only there during August.'

Janie Ingalls had been murdered in early June.

'How old was Willie Burns?'

'Not much older than Caroline – maybe twenty, twenty-one. I thought it was nice, someone paying attention to her. Do you know something about him?'

I shook my head. 'You didn't read the chart, but did you ever hear why Caroline was sent to Achievement House?'

'I assumed the same reason every other kid was: unable to jump high hurdles. I know that world, Alex. Grew up in Beverly Hills, my dad was an assistant attorney general. I thought I wanted something simple, would never return to California.'

'Larry said you went to Penn for grad school.'

'Went to Penn and loved it. Then I spent a couple of years at Ann Arbor, came back to Penn and took an assistant professorship. If it had been up to me, I'd have stayed back East. But I married a Wharton guy and he got a fantastic job offer at Union Oil here in L.A. and all of a sudden we were living in a condo on the Wilshire Corridor and I was cramming for the California boards.'

'Sounds like things have worked out,' I said.

She'd speared steak on her fork and dipped it in béarnaise. The meat remained suspended for a moment, then she placed the fork down on her plate. 'Life *was* rolling along quite nicely, then three summers ago, my father woke up at 4 A.M. with chest pains and my mom called us in a panic. Grant – my husband – and I rushed over and the three of us took Dad to the hospital and while they were working him up, Grant wandered off. I was so caught up supporting Mom and waiting for the verdict on Dad that I didn't pay much attention. Finally, just as they told us Dad was fine – gastric reflux – and we could take him home, Grant showed up and from the look on his face, I knew something was wrong. We didn't talk until after we dropped Mom and Dad off. Then he told me he hadn't been feeling well for a while – bad stomachaches. He'd figured it was job stress, kept thinking the pain would go away, was eating antacids like candy, hadn't wanted to alarm me. But then the pain got unbearable. So while we were at the hospital, he got hold of a doctor he knew – a Penn golfing buddy – and had x rays taken. And they found spots all over. A rare bile-duct tumor that had spread. Five weeks later, I was the mourning widow, living back with Mom and Dad.'

'I'm sorry.'

She nudged her plate away. 'It's rude of me to unload like this.' Another tentative smile. 'I'll blame it on your being too good a listener.'

Without thinking, I reached out and patted her hand. She squeezed my fingers, then spider-walked away, took hold of her wineglass, drank while staring past me.

I took a healthy swallow of beer.

'Want to hear something funny?' she said. 'Tonight I'm lecturing about post-traumatic stress. Listen, Alex, it's been nice meeting you, and good luck with whatever you're trying to do, but I've really got to run.'

She summoned the waiter, and, over her objections, I

paid the check. She removed a gold compact and lipstick from her bag, freshened her mouth, touched a long, black eyelash, checked her face in the mirror. We got up from the table. I'd figured her for tall, but in three-inch heels she wasn't more than five-five. Another little looker. Just like Robin.

We left the restaurant together. Her car was a ten-year-old black Jaguar XJS convertible that she stepped into with agility and revved hard. I watched her drive away. Her eyes stayed fixed on the road.

sixteen

Two new names:
Michael Larner.
Willie Burns.

Perhaps both were irrelevant, but I drove south into Cheviot Hills, located Achievement House on a cul-de-sac just east of Motor and south of Palms, idled the Seville across the street.

The building was an undistinguished two-story box next to an open parking lot, pale blue in the moonlight, surrounded by white iron fencing. The front façade was windowless. Glass doors blocked entry to what was probably an interior courtyard. Half a dozen cars sat in the lot under high-voltage lighting, but the building was dark and there was no signage I could see from this distance. Wondering if I had the right location, I got out and crossed the street and peered through the fence slats.

Tiny white numbers verified the address. Tiny white letters, nearly invisible in the darkness, spelled out:

Achievement House
Private Property

I squinted to get a look at what was behind the glass

182

doors, but the courtyard – if that's what it was – was unlit, and all I made out was reflection. The street was far from quiet; traffic from Motor intruded in bursts, and the more distant rumble of the freeway thrummed nonstop. I got back in the car, drove to the U, returned to the Research Library, got my itchy hands on that old friend, the periodicals index.

Nothing on Willie Burns, which was no surprise. How many janitors made the news? But Michael Larner's name popped up twelve times during the past two decades.

Two citations were dated from Larner's tenure as director of Achievement House: coverage of fund-raising events, no photos, no quotes. Then nothing for the next three years, until Larner popped up as official spokesman for Maxwell Films, demeaning the character of an actress sued by the film company for breach of contract. No follow-up on how that case resolved, and a year later Larner had made another occupational change: an 'independent producer' inking a deal with the very same actress for a sci-fi epic – a movie I'd never heard of.

The Industry. Given Larner's sexual aggressiveness, it was either that or politics.

The next four citations caught my eye because of Larner's *new* affiliation: director of operations for Cossack Development.

These were brief items from the business section of the *Times*. Larner's job seemed to be lobbying council members for Garvey and Bob's development deals.

Caroline Cossack shunted to Achievement House soon after Janie Ingalls's murder. Not the kind of kid Achievement House accepted but a few years later the director was working for the Cossack family.

I'd be brightening Milo's evening.

★ ★ ★

I got home and checked my phone machine. Still nothing from Robin.

Not like her.

Then I thought: *Everything's new, the rules have changed.*

I realized I'd never gotten an itinerary of the tour. I hadn't asked, and Robin hadn't offered. No one's fault, both of us caught up, everything moving so fast. The two of us tripping through the calisthenics of separation.

I went into my office, booted up the computer, found the Kill Famine Tour's homepage. PR shots and cheerful hype, links to mail-order CD purchases, photo-streams of previous concerts. Finally, times and dates and venues. Eugene, Seattle, Vancouver, Denver, Albuquerque . . . everything subject to change.

I phoned the Vancouver arena. Got voice mail and entered a pushbutton maze to learn *Our offices are closed . . . open tomorrow at 10 A.M.*

Left out in the cold.

I'd never set out to exclude Robin from my life. Or had I? During all the time we'd spent together I'd kept my work to myself – kept her at arm's length. Claiming confidentiality even when it didn't apply. Telling myself it was for her good, she was an artist, gifted, sensitive, needed to be protected from the ugliness. Sometimes she'd learned what I'd been up to the hard way.

The night I'd blown it, she'd left the house for a recording studio, full of trust. The moment she was gone, I left for a meeting with a beautiful, crazy, dangerous young woman.

I'd screwed up royally, but hadn't my intentions been noble? Blah blah blah.

Two tickets to Paris; pathetic. A sudden rush of

memories took hold. Exactly what I'd worked hard at forgetting.

The other time we'd separated.

Ten years ago, nothing to do with my bad behavior. That had been all Robin, needing to find her own way, forge her own identity.

Lord, rephrased that way it sounded like a pop-psych cliché, and she deserved better.

I loved her, she loved me. So why wasn't she calling?

Grow up, pal, it's only been two days and you weren't exactly Mr Charming the last time she tried.

Had I failed some kind of test by letting her go too easily?

Ten years ago she'd come back but not before . . .

Don't get into that.

But at that moment, I wanted nothing but punishment. Opened the box, let loose the furies.

The first time, she'd stayed away for a long time and eventually I'd found another woman. Then that had ended well before Robin returned.

When we reunited, Robin had seemed a bit more fragile, but otherwise everything seemed to be fine. Then one day, she broke down and confessed. She'd found someone, too. A guy, just a guy, a stupid guy, she'd been stupid.

Really stupid, Alex.

I'd held her, comforted her. Then she told me. Pregnancy, abortion. She'd never told the guy – Dennis, I'd blocked out his name – goddamn Dennis had gotten her pregnant, and she'd left him, gone through the ordeal alone.

I kept holding her, said the right things, what a

sensitive guy, the essence of understanding. But a nagging little voice in my head refused to let go of the obvious:

All those years together, she and I had waltzed around the topic of marriage and kids. Had been *careful.*

A few months away from me, and another man's seed had found its way—

Had I ever really forgiven her?

Did she wonder about that, too? What was she thinking about, right now?

Where the hell *was* she?

I picked up the phone, wondered who to call, swept the damn thing off the desk and onto the floor – screw you, Mr Bell.

My face was hot and my bones twitched and I began pacing, the way Milo does. Not limiting myself to one room, racing around the entire house, unable to burn off the pain.

Home smothering home.

I headed for the front door, threw it open, threw myself into the night.

I walked the glen, north, up into the hills. Did it the stupid way – with the traffic to my back, undeterred by the rush of approaching engines, the flash-freeze of headlights.

Drivers sped by honking. Someone yelled, *'Idiot!'*

That felt right.

It took miles before I was able to conjure up Janie Ingalls's corpse and relax.

When I got back to the house, the front door was ajar – I'd neglected to shut it – and leaves had blown into the entry. I got down on my knees, picked up every speck, returned to my office. The phone remained on the floor. The answering machine had tumbled, too, and lay there, unplugged.

But the machine in the bedroom was blinking.

One message.

I ignored it, went to the kitchen, got the vodka out of the freezer. Used the bottle to cool my hands and my face. Put it back.

I watched TV for hours, ingested hollow laughter, tortured dialogue, commercials for herbal sexual potency remedies and miracle chemicals that attacked the most hideous of stains.

Shortly after midnight, I punched the bedroom machine's PLAY button.

'Alex? . . . I guess you're not in . . . we were supposed to fly to Canada, but we've been held over in Seattle – doing an extra show . . . there were some equipment modifications that needed to be done before the concert, so I was tied up . . . I guess you're out again . . . anyway, I'm at the Four Seasons in Seattle. They gave me a nice room . . . it's raining. Alex, I hope you're okay. I'm sure you are. Bye, honey.'

Bye, honey.

No *I love you.*

She always said *I love you.*

seventeen

At 1 A.M., I called the Four Seasons in Seattle. The operator said, 'It's past the time where we put calls through, sir.'

'She'll talk to me.'

'Are you her husband?'

'Her boyfriend.'

'Well . . . actually, it looks like you're going to have to leave a message. I've got her as out of her room, her voice mail's engaged, here you go.'

She put me through. I hung up, trudged to bed, fell into something that might've been called sleep had it been restful, found myself sitting up at 6:30 A.M. dry-mouthed and seeing double.

At seven, I phoned Milo. His voice was fuzzy, as if filtered through a hay bale.

'Yo, General Delaware,' he said, 'isn't it a little early for my field report?'

I told him what I'd learned about Caroline Cossack and Michael Larner.

'Jesus, I haven't even brushed my teeth . . . okay, let me digest this. You figure this Larner did a favor for the Cossacks by stashing Caroline and they paid him back – what – fifteen years later? Not

188

exactly immediate gratification.'

'There could've been other rewards along the way. Both Larner and the Cossacks were involved in independent film production.'

'You find any film link between them?'

'No, but—'

'No matter, I'll buy a relationship between Larner and Caroline's family. She was a screwy kid, and Larner ran a place for screwy kids. It says nothing about what got her in there in the first place.'

'The behavioral warning on her chart says plenty. My source says Caroline was the only one tagged. Anyway, do what you want with it.'

'Sure, thanks. You all right?'

Everyone kept asking me the same damn question. I forced amiability into my voice. 'I'm fine.'

'You sound like me in the morning.'

'You rarely hear me this early.'

'That must be it. Behavioral warning, huh? But your source didn't know why.'

'The assumption was some kind of antisocial or aggressive behavior. Add to that Dr Schwartzman's dead Akita, and a picture starts forming. A rich kid doing very bad things would explain a cover-up.'

'Your basic disturbed loner,' he said. 'What would we homicide folk do without them?'

'Something else,' I said. 'I was thinking maybe the reason Caroline never got a social security card was because eventually she did act out and ended up in—'

'Lockup. Yeah, I thought of that right after we talked. Stupid of me not to jump on that sooner. But, sorry, she's not in any state penitentiary in the lower forty-eight, Hawaii or Alaska. I suppose it's possible she's stashed at some Federal pen, or maybe you were right about them shipping her to some nice little villa in Ibiza, sun-splashed exterior, padded walls. Know of anyone who'll fund a fact-finding Mediterranean tour for a deserving detective?'

'Fill out a form and submit it to John G. Broussard.'

'Hey, gosharoo, why didn't *I* think of that? Alex, thanks for your time.'

'But . . .'

'The whole thing is still dead-ending, just like twenty years ago. I've got no files, no notes to fall back on, can't even locate Melinda Waters's mother. And I was thinking about something: I gave Eileen Waters my card. If Melinda never returned home, wouldn't she have called me back?'

'Maybe she did, and you never got the message. You were in West L.A. by then.'

'I got other calls,' he said. 'Bullshit stuff. Central forwarded them to me.'

'Exactly.'

Silence. 'Maybe. In any event, I can't see anywhere to take it.'

'One more thing,' I said. I told him about Willie Burns, expected him to blow it off.

He said, 'Willie Burns. Would he be around . . . forty by now?'

'Twenty or twenty-one then, so yeah.'

'I knew a Willie Burns. He had a baby face,' he said. 'Woulda been . . . twenty-three back then.' His voice had changed. Softer, lower. Focused.

'Who is he?' I said.

'Maybe no one,' he said. 'Let me get back to you.'

He phoned two hours later sounding tight and distracted,

as if someone was hovering nearby.

'Where are you?' I said.

'At my desk.'

'Thought you were taking vacation time.'

'There's paper to clear.'

'Who's Willie Burns?' I said.

'Let's chat in person,' he said. 'Do you have time? Sure you do, you're living the merry bachelor life. Meet me out in front of the station, let's say half an hour.'

He was standing near the curb and hopped into the Seville before the car had come to a full stop.

'Where to?' I said.

'Anywhere.'

I continued up Butler, took a random turn, and cruised the modest residential streets that surround the West L.A. station. When I'd put half a mile between us and his desk, he said, 'There is definitely a God and He's jerking my chain. Payment for old sins.'

'What sins?'

'The worst one: failure.'

'Willie Burns is another cold one?'

'Willie Burns is an old *perp* on a cold one. Wilbert Lorenzo Burns, DOB forty-three and a half years ago, suspicion of homicide; I picked it up right after I transferred. And guess what, another file seems to have gone missing. But I did manage to find one of Burns's old probation officers, and he came up with some old paper and there it was: Achievement House. Willie'd finagled a summer placement there, lasted less than a month, and was booted for absenteeism.'

'A homicide suspect and he's working with problem teens?'

191

'Back then he was just a junkie and a dealer.'

'Same question.'

'Guess Willie never told him about his background.'

'Who'd he kill?'

'Bail bondsman name of Boris Nemerov. Ran his business right here in West L.A. Big, tough guy, but he sometimes had a soft heart for cons because he himself had spent some time in a Siberian gulag. You know how bail bonds work?'

'The accused puts up a percentage of the bail and leaves collateral. If he skips trial, the bondsman pays the court and confiscates the collateral.'

'Basically,' he said, 'except generally the bondsman doesn't actually pay the initial bail with his own money. He buys a policy from an insurance company for two to six percent of the total bail. To cover the premiums and make a profit, he collects a fee from the perp – usually ten percent, nonrefundable. If the perp goes fugitive, the insurance company shells out to the court and has the right to collect the collateral. Which is usually a piece of property – Grandma letting her beloved felon offspring tie up the cute little bungalow where she's lived for two hundred years. But seizing the cottage from poor old Grandma takes time and money and gets bad press and what do insurance companies want with low-rent real estate? So they'd always rather have the perp in hand. That's why they send out bounty hunters. Who take *their* cut.'

'Trickle-down economics,' I said. 'Crime's good for the GDP.'

'Boris Nemerov made out okay as a bondsman. Treated people like human beings and had a low skip rate. But he sometimes took risks – forgoing collateral, discounting his ten percent. He'd done that for Willie Burns because Burns was a habitual client who'd never let him down before. Last time Burns presented himself to Nemerov, he had no collateral.'

'What was the charge?'

'Dope. As usual. This was after he was fired at Achievement House and didn't show up at his probation appointment. Up till then, Burns had been nonviolent, as far as I could tell. His juvey record began at age nine and it was sealed. His adult crime career commenced the moment he was old enough to be considered an adult: one week after his eighteenth birthday. Petty theft, drugs, more drugs. Yet more drugs. A whole bunch of plea bargains put him back on the street, then he finally had to stand trial and got probation. The last bust was more serious. Burns was caught trying to peddle heroin to some junkies on the Venice walkway. The junkie he picked was an undercover officer and the arrest came during one of those times when the department claimed to be fighting The War On Drugs. All of a sudden, Burns faced a ten-year sentence and the court imposed a fifty-thousand-dollar bond. Burns went to Boris Nemerov, as usual, and Nemerov posted for him and accepted Burns's promise to work off the five grand. But this time, Burns skipped. Nemerov called around, trying to locate Burns's family, friends, got zilch. The address Burns had listed was a parking lot in Watts. Nemerov started to get irritated.'

'Started?' I said. 'Patient fellow.'

'Cold winters on the steppes can teach you patience. Eventually, Nemerov put the bounty hunters on Burns's trail, but they got nowhere. Then out of the blue, Nemerov got a call from Burns. Guy claimed to want to give himself up but was scared the hunters were gonna shoot him in his tracks. Nemerov tried to put his mind at ease, but Burns was freaking out. Paranoid. Said people were after him. Nemerov agreed to pick up Burns personally. East of Robertson, near the 10 East overpass. Nemerov set out late at night in this big old gold Lincoln he used to tool around in, never came home. Mrs Nemerov went crazy, Missing Persons prioritized it because Boris was well known at the station. Two days later, the Lincoln was found in an alley behind an apartment on Guthrie, not far from the meeting place. Those days, the neighborhood was serious gang territory.'

'Meeting Burns alone there didn't worry Nemerov?'

'Boris was self-confident. Big, jolly type. Probably thought he'd seen the worst and survived. The Lincoln was stripped and gutted and covered with branches – someone had made a half-baked attempt to conceal it. Boris was in the trunk, bound and gagged, three holes in the back of his head.'

'Execution,' I said.

'No good deed goes unpunished. Del Hardy and I got the case and worked it all the way to nowhere.'

'You would think something like that would make the papers. Burns's name pulled up zilch.'

'That I can explain. Nemerov's family wanted it kept quiet, and we obliged. They didn't want Boris's lapse in judgment made public – bad for business. And they had quite a few favors to pull in – reporters' kids who'd been bailed out. Cops' kids, too. Del and I were ordered to do our job but to do it very quietly.'

'Did that hamstring you?'

'Not really. Finding Burns wasn't going to be

accomplished by feeding the press. The Nemerovs were decent folk – first everything they'd gone through in Russia and now this. We didn't want to upset them, everyone felt bad about the whole thing. The business almost went under, anyway. The insurance companies weren't pleased, wanted to sever all ties. Nemerov's widow and son agreed to eat all fifty grand of Burns's forfeited bail and begged for a chance to prove themselves. They managed to hold on to most of their policies. Eventually, they got their heads above water. They're still in business – same place, right around the corner from the station. Nowadays they're known for never giving an inch.'

'And Willie Burns's trail went cold,' I said.

'I dogged him for years, Alex. Anytime I had a lull, I checked on the asshole. I was sure he'd turn up eventually because a junkie's unlikely to change his ways. My bet was he'd end up incarcerated or dead.'

'Maybe he did end up dead,' I said. 'The Nemerov family had access to professional searchers. Even good folk can develop a thirst for revenge.'

'My gut says no, but if that's what happened, it's a definite dead end. I'm starting to feel like I'm back in junior high, staring at tests I flunked.'

'Maybe it's only one big test,' I said. 'Maybe Willie Burns knew Caroline before she was sent to Achievement House – one of the black guys Dr Schwartzman saw Caroline hanging with. Burns's murdering Nemerov could've been nothing new for him, because he'd killed before. At a party in Bel Air.'

'Burns's record was nonviolent, Alex.'

'Till it wasn't,' I said. 'What if the nonviolent crimes were the ones he never got caught for. Was he only into heroin?'

'No, poly-drug addict. Heroin, acid, pills, meth. Since the age of ten.'

'Ups and downs,' I said. 'Unpredictable behavior. Put someone like that in contact with an unbalanced kid like Caroline, stick both of them at a dope party where two not-too-bright street girls show up, and who knows what might happen? Caroline's family suspected – or knew she'd been part of something bad and sent her to Achievement House. Willie split back to the streets but found his way over to Achievement House to visit Caroline. Stupid move, but junkies are impulsive. And no one caught on. He worked there for a month, was fired because of absenteeism.'

He drummed his fingers on his knees. 'Burns and Caroline as a killing couple.'

'With or without additional friends. Burns participating in a murder could also explain his skipping out on Nemerov. The city was clamping down on dope dealers, and he knew he was likely to serve time. That would've made him a captive audience if Janie Ingalls's murder came to light.'

'Then why'd he call Nemerov and offer to turn himself in?'

'To accomplish exactly what he did: ambush Nemerov, rob him, take his car – it was stripped. For all we know, Burns fenced the stereo and the phone. And that half-baked attempt at hiding it is pure hype. Also, Caroline's disappearance could be Willie taking no chances. Figuring she was high risk to talk.'

'If Burns or anyone else disappeared Caroline, you don't think her family would've reacted? Leaned on the department to solve it?'

'Maybe not. Caroline had been an embarrassment to them all through childhood – the weird sib – and if they knew she'd been an accomplice to murder, they'd have wanted to keep it quiet. It's consistent with sequestering her at Achievement House.'

'With a pink tab,' he said.

'Burns found her anyway. Maybe *she* contacted *him*. For all we know, she was with him when he ambushed Boris Nemerov. When exactly was Nemerov executed?'

'December, right before Christmas. I remember Mrs Nemerov talking about it. How they were Russian Orthodox, celebrated in January, there'd be nothing to celebrate.'

'Caroline was at Achievement House in August,' I said. 'Four months later, she could've been out of there. Willie could've broken her out. Perhaps they were planning to cut town all along, and that's why Burns was trying to sell dope in Venice.'

'My, my, so many possibilities,' he said. 'Ah.'

He had me drive in the direction of the station, then turn onto Purdue and park in front of an old redbrick building just south of Santa Monica Boulevard.

The entrance to Kwik 'n' Ready Bail Bonds was a glass-fronted storefront heralded by neon above the door and gold leaf on the glass. Unlike Achievement House, this placed welcomed attention.

I pointed to the *No Stopping, Tow Away* warning.

Milo said, 'I'll watch out for the parking Nazis. Failing that, I'll go your bail.'

The front office was a stuffy sliver of fluorescence with

a high counter and walls paneled in something mustard-colored that bore no biological link to trees. A knobless door was cut into the rear paneling. A single Maxfield Parrish print – purple mountains' majesty – hung to the left of the doorway. Behind the counter, a round-faced man in his late thirties sat on an old oak swivel chair and ate a big wet sandwich wrapped in wax paper. A coffeemaker and a computer sat to his left. Cabbage and slabs of meat and something red protruded from the sandwich. The man's short-sleeved white shirt was clean but his chin was moist, and as the door closed behind us he swiped at himself with a paper napkin and aimed cautious gray eyes at us. Then he grinned.

'Detective Sturgis.' He hauled a thick body out of the chair and a pink forearm shot across the counter. An anchor tattoo blued the smooth flesh. His brown hair was cropped to the skull and his face was a potpie that had been nibbled at the edges.

'Georgie,' said Milo. 'How's everything?'

'People are very bad, so everything's very good,' said Georgie. He glanced at me. 'He doesn't look like a business opportunity for me.'

'No business today,' said Milo. 'This is Dr Delaware. He consults for the department. Doctor, George Nemerov.'

'A doctor for the cops,' said Georgie, pumping my hand. 'What do you specialize in, sexually transmitted diseases or insanity?'

'Good guess, Georgie. He's a shrink.'

Nemerov chuckled. 'People are nuts, so everything's good for *you*, Doctor. If you knew more about this business, you'd try to lock me up, too.' Heavy eyelids drooped, and the gray eyes narrowed. But the rest of the soft, doughy face remained placid. 'So what's up, Detective Milo?'

'This and that, Georgie. Eating your spinach?'

'Hate that stuff,' said Nemerov, patting his anchor tattoo. To me: 'When I was a kid, I was a big cartoon fan, Popeye the Sailor. One night, when I was a high school punk, me and some friends were over at the Pike in Long Beach and I got this shit put on me. My mother almost skinned me alive.'

'How is your mom?' said Milo.

'Good as can be expected,' said Nemerov. 'Next month she's seventy-three.'

'Give her my best.'

'Will do, Milo. She always liked you. So . . . why you here?' Nemerov's smile was angelic.

'I've been looking into some old files, and your dad's case came up.'

'Oh, yeah?' said Nemerov. 'Came up how?'

'Willie Burns's name surfaced with regard to another 187.'

'That so?' Nemerov shifted his weight. His smile had died. 'Well, that wouldn't surprise me. The guy was lowlife scum. You telling me he's been spotted around?'

'No,' said Milo. 'The other case is also old and cold. Actually went down before your dad.'

'And this never came to light when you guys were looking for that murderous fuck?'

'No, Georgie. Burns isn't officially a suspect on the other one. His name just came up, that's all.'

'I see,' Georgie said. 'Actually, I don't.' He rolled a wrist, and muscles bulged in his forearm. 'What, things are so relaxed around the corner that they've got you chasing ghosts?'

'Sorry to bring up old crap, Georgie.'

'Whatever, Milo, we all got our jobs. Back then I was a kid, first-year college, Cal State Northridge, I was going to become a lawyer. Instead, I got this.' Pudgy hands spread.

Milo said, 'I just wanted to verify that you guys never caught any wind of Burns.'

Nemerov's eyes were ash-colored slits. 'You don't think I'd tell you if we did?'

'I'm sure you would, but—'

'We go by the law, Milo. Making our living depends on it.'

'I know you do, Georgie. Sorry—'

Georgie picked up his sandwich. 'So who else did Burns off?'

Milo shook his head. 'Too early to let that out. When you guys were looking for him did you uncover any known associates?'

'Nah,' said Nemerov. 'Guy was a fucking loner. A dope-head and a bum and a scumbag. Today, those Legal Aid assholes would call him a poor, poor pitiful homeless citizen and try to get you and me to pay his rent.' His mouth twisted. 'A bum. My dad always treated him with respect and that's how the fuck repaid him.'

'It stinks,' said Milo.

'It stinks bad. Even after all this time.'

'Your dad was a good guy, Georgie.'

Nemerov's gray slits aimed at me. 'My dad could read people like a book, Doctor. Better than a shrink.'

I nodded, thinking: Boris Nemerov had misread Willie Burns in the worst possible way.

Georgie rested one beefy arm on the countertop and favored me with a warm gust of garlic and brine and mustard.

'He could read 'em, my dad could, but he was too damn good, too damn soft. My mom tortured herself for not stopping him from going to meet the fuck that night. I told her she couldn'ta done nothing – Dad got an idea in his head, you couldn't stop him. That's what kept him alive with the communists. Heart of gold, head like a rock. Burns, the fuck, was a loser and a liar but he'd always made his court dates before so why wouldn't my dad see the best in him?'

'Absolutely,' said Milo.

'Ah,' said Nemerov.

The door in the rear panel was pushed open and seven hundred pounds of humanity emerged and filled the office. Two men, each close to six-six, wearing black turtlenecks, black cargo pants, black revolvers in black nylon holsters. The larger one – a fine distinction – was Samoan, with long hair tied up in a sumo knot and a wispy mustache-goatee combo. His companion wore a red crew cut and had a fine-featured, baby-smooth face.

Georgie Nemerov said, 'Hey.'

Both monsters studied us.

'Hey,' said Sumo.

Red grunted.

'Boys, this is Detective Milo Sturgis, an old friend from around the corner. He investigated the scumfuck who murdered my dad. And this is a shrink the department uses because we all know cops are crazy, right?'

Slow nods from the behemoths.

Georgie said, 'These are two of my prime finders, Milo. This here's Stevie, but we call him Yokuzuna, 'cause he used to wrestle in Japan. And the little guy's Red Yaakov, from the Holy Land. So what's new, boys?'

'We got something for you,' said Stevie. 'Out back, in the van.'

'The 459?'

Stevie the Samoan smiled. 'The 459 and guess what? A bonus. We're leaving the 459's crib – idiot's right there in bed, like he doesn't believe anyone's gonna come looking for him and in two secs we've got him braceleted, are taking him out to the car and a window shade in the next-door house moves and some other guy's staring out at us. And Yaakov says, waitaminute, ain't that the 460 we been looking for since the Democratic convention?'

Yaakov said, 'Det stoopid guy Garcia, broke dose windows and reeped off all dot stereo.'

'Raul Garcia?' said Georgie. He broke into a grin. 'No kidding.'

'Yeah, him,' said Stevie. 'So we go in and get him, too. Both of them are out there in back, squirming in the van. Turns out they played craps together – neighborly spirit and all that. They actually asked us to loosen the brace-lets so they could play in the van.'

Georgie high-fived both giants. 'Two for one, beautiful. Okay, let me process the papers, then you can take both geniuses over to the jail. I'm proud of you boys. Come back at five and pick up your checks.'

Stevie and Yaakov saluted and left the way they'd come in.

'Thank God,' said Georgie, 'that criminals are retarded.' He returned to his chair and picked up his sandwich.

Milo said, 'Thanks for your time.'

The sandwich arced toward Nemerov's mouth, then paused inches from its destination. 'You actually going to be looking for Burns again?'

'Should I?' said Milo. 'I figure if he was findable, you guys woulda brought him in a long time ago.'

'You got that,' said Georgie.

Knots formed along Milo's jawline as he sauntered closer to the counter. 'You think he's dead, Georgie?'

Nemerov's eyes shifted to the left. 'That would be nice, but why would I think that?'

'Because you never found him.'

'Could be, Milo. 'Cause we're good at what we do. Maybe when it first happened we weren't. Like I said, I was a college kid, what did I know? And Mom was all torn up, you remember how the insurance companies were jerking us around – one day we're doing the funeral, the next day we're fighting to stay out of bankruptcy. So maybe Burns didn't get looked for like he should. But later I sent guys out for him, we've still got him on our list – look, I'll show you.'

He got up, pushed the paneled door hard, was gone for a few moments, came back with a piece of paper that he dropped on the counter.

Wilbert Lorenzo Burns's wanted sheet. Mug shot in full face and profile, the usual necklace of numbers. Medium-dark face, well-formed features that were soft and boyish – what would have been a pleasant face but for the hype eyes. Burns's long hair protruded in wooly tufts, as if it had been yanked. His statistics put him at six-two, one-sixty, with knife-scars on both forearms and the back of the neck, no tattoos. Wanted for PCs 11375, 836.6., 187. Possession with intent to sell, escape after remand or arrest, homicide.

'I think of him from time to time,' said Georgie, between bites of wet sandwich. 'Probably he is dead. He was a hype, what's those fuckheads' life expectancies, anyway? But you learn different, call me.'

eighteen

As we left the bail bond office, a meter reader's go-cart pulled up behind the Seville. Milo said, 'Let's get going,' and we ran for the car. The reader got out with his little computerized instrument of evil, but I peeled away before he could punch buttons.

'Close call,' said Milo.

'Thought you had clout,' I said.

'Clout's an ephemeral thing.'

I turned the corner, headed back to the station.

He said, 'So what do you think?'

'About what?'

'Georgie's demeanor.'

'I don't know Georgie.'

'Even so.'

'He seemed to get edgy when you brought up Burns.'

'He did, at that. Normally, he's even-tempered, you never hear him swear. This time he was tossing out the f-word.'

'Maybe recalling his father's murder got him worked up.'

'Maybe.'

'You're wondering if he did take care of Burns. But you're unlikely to ever know.'

'Thought you were supposed to make people feel better.'

'Purification through insight,' I said, pulling up near the Westside staff parking lot and letting the Seville idle. Milo remained in place, long legs drawn up high, hands flat on the seat.

'Screw Schwinn,' he finally said.

'That would be easy,' I said. 'If it was really about Schwinn.'

He glared at me. 'More purification?'

'What are friends for?'

A few minutes later: 'Why the murder book? If he really wanted to help, all he had to do was call and give me the facts.'

'Maybe there's more to the book than just Janie's photo.'

'Such as?'

'I don't know, but it's worth a second look.'

He didn't answer. Made no effort to leave the car.

'So,' I said.

'So . . . I was thinking of a visit to Achievement House, maybe pick up on the latest trends in special education.'

'You're still on it.'

'I don't know what I am.'

I took Pico east to Motor, sped past Rancho Park and into Cheviot Hills. In the daylight, Achievement House didn't look any more impressive. The light stucco I'd seen last night was baby blue. A few more cars occupied the lot, and a dozen or so adolescents hung in loose groups. When we pulled up to the curb, they paid scant notice. The kids were a varied bunch ranging from black-lipped Goths to preppy chirpers who could've been extras on the *Ozzie and Harriet* set.

Milo rang the bell on the gate, and we were buzzed in without inquiry. Another buzz got us through the door. The lobby smelled of room freshener and corn chips. A reception desk to the right and an office door marked ADMINISTRATION were separated by a hallway that emptied to a softly lit waiting room where no one waited. Cream walls hung with chrome-framed floral prints, plum-colored carpeting, neatly arranged magazines on teak tables, off-white, overstuffed chairs. Glass panes in the rear double doors provided a view of more corridor and bursts of gawky adolescent movement.

The receptionist was a young Indian woman in a peach sari, surprised, but untroubled, by Milo's badge.

'And this is about?' she said, pleasantly.

'An inquiry,' said Milo, with downright good cheer. During the ride he'd been tense and silent, but all that was gone now. He'd combed his hair, tightened his tie, was coming across like a man with something to look forward to.

'An inquiry?' she said.

'A look at some student records, ma'am.'

'I'll get you Ms Baldassar. She's our director.'

She left, returned, said, 'This way,' and showed us to the door across the hall. We entered a front office and a secretary ushered us through a door to a tidy space where an ash blonde woman in her forties sat behind a desk and stubbed out a cigarette.

Milo offered the badge, and the blonde said, 'Marlene Baldassar.' Thin, tan, and intensely freckled, she had hollow cheeks, golden brown eyes, and a knife-point chin. Her navy blue A-line dress was piped with white and bagged on her bony frame. The ash hair was blunt-cut to mid-neck, bangs feathered to fringe. She wore a gold wedding band and an oversize black plastic diver's watch. Tortoise-framed glasses hung on a chain. The big glass ashtray on her desk was half-filled with lipstick-tipped butts. The rim read *Mirage Hotel, Las Vegas*. The rest of the desk was taken up with books, papers, framed photos. And a shiny silver harmonica.

She saw me looking at the instrument, picked it up with two fingers, tooted twice, put it down, smiling. 'Tension reliever. I'm trying to quit smoking. And obviously not doing very well.'

'Old habits,' I said.

'Very old. And yes, I *have* tried the patch. All of them. My DNA's probably saturated with nicotine.' She ran a finger along the edge of the harmonica. 'So, what's this Shoba tells me about a police inquiry? Has one of our alumni gotten into trouble?'

'You don't seem surprised by that possibility,' said Milo.

'I've worked with kids for going on twenty years. Very little surprises me.'

'Twenty years here, ma'am?'

'Three here, seventeen with the county – Juvenile Hall, community mental health centers, gang-violence prevention programs.'

'Welcome change?' I said.

'For the most part,' she said. 'But county work could even be fun. Lots of futility, but when you do come across a gem in the trash pile, it's exciting. Working here's extremely predictable. By and large, the kids are a decent bunch. Spoiled but decent. We specialize in serious learning disabilities – chronic school failure, severe dyslexia, kids who just can't get it together educationally. Our goal's specific: try to get them to a point so that when they get hold of their trust funds they can read the small print. So if your *inquiry* is about one of my current charges, I'd be surprised. We steer away from high-risk antisocials, too much maintenance.'

Milo said, 'Are the kids confined twenty-four hours a day?'

'Heavens no,' she said. 'This isn't prison. They go home on weekends, earn passes. So what do you need to know and about whom?'

'Actually,' said Milo, 'this is more of a historical venture. Someone who was here twenty years ago.'

Marlene Baldassar sat back, fooled with her eyeglasses. 'Sorry, I'm not free to talk about alumni. An emergent situation with a current student would be something else – someone in the here and now posing a danger to themselves and/or others. The law would require me to work with you on that.'

'Schools have no confidentiality, ma'am.'

'But psychotherapists do, Detective, and many of our files contain psychotherapeutic records. I'd love to help, but—'

'What about personnel records?' said Milo. 'We're also looking into someone who worked here. There'd be no protection of any sort, there.'

Baldassar fiddled with her glasses. 'I suppose that's true, but . . . twenty years ago? I'm not sure we even have records going back that far.'

'One way to find out, ma'am.'

'What's this person's name?'

'Wilbert Lorenzo Burns.'

No recognition on the freckled face. Baldassar got on the phone, asked a few questions, said, 'Wait right here,' and returned a few moments later with a scrap of pink paper.

'Burns, Wilbert L.,' she said, handing it to Milo. 'This is all we've got. Mr Burns's notice of termination. He lasted three weeks. August third through the twenty-fourth. Was terminated for absenteeism. See for yourself.'

Milo read the scrap and handed it back.

'What did Mr Burns do?'

'There's a fugitive warrant out on him. Mostly he was a narcotics violator. Kind of alarming that when he worked here he was on probation for a drug conviction. About to face trial for selling heroin.'

Baldassar frowned. 'Wonderful. Well, that wouldn't happen today.'

'You vet your employees carefully?'

'A pusher wouldn't get by me.'

'Guess the former director wasn't that picky,' said Milo. 'Do you know him – Michael Larner?'

'The only one I know is my immediate predecessor. Dr Evelyn Luria. Lovely woman. She retired and moved to Italy – she's at least eighty. I was told that she was brought in to beef up clinical services. I was brought in to organize things.' She poked the harmonica. 'You're not implying this Burns was dealing to the kids here.'

'Do the kids here have drug problems?'

'Detective, please,' said Baldassar. 'They're teenagers with poor self-esteem and plenty of disposable income. You don't need a PhD to figure it out. But believe me, I don't allow any species of felon to pass through our gates. As far as what happened twenty years ago . . .'

She picked up the harmonica, put it down. 'If that's all . . .'

'Actually,' said Milo, 'the investigation's not just about Willie Burns. It's about a student Burns was friendly with. A girl named Caroline Cossack.'

210

Baldassar stared. Then she snorted – I suppose it was laughter, but she looked anything but happy. She said, 'Let's go outside. I want to smoke, but I don't want to poison anyone else.'

She took us through the glass-paned double doors, past ten rooms, some of which had been left open. We walked by carelessly made beds, piles of stuffed animals, movie and rock star posters, boom boxes, guitars, books stacked in little wooden desks. A few teens were stretched across beds listening to music through earphones, one boy did push-ups, a girl read a magazine – brow knitted, lips moving laboriously.

We followed Marlene Baldassar under a rear staircase, where she pushed a door marked EXIT and let us pass through to an alley behind the building. Two dumpsters were pushed against a cinder-block wall. Nearby stood a chesty girl with her elbows to the block, hips thrust at a tall, buzz-cut boy wearing low pants that puddled around his unlaced sneakers. He looked like a scarecrow about to come apart. Moved in for a kiss but stopped as the girl said something, turned and frowned.

Baldassar said, 'Hi, guys.' Expressionless, the couple ambled off and disappeared around a corner.

'Somethingus interruptus,' said Baldassar. 'I almost feel guilty.'

Power lines were strung ten feet above the wall, and I could hear them buzzing. A pigeon soared overhead. Baldassar lit up, dragged hungrily, smoked down a half inch of her cigarette.

'Is there any chance we can talk confidentially?' she said.

'I'd like to promise you that,' said Milo. 'But if you've got knowledge of a crime—'

'No, it's nothing like that. And I never met the Cossack girl, though I do know that she was once a resident. But in terms of her family . . . let's just say they're not very popular around here.'

'Why's that, ma'am?'

Baldassar smoked and shook her head. 'I suppose if you dug around enough, you'd find out, anyway.'

'Where should I be digging?'

'What, I should do your job for you?'

'I'll take anything I can get, ma'am,' said Milo.

She smiled. 'County records. I'll tell you what I know, but I can't have any of it traced back to me, okay?'

'Okay.'

'I'm trusting you, Detective.'

'Thank you, ma'am.'

'And no more ma'ams please,' she said. 'I'm starting to feel like I'm in some old *Dragnet* script.'

'Fair enough, Ms—'

Baldassar cut him off with a wave of her cigarette. 'To make a long story exquisitely short, several years ago, seventeen or eighteen years ago, Achievement House ran into some severe financial problems due to bad investments. The board was comprised of stuffy old farts who were conservative with their personal fortunes but turned out to be a good deal more adventurous with Achievement House's endowment. Remember all that junk-bond foolishness? The board hired a money manager who traded Achievement House's blue chips for a whole slew of what ended up as worthless paper. At the time, the interest rates were enticing, and the income allowed the school to run at such a high paper profit that the board was starting to think Achievement House would pay for itself. Then everything crashed. And to make matters worse, the manager had taken out a second mortgage and bought additional bonds on margin. When everything hit the fan, Achievement House was way in the hole and facing foreclosure on the property.'

'The rich old farts would've let that happen?'

'The rich old farts served on the board in order to feel noble and to get their names in the social pages during gala season. To make matters worse, there'd been a bit of unpleasantness with the director – your Mr Larner. I know all this from Evelyn Luria. She briefed me before she left for Europe, but wouldn't give me details. But she did hint that it had been something of a sexual nature. Something that might've gotten the board members the worst type of publicity.'

'So the school was in danger of closing down, and the board wouldn't go to bat.'

'God, I hope this doesn't blow up, after all these years. I was looking at this job as a way to relax.'

'Nothing will get traced to you, Ms. Baldassar. Now tell me why the Cossacks aren't popular.'

'Because they came to the rescue – white knights – and then turned into something quite different.'

'Caroline's father?'

'Caroline's father and brothers. The three of them had some kind of real estate business and they stepped in and renegotiated with the bank and got a better rate for the mortgage, then had Achievement House's deed signed over to them. For a while, they made payments, no questions asked. Then a couple of years later, they announced they were evicting the school because the land was too valuable for a nonprofit – they'd been buying up lots, had plans to develop the entire block.'

She dropped her cigarette, ground it out with the toe of her pump.

'Achievement House is still here,' said Milo. 'What happened?'

'Threats, accusations, lawyers. The board and the Cossacks finally reached an agreement, but it meant dipping into some deep pockets in order to pay the Cossacks off. From what I was told, the outrage was compounded by the fact that Caroline Cossack's stay here had been a favor to the family. She didn't qualify.'

'Why not?'

'She was a psychiatric case – severe behavior problems, not learning disabilities.'

'Custodial care?' I said.

'Yes, the rules were bent for her. Then, for her family to do *that*.'

Milo said, 'Do you have any records on Caroline?'

Baldassar hesitated. 'Let me check – wait out here, please.'

She reentered the building. I said, 'I wonder if Michael Larner had something to do with the Cossacks trying to evict the school. After the board fired him, he wouldn't have been fond of the institution.'

Milo kicked one of the dumpsters. Another pigeon flew overhead. Then three more. 'Airborne rats,' he muttered. Barely audible, but the vibrations must have reached the birds, and they scattered.

Marlene Baldassar returned, another cigarette in one hand, a pink index card in another.

'No chart. All I found was this, listing the dates of her stay.'

Milo took the card. 'Admitted 9 August, discharged

214

22 December. But it doesn't say where she went.'

'No, it doesn't,' said Baldassar.

'You don't hold on to old charts?'

'We do. It should be here.' She studied Milo's face. 'You're not shocked.'

'Like you, I'm pretty much beyond being shockable, Ms Baldassar. And I'm going to ask you to return the favor: keep this visit confidential. For everyone's sake.'

'No problem with that,' said Baldassar. She took a deep drag, blew a smoke ring. 'Here I thought it was going to be a lazy day, and it turned out to be heavy-duty déjà vu. Gentlemen, you brought back memories of my days with the county.'

'How so?' I said.

'Problems that can't be solved with phonics and a credit card.'

nineteen

'Interesting time line,' I said, as we headed for the car under the now-watchful eyes of the kids in the parking lot. 'Janie Ingalls is murdered in early June. Two months later, Caroline gets checked into Achievement House and Willie shows up and works there for three weeks. Willie's fired, then he's busted for dope, gets Boris Nemerov to bail him out. When was Nemerov ambushed?'

'23 December,' said Milo.

'The day after Caroline leaves Achievement House – voluntarily or otherwise. Maybe Willie took his girlfriend out, then took care of her. Or Cossack family money found both of them a nice safe place to hide out. And one more thing: Georgie could've gotten nervous when you brought up Burns not because his men finished off his dad's killer but because they didn't. Were paid off not to.'

'He accepted money to let his dad's murderer off the hook? Uh-uh, not Georgie.'

'He and his mother were in severe financial straits. Maybe it took more than twenty-hour days and clever negotiating to keep the business going.'

'No, I can't see it,' he said. 'Georgie's always been a straight-ahead guy.'

'You'd know.'

'Yeah, I'm a font of knowledge. C'mon, let's go over to my place, have another look at that damn book.'

Rick and Milo lived in a small, well-kept bungalow in West Hollywood, on a quiet, elm-darkened street further shadowed by Design Center's alarming blue bulk. Rick's white Porsche was gone and the blinds were drawn. A few years ago, L.A. suffered through a drought and Rick had the lawn dug up and replaced with pea gravel and gray-leafed desert plants. This year, L.A. had plenty of water but the xeriscape remained in place, bursts of tiny yellow blossoms punctuating the pallid vegetation.

I said, 'The cactus are thriving.'

Milo said, 'Great. Especially when I come home in the dark and snag my pants.'

'Nothing like seeing the bright side.'

'That's my core philosophy,' he said. 'The glass is either half-empty or broken.'

He unlocked the front door, disarmed the alarm, picked up the mail that had fallen through the slot and tossed it on a table without breaking stride. The kitchen often lures him in his own digs, too, but this time he walked through it into the service porch nook that serves as his office: a cramped, dim space, sandwiched between the washer-dryer and the freezer and smelling of detergent. He'd set it up with a hideous metal desk painted school-bus yellow, a folding chair, and a painted wooden shark-face lamp from Bali. The blue book sat in an oversize Ziploc bag, on the top shelf of a miniature bookcase bolted above the desk.

He gloved up, unbagged the book, flipped to Janie Ingalls's photo, and studied the death shot. 'Any sudden insights?'

'Let's see what follows.'

Only three more pages after Janie. A trio of crime-scene photos, all of the victims young men. One black youth, two Hispanics, each sprawled on blood-splotched pavement. White lights on the corpses and dark periphery said nighttime death. A shiny revolver lay near the right hand of the final victim.

The first photo was labeled 'Gang drive-by, Brooks St, Venice. One dead, two wounded.'

Next: 'Gang drive-by, Commonwealth and Fifth, Rampart.'

Finally: 'Gang drive-by, Central Ave.'

'Three of a kind,' I said. 'That's kind of interesting.'

'Why?'

'Until now there was variety.'

Milo said, 'Gang stuff . . . business as usual. Maybe Schwinn ran out of interesting pictures – if these took place after Janie, when he was already out of the department, he coulda had trouble getting hold of crime-scene shots. God only knows how he managed to get these.' He closed the book. 'You see any way drive-bys could be connected to Janie? I sure don't.'

'Mind if I take another look?'

'Take as many looks as you want.' He produced another pair of gloves from a desk drawer, and I slipped them on. As I turned to the first photo, he stepped around the washer-dryer and into the kitchen. I heard the fridge door creak open.

'Want something to drink?'

'No, thanks.'

Heavy footsteps. A cabinet opened. Glass touched tile. 'I'm gonna go check the mail.'

I took my time with the crime-scene shots. Thinking about Schwinn, addicted to speed and divesting himself

218

of worldly goods even as he held on to his purloined photos. Moving on to a life of serenity but assembling this leather-bound monstrosity in secrecy. As I turned pages – now-familiar pages – and images began to blur, I tore myself away from speculation and tried to focus on each brutal death.

The first go-round, I came up with nothing, but on the second circuit something made me pause.

The two photos that *preceded* Janie's death shot.

The second page back was a full-color medium-range shot of a thin, rangy black man whose skin had begun to fade to postmortem gray. His long body lay on brown dirt, and one arm curled toward his face, protectively. Gaping mouth, half-open, lifeless eyes, splayed limbs.

No blood. No visible wounds.

Drug OD, possible 187 hotshot.

The next page faced Janie's. I'd avoided it because it was one of the most repellent images in the book.

The camera had focused on a heap of mangled flesh, beyond recognition as human.

Hairless legs and a battered, concave pelvic section suggested a woman. The caption precluded the need for deduction.

Female Mental Case, fell or thrown in front of double tractor trailer.

I flipped back to the skinny black man.

Returned to the beginning of the murder book and double-checked.

Then I went to get Milo.

He was in the living room, studying his gas bill, a shot glass of something amber in his paw. 'Finished?'

I said, 'Come look at this.'

219

He tossed back the rest of his drink, held on to the glass, and followed me.

I showed him the pictures preceding Janie. He said, 'What's your point?'

'Two points,' I said. 'First of all, content: right before Janie are a black drug-using male and a white woman with mental problems. Sound familiar? Second, context: these two deviate *stylistically* from every other photo in the book. Forty-one photos, including Janie's, list the location and the police division where the murder took place. These are the only two that don't. If Schwinn lifted the photos from police files, he had access to the data. Yet he left the locales out. Are you willing to consider a bit of psychological interpretation?'

'Schwinn being symbolic?' he said. 'These two represent Willie Burns and Caroline Cossack?'

'They're missing information because they represent the *missing* Willie Burns and the *missing* Caroline Cossack. Schwinn designated no locations because Burns's and Cossack's whereabouts remain unknown. Then he followed up with Janie's picture and wrote NS for No Solve. Right *after* Janie, he placed three drive-bys, grouped together. I don't think that's a coincidence, either. He knew how you'd see them: business as usual, just like you said. He's outlining a process here: a missing black man and mentally ill white woman are connected to Janie, whose murder is never solved. On the contrary: she's abandoned, and then it's business as usual. He's describing the cover-up.'

He pulled at his lower lip. 'Games . . . pretty subtle.'

'You said Schwinn was a devious sort,' I said. 'Suspicious, verging on paranoid. LAPD dumped him, but he continued to think like a rogue cop, played games to the end, in order to cover his rear. He decided to communicate with you, but set it up so that only you would get it. That way, if the book went astray, or was ever traced back to him, he could disclaim ownership. He took pains to make sure it *wasn't* traced to him – no fingerprints. Only you were likely to recall his photography hobby and make the connection. He might have planned to send you the book himself, but changed his mind and chose someone else as a go-between, as another layer of security.'

He studied the dead black man. Paged to the truck-crash nightmare, then Janie. Repeated the process.

'Willie and Caroline's surrogates . . . too weird.'

I pointed to the black man's corpse. 'How old does he look to you?'

He squinted at the ashen face. 'Forties.'

'If Willie Burns were alive today, he'd be forty-three. That means Schwinn saw the dead man as a surrogate for Willie *in the here and now*. Both the pictures are faded, probably decades old. But Schwinn oriented them toward the present. Meaning he finished the book fairly recently, wanted to focus *you* on the present.'

He rolled the empty shot glass between his palms. 'Bastard was a good detective. If the department got rid of him because someone was worried about what he knew about Janie, that means they didn't worry about me.'

'You were a rookie—'

'I was the dumb shit they figured would just follow orders. And guess what?' He laughed.

'It's likely when Schwinn learned he'd been forced out and you hadn't, it confirmed his suspicions of you. Maybe he figured you'd played a role in his dismissal. That's why he didn't tell you what he'd learned about Janie for years.'

'And then he changed his mind.'

'He came to admire you. Told Marge.'

'Mr Serenity,' he said. 'So he enlists his girlfriend or some old cop washout to serve as go-between. Why'd whoever it was wait until seven months after Schwinn died?'

I had no answer for that. Milo tried to pace, but the confined quarters of the laundry area made it a two-step exercise.

He said, 'Then the guy falls off a horse.'

'A horse so gentle Marge felt comfortable with Schwinn riding up into the hills alone. But Akhbar got spooked, anyway. Marge said by "something." Maybe it was some*one*.'

He stared past me, reentered the kitchen, washed out the shot glass, returned, and glared at the book. 'Nothing says Schwinn's death wasn't an accident.'

'Nothing at all.'

He pressed his hands flat against the wall as if straining to push it down.

'Bastards,' he said.

'Who?'

'Everyone.'

We sat down in his living room, each of us thinking in silence, neither of us coming up with anything. If he felt as weary as I did, he needed a break.

The phone rang. He snatched up the receiver. 'This is him . . . what? Who – yes . . . one week. Yeah . . . I did . . . that's right. What's that? Yeah, I just told you that, anything else? Okay, then. Hey, listen, why don't you give me your name and number and I'll—'

The other party cut him off. He held the phone at

arm's length, began gnawing his upper lip.

'Who was that?' I said.

'Some guy claiming to be from Department Personnel downtown, wanting to verify that I was indeed taking vacation time and how long did I plan to be away. I told him I'd filled out the forms.'

'*Claiming* to be from Personnel?'

'I've never known the department to make calls like that, and he hung up when I asked his name. Also, he didn't sound like a department clerk.'

'How so?'

'He sounded like he gave a damn.'

twenty

He slipped the murder book back into the plastic bag, and said, 'This goes in the safe.'

'Didn't know you had a safe,' I said.

'For all my Cartier and Tiffany. Wait here.'

He disappeared and I stood there, humbled once more by the truism I'd learned a thousand patients ago: Everyone has secrets. At the core, we're alone.

That made me think of Robin. Where was she? What was she doing? With whom?

Milo returned, minus his necktie. 'Hungry?'

'Not really.'

'Good, let's eat.'

He locked up and we got back in the car. I said, 'That call from Personnel. Maybe procedures have tightened up with John Broussard in charge. Isn't troop discipline his pet issue?'

'Yeah. How about Hot Dog Heaven?'

I drove to San Vicente just north of Beverly and parked at the curb. Hot Dog Heaven was built around a giant hot dog, yet another testament to L.A.'s literal thinking. The fast-food joint became a landmark when the pony ride

224

that had occupied the corner of La Cienega and Beverly for decades was replaced by the neon-and-concrete assault known as the Beverly Center. Too bad Philip K. Dick had committed suicide. A few years later and he'd have seen *Blade Runner* spring to life. Or maybe he'd known what was coming.

Back during pony-ride days, the dirt track had been a favorite weekend visitation hangout for divorced dads and their kids. Hot Dog Heaven had thrived peddling nitrites to lonely men who smoked and hung around the low-slung corral, watching their progeny go round and round. Where did displaced dads go now? Not the mall. The last thing kids at the mall wanted was proximity to their parents.

Milo ordered two jumbo chili cheese dogs with extra onions, and I got a knockwurst. We filled out the bill with two large Cokes and sat down to eat as traffic roared by. It was late for lunch and early for dinner and only two other tables were occupied, an old woman reading the paper and a tall, long-haired youth in hospital blues – probably a Cedars-Sinai intern.

Milo wolfed the first chili dog without the aid of respiration. After tweezing every scrap of cheese from the wax paper with his fingers, he gulped Coke and got to work on the second. He finished that one, too, sprang up, and bought a third. My wurst tasted fine, but it was all I could do to feign hunger.

He was counting his change when a bronze Jeep Cherokee parked in front of my Seville and a man got out and walked past me toward the counter. Black suit, pearl shirt, soot-colored tie. Smiling. That's what made me notice him. A big, wide, toothy grin, as if he'd just received terrific news. I watched him stride quickly to the counter and come to a stop just behind Milo, where he

225

waited, bouncing on his heels. His black suede loafers were lifted by two-inch heels. Without them he was an easy six feet. He stood close to Milo, kept bouncing. Milo didn't seem to notice. Something made me put down the wurst and keep my eyes on both of them.

Smiley was thirty or so, with dark hair gelled and combed back, curling over his collar. Big-jawed face, prominent nose, golden tan. The suit was well cut – Italian or pretending to be, and it looked brand-new, as did the suede shoes. The gray shirt was satin-finish silk, the tie a bulky knit. Dressed for an audition as a game show host?

He edged even closer to Milo. Said something. Milo turned and answered.

Smiley nodded.

Milo picked up his food and returned to the table.

'Friendly sort?' I said.

'Who?'

'The guy behind you. He's been smiling since he left that Jeep.'

'So?'

'So what's to smile about?'

Milo allowed his own mouth to curl upward. But he let his eyes drift back to the counter, where the smiling man was now conversing with the counter girl. 'Anything other than that bother you about him?'

'He was standing close enough to you to smell your cologne.'

'If I wore any,' he said, but he continued to watch the goings-on at the counter. Finally sat back and sank his teeth into the third chili dog. 'Nothing like health food.' He regarded my half-finished wurst. 'What's with the anorexia?'

'Just out of curiosity, what did he say to you up there?'

'Oh, boy . . .' He shook his head. 'He wanted to know what was good, okay? I told him I liked anything with chili. Heavy-duty intrigue.'

I smiled. 'Or flirting.'

'Me?'

'Him.'

'Oh, sure, strangers always come up and hit on me. The old fatal charm and all that.'

But he hazarded another glance at the counter, where Smiley was still gabbing with the girl as he paid for his dog. Plain, no chili. He sat down at the table closest to ours, unfolded a napkin over his lap, flipped his hair, beamed at Milo, said, 'Chickened out on the chili.'

'Your loss.'

Smiley laughed. Tugged at his lapel. Took a bite. A dainty little bite that didn't alter the shape of the hot dog.

I mumbled, 'Fatal charm.'

Milo said, 'Enough,' and wiped his face.

Smiley continued to nibble without making much progress. Dabbed his chin. Showed off his dental work. Made several attempts at catching Milo's eye. Milo moved his bulk around, stared at the ground.

Smiley said, 'These really *are* a mouthful.'

I fought back laughter.

Milo nudged my arm. 'Let's go.'

We stood. Smiley said, 'Have a nice day.'

He got to his feet as we reached the car and jogged toward us, sandwich in one hand, the other waving.

'What the hell,' said Milo, and his hand sidled under his coat.

Smiley reached into his own jacket and all at once Milo had interposed himself between the stranger and me. A flesh barrier, immense; tension seemed to enlarge him. Then he relaxed. Smiley was still waving, but the something in his hand was small and white. A business card.

'Sorry for being so forward, but I . . . here's my number. Call me if you'd like.'

'Why would I do that?' said Milo.

Smiley's lips drew back, and his grin morphed into something hungry and unsettling. 'Because you never know.'

He dangled the card.

Milo stood there.

Smiley said, 'Oh, well,' and placed the card on the hood of the Seville. His new face was serious, vulpine, purposeful. He trotted away from us, tossed the uneaten hot dog in the trash, got into the Jeep, and sped away as Milo hustled to copy down his license plate. He picked the card off the hood, read it and handed it to me.

Off-white vellum with a faintly greasy feel, engraved letters.

Paris M. Bartlett
Health Facilitator

Below that, a cell-phone number.

' "Because you never know," ' said Milo. 'Health facilitator. Do I look sick?'

'Other than stains on your shirt you look perfectly put-together.'

'Health facilitator,' he repeated. 'Sounds like something from the AIDS industry.' He pulled out his cellphone and jabbed in Paris Bartlett's number. Frowned again. 'No longer in service. What the hell . . .'

'Time to DMV the plates?' I said.

'DMVing is illegal when I'm on vacation. Using departmental resources for personal reasons, big no-no.'

'John G. would disapprove mightily.'

'Mightily.' He made the call to State Motor Vehicles, recited the plate, waited a while, wrote something down. 'The plates belong to a two-year-old Jeep, so that's kosher. Registered to the Playa del Sol Corporation. The address is right here in West Hollywood. I recognize it. Parking lot of the Healthy Foods market on Santa Monica. There's a post–office box outlet there. I know because I used to rent there myself.'

'When?'

'Long time ago.'

A safe. A POB. All the new things I was learning about my friend.

'Dead number, shadow address,' I said. 'Playa del Sol could be nothing more than a cardboard box in someone's apartment, but it does have the ring of a real estate outfit.'

'As in the Cossacks.' He studied the card. 'That and the call about my vacation time. Right after we talk to Marlene Baldassar. Maybe she *can't* be trusted.'

Or maybe he hadn't covered his trail. I said, 'It could be just a pickup attempt.' But I knew that was wrong. Paris Bartlett had bounded out of his car with clear intention.

He slipped the card in his pocket. 'Alex, I grew up in a big family, never got much attention, never developed a taste for it. I need some alone time.'

I drove him back to his place, and he hurtled out of the Seville, mumbled something that might've been 'Thanks,' slammed the door, and loped toward his front door.

I made it to my own front door thirty-five minutes later, told myself I'd be able to walk right past the phone. But the red blinking 1 on the answering machine snagged me, and I stabbed the message button.

Robin's voice: 'Looks like I missed you again, Alex. There's another change in schedule, we're adding an extra day in Vancouver, maybe the same in Denver. It's crazy around here, I'll be in and out.' Two-second delay, then several decibels lower: 'I love you.'

Obligatory add-on? Unlike Pierce Schwinn, I didn't need drugs to prime the paranoia pump.

I phoned the Four Seasons Seattle again and asked for Ms Castagna's room. This time if they gave me voice mail, I'd leave a message.

But a man answered. Young, one of those laughing voices. Familiar.

Sheridan. He of the ponytail, the cheerful outlook, and the Milk-Bone for Spike.

'Robin? Oh, hi. Yeah, sure.'

Seconds later: 'This is Robin.'

'And this is Alex.'

'Oh . . . hi. Finally.'

'Finally?'

'Finally we connect. Is everything okay?'

'Everything's peachy,' I said. 'Am I interrupting something?'

'What – oh, Sheridan? No, we were just finishing up a meeting. A bunch of us.'

'Busy busy.'

'I've got time now. So how *are* you? Busy yourself?'

This was too much like small talk, and it depressed me. 'Muddling along. How's Spike?'

'Thriving. There's a bunch of other dogs along for the

230

ride, so there's a nice kennel space. Spike's getting pretty sociable. There's an eighty-pound shepherd bitch who seems to have caught his fancy.'

'Does the kennel space include a ladder for him to reach her?'

She laughed, but sounded tired. 'So . . .'

I said, 'So are you getting in any social time?'

'I'm working, Alex. We're putting in twelve-, thirteen-hour days.'

'Sounds tough. I miss you.'

'Miss you, too. We both knew this would be difficult.'

'Then we were both right.'

'Honey – hold on, Alex . . . someone just stuck their head in.' Her voice got muffled and distant; hand over the phone. *'I'll see what I can do, give me a little time on it, okay? When's sound-check? That soon? Okay, sure.'* Back to me: 'As you can see I haven't had much solitude.'

'I've had plenty.'

'I'm jealous.'

'Are you?'

'Yes,' she said. 'We both like our solitude, right?'

'You can have yours back anytime.'

'I can't exactly walk out on everyone.'

'No,' I said. 'As Richard Nixon said, that would be wrong.'

'I mean I – if there was some easy – if that would really make you happy, I'd do it.'

'It would ruin your reputation.'

'It sure wouldn't help it.'

'You're committed,' I said. 'Don't worry about it.' *Why the hell is Sheridan so happy?*

'Alex, when I do get a minute to breathe, I think of you, wonder if I did the right thing. Then I plan all the things I'm going to tell you, but then when we finally talk . . . it doesn't seem to go the way I'd planned.'

'Absence makes the heart cranky?'

'Not my heart.'

'Guess it's me, then,' I said. 'Guess I don't do well with separation. Never got used to it.'

'Used to it?' she said. 'Your parents?'

My parents were the last thing I'd been thinking of. Now bad old memories ignited: the wasting away of the two people who'd brought me into this world, bedside vigils, a pair of funerals in as many years.

'Alex?'

'No,' I said. 'I was just talking generally.'

'You sound upset,' she said. 'I didn't mean to—'

'You didn't do anything.'

'What did you mean by that? Never getting used to separation?'

'Random blather,' I said.

'Are you saying that even when we were together you felt abandoned? That I neglected you? Because I—'

'No,' I said. 'You've always been there for me.' *Except for the other time you left.*

Except for finding another man and— 'It really was blather, Rob. Put it down to missing you.'

'Alex, if this is really bad for you, I'll come *home*.'

'No,' I said. 'I'm a big boy. It wouldn't be good for you. For either of us.'

And I've got things on my *plate. Little odd jobs, the kind you hate.*

'That's true,' she said. 'But just say the word.'

'The word is I love you.'

'That's three words.'

'Picky picky.'

She laughed. Finally. I uttered a few pleasantries, and she did the same. When we hung up she sounded okay, and I figured I faked it pretty well.

Milo claimed to want 'alone time,' but I figured he'd be nosing around on the fringes of the LAPD bureaucracy.

If the call from Personnel and/or the encounter with the toothy Paris Bartlett did have something to do with his raking up the Ingalls case, that meant he – *we* – had been tagged, were being watched.

Marlene Baldassar as the source didn't sit right with me, and I thought about the trail we might've left.

My solo activities had consisted of the call to Larry Daschoff, dinner with Allison Gwynn, computer work at the Research Library. None of that was likely to attract attention.

Together, Milo and I had interviewed Marge Schwinn and Baldassar and Georgie Nemerov. I supposed either woman could've reported the conversation, but neither had been hostile, and I couldn't see why they'd have bothered.

Nemerov, on the other hand, had grown antsy when talking about his father's murder and Willie Burns's skip. Nemerov's bail bond business gave him close ties to the department. If John G. Broussard had been part of a fix, the department would care.

A third possibility was Milo's solo work on Janie Ingalls had attracted attention. As far as I knew that had been limited to phone work and unearthing old files. But he'd worked at the West L.A. station, sneaked around Parker Center.

Thinking he'd been discreet but he could've invited scrutiny – from clerks, other cops, anyone in a position to witness him nosing. John G. Broussard had sent a clear directive to tighten up discipline among the rank and file. The new chief had also waged war on the blue code of silence – talk about irony. Maybe cops informing on cops was the new LAPD Zeitgeist.

The more I thought about that, the more it made sense: Milo was a pro, but he'd taken too much for granted.

Procedurally, he'd been outed.

That made me think about his continuing vulnerability. Twenty years in the department with one of the highest solve rates in Homicide, but that wasn't enough, would never be enough.

For two decades he'd functioned as a gay man in a paramilitary organization that would never be free of gut-level bias and still hadn't acknowledged the existence of homosexual cops. I knew – everyone knew – that scores of gay officers patrolled the streets, but not a single one had gone public. Neither had Milo, in a strict sense, but after those first brutal years of self-torment he had stopped hiding.

Department statisticians were happy to file his solves in the Assets column but the brass continued to retard his progress and made periodic attempts to get rid of him. Milo had collected secrets of his own along the way, finally managed to leverage his way to relative job security and seniority. He'd turned down the offer to take the lieutenant's exam twice because he knew the department's real intention was to shunt him to some desk job where they could pretend he didn't exist, while boring him to the point of voluntary retirement. Instead, he'd stayed on the detective track, had taken it as far as it would go: to Detective-III.

Maybe Pierce Schwinn had followed all that, come to respect Milo for holding his own. Offered Milo a perverse gift.

Normally, nothing heated Milo's blood like a good cold case. But this was a rethaw from his own past, and perhaps he'd gotten careless and turned himself into prey.

I thought of how Paris Bartlett had targeted Milo, ignored me.

Meaning I had room to move.

The timing was perfect, the logic exquisite: what were friends for?

twenty-one

Alone, at his crappy little piss-colored desk, the washer churning the clothes he'd just loaded for background noise, Milo felt better.

Free of *Alex*, he felt better.

Because Alex's mind could be a scary thing – cerebral flypaper; stuff flew in but never left. His friend was capable of sitting quietly for long stretches when you'd think he was listening – actively listening the way they'd taught him in shrink school – then he'd let loose a burst of associations and hypotheses and apparently unrelated trivialities that turned out too often to be right-on.

Houses of cards that, more often than not, withstood the wind. Milo, on the receiving end of the nonstop volleys, felt like a wobbly sparring partner.

Not that Alex pushed. He just kept *supposing. Suggesting.* Another shrink tactic. Try ignoring any of it.

Milo had never met anyone smarter or more decent than Alex, but hanging with the guy could be draining. How many nights' sleep had he lost because one of his friend's *suggestions* had hooked a barb in his brain?

But for all his bloodhound instincts, Alex was a civilian and out of his element. And he'd failed to mature in one regard: had never developed a proper sense of threat.

In the beginning, Milo had attributed it to the carelessness of an overenthusiastic amateur. It hadn't taken long to learn the truth: Alex got off on danger.

Robin understood that, and it scared her. Over the years she'd confided her fears to Milo – more nuance than complaint. And when the three of them were together and Alex and Milo lapsed into the wrong type of conversation and her face changed, Milo caught it quickly and changed the subject. Strangely enough, Alex, for all his perceptiveness, sometimes missed it.

Alex had to realize how Robin felt, yet he made no effort to change. And Robin put up with it. Love is blind and deaf and dumb . . . maybe she'd simply made a commitment and was smart enough to know it was damn near impossible to change anyone.

But now, she'd gone on that tour. And taken the dog. For some reason that felt wrong – the damn pooch. Alex was claiming to be okay, but that first day Milo'd dropped in, he'd looked really bad, and even now, he was different . . . distracted.

Something was off.

Or maybe not.

He'd poked a bit at Alex's resistance. Playing shrink to the shrink, and why the hell shouldn't he? How could you have a real friendship when the therapy went only one way? But no luck. Alex talked the talk – openness, communication, blah blah blah, but in his own articulate, empathetic, ever-so-disgustingly *civilized* way, the guy was pain-in-the-ass, dead-end *immovable*.

Now that he thought about it, had Alex *ever* been deterred? Milo couldn't remember a single instance.

Alex did exactly what Alex wanted to do.

And Robin . . . Milo'd offered his smoothest

reassurances. And he supposed he'd done a decent job of keeping Alex out of harm's way. But there were limits.

Everyone stood alone.

He got up, poured himself a vodka and pink-grapefruit juice, rationalizing that the vitamin C counteracted the oxidation, but wondering how closely his liver resembled that medical journal photo Rick had shown him last month.

Erosion of hepatic tissue and replacement with fatty globules due to advanced cirrhosis.

Rick never pushed either, but Milo knew he wasn't happy with the fresh bottle of Stoli in the freezer.

Switch channels: back to Alex.

Other people's problems were so much more engaging.

He walked half a mile to a Budget Rent-a-Car on La Cienega and got himself a fresh blue Taurus. Driving east on Santa Monica, he crossed into Beverly Hills, then West Hollywood. Not much traffic past Doheny Drive, but at the West Hollywood border the boulevard had been narrowed to one lane in either direction and the few cars in sight were crawling.

West Hollywood, The City That Never Stopped Decorating, had been digging up the streets for years, plunging businesses into bankruptcy and accomplishing little Milo could see other than a yawning stretch of dirt piles and ditches. Last year, the ribbon had been cut on a spanking new West Hollywood fire station. One of those architectural fancies – peaks and troughs and gimcracks and weird-shaped windows. Cute, except the doors had proved too narrow for the fire engines to squeeze through, and the poles didn't allow the firefighters to slide down. This year, West Hollywood had embarked on a sister-city deal with Havana. Milo doubted Fidel would approve of Boystown nightlife.

Among the few businesses the roadwork couldn't kill were the all-night markets and the gay bars. A guy had to eat and a guy had to party. Milo and Rick stayed in most nights – how long had it been since he'd cruised?

And now, here he was.

He found himself smiling, but it felt like someone else's mirth.

Because what the hell was there to be happy about? Pierce Schwinn and/or a confederate had manipulated him into warming up Ingalls, he'd accomplished nothing but had managed to screw up royally.

Attracting attention.

Playa del Sol. That toothy putz Paris Bartlett. First thing he did after ditching Alex was to check city records for a business registration on Playa. Nothing. Then he ran Bartlett through every database he could think of. Like that could be a real name.

Taking a giant risk because what he'd told Alex had been true: as a civilian he was forbidden to use departmental resources, he was treading felonious water. He'd put up a firewall by using the ID numbers of other cops for the requests. Half a dozen IDs of cops he didn't care for, jumping around different divisions. His version of identity theft; he'd been collecting data for years, stashing loose bits of paper in his home safe because you never knew when your back was gonna be against the wall. But if someone tried hard enough, the calls could be traced back to him.

Clever boy, but the search had been futile: no such person as Paris Bartlett.

Which he supposed he'd known right away – apart from the moniker having a phony ring, Bartlett, all hair and teeth and eagerness, had had that *actor* thing going on. In L.A. that didn't necessarily mean a SAG card and a portfolio full of headshots. LAPD liked guys who were good at pretending, too. Channeled them into undercover work. Nowadays, that meant mostly Narcotics, occasionally Vice when the word came down to run yet another week or two of hooker rousts for public relations.

Years ago undercover had meant another Vice game, a regularly scheduled weekend production: Friday and Saturday night operations put together with military lust. Staking out targets and delineating the enemy and moving in for the attack.

Bust the queers.

Not naked aggression, the way it had been back before Christopher Street, when gay bars were ripe for routine, big-time head-breaking. Most of that ended by the early seventies, but Milo had caught the tail end of the department's fag-bashing fervor: LAPD masked the raids as drug busts, as if hetero clubs weren't fueled by the same dope. During his first month at West L.A. he'd been assigned to a Saturday night bivouac against a private club on Sepulveda near Venice. Out-of-the-way dive in a former auto-painting barn where a hundred or so well-heeled men, believing themselves to be secure, went to talk and dance and smoke grass and gobble Quaaludes and enjoy the bathroom stalls. LAPD had a different notion of security. The way the supervisor – a hyper-macho D II named Reisan who Milo was certain was tucked deeply in the closet – laid out the plan, you'da thought it was a swoop on some Cong hamlet. Squinty eyes, military lingo, triangulated diagrams scrawled on the board, give me a break.

Milo sat through the orientation, struggling not to succumb to a full-body sweat. Reisan going on about coming down hard on resisters, don't be shy about using your batons. Then, leering, and warning the troops not to kiss anyone because you didn't know where those lips had been. Looking straight at Milo when he'd cracked wise, Milo laughing along with the others and wondering: *Why the hell is he doing that?* Fighting to convince himself he'd imagined it.

The day of the raid, he called in sick with the flu, stayed in bed for three days. Perfectly healthy, but he worked hard at degrading himself by not sleeping or eating, just sucking on gin and vodka and rye and peach brandy and whatever else he found in the cupboard. Figuring if the department checked on him, he'd look like death warmed over.

VN combat vet, now a real-life working detective, but he was still thinking like a truant high school kid.

Over the three days, he lost eight pounds, and when he stood his legs shook and his kidneys ached and he wondered if that yellow tinge in his eyes was real or just bad lighting – his place was a dingy hovel, the few windows it offered looked out to airshafts, and no matter how many bulbs he used, he could never get the illumination above tomb-strength.

The first time in three days that he tried food – a barely warmed can of Hearty Man chili – what he didn't heave whooshed out the other end. He smelled like a goat pen, his hair felt brittle, and his fingernails were getting soft.

For a full week later, his ears rang and his back hurt and he drank gallons of water a day just in case he'd damaged something. The day he returned to the station, a transfer slip – Vice to Auto Theft, signed by Reisan – was in his box. That seemed a fine state of affairs. Two days later, someone slipped a note through the door of his locker.

How's your bunghole, faggot?

He pulled into the Healthy Foods lot, stayed in the Taurus, scanned the parking lot for anything out of the ordinary. During the drive from his house to the station, then from Budget to the market, he'd been on alert for a tail. Hadn't picked up any, but this wasn't the movies, and the hard truth was, in a city built around the combustion engine, you could never be sure.

He watched shoppers enter the market, finally satisfied himself that he hadn't been followed, and crossed over to the row of small stores – rehabbed shacks, really – that sat across from Healthy Foods. Locksmith, dry cleaners, cobbler, West Hollywood Easy Mail Center.

He flashed his badge to the Pakistani behind the mail-drop counter – pile up those violations, Sturgis – and inquired about the box number listed on the Jeep's registration. The clerk was sullen, but he thumbed through his circular Rolodex and shook his head.

'No Playa del Sol.' Behind him was the wall of brass boxes. A sign advertised FedEx, UPS, rubber stamps, *While-U-Wait* gift-wrapping. Milo spotted no ribbons or happy-face wrapping paper. This was all about secrets.

'When did they stop renting?' he said.

'Had to be at least a year ago.'

'How do you know?'

'Because the current tenant has been renting for thirteen months.'

Tenant. Milo pictured some leprechaun setting up house in the mailbox. Tiny stove, refrigerator, Murphy bed, thumbnail-sized cable TV blaring *The Pot of Gold Network.*

'Who's the current tenant?' he said.

'You know I can't tell you that, sirrr.'

'Aw, shucks,' said Milo, producing a twenty-dollar bill. Keep those felonies coming . . .

The Pakistani stared at the bill as Milo placed it on the counter, closed his hand over Andrew Jackson's gaunt visage. Then he turned his back on Milo and began fiddling with one of the empty mailboxes and Milo reached over and took hold of the Rolodex and read the card.

Mr and Mrs Irwin Block

Address on Cynthia Street. Just a few blocks away.

'Know these people?' said Milo.

'Old people,' said the Pakistani, still showing his back. 'She comes in every week, but they don't get anything.'

'Nothing?'

'Once in a while, junk.'

'Then why do they need a POB?'

The clerk faced him and smiled. 'Everyone needs one – tell all your friends.' He reached for the Rolodex, but Milo held on to it, thumbing back from *Bl* to *Ba*. No Bartlett. Then up to *P*. No Playa del Sol.

The Pakistani said, 'Stop, please. What if someone comes in?'

Milo released the Rolodex, and the clerk placed it under the counter.

'How long have you been working here?'

'Oh,' said the clerk, as if the question was profound. 'Ten months.'

'So you've never dealt with anyone from Playa del Sol.'

'That is true.'

'Who worked here before you?'

'My cousin.'

'Where is he?'

'Kashmir.'

Milo glared at him.

'It's true,' said the man. 'He had enough of this place.'

'West Hollywood?'

'America. The morals.'

No curiosity about why Milo wanted to know about Playa del Sol. Given the guy's line of work, Milo supposed he'd learned not to be curious.

Milo thanked him, and the clerk rubbed his index finger with his thumb. 'You could show your thanks in another way.'

'Okay,' said Milo, making a very low bow. 'Thank you *very much*.'

As he left, he heard the man utter something in a language he didn't understand.

He drove to the Cynthia Street apartment of Mr and Mrs Irwin Block, pretended to be a census taker, and enjoyed an affable five-minute chat with the possibly hundred-year-old Selma Block, a blue-caftaned, champagne-haired pixie of a woman so bent and tiny she might very well have fit into one of the mailboxes. Behind her sat Mr Block on a green-and-gold sofa, a mute, static, vacant-eyed apparition of similar antiquity whose sole claim to physiologic viability was the occasional moist and startling throat clear.

Five minutes taught Milo more about the Blocks than he'd wanted to know. Both had worked in the Industry – Selma as a costume mistress for several major studios, Irwin as an accountant for MGM. Three children lived back East. One was an orthodontist, the middle one had gone into 'the financial world and became a Republican, and our daughter weaves and sews hand-fashioned—'

'Is this the only address you keep, ma'am?' said Milo, pretending to write everything down but doodling curl-icues. No chance of Mrs B spotting the ruse. The top of her head was well below the pad.

'Oh, no, dear. We keep a post-office box over by the Healthy Foods.'

'Why's that, ma'am?'

'Because we like to eat healthy.'

'Why the post-office box, ma'am?'

Selma Block's tiny claw took hold of Milo's sleeve, and he felt as if a cat was using his arm for a spring post.

'Politics, dear. Political mailers.'

'Oh,' said Milo.

'What party do you belong to, dear?'

'I'm an independent.'

'Well, dear, we like the Green Party – rather subversive, you know.' The claw dug in deeper.

'You keep the box for Green Party mailers?'

'Oh, yes,' said Selma Block. 'You're too young, but we remember the way it used to be.'

'The way it used to be when?'

'The old days. Those House UnAmerican fascists. That louse McCarthy.'

Refusing the invitation to stay for tea and cookies, he

extricated himself from Mrs Block and drove around aimlessly, trying to figure out his next move.

Playa del Sol. Alex was right, it did have that real estate ring, so maybe the Cossacks did have their hand in this – assisted by LAPD.

The fix. Again.

Early on, he'd looked up Cossack Development's address, found it on Wilshire in Mid-City, but he hadn't retained the numbers in his head – those days were gone – so he called Information and fixed the placement between Fairfax and La Brea.

The sky was dark and traffic had started to thin and he made it over in less than a quarter-hour.

The Cossack brothers had headquartered themselves in a three-story pink granite, ziggurat-dominated complex that occupied a full city block just east of the County Art Museum. Years ago, this had been junk real estate – the fringes of the pathetically misnamed Miracle Mile. Back in the forties, The Mile's construction had been an historic first: a commercial strip with feeble street appeal but entry through the rear parking lots – yet another symptom of L.A.'s postwar infatuation with The Car. Twenty years later, westward flight had left the central city area a sump of poorly maintained buildings and low-rent businesses, and the only miracle was that any part of The Mile survived.

Now, the current cycle: urban renewal. County Art – not much in the way of a museum, but the courtyard did offer free concerts and L.A. didn't expect much – had spawned other museums – tributes to dolls, folk art, and most effectively, The Car. Big, glossy office structures had followed. If the Cossacks had gotten in early and owned the land under the pink granite thing, they'd made out well.

He parked on a side street, climbed wide, slick granite steps past a huge, shallow black pool filled with still water and dotted with pennies, and entered the lobby. Guard desk to the right, but no guard. Half the lights were off and the cavernous space echoed. The complex was divided into east and west wings. Most of the tenants were financial and showbiz outfits. Cossack Development took up the third floor of the east wing.

He rode the elevator, stepped into an unfurnished, white-carpeted, white-walled space. One big abstract lithograph greeted him – yellow and white and amorphous, maybe some genius's notion of a soft-boiled egg – then, to the left, double white doors. Locked. No sound from the other side.

The elevator door closed behind him. Turning, he stabbed the button and waited for it to return.

Back on Wilshire, he continued to study the building. Lot of lights were on, including several on the third floor. A couple of weeks ago, the state had warned of impending power shortages, urged everyone to conserve. Either the Cossacks didn't care, or someone was working late.

He rounded the corner, returned to the Taurus, reversed direction, and parked with a clear view of the building's subterranean parking lot. Fighting back that old feeling: wasted hours, stakeout futility. But stakeouts were like Vegas slots: once in a great while something paid off, and what better basis for addiction?

Twenty-three minutes later, the lot's metal grate slid open and a battered Subaru emerged. Young black woman at the wheel, talking on a cell-phone. Six minutes after that: a newish BMW. Young white guy with spiked hair – also gabbing on cell, oblivious, he narrowly missed colliding with a delivery truck. Both drivers traded insults and bird-flips. The streets were safe, tonight.

Milo waited another half-hour, was just about to split when the grate yawned once more and a soot-gray Lincoln Town Car nosed out. Vanity plates: CCCCCCC. Windows tinted well past the legal limit – even the driver's pane – but otherwise nice and conservative.

The Lincoln stopped at the red light at Wilshire, then turned west. Traffic was heavy enough for Milo to obtain cover two lengths behind, but sufficiently fluid to allow a nice, easy tail.

Perfect. For what it was worth.

He followed the gray Lincoln half a mile west to San Vicente Boulevard, then north to Melrose and west again on Robertson, where the Town Car pulled into the front lot of a restaurant on the southwest corner.

Brushed steel door. Matching steel nameplate above the door, engraved heavily:

Sangre de Leon

New place. The last time Milo had taken the time to look, an Indonesian–Irish fusion joint had occupied the corner. Before that had been some kind of Vietnamese bistro run by a celebrity chef from Bavaria and bank-rolled by movie stars. Milo figured the patrons had never served in the military.

Before *that*, he recalled at least six other start-up trendolas in as many years, new owners refurbishing, grand opening, garnering the usual breathless puff pieces in *L.A. Magazine* and *Buzz*, only to close a few months later.

Bad-luck corner. Same for the site across the street – the bamboo-faced one-story amorphoid that had once been a Pacific Rim seafood palace was now shuttered, a heavy chain drawn across its driveways.

Sangre de Leon. Lion's Blood. Appetizing. He wouldn't take bets on this one enduring longer than a bout of indigestion.

He found a dark spot across Robertson, parked diagonal to the restaurant, turned off his headlights. The rest of the decor was windowless gray stucco and sprigs of tall, bearded grass that looked like nothing other than dry weeds. An army of pink-jacketed valets – all good-looking and female – hovered at the mouth of the lot. Stingy lot; the seven Mercedes parked there filled it.

The Town Car's chauffeur – a big, thick bouncer type nearly as large as Georgie Nemerov's hunters – jumped out and sprang a rear door. A chesty, puffy-faced guy in his forties with sparse, curly hair got out first. His face looked as if it had been used as a waffle iron. Milo recognized Garvey Cossack right away. The guy had put on weight since his most recent newspaper photo, but not much else about him had changed. Next came a taller, soft-looking character with a shaved bullet head and a Frank Zappa mustache that drooped to his chin – little brother Bobo, minus his slicked-back hairdo. Middle-aged sap doing the youth-culture thing? Cranial skin as a proud badge of rebellion? Either way, the guy enjoyed mirror time.

Garvey Cossack wore a dark sport coat with padded shoulders over a black turtleneck, black slacks. Below the slacks, white running shoes – now there was a touch of elegance.

Bobo had on a too-small black leather bomber jacket, too-tight black jeans and black T-shirt, too-high black boots. Black-lensed shades, too. Call the paramedics, we've got an emergency overdose of cool.

A third man exited the Lincoln, and the big chauffeur let him close his own door.

Number Three was dressed the way businessmen used to dress in L.A. Dark suit, white shirt, undistinguished tie, normal shoes. Shorter than the Cossack brothers, he had narrow shoulders and a subservient stoop. Saggy, wrinkled face, though he didn't appear any older than the Cossacks. Minuscule oval eyeglasses and long, blond hair that shagged over his collar fought the Joe Corporate image. The top of his scalp was mostly bald spot.

Mini-Specs hung back as the Cossacks entered the restaurant, Garvey in a flat-footed waddle, Bobo swaggering and bopping his head in time to some private melody. The chauffeur returned to the car and began backing out, and Specs walked past the pink ladies' expectant smiles. The Town Car turned south on Robertson, drove a block, pulled to the curb, went dark.

Specs remained out in the lot for a few seconds, looking around – but at nothing in particular. Facing the Taurus, but Milo caught no sign the guy saw anything that bothered him. No, this one was just full of random nervous energy – hands flexing, neck rotating, mouth turned down, the tiny lenses of his glasses darting and catching street light, a pair of reflective eggs.

Guy made him think of a crooked accountant on audit day. Finally, Specs ran his finger under his collar, rotated his shoulders, and made his way to the pleasures of leonine hemoglobin.

★ ★ ★

No additional diners materialized during the thirty-seven minutes Milo sat there. When one of the untipped valets looked at her watch, stepped out to the sidewalk, and lit up a cigarette, he got out of the Taurus and loped across the street.

The girl was a gorgeous little red-haired thing with blue-blue eyes so vivid the color made its way through the night. Maybe twenty. She noticed Milo approaching, kept smoking. The cigarette was wrapped in black paper and had a gold tip. Shermans? Did they still make those?

She looked up when he was three feet away and smiled through the cloud of nicotine that swirled in the warm night air.

Smiling because Milo had his latest bribe visible. Two twenties folded between his index and tall fingers, backed by a freelance journalist cover story. Forty bucks was double what he'd paid the Pakistani POB clerk but the valet – her tag said Val – was a helluva lot cuter than the clerk. And as it turned out, a lot easier to deal with.

Ten minutes later he was back in the Taurus, cruising past the Town Car. Mr Chauffeur was snoozing with his mouth open. A shaved-head Latino guy. The redhead had supplied Mini-Specs's ID.

'Oh, that's Brad. He works with Mr Cossack and his brother.'

'Mr Cossack?'

'Mr Garvey Cossack. And his brother.' Blue-eyed glance back at the restaurant. 'He co-owns this place, along with . . .' A string of celebrity names followed. Milo pretended to be impressed.

'Must be a jumping place.'

'It was when it opened.'

'No more, huh?'

'You know,' she said, rolling her eyes.

'How's the food?'

The parking cutie smiled and smoked and shook her head. 'How would I know? It's like a hundred bucks a plate. Maybe when I get my first big part.'

Her laugh was derisive. She added: 'Maybe when pigs fly.' So young, so cynical.

'Hollywood,' said Milo.

'Yeah.' Val looked back again. All the other girls were loafing, and a few were smoking. Probably keeping their weight down, thought Milo. Any of them could've modeled.

Val lowered her voice to a whisper: 'Tell the truth, I hear the food sucks.'

'The name can't help. Lion's Blood.'

'Ick. Isn't that gross?'

'What kind of cuisine is it?'

'Ethiopian, I think. Or something African. Maybe also Latino, I dunno – Cuban, maybe? Sometimes they've got a band and from out here it sounds kind of Cuban.' Her hips pistoned, and she snapped her fingers. 'I hear it's on its way out.'

'Cuban music?'

'No, silly. This place.'

'Time for a new job?' said Milo.

'No prob, there's always bar mitzvahs.' Stubbing out her cigarette, she said, 'You don't happen to ever work for *Variety*, do you? Or the *Hollywood Reporter*?'

'Mostly I do wire service stuff.'

'Someone's interested in the restaurant?'

Milo shrugged. 'I drive around. You've got to dig if you wanna find oil.'

She looked at the Taurus and her next smile was ripe

with sympathy. *Another L.A. loser.* 'Well, if you ever do *Variety*, remember this name: Chataqua Dale.'

Milo repeated it. 'Nice. But so is Val.'

A cloud of doubt washed over the blue eyes. 'You really think so? 'Cause I was wondering if Chataqua was maybe, you know, over the top.'

'No,' said Milo. 'It's great.'

'Thanks.' She touched his arm, let the cigarette drop to the pavement, ground out the butt, got a dreamy look in her eyes. Audition fever. 'Well, gotta go.'

'Thanks for your time,' said Milo, reaching into his pocket and slipping her another twenty.

'You are *soooo* nice,' she said.

'Not usually.'

'Oh, I bet you are – let me ask you, you meet people, right? Know any decent agents? 'Cause mine is an asshole.'

'Only agents of destruction,' he said.

Puzzlement lent the beautiful young face temporary complexity. Then her actor's instincts cut in: Still not comprehending, but recognizing a cue, she smiled and touched his arm again. 'Right. See you around.'

'Bye,' said Milo. 'By the way, what does Brad do?'

'Walks around with them,' she said.

'A walking-around guy.'

'You got it – they all need them.'

'Hollywood types?'

'Rich types with gross bodies.'

'Know Brad's last name?'

'Larner. Brad Larner. He's kind of a jerk.'

'How so?'

'He's just a jerk,' said Val. 'Not friendly, never smiles, never tips. A jerk.'

He drove the two blocks to Santa Monica Boulevard, made a right turn, and circled back to Melrose, this time approaching the corner from the east and parking just up from the shuttered Chinese place. The rest of the boulevard was taken up by art galleries, all closed, and the street was dark and quiet. He got out, stepped over the Chinese place's heavy chain, and walked across a lot starting to sprout weeds through the cracks and dotted with mounds of dry dog shit. Finding himself a nice little vantage point behind one of the dead restaurant's gateposts, he waited, taking in the Chinese place's grimness up close – black paint flaking, bamboo shredding.

Another dream rent asunder; he liked that.

Nowhere to sit, so he continued to stand there, well concealed, watching nothing happen at Sangre de Leon for a long time. His knees and back began to hurt, and stretching and squatting seemed to make matters worse. Last Christmas, Rick had bought a treadmill for the spare bedroom, used it religiously every morning at five. Last month, he'd suggested that Milo give regular exercise a try. Milo hadn't argued, but neither had he complied. He was no good in the morning, usually pretended to be asleep when Rick left for the ER.

He checked his Timex. The Cossacks and Brad 'the jerk' Larner had been inside for over an hour, and no other patrons had materialized.

Larner was no doubt the Achievement House director's son. The harasser's son. Yet another link between the families. Daddy putting up Crazy Sister Caroline at Achievement House, buying jobs for himself *and* Junior.

Connections and money. So what else was new? Presidents were selected the same damn way. If any of this provided a hook to Janie Ingalls, he couldn't see it. But he knew – on a gut level – that it *did* matter. That Pierce Schwinn's forced retirement and his own transfer to West L.A. had resulted from more than Schwinn's dalliances with street whores.

Twenty-year-old fix, John G. Broussard doing the dirty work.

Schwinn had sat on whatever he'd known for two decades, pasted photos in an album, finally decided to break silence.

Why now?

Maybe because Broussard had reached the top and Schwinn wanted his revenge to be a gourmet dish.

Using Milo to do the dirty work . . .

Then he falls off a docile horse . . .

Headlights from the north end of Robertson slapped him out of his rumination. Two sets of lights, a pair of vehicles approaching the Melrose intersection. The traffic signal turned amber. The first car passed through legally and the second one ran the red.

Both pulled up in front of Sangre de Leon.

Vehicle Number One was a discreet, black, Mercedes coupe – surprise, surprise! – whose license plate he copied down quickly. Out stepped the driver, another business-suit, moving so quickly the pink ladies had no time to get his door. He slipped a bill to the nearest valet, anyway, let Milo have a nice, clean look at him.

Older guy. Late sixties to midseventies, balding, with a sparse gray comb-over, wearing a boxy beige suit, a white shirt, and a dark tie. Medium height, medium build, clean-shaven, the skin falling away from the bone at jowls and neck. No expression on his face. Milo wondered if this was Larner, Senior. Or just a guy out for dinner.

If so, it wouldn't be a solo dinner, because the

occupants of the second car nearly tripped over themselves to get to his side.

Vehicle Two was also black, but no feat of German engineering. Big, fat Crown Victoria sedan, anachronistically oversize. The only places Milo'd seen those things, recently, were government offices, but this one didn't have state-issue e plates.

But neither did lots of unmarkeds, and for a second he thought, *Department brass?* and experienced a rush of expectations met too easily: documenting cop honchos with the Cossacks, why the hell hadn't he remembered to bring a damn *camera*?

But the moment the first guy out of the Crown Victoria turned and showed his face, it was a whole different story.

Long, dark, lizard face under a black pompadour.

City Councilman Eduardo 'Ed the Germ' Bacilla, the official representative of a district that encompassed a chunk of downtown. He of the serious bad habits and poor work habits – Bacilla attended maybe one out of every five council meetings and a couple of years ago he'd been nabbed in Boyle Heights trying to buy powdered coke from an undercover narc. Quick and frantic negotiations with the DA's Office had led to the draconian sentence of public apology and public service: two months on graffiti-removal detail, Bacilla working alongside some of the very gang-bangers he'd favored with city-funded scam rehab programs. Lack of a felony conviction meant the councilman could keep his job, and a recall effort by a leftist homeboy reformer sputtered.

And now here was ol' Germ, kissing up to Tan Suit.

So was Crown Victoria Rider Two, and guess what: another civil stalwart.

This guy had looped his arm around Tan Suit's shoulder and was laughing about something. No expression on Suit's CEO face.

Mr Jocular was older, around Tan Suit's age, with white temples and a bushy, white mustache that concealed his upper lip. Tall and narrow-shouldered, with an onion-bulb body that a well-cut suit couldn't enhance, and the ice-eyed cunning of a cornered peccary.

City Councilman James 'Diamond Jim' Horne. He of the suspected kickbacks and briberies and ex-wives hush-moneyed to silence back in the good old days when domestic violence was still known as wife-beating.

Milo knew through the LAPD grapevine that Horne was a longtime, serious spouse-basher with a penchant for pulverizing without leaving marks. Like Germ Bacilla, Diamond Jim had always managed to squeak through without arrest or conviction. For over thirty years, he'd served a district that bordered Bacilla's, a north-central strip filled with ticky-tack houses and below-code apartments. Once solidly working-class white, Horne's constituency had turned 70 percent poor Hispanic, and the councilman had watched his vote pluralities tumble. From 90 percent to 70. A series of opponents with surnames ending in 'ez' had failed to topple Horne. The corrupt old bastard got the potholes fixed, and plenty else.

Germ and Diamond Jim, walking arm in arm with Tan Suit, heading for the steel door of Sangre de Leon.

Milo returned to the Taurus and, using the ID of a Pacific Division Vice detective he despised, pulled up the Mercedes coupe's plates.

He half expected another corporate shield, but the

numbers came back matching a four-year-old Mercedes owned by a real-life person.

W.E. Obey

The three hundred block of Muirfield Road in Hancock Park.

Walter Obey. He of the billion-dollar fortune.

Nominally, Walt Obey was in the same business as the Cossacks – concrete and rebar and lumber and drywall. But Obey occupied a whole different galaxy from the Cossacks. Fifty years ago, Obey Construction began nailing up homes for returning GIs. The company was probably responsible for 10 percent of the tracts that snaked parallel to the freeways and sprawled across the smog-choked basin that the Chumash Indians had once called the Valley of Smoke.

Walt Obey and his wife, Barbara, were on the board of every museum, hospital, and civic organization that meant anything in the lip-gnawing, over-the-shoulder uncertainty known as L.A. Society.

Walt Obey was also a model of rectitude – Mr Upright in a business that claimed few saints.

The guy had to be at least eighty, but he looked a good deal younger. Good genes? Clean living?

Now here he was, supping with Germ and Diamond Jim.

The Cossacks and Brad Larner had been inside for one hour. No shock, it was their restaurant. Still the question hung: table for three, or six?

He obtained Sangre de Leon's number from Information and called the restaurant. Five rings later a bored, Central European-accented male voice said, 'Yes?'

'This is Mr Walter Obey's office. I've got a message for Mr Obey. He's dining with the Cossacks, I believe they're in a private room—'

'Yes, they are. I'll get the phone to him.' Eagerness to please had wiped out the boredom.

Milo hung up.

He drove home trying to piece it all together. The Cossacks and Walt Obey and two city councilmen noshing on designer grub. Brad Larner along as a gofer, or his dad's surrogate? Alex had pulled up something about the Cossacks trying to bring a football team to L.A., maybe reactivating the Coliseum. The scheme had died, as had nearly everything else the Cossacks had tried – movies, tearing down landmarks. On the face of it the brothers were losers. Yet they had enough clout to bring Walt Obey from Hancock Park to West Hollywood.

The Cossacks in their chauffeured Town Car with personalized plates screamed new money. But Obey, the real money man, drove himself in an anonymous, four-year-old sedan. The billionaire was so unobtrusive he could pass for your average, middling CPA.

What got vulgarians and bluenoses together? Something big. The Coliseum sat in Germ Bacilla's district, and next door was Diamond Jim Horne's domain. Was this one of those complicated deals that always managed to elude zoning laws and whatever else stood in its way? Taxpayers footing the bill for rich guys' indulgences? Something that might be jeopardized by the rehash of a twenty-year-old murder and the exposure of the Cossacks' role in covering up for their crazy sister and junkie-murderer Willie Burns?

Why *had* Georgie Nemerov gotten so antsy?

The only possible thread between Nemerov and the rest of it was the department.

And now the department was verifying his vacation time and maybe sending that Bartlett asshole to spook him.

Health facilitator. Meaning what? Be careful not to get *un*healthy?

Suddenly, he wanted very much to make someone else deathly ill.

When he pulled into his driveway, the white Porsche was parked up near the garage, little red alarm light blinking on the dash, extra-strength lock bar fixed to the steering column. Rick loved the car, was as careful with it as he was with everything else.

He found Rick at the kitchen table, still wearing his scrubs and eating warmed-up Chinese food from last night. A glass of red wine was at his elbow. He saw Milo and smiled and gave a weak wave and the two of them shared a brief hug, and Rick said, 'Working late?'

'The usual. How'd your day go?'

'The usual.'

'Heroics?'

'Hardly.' Rick pointed to the empty chair across the table. The final dark hairs in his dense cap of curls had faded to gray last summer, and his mustache was a silver toothbrush. Despite being a doctor and knowing better, he liked to tan out in the backyard and his skin had held on to summer color. He looked tired. Milo sat down opposite him and began picking at orange chicken.

'There's more in the refrigerator,' said Rick. 'The egg rolls, the rest of it.'

'No, I'll just take yours.'

Rick smiled. Weary.

'Bad stuff on shift?' said Milo.

'Not particularly. Couple of heart attacks, couple of false alarms, kid with a broken leg from falling off a Razor scooter, colon cancer patient with a serious gut bleed that kept us busy for a long time, woman with a darning needle in her eye, two auto accidents, one accidental shooting – we lost that one.'

'The usual trivia.'

'Exactly.' Rick pushed his food away. 'There was one thing. The shooting was the last case I pulled. I couldn't do anything for the poor guy, he came in flat, never beeped. Looks like he was cleaning his nine-millimeter, stared into the barrel, maybe making sure it was clear, and boom. The cops who came in with the body said they found gun oil and rags and one of those barrel-reaming tools on the table next to him. Bullet entered here.' Rick touched the center of his mustache, under his nose.

'An accident?' said Milo. 'Not suicide? Or anything else?'

'The cops who came in kept calling it an accident, maybe they knew something technical. It'll go to the coroner.'

'Sheriff's cops?' said Milo.

'No, you guys. It happened near Venice and Highland. But that's not what I want to tell you. The body had just gone to the morgue, and I came back to chart and the cops who brought the guy in were in the cubicle next door and I heard them talking. Going on about their pensions, sick leave, department benefits. Then one said something about a detective in West L.A. division who'd tested HIV-positive and put in for retirement. The other cop said, "Guess what goes 'round comes round." Then they both laughed. Not a joyful laugh. A mean laugh.'

Rick picked up a chopstick and seesawed it between two fingers. Looked into Milo's eyes. Touched Milo's hand.

Milo said, 'I haven't heard anything about that.'

'Didn't assume you had, or you'd have told me.'

Milo withdrew his hand, stood, and got himself a beer.

Rick stayed at the table, continued to play with the chopstick. Tilting it deftly, precisely. A surgeon's grace.

Milo said, 'It's bullshit. I'da heard.'

'I just thought it was something you'd want to know.'

'Highland and Venice. What the hell would Wilshire Division know about West L.A.? What the hell would *blues* know about *Ds?*'

'Probably nothing . . . Big guy, is there something I should know? Some tight spot you've gotten yourself into?'

'Why? What does this have to do with me?' Milo didn't like the defensiveness in his own voice. Thinking: the goddamn department rumor mill. Then thinking: *Health Facilitator. You never know . . .*

Rick said, 'Okay,' and started to get up.

Milo said, 'Wait,' and came around and stood behind Rick and put his hands on Rick's shoulders. And told him the rest of it.

twenty-two

I got on the computer, typed in 'Paris Bartlett' as a keyphrase on several search engines, and came up with nothing.

Next, I tried 'Playa del Sol' and its English translation: *Sun Beach*, and connected to hundreds of resort links all over the world. Costa del Sol. Costa del Amor. Playa Negra. Playa Blanca. Playa Azul. Sun City. Sunrise Beach. Excursion packages, time shares, white sand, blue water, adults only, bring the kids. Also, a guy who'd devoted an obsessive site to the old song *'Cuando Caliente El Sol.'* The joys of the information age . . .

I stuck with it for hours, felt my eyes crossing and broke for a midnight sandwich, a beer, and a shower before returning to the screen. By 2 A.M., I was fighting sleep and nearly missed the article in a three-year-old issue of the *Resort Journal* elicited by yet another try at Playa del Sol. This time, I'd logged on to a pay service – a business-oriented data bank that I hadn't used since last fall, when I'd considered selling a lot of municipal bonds. I clicked my assent to pony up by credit card and continued.

What I got was a rear-of-the-magazine piece entitled 'Seeking the Good Life on Distant Shores: Americans

263

Looking for Foreign Bargains Often Find Themselves on the Losing End.' The article recounted several real estate deals gone sour, among them a construction project down in Baja named Playa del Sol: high-end condos peddled to American retirees lured by American-style luxury living at Mexican prices. Two hundred units out of a planned four hundred fifty had been built and purchased. The first wave of retirees hadn't yet moved in when the Mexican government invoked a fine-print provision of an obscure regulation, confiscated the land, and sold it to a Saudi Arabian consortium who turned the condos into a hotel. The Playa del Sol Company, Ltd, incorporated in the Cayman Islands, dissolved itself and its American subsidiary, Playa Enterprises, declared Chapter 11. The retirees lost their money.

No comment from the president of Playa Enterprises, Michael Larner.

Recalling the obscure business journal references that had come up on my first search for Larner – magazines not in the Research Library's holdings – I looked for anything else I could find on the former Achievement House director and came across several other deals he'd put together during the past five years.

Larner's specialty was real estate syndication – getting moneyed people together to buy out incomplete building projects that had run into trouble. High-rise apartments in Atlanta, defunct country clubs in Colorado and New Mexico, a ski lodge in Vermont, a golf course in Arizona. Once the deal was inked, Larner took his cut and walked away.

All the subsequent articles had the rah-rah tone of paid ads. None mentioned the Mexican debacle, Playa Enterprises, or the Playa del Sol Company, Ltd. Larner's corporate face was now the ML Group.

No mention of the Cossack brothers, either. Or any of Larner's fellow venture capitalists, though showbiz and Wall Street affiliations were implied. The only other ML staffer named was Larner's son, Bradley, executive vice-president.

Using 'ML Group' as a keyphrase, I retraced all the search machines and obtained the exact same articles, plus one more: a two-year-old stroke job in a glossy rag titled *Southwest Leisure Builder*.

Centered amid the text was a color photo: Larners, father and son, posing on a bright day in Phoenix, wearing matching royal blue golf shirts, white canvas slacks, white smiles.

Michael Larner looked around sixty-five. Square-faced and florid, he wore wide steel-framed aviator's glasses turned to mirrors by the Arizona sun. His smile was self-satisfied and heralded by overly large capped teeth. He had a drinker's nose, a big, hard-looking belly, and meticulously styled white hair. A casting agent would've seen Venal Executive.

Bradley Larner was thinner and smaller and paler – barely a nuance of his father. Late thirties or early forties, he was also bespectacled, but his choice of eyewear ran to gold-framed, narrow, oval lenses so tiny they barely covered his irises. His hair was that lank, waxy blond destined to whiten, and it trailed past his shoulders. Less enthusiasm in his expression. Barely a smile at all, though to read the article, the Larners were riding the crest of the real estate wave.

Bradley Larner looked like a kid forced to sit for yet another obnoxious family snapshot.

An accompanying picture on the following page

showed Michael Larner in an ice-cream suit, blue shirt, and pink tie posed next to a white-on-white Rolls-Royce Silver Spirit. To his father's right, Brad Larner perched atop a gold Harley-Davidson, wearing black leather.

The caption read: **Different generations, but the same flair for the Ultimate Ride.**

The Playa del Sol link meant 'Paris Bartlett' was likely an envoy to Milo from the Larners.

Warning him off the trail of Caroline Cossack.

Because the Larners and the Cossacks went way back.

The families had something else in common: big deals that often went bad. But all of them managed to stay on top, maintaining the good life.

The Ultimate Ride.

In the Cossacks' case, inherited wealth might've provided a nice safety blanket. Michael Larner, on the other hand, had bounced from job to job and industry to industry, leaving scandal or bankruptcy in his wake but always managing to position himself higher.

That smile, teeth as white and gleaming as his Rolls-Royce. A man willing to do whatever it took? Or friends in the right places? Or both.

Back when Larner had bent the rules and admitted Caroline Cossack to Achievement House, her brothers had been barely out of adolescence but already in the real estate business. Larner might have dealt initially with Garvey Cossack, Senior, but the relationship endured well after Senior's demise and found Larner working for men twenty-five years his junior. Then I thought of something: *Bradley* Larner was about the same age as the Cossack brothers. Was there some link there? Something that went beyond business?

When searching for school data on Caroline, Milo hadn't gotten very far with the local high schools. Because everyone was litigation-wary and watched episodic TV and believed cops without warrants were impotent.

Maybe also because Caroline's emotional problems meant she hadn't enjoyed much of a school history. But perhaps tracking her brothers would be easier.

The next morning, I was back at the library thumbing through *Who's Who*. Neither Bob Cossack nor Bradley Larner was listed, but Garvey Cossack had merited a biography: a single paragraph of puffery, mostly what I'd already learned from the Web.

Tucked among all the corporate braggadocio was Garvey's educational history. He'd completed two years of college at Cal State Northridge but hadn't graduated. Maybe that's why he'd bothered to list his high school. And the fact that he'd been student body treasurer during his senior year.

University High.

I checked with the reference desk and found that the library maintained three decades of local yearbooks in the reference section. Uni was as local as it got.

Finding the right volume wasn't hard. I estimated Garvey's age and nailed it on the second try.

His graduation picture revealed a full-faced, acne-plagued eighteen-year-old with long, wavy hair, wearing a light-colored turtleneck. Sandwiched between the top of the sweater's collar and the boy's meaty chin was a puka-shell necklace. His grin was mischievous.

Listed under his picture were memberships in the Business Club, the 'managerial staff' of the football team, and something called the King's Men. But there was no mention of his being treasurer. According to the Student Council page, the treasurer was a girl named Sarah Buckley. Thumbing through the three preceding year-books taught me that Garvey Cossack had never served in any student-government capacity.

Petty fib for a middle-aged millionaire; that made it all the more interesting.

I located Robert 'Bobo' Cossack's headshot one class back. He'd come to photo day wearing a black shirt with a high collar and a choker-length chain. Equine face, hair darker and even longer than his brother's, a more severe blemish. Bobo wore a sullen expression and his eyes were half-shut. Sleepy or stoned – or trying to look the part. His attempts to grow a beard and mustache had resulted in a halo of dark fuzz around his chin and spidery wisps above his upper lip.

No affiliations below his picture other than the King's Men.

Also in the junior class was a very skinny Bradley Larner, wearing tinted aviator glasses, a button-down shirt, and peroxide surfer-do that obscured half his face. The part that was visible was as dispirited as Bobo Cossack's.

Another King's Man.

I searched the yearbook for mention of the club, found a listing in the roster of school service organizations but no details. Finally, in a breathless account of the home-coming game, I spotted a reference to *'the revelry, high jinks (and other good stuff) perpetrated by the King's Men.'*

An accompanying snapshot showed a group of six boys at the beach, wearing bathing trunks and striped beanies and clowning around with cross-eyed grins, goofy poses, behind-the-head rabbit ears. The beer cans in their hands had been blacked out clumsily. In one case, the Miller logo was still visible. The caption: **Surf's Up! but the King's Men crave other liquid entertainment! Partying at Zuma: G. Cossack, L. Chapman, R. Cossack, V. Coury, B. Larner, N. Hansen**.

The Cossack brothers had been high school party animals, and the Bel Air bash a couple of years later was just more of the same. And the link between them and the Larners had been forged on the sands of Zuma, not in the boardroom.

That made me wonder if the idea for secreting problematic sister Caroline might have originated with the boys, not their father. *'Hey, Dad, Brad's dad works at this place for weirdos, maybe he can help out.'*

I searched the yearbooks for mention or a picture of Caroline Cossack.

Nothing.

I drove around the pretty residential streets of Westwood, thinking about Pierce Schwinn and what he'd really wanted from Milo. Had the former detective finally decided to come clean with secrets held for two decades, as I'd suggested, or had he undertaken his own freelance investigation late in life and come up with new leads?

Either way, Schwinn hadn't been as serene as his second wife believed. Or as faithful: he'd found a confidante to mail the murder book.

As I'd told Milo, Ojai was a small town and it was doubtful Schwinn could've pulled off a regular assignation there without Marge finding out. But before he'd married Marge, he'd lived in Oxnard in a fleabag motel.

Marge hadn't mentioned the name, but she had given us the site of Schwinn's minimum-wage job, and said Schwinn hadn't owned a car. Taking out the trash at Randall's Western Wear. Somewhere within walking distance.

The place was still in business, on Oxnard Boulevard.

I'd taken the scenic route because it was the quickest way and I had no stomach for the freeway: Sunset to PCH, then north on the coast highway past the L.A.–Ventura line and Deer Creek Road and the campgrounds of Sycamore Creek – fifteen miles of state land that kissed the ocean and separated the last private beach in Malibu from Oxnard. The water was sapphire blue under a chamber-of-commerce sky, and the bodies that graced the sand were brown and perfect.

At Las Posas Road, I avoided the eastern fork that swoops into glorious, green tables of farmland and up to the foothills of Camarillo and continued on Route 1.

Nature's beauty gave way, soon enough, to dinge and depression and seventy-five minutes after leaving the house I was enjoying the sights of central Oxnard.

Oxnard's a funny place. The town's beach sports a marina and luxury hotels and fishing excursions and tour boats to the Channel Islands. But the core is built around agriculture and the migrant workers whose dreadful lives put food on the nation's tables. The crime rate's high, and the air stinks of manure and pesticide. Once you get past the marina turnoff, Oxnard Boulevard is a low-rent artery lined with trailer parks, auto-parts yards, thrift shops, taco bars, taverns blaring Mexican music, and more Spanish than English on the signage.

Randall's Western Wear was a red barn in the center of the strip, stuck between Bernardo's Batteries and a windowless bar called El Guapo. Plenty of parking in back; only two pickups and an old Chrysler 300 in the lot.

Inside was the smell of leather and sawdust and sweat, ceiling-high racks of denim and flannel, Stetsons stacked like waffles, cowboy boots and belts on sale, one corner devoted to sacks of feed, a few saddles and bridles off in another. Travis Tritt's mellow baritone eased through scratchy speakers, trying to convince some woman of his good intentions.

Slow day in the ranch-duds biz. No customers, just two salesmen on duty, both white men in their thirties. One wore gray sweats, the other jeans and a black Harley-Davidson T-shirt. Both smoked behind the counter, showing no interest in my arrival.

I browsed, found a tooled cowhide belt that I liked, brought it to the counter and paid. Harley-D rang me up, offering no eye contact or conversation. As he handed back my credit card, I let my wallet open and showed him my LAPD consultant badge. It's a clip-on deal with the department's badge as a logo, not good for much and if you look closely it tells you that I'm no cop. But few people get past the insignia, and Harley was no exception.

'Police?' he said, as I closed the wallet. He wore a bad haircut like his own badge of honor, had a handlebar mustache that drooped to his chin, and a clogged-sinus voice. Stringy arms and stringy hair, a scatter of faded tattoos.

I said, 'Thought maybe you could help me with something.'

'With what?'

271

Sweats looked up. He was a few years younger than Harley, with a blond-gray crew cut, a square shelf of a chin finishing a florid face. Stocky build, quiet eyes. My guess was ex-military.

'A few questions about a guy who worked here a while back. Pierce Schwinn.'

'Him?' said Harley. 'He hasn't been here for what – coupla years?' He looked back at Sweats.

'Coupla,' Sweats agreed.

Harley looked at the belt. 'What, you bought that to get friendly or something?'

'I bought it because it's a nice belt,' I said. 'But I have no problem with being friendly. What do you remember about Schwinn?'

Harley frowned. 'When he worked here he was a bum. What's up with him now?'

'Have you seen him since he stopped working here?'

'Maybe once,' he said. 'Or maybe not. If he did come in, it was with his wife – that right?' Another consultation with Sweats.

'Probably.'

'Why?' said Harley. 'What he do?'

'Nothing. Just a routine investigation.' Even as I said it, I felt ridiculous, not to mention criminal. But if Milo could risk violations of the public order, so could I. 'So the last time Mr Schwinn worked here was a couple of years ago?'

'That's right.' Harley's smile was derisive. 'If you wanna call it work.'

'It wasn't?'

'Man,' he said, leaning on the counter, 'let me tell you: it was a gift. From our mom to him. She owns the place. He used to live down the block, at the Happy Night.

272

Mom felt sorry for him, let him clean up for spare change.'

'The Happy Night Motel?' I said.

'Right down the block.'

'So it was a sympathy thing,' I said. 'From your mother.'

'She's got a soft heart,' said Harley. 'Ain't that so, Roger?'

Sweats nodded and smoked and turned up the volume on Travis Tritt. The singer's voice was plaintive and rich; I'd have been convinced.

'Schwinn have any friends?' I said.

'Nope.'

'What about Marge – the woman who married him.'

'She comes in for feed when she runs out on her bulk order,' said Harley. 'Yeah, she married him, but that makes her his wife, not his friend.'

And when are you entering law school, F. Lee Picky?

I said, 'Marge met him here.'

'Guess so.' Harley's brows knitted. 'Haven't seen her either, for a while.'

Roger said, 'She's probably ordering off the Internet, like everyone. We gotta get with that.'

'Yeah,' said Harley, listlessly. 'So, c'mon, tell me, man, why're you asking about him? Someone off him or something?'

'No,' I said. 'He's dead, all right. Fell off a horse a few months ago.'

'That so. Well, she never mentioned it. Marge didn't.'

'When's the last time you saw her?'

Harley looked back at Roger. 'When's the last time I saw her?'

Roger shrugged. 'Maybe four, five months ago.'

'Mostly everyone orders bulk from suppliers,' said Harley. 'And the Internet. We do gotta get hooked up.'

'So Marge has been in since Schwinn died, but she never mentioned his death.'

'Probably – I couldn't swear to it, man. Listen, don't pin me down on any a this.'

Roger gave another sweat-suited shrug. 'Marge don't talk much, period.'

Travis Tritt bowed out and Pam Tillis weighed in about 'The Queen of Denial.'

Harley said, 'Is this about drugs, or something?'

'Why do you say that?'

Harley fidgeted. His brother said, 'What Vance means is that the Happy Night – everyone knows about it. People go in and out. You wanna do us a favor? Get it moved outta here. This block used to be a nice place.'

I kept my car in the Randall's lot and walked the block to the motel. The place was a twelve-unit gray stucco C built around a central courtyard and open to the street. The yard was tiled with crumbling bricks, didn't look as if it had been designed for parking, but four dirty compact cars and an equally grubby truck with a camper shell occupied the space. The office was off to the right – a cubicle that smelled of gym sweat manned by a young skin-headed Hispanic man wearing an aqua blue cowboy shirt with blood-red piping. Spangling on the yokes, too, but oily splotches in the armpits and ketchup-colored freckles across the front mitigated the garment's charm. Resting on the pleat was a heavy iron crucifix attached to a stainless-steel chain.

My entry rang a bell over the door and the clerk shot a look at me then glanced under the counter. Reflexively.

Probably checking out the requisite pistol. Or just wanting to let me know he was armed. A sign on the wall behind him said CASH ONLY. Same message in Spanish, right below. He didn't move but his eyes jumped around and the left lid twitched. He couldn't be more than twenty-two or -three, could probably take the adrenaline surges and blood-pressure spikes for a few more years.

I showed him the badge, and he shook his head. Atop the counter was a *novella* – black-and-white photos of characters speaking in captions, storyboard laid out like a comic book. Upside down I caught a few words: '*sexualismo*', '*con pasión.*'

He said, 'Don' know nothin'.' Heavy accent.

'I haven't asked anything.'

'Don' know nothin'.'

'Good for you,' I said. 'Ignorance is bliss.'

His stare was dull.

'Pierce Schwinn,' I said. 'He used to live here.'

No answer.

I repeated the name.

'Don' know nothin'.'

'An old man, Anglo, white hair, white beard?'

Nothing.

'He used to work at Randall's.'

Uncomprehending look.

'Randall's Western Wear – down the block?'

'Don't know nothin'.'

'What's your name?'

'Don' kno—' Lights on in the brown eyes. 'Gustavo.'

'Gustavo what?'

'Gustavo Martinez Reyes.'

'You speak any English, Mr Martinez Reyes?'

Headshake.

'Anyone work here who does?'

'Don' know noth—'

So much for ace detective work. But I'd come this far, why not give Ojai another try – check out a place I knew Marge Schwinn had frequented. The shop where she'd bought the blue albums – *O'Neill & Chapin . . . over by the Celestial Café . . . from England . . . discontinued . . . I bought the last three.*

Maybe she hadn't. Or maybe Schwinn had also shopped for himself.

I continued to the next freeway on-ramp and was back on Highway 33 within minutes. The air was cold and clean, every color on full volume, and I could smell ripening fruit in the neighboring groves.

O'Neill & Chapin sat in one of those cozy commercial groupings that had sprouted along the road, this one a well-shaded segment just past the center of Ojai but several miles before the turnoff to Marge Schwinn's ranch. The shop was a minuscule, shingle-roofed, clapboard cottage dominated by live oaks. The boards were painted forest green, and the store was fronted by five feet of cobblestones running from the earthen curb to Dutch doors painted creamy mint. Gold leaf lettering across the front window proclaimed:

O'Neill & Chapin,
Purveyors of Fine Paper and Pigments.
Est. 1986

Behind the windows were dark oak shutters. A sign leaning against the slats said:

On a buying trip in Europe. Back soon

I checked out the neighboring business. To the right was the candlery, also shuttered. Then Marta, Spiritual Counselor, and the Humanos Theosophic Institute. To the left was a one-story office building faced in river rock: chiropractor's office, a notary public-cum-insurance broker, a travel agent specializing in 'nature-friendly excursions.' Next to that, in a sunnier spot, sat an adobe cube with a wooden sign over the door.

Celestial Café

Gold stars danced around the edges of the signs. Lights flickered behind blue gingham curtains. It was nearly 3 P.M. and I'd fed neither my brain nor my gut. Times like this, I supposed, organic muffins and herbal tea wouldn't be half-bad.

But according to the blackboard mounted above the open kitchen, the café specialized in country French food – crêpes, quiche, soufflés, chocolate desserts. Real coffee, Lord almighty.

Some kind of New Age soundtrack – tinkly bells, flute, and harp – eased out of speakers set into the low, wood-beam ceiling. More blue gingham covered half a dozen tables. A woman with elaborately braided gray hair wearing a buckskin jacket over a crinkly, pink dress sat enjoying what looked to be ratatouille. No server was in sight, just a pasty-faced, heavyset, white-aproned woman wearing a blue bandana over her hair cutting vegetables in the kitchen. At her elbow was a six-burner Wolfe range, with one flame aglow under a cast-iron crêpe pan. Fresh batter had just been poured into the pan, and the

277

cook stopped cutting long enough to grab a towel and take hold of the handle. Tilting deftly, she created a perfect disc that she slid onto a plate, then topped with creamed spinach. A dash of nutmeg, and the crêpe was rolled and placed on the counter. Then back to the vegetables.

The gray-haired woman got up and took the crêpe. 'Beautiful, Aimee.'

The cook nodded. She looked to be forty or so, had a squashed face and downturned eyes. The hairs that had peeked out from under the bandana were light brown and silver.

I smiled at her. Her face registered no expression, and she continued chopping. I read the blackboard. 'How about a mixed-cheese crêpe and coffee?'

She turned around, left the kitchen through a side door. I stood there, listening to bells and flute and harp.

Behind me, the gray-braided woman said, 'Don't worry, she'll be back.'

'I was wondering if it was something I said.'

She laughed. 'No, she's just shy. Heck of a cook, though.'

Aimee returned with a small wheel of white cheese. 'You can sit,' she said, in a very soft voice. 'I'll bring it to you.'

'Thanks much.' I tried another smile, and her mouth quivered upward for less than a second, and she began wiping the crêpe pan.

The gray-haired woman finished her meal just as Aimee brought me my plate, a mug of coffee, utensils wrapped in a heavy yellow linen napkin. She returned to her vegetables and the gray-braided woman said, 'Here you are, dear,' and paid her cash. No change exchanged.

No credit card signs anywhere in the café.

I unfolded the napkin, looked at my plate. Two crêpes.

With her back to me, Aimee said, 'You only have to pay for one. I had lots of cheese.'

'Thank you,' I said. 'They look delicious.'

Chop chop chop.

I cut into the first crêpe and took a bite and flavor burst on my tongue. The coffee was the best I'd had in years, and I said so.

Chop chop chop.

I was working on the second crêpe when the front door opened, and a man walked in and headed for the counter.

Short, chubby, white-haired, he wore a purplish red polyester jumpsuit, zipped in front, with big floppy lapels. Crimson clogs and white-socks-clad stubby feet. His fingers were attenuated, too, the thumbs little more than arced nubs. His ruddy face was impish but peaceful – an elf in repose. A leather-thonged bolo tie was held in place by a big, shapeless purple rock. Flashing on his left hand was a huge gold pinkie ring set with a violet cabochon.

He looked to be in his midsixties, but I knew he was seventy-seven because I knew him. I also understood why he wore a single color: it was the only hue he could perceive in an otherwise black-and-white world. A rare form of color blindness was one of a host of physical anomalies he'd been born with. Some, like the shortened digits, were visible. Others, he'd assured me, were not.

Dr Wilbert Harrison, psychiatrist, anthropologist, philosopher, eternal student. A sweet and decent man, and even a murderous psychopath bent on revenge had recognized that, sparing Harrison as he conducted a rampage against the doctors he believed had tormented him.

I hadn't been spared, and I'd met Bert Harrison years

ago, trying to figure all of that out. Since then we talked occasionally – infrequently.

'Bert,' I said.

He turned, smiled. 'Alex!' Holding up a finger, he greeted Aimee. Without making eye contact, she poured him tea and selected an almond-crusted pastry from the glass case beneath the blackboard.

A regular.

He said, 'Thank you, darling,' sat down at my table, placed his cup and plate in front of him, and grasped my hand with both of his.

'Alex. So good to see you.'

'Good to see you too, Bert.'

'What have you been up to?'

'The usual. And you?'

Soft gray eyes twinkled. 'I've embarked on a new hobby. Ethnic instruments, the more esoteric the better. I've discovered eBay – how wonderful, the global economy in its finest form. I find bargains, wait like a child on Christmas Eve for the packages to arrive, then try to figure out how to play them. This week my project is a one-stringed curiosity from Cambodia. I haven't learned its proper name, yet. The seller billed it as a "Southeast Asian thingamajig." Sounds dreadful, so far – like a cat with indigestion, but I have no neighbors, per se.'

Harrison's home was a purple cottage, high on a hill above Ojai, bordered by olive groves and empty fields and nearly hidden by snarls of agave cactus. Bert's old Chevy station wagon sat in a dirt driveway, always freshly waxed. Each time I'd visited, the house's front door had been unlocked.

'Sounds like fun,' I said.

'It's great fun.' He bit into the pastry, let loose a flow of custard, licked his lips, wiped his chin. 'Delicious. What have *you* been doing for fun, Alex?'

Figuring out how to answer that must have done something to my face, because Harrison placed his hand atop mine and looked like a concerned parent.

'That bad, son?'

'Is it that obvious?'

'Oh, yes, Alex. Oh, yes indeed.'

I told him about Robin. He thought a while, and said, 'Sounds like small things have been amplified.'

'Not so small, Bert. She's really had it with my risk-taking behavior.'

'I was referring to *your* feelings. Your anxiety about Robin.'

'I know I'm being paranoid, but I keep flashing back to the last time she left.'

'She made a mistake,' he said. 'But she bore the brunt of it, and you might think about disconnecting yourself from her pain.'

'Her pain,' I said. 'Think it still bothers her after all these years?'

'If she allows herself to focus on it, my guess is she feels a good deal worse about it than you do.'

He'd met Robin twice, and yet I didn't feel him presumptuous. A few months after our house had burned down, we'd driven up to Santa Barbara for a change of scenery and had run into Bert at an antiquarian book-store on State Street. He'd been browsing through eighteenth-century scientific treatises. In Latin. ('My current hobby, kids.') Dust had speckled the front of his jumpsuit.

'She loves you deeply,' he said. 'At least, she did when I

saw her, and I have my doubts about that depth of feeling just vanishing.' He ate more pastry, picked almond slivers from his plate, and slipped them between his lips. 'The body language, the mind language, was all there. I remember thinking, "This is the girl for Alex." '

'I used to think so.'

'Cherish what you've got. My second wife was like that, accepted me with all my irregularities.'

'You think Robin accepts me, no matter what.'

'If she didn't, she'd have left long ago.'

'But putting her through more of my risk-taking would be cruel.'

He squeezed my hand. 'Life is like a bus stop, Alex. We map out our route but linger briefly between adventures. Only you can chart your itinerary – and hope God agrees with it. So what brings you to Ojai?'

'Enjoying the scenery.'

'Then come up to my house, let me show you my acquisitions.'

We finished our food and he insisted on paying. The old station wagon was parked out front, and I followed him into town and onto Signal Street, where we climbed past a drainage ditch paved with fieldstones and spanned by footbridges, up to the top of the road.

The front door to the purple house was open and shielded by a well-oxidized screen. Bert climbed the steps with agility and ushered me into the living room. The space was exactly as I remembered: small, dark, plank-floored, crammed with old furniture, shawls, throw pillows, an upright piano, the bay window lined with dusty bottles. But now there was no room to sit: a gigantic, hammered-bronze gong nudged the piano. Every couch and chair bore drums and bells and lyres and zithers and

Pan pipes and harps and objects I couldn't identify. The floor space behind the piano bench was taken up by a six-foot dragon-shaped contraption topped with corrugated wood. Harrison ran a stick along the ridges and set off a percussive but melodic scale.

'Bali,' he said. 'I've learned "Old MacDonald" on it.' Sigh. 'One day, Mozart.'

He cleared instruments from a sagging sofa, and said, 'Be comfortable.'

As I sat, something metallic behind the couch caught my eye. A folded-up wheelchair.

Bert said, 'I'm storing it for a friend,' and settled his small frame on a hard-backed chair. The fingers of his right hand brushed against a pedal harp, but not hard enough to make a sound. 'Despite your stress you look well.'

'As do you.'

'Knock wood.' He rapped the rim of the harp, and this time a note rang out. 'G sharp . . . so you're just passing through? Next time, call and we can have lunch. Unless, of course, you need solitude.'

'No, I'd love to get together.'

'Of course, we all need solitude,' he said. 'The key is finding the right balance.'

'You live alone, Bert.'

'I have friends.'

'So do I.'

'Milo.'

'Milo and others.'

'Well, that's good – Alex, is there anything I can do for you?'

'No,' I said. 'Like what?'

'Anything, Alex.'

'If you could solve cold cases, that would be helpful.'

'Cold cases,' he said. 'A murder.'

I nodded.

'The body may be cold,' he said, 'but I wonder if the memory ever really cools. Care to tell me about it?'

I didn't. Yes, I did.

twenty-three

I described the Ingalls murder without mentioning names or places or the murder book. But there was no sense withholding Milo's name. Bert Harrison had met Milo, had given a statement to Milo on the Bad Love case.

As I talked, he rarely allowed his gaze to wander from my face.

When I finished, he said, 'This girl – the one who poisoned the dog – sounds monstrous.'

'At the very least, severely disturbed.'

'First a dog, then a person . . . that's the typical pattern . . . though you have only the neighbor's accusation to go on.'

'The behavioral warning in the girl's chart is consistent with the neighbor's report. She didn't belong in that school, Bert. String-pulling by her family probably got her in – safe hiding during the investigation of the murder.'

He folded his hands in his lap. 'And no word on the other possible victim . . . I assume Milo's been looking for her.'

'No sign of her, yet,' I said. 'Most likely she's dead. The disturbed girl seems to have vanished, completely.

No paper trail at all. That reeks of more string-pulling.'

'A supportive family,' he said.

'In terms of aiding and abetting.'

'Hmm . . . Alex, if the case was taken out of Milo's hands twenty years ago, how did he manage to be reassigned?'

'He was unofficially reassigned,' I said. 'By someone who knew we worked together and was sure I'd give him the message.'

'What message, Alex?'

I thought about how much to say. Told him about the murder book and its probable link to Pierce Schwinn.

'Pierce?' he said. 'So that's why you're here.'

'You knew him?'

'I did. I know his wife, Marge, as well. Sweet woman.'

'Milo and I were up at her ranch a few days ago,' I said. 'It's a good bet Schwinn assembled that book, but the only photos of his she claims to know about are nature shots.'

'Claims?' said Harrison. 'You doubt her?'

'She seemed truthful.'

'I'd believe her, Alex.'

'Why's that?'

'Because she's an honest woman.'

'And Schwinn?'

'I have nothing bad to say about him either.'

'How well did you know him, Bert?'

'We ran into each other from time to time. In town – shopping, at the Little Theater.'

'Are you aware of any confidante he might've had other than Marge? Someone he'd have trusted to send the book? Because it was mailed to me seven months after he died.'

'You're certain it emanated from Pierce?'

'The photos are LAPD crime-scene shots, probably purloined from old files. Schwinn was a shutterbug, used to bring his own camera to crime scenes in order to snap his own pictures. On top of that, Marge Schwinn said she purchased three identical blue leather albums for Pierce, over at O'Neill & Chapin. She showed us two but the third was missing and she had no idea where it was. That's what drew me back here. I wanted to speak to the shop's owners to see if they'd sold any others.'

'The owner,' he said, 'is a lovely woman named Roberta Bernstein, and she's in Europe. O'Neill & Chapin are her pet terriers.' He pressed a blunt little index finger to his lips. 'Sounds like the totality of evidence does point to Pierce . . .'

'But?'

'No buts, Alex. You've put together a solid argument.'

'Any idea who he might've passed it to?'

He crossed his legs, hooked a finger under the hem of a purple trouser leg. 'The only person I ever saw Pierce with was Marge. And as I said, I doubt she's involved.'

'Because she's honest.'

'And because Pierce was protective of her, Alex. I can't see him exposing her to something like that.'

'Sounds like you knew them both pretty well,' I said.

He smiled. 'I'm a psychiatrist. I'm allowed to theorize. No, we never really socialized, but this is a small town. You meet the same people over and over. I suppose I'm drawing upon Pierce's body language when they were together.'

'Protective.'

'Very much so. Marge seemed to take well to that. I found that interesting. She'd never lived with anyone before. Her family goes way back in this region, and she's taken care of that ranch nearly single-handedly for years. People of a certain age can get set in their ways, not take well to the demands of a relationship. But Marge seemed quite content with domestic life. They both did.'

'Did you know Pierce had been a detective?'

'Marge told me,' he said. 'Soon after Pierce moved in. I believe it was at the theater, as a matter of fact. Out in the lobby, during intermission. She introduced me, and we began chatting about a crime story in the newspaper – something down your way, bank robbers, a shoot-out, the criminals had escaped. Marge said something along the lines of "If Pierce were still on the force, he'd solve it." '

'How'd Pierce react to that?'

'If I recall correctly, *un*reactive. Didn't say much of anything. That's the way he usually was. Reserved.'

Milo had described Schwinn as verbally aggressive, prone to sermonizing. Lots had changed over twenty years.

I said, 'Marge told us Pierce had grown serene.'

'She'd know best . . . so Pierce was Milo's partner. How interesting. The world grows smaller yet.'

'The way he died,' I said. 'Falling off that horse. Any thoughts about that?'

He uncrossed his leg, tapped a rosy cheek, and allowed his hand to brush against an ornate concertina. 'You suspect something other than an accident? Why, Alex?'

'Because that's the way my mind works.'

'Ah,' he said.

I could hear Milo laughing.

'Small world,' he repeated. 'That's about all I can tell you . . . can I fix you some tea, Alex? Wait – you're a guitarist, aren't you? I've got something in back that might interest you. A turn-of-the-century Knutsen Hawaiian harp-guitar. Perhaps you can tell me how to tune the drone strings.'

His spare bedroom was filled with instruments and antique music stands, and I hung around for a while watching him fiddle and tinker, listened to him expound on music and rhythm and culture. He began to reminisce about his time in Chile. Ethnographic research in Indonesia, a summer of musicology in Salzburg, ministering to Israeli kibbutz children who'd been traumatized by terrorism.

No mention of his Santa Barbara days – the years he'd spent at a school for troubled kids, just a few miles away. The kind of place someone like Caroline Cossack might easily have ended up. That high-priced travesty had caused more problems than it had solved.

Bert had a selective memory for the positive. Perhaps that's why he'd seemed reluctant to imagine a young girl evincing brutality.

He stopped narrating and threw up his hands. 'I'm such a bore – you've probably begun wondering if I'm going senile.'

'I haven't at all, Bert.' Though I had thought: *He seems distracted.*

'The truth is, I have lost some short-term memory. But nothing beyond my age norms.'

'Your memory seems fine to me,' I said.

'That's kind of you to say . . .' He gestured around the room. 'All this – all these toys, Alex, they're a wonderful distraction. A boy needs a hobby.' Pudgy fingers took hold of my forearm. His grip was forceful. 'We both know that, don't we?'

★ ★ ★

289

I stuck around for tea, finally told him I needed to get back to L.A.

As he walked me to my car, he said, 'That girl. So monstrous, if it's true.'

'You seem skeptical.'

He nodded. 'I do find it hard to believe that a young female would be capable of such savagery.'

'I'm not saying she acted alone, Bert, or even initiated the murder. But she could've lured the victims, and either receded into the background or participated.'

'Any theories about the main perpetrator?'

'The girl had a boyfriend, six years older, with a criminal history, including murder.'

'Sexual murder?'

'No, an ambush killing.'

'I see,' he said. 'Any particular reason you didn't mention him, initially?'

'The cover-up's more likely related to the girl.'

'This fellow wasn't wealthy.'

'Young black street pusher.'

'I see – and what became of this murderous young felon?'

'He vanished, too.'

'A girl and a young man,' he said. 'That would change things. Psychosocially.'

'A killing team,' I said. 'One scenario is the two of them picked up the victims at the party and took them somewhere to be raped and murdered.'

'A Svengali-Trilby situation,' he said. 'Dominant male, submissive female . . . because that's what it usually takes to get an impressionable young female involved in extremely violent behavior. Nearly all sexual violence seems to emanate from the Y chromosome, doesn't it?

What else do you know about this boyfriend?'

'Apart from being a junkie and a pusher, he was manipulative enough to get a street-smart bail bondsman to forgo a bond. And calculated enough to ambush the bondsman – that's the homicide he's wanted for. Still wanted. Another of Milo's open cases.'

'Sad convergence for Milo,' he said. 'A junkie in the strict sense – heroin?'

'Heroin was his first choice, but he was eclectic.'

'Hmm . . . then I suppose that would explain it.'

'Explain what?' I said.

'With sexual sadists, one usually thinks of alcohol or marijuana as the drugs of choice, correct? Something mild enough to take the edge off inhibition, but not sufficiently incapacitating to blunt the libido. Other drugs – amphetamines, cocaine – can foster violence, but that's usually more of a paranoid reaction. But heroin?' He shook his head. 'Opiates are the great pacifiers. Take away the necessity to steal in order to obtain heroin and no place would be safer than a city full of addicts. I've certainly never heard of a junkie acting out in such a sexually violent manner.'

'Not while high,' I said. 'But a heroin addict in need of a fix wouldn't be good company.'

'I suppose.' He scratched an ear. 'Even then, Alex, wouldn't the violence be impulsive – born of frustration? An addict would be interested in the needle, not luring and raping and cutting up young girls. Just garnering the concentration would be difficult, wouldn't you say? At least that's the way it was years ago when I worked with addicts.'

'When was that?'

'During my internship, I rotated through the Federal hospital in Lexington.'

'Where haven't you been, Bert?'

'Oh, lots of places . . . do forgive my rambling, Alex. What do I know about crime? You're the expert.'

As I got in the Seville, he said, 'What I told you before about Robin. I didn't mean to presume to instruct you how to live your life. I've presumed an awful lot today, haven't I?'

'I didn't take it that way, Bert.'

He sighed. 'I'm an old man, Alex. Most of the time I *feel* young – sometimes I wake up in the morning ready to dash to the lecture hall and take notes. Then I look in the mirror . . . the life cycle. One regresses. Loses one's sense of propriety. Forgive me.'

Tears welled in the gray eyes.

'There's nothing to forgive—'

'You're kind to say that.'

I placed a hand on his shoulder. Beneath the purple polyester he was soft and frail and small. 'Is everything okay, Bert?'

'Everything is as it should be.' He reached up and patted my hand. 'Lovely seeing you, son. Don't give up.'

'On the case?'

'On anything that matters.'

I drove down the hill, paused to look through the rearview mirror. He remained standing in the driveway. Waved. A tired wave.

Definitely distracted, I thought as I drove away. And the sudden mood swings – the tears. A different Bert from the buoyant man I'd known.

The allusions to senility.

Nothing beyond my age norms.

As if he'd tested himself. Maybe he had.

An impressive man, afraid . . .

He called me *son* several times. I realized that for all his travels and adventures, the first-time mention of being married, he'd never spoken of having children.

Alone, in a house full of toys.

If I reached his age, how would I be living?

I got home just before dark, with a head full of road glare and lungs teeming with smog. No numeral blinked on my phone machine, but two messages had been left with my service: someone wanting to sell me earthquake insurance and a request to call Dr Allison Gwynn.

A young female voice answered at Allison's office.

'Hi, Dr Delaware, I'm Connie Martino, Dr Gwynn's psych assistant. She's in session right now but she told me to let you know that she'd like to speak with you. Her last patient's finished by eight and you can drop by the office if you'd like. Or let me know what works for you.'

'Eight works for me.'

'Great. I'll tell her.'

At seven-forty, I set out for Santa Monica. Allison Gwynn's building was on Montana Avenue, just east of the beach city's boutique row, a pale, one-story late-forties moderne affair with rounded corners and grilled slat windows and apricot-tinted accent lighting. A small patch of daylilies sprouted near the front door, bleached white by the night. Inside were four suites: a three-woman obstetric-gynecology group, a plastic surgeon, an endodontist, and, at the rear, A. GWYNN, PHD, AND ASSOCIATES.

Allison's waiting room was empty and smelled of face powder and perfume and the merest nuance of stress.

The decor was soft chairs and thick wool carpeting and marine prints, everything tinted in variants of soft aqua and beige, as if someone were trying to bring the beach indoors. Halogen spots tuned to dim cast a golden white glow – the beach at twilight. Magazines were stacked neatly. A trio of red call buttons next to the door listed Allison's name above those of two assistants: C. MARTINO, MA, AND E. BRACHT, PHD. I rang in, and, a moment later, she opened the door.

Her black hair was tied back into a ponytail and she wore an ankle-length, navy crêpe dress above matte brown boots. The dress had a scoop neck that dipped just below her collarbone. The same meticulously applied makeup. Same diamond accents at wrist and neck and ears, but tension played around the big blue eyes. The first time I'd met her, she'd maintained steady eye contact. Now she was focused somewhere over my left shoulder.

'Sorry for bringing you all the way here,' she said, 'but I didn't want to talk over the phone.'

'I don't mind being here.'

Her eyebrows rose. 'Well, then, come in.'

Her inner office was more of the same maritime hues and compassionate lighting. The room was large enough for group therapy, but set up for individual work, with a desk in the corner, a sofa and a pair of facing easy chairs. She took one of the chairs, and I sat down opposite her. The navy dress covered most of her but clung to her body, and as she positioned herself I saw muscle and curve, the sweep of thigh, the tug of bosom.

Remembering her history with Michael Larner, I switched mental gears.

She said, 'This may turn out to be nothing, but given

the seriousness of what you're doing, I thought it best that I tell you.'

She shifted in the chair, showed me another aspect of her figure. Not seductively; her mouth was set tight.

I said, 'I appreciate any help you can give me.'

The edge of her lower lip insinuated itself between her teeth, and she chewed. Her hands flexed. She shook her head.

Neither of us spoke. Two therapists measuring the silence.

She said, 'I recalled something right after we talked. I'd forgotten about it – or maybe it never really registered because at the time . . . I'm sure it's nothing, but a short while after Willie Burns left Achievement House – maybe a week later – I was with *him*. Larner. And he was angry about Willie. Worked up. I know because he called me into his office and his anger was obvious. I never really thought about it in terms of Willie because I had my own issues . . .' She chewed her lip, again. 'Let me back up . . .'

Undoing her ponytail, she shook her hair loose in a sable billow, tied it up again. Tucking her legs under her, she hugged herself and studied the carpet.

'Larner had been bothering me for a while. It began soon after I started volunteering. Nothing blatant – looks, smiles, little asides about my clothes – how cute they were, what a nice healthy girl I was. He'd pass me in the hall and pat me on the head or brush my hip or chuck my chin. I knew what was going on, but what I didn't realize was just how wrong it was.' She took hold of her hair, smoothed the ends. 'I didn't want to leave Achievement House, thought it would be a good summer experience. And even if I'd told someone, what was he really doing to me?'

'Insidious,' I said.

'Insidious and devious and altogether creepy. I tried to avoid him. For the most part, it worked. But that day – it was a Monday, I remember that because I'd been to the beach over the weekend, had gotten a tan. Willie Burns had been gone a good week, maybe more. I remember asking about Willie because with him gone the halls were quiet. When he worked, he'd usually be humming, low-key, some kind of bluesy thing. He always looked stoned, but he did have a good voice. And he was friendly, would generally look up and smile, and say, "Hi." '

'Friendly to everyone?'

'To the kids. They seemed to like him, though I got the feeling some of them were making fun of him – that drugged-out demeanor. The only time he got furtive was when he was with Caroline. Anyway, he was gone, and an older woman was doing his job – an old Latina who didn't speak English. I asked people what had happened to Willie, but no one seemed to know.'

She twisted in her chair, cupped one hand over a knee. 'That Monday, I'd been delivering charts when Larner called me into his office. Something about new filing procedures. That sounded strange – why would the director want to talk to a student volunteer about procedure? I didn't want to go, but I couldn't see any way out. If I refused, that would be insubordination. When I got there, Larner's secretary was out in front, and that made me feel better. But then she told me to go right in and closed the door after me. It was summer and I was wearing a sleeveless white sundress and my tan was pretty blatant and I just knew he'd say something about it and started to tell myself I was stupid for not covering up more. But Larner didn't even look at me. He was standing, sleeves rolled up, a cigar in one hand, his back turned, on the phone, listening. I stood near the door. He was rocking on his heels and clenching the phone tight – he was a big, pink disgusting thing, and his hands were tight around the receiver – mottled, like lunch meat. Then he half turned, but he still didn't acknowledge me. His face was different from all the other times I'd seen him. In the past he'd always smiled. Leered. Now he looked furious. Red-faced – he's naturally ruddy, but this time he was like a beet. I remember the contrast with his hair – he had this blond-white hair that looked as if he waxed it. I just stayed there, with my back against the door, and he barked something into the phone and slammed it down. All I caught was Willie Burns's name. Then something about "We'd better do something about it." Then he hung up.' She held out one hand. 'That's it. I never paid much attention to that, because it really wasn't the focus of my memories.'

'You had your own issues,' I said.

She lowered her head, then raised it very slowly. Her eyes were closed, and her face had lost color.

'After he slammed down the phone, he began to dial another number, then he saw me, gave me this surprised look – surprised and hateful. As if I wasn't supposed to be there. Then there it was – that smile of his. But the anger remained on his face, also, and the combination scared me – predatory. He came around from behind the desk, shook my hand, held on too long, told me to sit down, said something to the effect of "How's my favorite volunteer?" Then he walked behind me and just stood there, not talking or moving. I could smell his cigar, the smoke kept wafting toward me. To this day, I can't see a cigar without . . .'

She sprang up, strode to her own desk, and sat down, putting wood and space between us.

'He started talking – softly, in a singsong. How did I like working at Achievement House? Was I finding satisfaction? Had I thought about career choices? Maybe teaching would be good for me because I was clearly a people person. I didn't say much, he really didn't want answers. It was a monologue – droning, hypnotic. Then he stopped talking and I tensed up, and he said, "Don't be nervous, Allison. We're all friends, here." Nothing happened for what seemed to be forever. Then suddenly I felt his finger on my cheek, pressing, stroking, and he said something about my skin – how clean and fresh it was, how nice it was to see a young lady who cared about her hygiene.'

She caught hold of her hair with one hand and tugged hard. Then both hands slapped flat on the desk and she was staring at me – daring me to look away.

'He kept stroking,' she said. 'It was annoying – ticklish – and I twisted my head away. And then he chuckled and I looked up and I saw that it hadn't been his finger on my cheek. It was his thing – oh, listen to me, like a child – it was his *penis*, and he was rubbing it against my cheek, *pushing*. I was so freaked out that my mouth dropped open and that was the worst thing to do because he chuckled again and in it went and all of a sudden he was holding the back of my head with his other hand, the hand with the cigar, and the smoke wrapped around me, and he forced himself deeper into my mouth and I couldn't breathe, I was gagging. But my eyes were open, for some reason I kept them open, and I could see his white shirt and his tie – a striped tie, blue and black – and the bottom of his face, all that pink flab, quivering, his double chin and he was rocking on his heels again, but in a different way and the cigar smoke was burning my eyes and I started to cry.'

She turned icy and still. Didn't move for a long time. 'He didn't come. Thank God for that. I managed to wrench free first, made it to the door, ran out, never looked back. Drove home like a zombie, called in sick. Which wasn't much of a stretch because I felt sick as a dog. For the next few days, I took to bed. Threw up when my mother wasn't listening, lay there feeling degraded and scared and worst of all stupid – replaying it over and over, blaming myself. For the tan and the dress and not being on guard – I know it's never the victim's fault, God knows how many times I've told that to *patients*. But . . .'

'You were seventeen,' I said.

'I'm not sure I'd have handled it better – or felt differently – had I been twenty-seven. Not at the level of consciousness twenty years ago.' She slumped, loosened her hair again, fooled with it, flicked something away from the corner of one eye.

'The worst part was how *alone* I felt. Abandoned, with no one in my corner. I couldn't tell my parents, because I was too humiliated. I told Larry Daschoff a sanitized version, because even though Larry had been my mentor for the summer and he'd been kind and helpful, he was a *man*. And I couldn't get rid of the feeling that I was to blame. So I just kept calling in sick to Achievement House, told my mother I had some kind of flu, stayed holed up in my room. Obsessing about what had happened, dreaming about it – in the dreams it was worse. In the dreams I *didn't* get away and Larner came in my mouth and then he hit me and raped me and forced me to smoke the cigar. Finally, I realized I was falling apart – was *wasting*. I needed to do something. So I found out the name of the school's chairman of the board – some downtown lawyer – Preston something – and after agonizing about it for a whole week, I called his office, got through after several attempts, and told him what had happened. Only I didn't really tell him. I soft-pedaled it. Reduced it to grabbing – the same story I told Larry.'

Larry had told me, *Mashing and groping*.

'How'd Preston react?' I said.

'He listened. Didn't say anything at all, at first. Didn't ask any questions, which really upset me. I got the impression he thought I was crazy. Finally, he said he'd get back to me. Two days later a letter of dismissal arrived in the mail. I was being let go for poor work habits and excessive absenteeism. I never showed the letter to my parents, just told them I'd quit because the job wasn't challenging. They didn't care. My mother wanted me to swim at the club and play tennis and meet guys. What she *wasn't* happy about was that I just wanted to hang around the house and not be *social*. So she arranged a family cruise to Alaska. Big luxury liner cruising past the glaciers – baby otters nursing amid the ice floes. All that blue ice wasn't as cold as my heart was that summer.'

She stood, returned to the easy chair, tried to look comfortable but couldn't pull it off.

'I've never told anyone what really happened. Not until now. But this was the wrong time and place, wasn't it? Using a stranger. I'm sorry.'

'Nothing to be sorry for, Allison.'

'All these years,' she said. 'And it still eats at me – not going after that piece of dirt. Who knows how many

300

others he's done that to. What I could've prevented.'

'It would've been his word against yours, and he was in power,' I said. 'It wasn't your fault then, and it's not your fault, now.'

'Do you know how many women I've treated – how many patients I've helped deal with *exactly* this kind of thing? *Not* because I pursue those kinds of cases. *Not* because I'm using my patients to work through my own garbage. Because it's so damned *common*. I've helped my patients, but then when it comes to my own garbage, I repress. It's crazy, don't you think?'

'No,' I said. 'It's human. I've preached the virtues of talking it out, but when it comes to my own stuff, I usually go it alone.'

'Do you?'

I nodded.

'And you're going through something now, aren't you?'

I stared at her.

'Your eyes are sad,' she said.

'I'm going through a bit of something,' I said.

'Well, then,' she said, 'I guess we're kindred spirits. And I guess we'll leave it at that.'

She walked me to the waiting-room door. 'Like I told you the first time, you're just too good a listener, sir.'

'Occupational hazard.'

'Was it helpful? Telling you that Larner was angry about Willie Burns?'

'Yes,' I said. 'Thanks very much. I know it was an ordeal.'

She smiled. 'Not an ordeal, an experience. What you're going through – it has nothing to do with Caroline Cossack or Willie Burns, does it?'

I shook my head.

'Sorry,' she said. 'No more prying.' She reached for the doorknob and her shoulder brushed my arm. The contact sent something electrical down my arm. Suddenly I was rock-hard, fighting to keep my breathing even. To keep my hands off her.

She stared at me. No tension around the huge, blue eyes, just softness, sadness, maybe desire.

'It wasn't an ordeal,' she said. 'You said the right thing. Here's another confession: I was looking forward to seeing you again.'

'Me too,' I said.

I smiled and shrugged, and she did the same. Gracious mimickry.

'You too, *but*,' she said. 'That bit of something, right?'

I nodded.

'Well, maybe in another galaxy, Alex. You're very sweet. Good luck.'

'Good luck to you, too.'

She held the door open. Kept it open as I walked down the hall.

twenty-four

Milo woke up early the next morning, with the faces of the men at the Sangre de Leon meeting leering in his head. Thinking: *Too many ways to take it, not enough of me to go around.*

He stumbled to the shower, shaved, picked clothes randomly, got the coffee machine going, looked at the clock. Seven-thirteen. An emergency call had yanked Rick out of bed three hours ago. Milo had watched in the darkness as Rick slipped into the scrubs he kept neatly folded on a bedroom chair, picked up his Porsche keys from the nightstand, and padded out the door.

Rick stopped, returned to the bed, kissed Milo lightly on the forehead. Milo pretended to be sleeping, because he didn't feel like talking, not even 'Goodbye.'

The two of them had talked plenty all night, sitting up late at the kitchen table. Mostly Milo had blabbed and Rick had listened, maintaining a superficial calm, but Milo knew he was shaken by the Paris Bartlett encounter and the HIV rumor. All these years, and Milo's work had never intruded on their personal life.

Milo reassured him, and Rick nodded, complained of crushing fatigue and fell asleep the moment his head hit the pillow.

Milo cleaned up the Chinese takeout cartons and the dinner dishes and slipped into bed beside him, lying there for an hour or so, listening to Rick's even breathing, thinking.

The Cossacks, Walt Obey, Larner Junior, Germ Bacilla, Diamond Jim Horne.

Plus the player who *hadn't* shown up. He saw that face, clearly: a stoic ebony mask.

Smiley Bartlett, the personnel inquiry, and the HIV rumor said John G. Broussard's hand was in all of it.

He recalled Broussard – smelled Broussard's citrus cologne in the interview room, twenty years ago. The hand-stitched suit, all that confidence, taking charge. He and his pink pal – Poulsenn. Milo had no idea what had happened to *his* career, but look how far John G. had come.

A white man and a black man teamed up, and the black man had been the dominant partner.

A black man advancing that quickly, back in LAPD's bad old racist days. That had to mean Broussard had harpoons in all the right whales. Had probably used his IA dirt to build up leverage.

Mr Straight and Narrow. And he'd covered up Janie Ingalls and Lord knew what else. Milo had been part of it, allowed himself to be swept along, pretended he could forget about it.

Now he wondered what that had done to his soul.

He poured coffee but the muddy brew tasted like battery acid and he spit it out and gulped a glass of tap water. The light through the kitchen window was the yellow-gray of old phlegm.

He sat down, kept thinking about Broussard, a South Central guy who'd ended up in Hancock Park.

Neighbor to Walt Obey.

Every police chief before Broussard had lived in his own house, but John G. had convinced the mayor to give him an empty mansion on Irving Street, rent-free. The three-story edifice, donated to the city years ago by the heirs of a long-dead oil tycoon, was twelve thousand square feet of English Tudor with big lawns, a pool, and a tennis court. Milo knew because he'd done security years ago at a party for an ambassador – the envoy from some small Asian state that had since changed its name.

Set aside originally as a mayor's residence, the Irving house had sat dormant for years because the mayor's predecessor had his own place in Brentwood and the current mayor's even larger spread in Pacific Palisades was just fine, too.

John G. Broussard's crib, prior to his promotion, had been a too-small affair in Ladera Heights and John G. claimed he needed to be closer to headquarters.

Ladera Heights was a half-hour ride downtown, the mansion on Irving was fifteen minutes up Sixth Street. The mayor's drive from the Westside could stretch to over an hour, but no one saw the inconsistency in John G.'s logic, and the new chief got himself baronial lodgings.

Irving Street, less than a mile from Walt Obey's estate on Muirfield.

Obey was one of the mayor's big donors. Had supported Broussard for chief over three other candidates.

The mayor and Obey. Obey and Broussard. Obey and a bunch of lowlifes supping nouvelle-whatever cuisine in a private room at Sangre de Leon.

Private enterprise and municipal government and the long arm of the law arm in arm. And Schwinn had thrown him right into it.

★ ★ ★

He left his house, looking in all directions and over his shoulder, got into the rented Taurus, and drove north. IDing the asshole who claimed to be Paris Bartlett shouldn't be a problem, if his hunch about a department plant was true. Just head over to the police academy in Elysian Park and thumb through the face books. But that was too conspicuous; for all he knew it was his sneaky little trips to Parker Center and back to his West L.A. desk that had sicked the department on him in the first place. Besides, Bartlett was a minor player, just a messenger, and did it really matter who'd sent him?

Stay healthy . . .

Maybe he should return to Ojai and nose around a bit more up there. But what more could he learn? Schwinn was the Ojai link, and he was gone.

Falling off a goddamn horse . . .

He pulled over to the curb, yanked out his cell-phone, got the number of the Ventura County morgue. Using an insurance-investigator lie, he spent the next half hour being bounced from desk to desk, trying to get the full facts on Schwinn's death.

Finally, a coroner's assistant who knew something got on the line. The death was written up just as Marge Schwinn had described: massive head injuries and fractured ribs consistent with a fall, copious blood on a nearby rock. Ruled accidental, no suspicious circumstances. No dope or booze in Schwinn's system. Or the horse's, the clerk added. An equine drug scan seemed thorough, and Milo told the CA so.

'Special request of the widow,' said the guy, a middle-aged-sounding guy named Olivas. 'She wanted the horse tested and was willing to pay for it.'

306

'She suspect something?'

'All it says here is that she requested a full drug scan on Akhbar – that's the horse. We had a vet in Santa Barbara do it, and she sent us the results. Mrs Schwinn got the bill.'

'So the horse was clean,' said Milo.

'As a whistle,' said Olivas. 'It busted itself up plenty, though – two broken legs and a torsion injury of the neck. When the widow got there, it was down on the ground moaning, pretty much out of it. She had it put down. What's up, the insurance company has problems with something?'

'No, just checking.'

'It was an accident, he was an old guy,' said Olivas. 'Riding a horse at his age, what was he thinking?'

'President Reagan rode when he was in his eighties.'

'Yeah, well, he had Secret Service guys to look after him. It's like old people driving cars – my dad's eighty-nine, blind as a bat at night, but he insists on getting behind the wheel and driving to L.A. to get authentic *menudo*. That kind of thing and idiots on cell-phones, give me a break. You'd see what I see comes in here every day, you'd be scared.'

'I'm scared,' said Milo, hefting his phone.

'Pays to be scared.'

He craved caffeine and cholesterol, drove to Farmers Market at Fairfax and Third and had a green chili omelet and two stacks of toast at Du-Pars. Keeping his eye on a homeless guy in the next booth. The bum wore three jackets and hugged a battered, stringless guitar. The instrument made Milo think about Robin, but the psychosis in the homeless guy's eyes pulled him into the here and now.

They engaged in a staring contest until the homeless man finally threw down a couple of dollars and waddled off mumbling at unseen demons and Milo was able to enjoy his eggs.

Once again, he thought, *I've brought peace and light to the world.*

But then the waitress smiled with relief and gave him a thumbs-up, and he realized he'd really accomplished something.

Still hungry, he ordered a stack of hotcakes, drained everything down with black coffee, walked around the market, dodging tourists, figuring the distraction might get his brain in gear. But it didn't, and after inspecting produce stands full of fruit he didn't recognize and buying a bag of jumbo cashews, he left the market, drove south on Fairfax, turned left on Sixth, at the old May Company building, now an adjunct of the art museum, and kept going east.

Chief John G. Broussard's official residence was beautifully tended, with grass as green as Ireland and more flower beds than Milo remembered from that diplomatic party. A flagpole had been erected smack in the middle of the lawn and the Stars and Stripes and the California Bear swooshed in the midday breeze.

No walls or fences or uniformed officer on patrol, but the driveway had been gated with wrought iron, and through the stout bars Milo saw a black-and-white cruiser, and behind that a late-model white Cadillac. The Caddy was probably Mrs Broussard's wheels. He recalled her as a trim, pretty woman with henna-tinted, cold-waved hair and the resigned look of a political spouse. What was her name . . . Bernadette . . . Bernadine? Did she and John G. have kids? Milo'd never heard of any, and he realized how little he knew about the chief's personal life. How little the chief doled out.

Seven blocks west and a half mile south was Walt Obey's address on Muirfield. The billionaire's nest sat at the end of the road, where Muirfield terminated on the southern border of the Wilshire Country Club. No house in sight, just ten-foot stone walls broken by an opaque, black steel gate studded with enormous bolts. Closed circuit TV camera on one post. The implication was a grand place on multiple acres, and Milo flashed to Baron Loetz's spread, neighbor to the Cossack party house. Did Obey spend time on his veranda, sipping gin and enjoying what God had given him?

Eighty years old and still taking meetings with hustlers like the Cossacks. Some big deal on the verge?

He found himself staring at Obey's gate. The TV camera remained immobile. The place was close enough for an athletic guy like John G. to jog over. Obey and Broussard on the veranda? Making plans. Running things. All of a sudden Milo felt very small and vulnerable. He rolled down the window, heard birds peeping, a plink of running water behind Obey's walls. Then the camera began to rotate. An automatic circuit, or maybe his presence had attracted attention. He backed up halfway down the block, whipped a U-turn, and got the hell out of there.

A few minutes later, he was parked on McCadden near Wilshire, cell-phone hot against his ear. More DMV finagling gave him other addresses, and he had a look at all of them.

Michael Larner lived in a high-rise condo just east of Westwood, in the Wilshire Corridor. Pink stone and cheesy-looking brick, doorman out in front, an oversize fountain. Son Bradley's Santa Monica Canyon place turned out to be a smallish, blue frame house with stupendous ocean views and a FOR RENT sign out in front. No cars in the driveway, and the gardening looked a little lax, so Brad was living somewhere else.

Garvey Cossack Junior and brother Bob bunked together at a Carolwood address in Holmby Hills, not far, geographically, from Alex's place off Beverly Glen, but a whole different world financially.

Carolwood was a lovely, hilly block, leafy and sinuous, shaded by old-growth trees, one of the highest-priced stretches in L.A. Most of the houses were architectural masterpieces landscaped like botanical gardens, many of them cosseted by greenery and bearing that classy look that only came from durability.

The Cossack brothers' pad was an exceedingly vulgar, blue-tile-roofed and monstrously gabled heap of gray limestone perched atop a scarred dirt hill with no grass or trees in sight. Stone facing, only. The sides were lumpy stucco. Bad trowel job. Cheap-looking white metal fencing and an electric gate partitioned the front of the property from the street, but without benefit of vegetation the house sat in full view, baking in the sun, puffy flanks glaring white in spots.

A double-sized dumpster overflowing with trash advertised ongoing construction, but no workers were in sight, drapes covered the windows, and a mini car museum took up the rest of the massive driveway.

Plum-colored Rolls-Royce Corniche, black Humvee with blacked-out windows, red (what else?) Ferrari that came as close as Milo had seen to a penis on wheels, a taxi-yellow Pantera, a pair of Dodge Vipers, one white with a blue center stripe, the other anthracite-gray striped orange, and a white Corvette convertible. All under a drooping, makeshift canvas awning that stretched across listing metal stilts. Off to the side, in the full sun, was a ten-year-old Honda that had to be the maid's wheels.

Big house and all those cars, but no landscaping. Just the kind of eyesore a couple of teenagers would put together if they tumbled into endless cash, and Milo was willing to bet the Cossacks had six figures' worth of stereo equipment inside, along with a state-of-the-art screening room, a pub, a game room or two. He was starting to think of them as a dual case of profound arrested development.

The house was exactly the kind of eyesore that would provoke neighbor complaints in a blue-chip district, meaning now he had something to look for.

He drove downtown to the Hall of Records, made it through the traffic by 2 P.M., and combed through the zoning-board complaint files. Sure enough, three gripes had been lodged against the Cossacks, all by Carolwood residents, irritated about noise and dirt and other indignities caused by 'protracted construction.' All dismissed for lack of cause.

He moved over to the property files, ran searches on the Cossacks, Walt Obey, both Larners, John G. Broussard.

Obey's holdings were protected by a cadre of holding companies, a firewall that would take weeks, if not months, to break through. Same for the Larners and the Cossacks, although a few pieces of real estate were held privately by each duo. In the case of the Larners it was half a dozen condos in a Marina del Rey building owned jointly by father and son. Sixteen strip malls in low-rent exurbs were registered to the Cossack brothers.

311

The boys living together, working together. How touching.

Nothing was registered to Sister Caroline.

Shifting gears for a moment, he pulled up Georgie Nemerov's records. The bail bondsman and his mother co-owned a single-family dwelling in Van Nuys that Milo recognized as the family home from twenty years ago, and a six-unit apartment in Granada Hills, also jointly registered to Ivana Nemerov. Whatever Georgie had or hadn't done, building a real estate empire didn't seem part of the equation.

John G. Broussard and his wife – Berna*delle* – had held on to the house in Ladera Heights as well as three contiguous lots on West 156th Street in Watts. Maybe the chief's or his wife's parents' place, an inheritance.

Once again: no empire. If John G. was trading for something, it wasn't land. Unless he was embedded somewhere in Walt Obey's corporate acreage.

He ran searches on Melinda Waters and mother Eileen and came up empty, was thinking about what else to do when the records clerk came over and told him the building was closing. He left and drove up and down Temple Street, past the place where Pierce Schwinn had spotted Tonya Stumpf strutting. The block was a Music Center parking lot now, filled with its daytime load of municipal workers' and litigants' vehicles, owing to the Court Building down the street. Lots of people, lots of movement, but Milo felt out of it – out of the rhythm.

He drove toward home, slowly, not caring about rush-hour toxins, street-work delays, notably stupid driving by what seemed to be fifty percent of his fellow commuters. All the urban niceties that usually drove up his blood pressure and made him wonder why the hell he'd chosen to live like this.

He was sitting at a red light at Highland when his phone rang. Alex's voice said, 'I got you. Good.'

'What's up?'

'Maybe nothing, but my source – the woman Michael Larner molested – called me again, and I met with her last night. Seems the day Larner made his move on her, he was angry about Willie Burns. Enraged, talking to someone about Burns. Willie had been gone from Achievement House for a few days so it sounds like Larner found out who Burns was, was steamed because Burns disappeared.'

'Enraged,' said Milo.

'That's how she describes it. She walked into his office just as he got off the phone, said Larner was flushed and agitated. Then he composed himself and turned his attention to her. Which could be more than a coincidence. Harassers and rapists often get stoked by anger. Anyway, it's probably no big deal, but it does fit with our working hypothesis: the Cossack family contracted Larner to hide Caroline until Janie Ingalls's murder cooled down. Burns made contact with Caroline, then split, and the family panicked. But they never found him, he even managed to slip away after his dope arrest, because Boris Nemerov bailed him out immediately. Four months later he ambushed Nemerov.'

'Interesting,' said Milo. 'Good work.' He summarized what he'd seen at Sangre de Leon last night.

'Big money,' said Alex. 'Same old story. One more thing: when I was looking for Melinda Waters on the Internet, I got a few hits but dismissed them. Then I realized maybe I'd been too hasty about one in particular. An attorney in Santa Fe, New Mexico, specializing in bankruptcy and evictions. I'd been thinking about Melinda as a stoned-out truant, didn't see a pathway from that to a legal career, but your comment about her turning up with a family and picket fence got me thinking, so I pulled up her website again and checked her bio. She's thirty-eight years old, which would be exactly our Melinda's age. And she didn't graduate college until she was thirty-one, law school till thirty-four. Before that, she worked as a paralegal for three years but her résumé still leaves the years between eighteen and twenty-eight unaccounted for. Which would mesh with someone going through changes, pulling her life together. And get this: she was schooled in California. San Francisco State for undergrad, Hastings for law.'

'Hastings is a top school,' said Milo. 'Bowie Ingalls described Melinda as a loser.'

'Bowie Ingalls was not a sterling judge. And people change. If I didn't believe that, I'd choose another profession.'

'Bankruptcy and eviction . . . I guess anything's possible.'

'Maybe she's not our gal, but don't you think it's worth looking into?'

'Anything else interesting in her bio?'

'No. Married, two kids. Do they have picket fences in Santa Fe? Not that hard to find out. It's a ninety-minute flight to Albuquerque, another hour by car to Santa Fe, and Southwest Airlines has cheap flights.'

'Calling her on the phone would be too easy,' said Milo.

'If she's trying to put her past behind her, she may lie.

There's a flight at seven-forty-five tomorrow morning. I booked two seats.'

'Manipulative. I'm proud of you.'

'It's cold there,' said Alex. 'Twenty to forty Fahrenheit, some snow on the ground. So bundle up.'

twenty-five

B y seven-fifteen, Milo and I were at the back of a long queue at the Southwest Airlines gate. The terminal was Ellis Island minus the overcoats – weary posture, worried eyes, language-soup.

'Thought we had our seats,' he said, eyeing the front of the line.

'We have electronic tickets,' I said. 'Southwest's system is you wait for your seat assignment. They board in groups, give you little plastic number tags.'

'Great . . . I'll take half a dozen bagels, a rye sliced thin, and two onion rolls.'

The flight was booked full and cramped, but amiable, populated by seasoned, mostly easygoing passengers and flight attendants who fancied themselves stand-up comedians. We arrived early on a tarmac specked with snow and turned our watches ahead one hour. Sunport Airport was low-profile and blessedly quiet, done up in earth tones, turquoise, and mock adobe, and riddled with talismanic hints of a decimated Indian culture.

We picked up a Ford Escort at the Budget desk, and I drove north on Highway 25 toward Santa Fe, feeling the wind buffet the tiny car. Snow – clean white fluff – was banked up along the side of the road, but the asphalt was plowed clear and the sky was bluer and bigger than I'd ever imagined and when I opened the window to test the air, I got a faceful of pure, sweet chill.

'Nice,' I said.

Milo grunted.

City sprawl, fast-food franchises, and Indian casinos gave way soon enough to long, low vistas of desert, bounded by the purplish tips of the Sangre de Cristo Mountains and that vast sky that just seemed to grow bigger.

'Gorgeous,' I said.

'Hey, look at this,' said Milo. 'Seventy-five-mile-an-hour speed limit. Put some weight on that pedal.'

As we neared Santa Fe, the highway climbed and the altitude registers increased steadily to seven thousand feet. I was speeding across the highest of deserts, no cactus or sandy desolation. The mountains were green where the snow had melted and so were the lowlands, bearded by wind-hardy, drought-tolerant *piñon* trees, ancient and ragged and low to the ground – Darwinian victors – and the occasional vertical statement of bare-branch aspens. Millions of trees, tipped with white, not a cloud in the sky. I wondered if Melinda Waters, Attorney-at-Law, had woken up thinking this was going to be a great day. Would we be a petty annoyance or an intrusion she'd never forget?

I took the Saint Francis exit to Cerrilos Road and continued through the southern part of Santa Fe, which seemed not much different from any other small city, with shopping centers and auto dealers and gas stations

317

and the type of businesses that hug highways. Melinda
Waters's office was listed on a street called Paseo de
Peralta, and my reading of the map I'd grabbed at the
rental counter put that right off Cerrilos. But the address
numerals didn't check out and I followed the signs north
to City Center and the Plaza and suddenly we were in a
different world. Narrow, winding streets, some of them
cobbled, forced me to reduce my speed as I rolled past
diamond-bright, one-story adobe and Spanish colonial
buildings plastered in sienna and peach and dun and
gold. Pools of melting ice glistened like opals. The
luxuriant trees that lined the road had managed to shrug
off all but reminiscent flecks of snow, and through their
branches streamed the sky's blue smile.

Different businesses filled the north side: art galleries,
sculpture and glass studios, gourmet cookware emporia,
purveyors of fine foods, high-fashion clothing and hand-
hewn furniture, custom picture framers. Cafés and restaurants never tainted by corporate logos abounded,
promising everything from Southwestern to sushi. SUVs
were the steeds of choice, and sinuous, happy people in
jeans and suede and boots that had never known the kiss
of manure crowded the sidewalks.

We reached the central plaza, a square of tree-shaded
green set up with a bandstand and surrounded by low-
rise shops, drove past a covered breezeway where a
couple of dozen down-parkaed Indians sat behind blankets of silver jewelry near the Palace of the Governors.
Across the square was a massive blocky structure of
fieldstone that seemed more European than American.
More restaurants and galleries, a couple of luxury hotels,
and suddenly Paseo de Peralta had disappeared.

'Very pretty,' said Milo, 'but you're going in circles.'

At Washington Avenue, in the shadow of a salmon-pink Scottish Rite temple, I spotted a white-haired couple in matched shearling jackets walking an English sheepdog that could've supplied the garment's linings, and asked directions. The man wore a plaid cap, and the woman's hair was long and braided and gray and set off by silver butterflies. She wore the kind of makeup meant to convey no makeup at all, had crinkly eyes and a ready smile. When I showed her the address she chuckled.

'You want the northern part of Paseo de Peralta – it horseshoes at the Plaza. Herb, where's this address, exactly?'

The man shared her mirth. At least I'd made someone happy. 'Right there, my friend – just up the block.'

Melinda Waters's law office occupied one of eight suites in a sand-colored adobe building that abutted an Italian taverna. The restaurant's chimney billowed storybook puffs of smoke and cooking smells that got my salivary glands going. Then I thought about what lay ahead, and my appetites shifted.

The units faced a large, open parking lot backed by a high berm and an opaque stand of trees, as if the property – the town itself – terminated at a forest. We parked and got out. The air was frigid and perfect.

Each office had its own entrance. A wooden post hung with shingles served as a directory. Four other lawyers, a psychotherapist, a practitioner of therapeutic massage, an antiquarian book dealer, a print gallery. How far was Ojai?

Melinda Waters's door was unlocked and her front room smelled of incense. Big rust-and-wine-colored che-nille chairs with fringed pillows were arranged around a battered old, blackwood Chinese table. Atop the table were art books, magazines that worshipped style, a brass bowl full of hard candy, and straw baskets of potpourri. Would any of that ease the pain of bankruptcy and eviction?

Blocking the rear door, a round-faced Indian woman of thirty or so sat behind a weathered oak desk and pecked at a slate gray laptop. She wore a pink sweatshirt and big, dangling earrings – geometric and hard-edged and gold, more New York than New Mexico. As we approached her desk, she looked up without conveying much in the way of emotion and continued typing.

'How can I help you?'

'Is Ms Waters in?'

'Do you have an appointment?'

'No, ma'am,' said Milo, producing his card.

'L.A.,' said the receptionist. 'The police. You've come all that way to talk to Mel.'

'Yes, ma'am.'

Her eyes scanned the card. 'Homicide.' No surprise. No inflection at all. She reached for the phone.

Melinda Waters was five-five, curvy and chunky and busty in a tailored, moss-green pantsuit turned greener by the wall of maroon-bound law books behind her. Her eyes were a lighter green edged with gray and her hair was honey-blond, cut short and swept back from a well-formed face softened by full lips and the beginnings of a double chin. Big, round tortoiseshell eyeglasses were perfectly proportioned for the thin, straight nose upon which they rested. Her lips were glossed, her manicure was impressive, and the diamond ring on her finger looked to be two carats, minimum.

She barely looked at us, gave off an air of bored competence, but seemed to be working at that. The moment I saw her my heart jumped. Same face as in the Hollywood High yearbook. Milo knew it, too. His expression was pleasant, but cherry-sized lumps had formed where his jaw met his sideburns.

Melinda Waters stared at his card and waved us into two cane-backed chairs that faced her desk.

Her private office was rust-colored and small – tiny, really, with barely enough room for the bookcase and the desk and a red lacquer stand off to one side, set with a single white orchid in a blue-and-white pot. The walls perpendicular to the books were hung with watercolor landscapes – green hills above the ocean, live oaks, fields of poppies. California dreaming. The rest of the space bore family photos. Melinda Waters with a slim, tall, dark-bearded man and two mischievous-looking boys, around six and eight. Skiing, scuba diving, horseback riding, fishing. The family that plays together . . .

'Homicide detectives. Well, this is certainly different.' Soft voice, edged with sarcasm. Under normal circumstances, she was probably the image of professionalism, but a quaver at the tail end said she wasn't pretending this was routine.

'Different from what, ma'am?' said Milo.

'From what I thought I'd be doing right before lunch. Frankly, I'm confused. I'm not working on any L.A. cases at all, let alone homicide. I specialize in tenants' rights and financial—'

'Janie Ingalls,' said Milo.

Melinda Waters's sigh stretched for a very long time.

She fiddled with papers and pens, closed her laptop,

tamped her hair. Finally, she punched an intercom button on her phone, and said, 'Hold my calls please, Inez.'

Wheeling her chair back the few inches that remained between her and the law book backdrop, she said, 'That's a name from a long time ago. What happened to her?'

'You don't know?'

'Well,' she said, 'your card says homicide, so am I safe in assuming?'

'Very safe.'

Melinda Waters removed her glasses, made a fist, knuckled one eye. The glossy lips trembled. 'Oh, damn. I suppose I knew it all along. But . . . I didn't really – damn. Poor Janie . . . that is so . . . obscene.'

'Very,' said Milo.

She sat up straighter, as if drawing upon a reserve of strength. Now her eyes were different – searching, analytical. 'And you're here, after all this time, because . . . ?'

'Because it remains an open case, Ms Waters.'

'Open or reopened?'

'It was never closed, officially.'

'You're not saying the L.A. police have been working on this for twenty years?'

'Does that matter, ma'am?'

'No . . . I suppose not. I'm rambling . . . this is really . . . this takes me by total surprise. Why are you here?'

'Because you were one of the last people to see Janie Ingalls alive, but no one ever took your statement. In fact, it was only recently we learned you hadn't been a victim, yourself.'

'A victim? You thought . . . oh, my.'

'You've been hard to locate, Ms Waters. So has your mother—'

322

'My mother died ten years ago,' she said. 'Lung cancer, back in Pennsylvania, where she was from. Before that, she had emphysema. She suffered a lot.'

'Sorry to hear that.'

'So was I,' said Waters. She picked a gold pen from several resting in a cloisonné cup, balanced it between the index fingers of both hands. The office was a jewel box, everything arranged with care. 'All this time you really thought I might be . . . how strange.' Weak smile. 'So I'm reborn, huh?'

The pen dropped and clattered to the desk. She snatched it up, placed it back in the cup.

'Ma'am, could you please tell us everything you remember about that night.'

'I did try to find out where Janie was. Called her father – you've met him?'

'He's dead too, ma'am.'

'How'd he die?'

'Car accident.'

'Driving drunk?'

'Yes.'

'No surprise there,' said Waters. 'What a lowlife, always plastered. He couldn't stand me, and the feeling was mutual. Probably because I knew he'd grope me if he had a chance, so I never gave him one – always made sure to meet Janie outside her building.'

'He came on to you?' said Milo.

'I never gave him a chance, but his intentions were obvious – leering, undressing me mentally. Plus, I knew what he'd done to Janie.'

'He abused Janie sexually?'

'Only when he was drunk,' said Waters, in mocking singsong. 'She never told me until shortly before she

323

was . . . before I last saw her. I think what made her talk about it was she'd had a bad experience a month or so before that. She was hitching, got picked up by some deviant who took her to a hotel downtown, tied her up, had his way with her. When she first told me about it, she didn't seem very upset. Kind of blasé, really, and at first I didn't believe her because Janie was always making things up. Then she pulled up her jeans and her top and showed me the rope marks where he'd tied up her ankles and her wrists. Her neck, too. When I saw that, I said, "Jesus, he could've strangled you." And she just clammed up and refused to say any more about it.'

'What did she tell you about the man who did this?'

'That he was young and nice-looking and drove a great car – that's why she said she went with him. But to tell the truth, she probably would've gone with anyone. A lot of the time Janie was out of it – stoned or drunk. She didn't have much in the way of inhibitions.'

She removed her glasses, played with the sidepieces, glanced at the photos of her family. 'Some lawyer I am, running my mouth. Before we go any further, I need your assurance that anything I tell you will be kept confidential. My husband's a semipublic figure.'

'What does he do?'

'Jim's an aide to the governor. Liaison to the Highway Department. I keep my maiden name for work, but anything unsavory could still be traced back to him.'

'I'll do my best, ma'am.'

Waters shook her head. 'That's not good enough.' She stood. 'I'm afraid this meeting is adjourned.'

Milo crossed his legs. 'Ms Waters, all we came here for are your recollections about Janie Ingalls. No assumption was made of any criminal involvement on your part—'

'You bet your boots no assumption was made.' Waters jabbed a finger. 'That didn't even cross my mind, for God's sake. But what happened to Janie twenty years ago isn't my problem. Safeguarding my privacy is. Please leave.'

'Ms Waters, you know as well as I do that I can't guarantee confidentiality. That's the DA's authority. I'm being honest, and I'd appreciate the same from you. If you've done nothing wrong, you have nothing to worry about. And refusing to cooperate won't shield your husband. If I wanted to complicate his life, all I'd have to do is talk to my boss and he'd make a call, and . . .'

He showed her his palms.

Waters slapped her hands on her hips. Her stare was cold and steady. 'Why are you doing this?'

'In order to find out who murdered Janie Ingalls. You're right about one thing. It was obscene. She was tortured, burned with cigarettes, mutilat—'

'No, no, no! None of that shock treatment, give me some *credit*.'

Milo's palms pressed together. 'This has become needlessly adversarial, Ms Waters. Just tell me what you know, and I'll do my utmost to keep you out of it. That's the best I can offer. The alternative means a bit more overtime for me and a lot more complication for you.'

'You have no jurisdiction in New Mexico,' said Melinda Waters. 'Technically, you're trespassing.'

'Technically, you're still a material witness, and last time I checked New Mexico had diplomatic relations with California.'

Waters looked at her family again, sat back down, put her glasses back on, mumbled, 'Shit.'

The three of us sat in silence for a full minute before

she said, 'This isn't fair. I'm not proud of the kind of kid I was back then, and I'd like to forget it.'

I said, 'We've all been teenagers.'

'Well, I was a *rotten* teenager. A total screwup and a stoner, just like Janie. That's what drew us together. Bad behavior – Jesus, I don't think a day went by when we weren't getting loaded. And . . . other things that give me a migraine when I think about them. But I pulled myself out of it – in fact, the process *started* the day after Janie and I split up.'

'At the party?' said Milo.

Waters grabbed for another pen, changed her mind, played with a drawer-pull – lifting the brass and letting it drop, once, twice, three times.

She said, 'I've got kids of my own now. I set limits, am probably too strict because I know what's out there. In ten years, I haven't touched anything stronger than Chardonnay. I love my husband. He's going places. My practice is rewarding – I don't see why any of that should be derailed because of mistakes I made twenty years ago.'

'Neither do I,' said Milo. 'I'm not taking notes, and none of that goes in any file. I just want to know what happened to Janie Ingalls that Friday night. And anything else you can tell me about the man who raped her downtown.'

'I told you everything I know about him.'

'Young and nice-looking with a nice car.'

'The car could've been Janie's fantasy.'

'How young?'

'She didn't say.'

'Race?'

'I assume he was white, because Janie didn't say he

wasn't. And she would've. She was a bit of a racist – got it from her father.'

'Any other physical description?'

'No.'

'A fancy car,' said Milo. 'What kind?'

'I think she said a Jaguar, but I can't be sure. With fur rugs – I do remember that because Janie talked about how her feet sank into the rug. But with Janie, who knows? I'm trying to tell you: she was always fantasizing.'

'About what?'

'Mostly about getting loaded and partying with rock stars.'

'That ever happen?'

She laughed. 'Not hardly. Janie was a sad little girl from the wrong part of Hollywood.'

'A young guy with a Jaguar,' said Milo. 'What else?'

'That's all I know,' said Waters. 'Really.'

'Which hotel did he take her to?'

'She just said it was downtown, in an area full of bums. She also said the guy seemed to know the place – the desk clerk tossed him a key the moment he walked in. But she didn't think he was actually staying there because the room he took her to didn't look lived in. He wasn't keeping any clothes there, and the bed wasn't even covered. Just a mattress. And rope. He'd put the rope in a dresser drawer.'

'She didn't try to escape when she saw that?'

Waters shook her head. 'He gave her a joint on the ride over. A huge one, high-grade, maybe laced with hash, because she was really floating and that's what hash usually did to her. She told me the whole experience was like watching someone else. Even when he pushed her down on the bed and started tying her up.'

'Her arms and legs and her neck.'

'That's where the marks were.'

'What happened next?'

Anger flashed behind Waters's eyeglass lenses. 'What do you think? He did his thing with her. Used every orifice.'

'She said that?'

'In cruder terms.' The gray in her eyes had deepened, as if an internal light had been dampened. 'She said she knew what he was doing, but didn't even feel it.'

'And she was blasé about it.'

'At first she was. Later – a few days later – she got loaded on Southern Comfort and started talking about it again. Not crying. Angry. At herself. Do you know what *really* bugged her? Not so much what he did to her, she was out of it during the whole thing. What made her mad was that when he was finished, he didn't drive her all the way back home, just dropped her off in East Hollywood and she had to walk a couple of miles. *That* ticked her off. But even there, she blamed herself. Said something along the lines of, "It must be something about me, makes people treat me like that. Even *him*." I said, "Who's him?" and she got this really furious look on her face, and said, *"Him*. Bowie." *That* freaked me out – first the deviant, now incest. I asked her how long that had been going on, but she clammed up again. I kept nagging her to tell me, and finally she told me to shut up or she'd tell my mother what a slut I was.'

She laughed.

'Which was a viable threat. I was no poster child for wholesome living. And even though my mother was no Betty Crocker, she wasn't like Bowie, she would've cared. She would've come down on me, hard.'

'Bowie didn't care,' said Milo.

'Bowie was scum, total lowlife. I guess that explains why Janie would do anything to avoid going home.'

I thought of the bareness of Janie's room. Said, 'Did she have a crash pad, or somewhere else she stayed?'

'Nowhere permanent. She'd sleep at my house, crash once in a while in those abandoned apartments north of Hollywood Boulevard. Sometimes she'd be gone for days and wouldn't tell me where she'd been. Still, the day after the party, after Janie and I had split up, I called Bowie. I *despised* the ground that lowlife walked on, but even so, I wanted to know Janie was okay. That's what I was trying to tell you: I made an attempt. But no one answered.'

'When did you split up?'

'Soon after we got there. I *cared* about Janie. We were both so screwed up, that was our bond. I guess I had a bad feeling about the party – about her just disappearing in the middle of all that commotion. I never really forgot about her. Years later, when I was in college and learned how to use a computer, I tried to find her. Then after I got to law school and had access to legal databases, I tapped into all kinds of municipal records. California and the neighboring states. Property rolls, tax files, death notices. But she was nowhere—'

She picked up Milo's card. 'L.A. Homicide means she was murdered in L.A. So why wasn't an L.A. death notice ever filed?'

'Good question, ma'am.'

'Oh,' said Waters. She sat back. 'This is more than a reopened case, isn't it? Something got really screwed up.'

Milo shrugged.

'Great. Wonderful. This is going to suck me in and screw me up no matter what I do, isn't it?'

'I'll do my best to prevent that, ma'am.'

'You sound almost sincere.' She rubbed her forehead, took a bottle of Advil out of a desk drawer, extricated a tablet, and swallowed it dry. 'What else do you want from me?'

'The party,' said Milo. 'How'd you and Janie hear about it, for starters.'

'Just street talk, kids talking. There was always plenty of that, especially as the weekend approached. Everyone trying to figure out the best way to party hearty. So many of us hated our homes, would do anything to be away. Janie and I were a twosome, party-wise. Sometimes we'd end up at squat-raves – promoters sneaking into an abandoned building, or using an outdoors spot – some remote corner of Griffith Park, or Hansen Dam. We're talking bare minimum in terms of entertainment: some tone-deaf band playing for free, cheap munchies, lots of drugs. *Mostly* lots of drugs. Because the promoters were really dealers, and their main goal was bulk sales. Other times, though, it would turn out to be a real party, in someone's house. An open invitation, or even if it wasn't, there was usually no problem crashing.'

She smiled. 'Occasionally, we got bounced, but a girl could almost always crash and get away with it.'

'The party that night was one of those,' said Milo. 'Someone's house.'

'Someone's *big* house, a mansion, and the talk on the street was *mucho* drugs. Janie and I figured we'd check it out. To us a trip to Bel Air was like blasting off to a different planet. Janie was going on and on about partying with rich kids, maybe finding a rich boyfriend who'd give her all the dope she wanted. As I said, she loved to fantasize. The truth is we were both such losers, no wheels, no money. So we did what we always did: hitched. We didn't even have the address, guessed once we got to Bel Air we'd figure it out. I picked Janie up at her place Friday afternoon, and we hung out on Hollywood Boulevard most of the day – playing arcade games, shop-lifting cosmetics, panhandling for spare change but we didn't get much. After dark, we walked back down to Sunset where the best hitching was, but the first corner we tried was near some hookers and they threatened to cut our asses, so we moved west – between La Brea and Fairfax, where all the guitar stores are. I remember that, because while we waited for a ride, we were looking at guitars in windows and saying how cool it would be if we started a girl band and got rich. No matter that neither of us had a lick of talent. Anyway, finally – we must've been waiting there over an hour – we got picked up.'

'What time?' said Milo.

'Must've been nine, ten.'

'Who picked you up?'

'A college student – nerdy type, said he went to Caltech, but he was heading to the U because he had a date with a girl there and that was really close to Bel Air. *He* had to tell us that, because we had no idea – I don't think either of us had ever been west of La Cienega, unless we were taking the bus straight to the beach, or, in my case, when I visited my father at the Navy base in Point Mugu. The nerd was a nice guy. Shy, probably picked us up on impulse and regretted it. Because we immediately started hassling him – turning the radio to our station, blasting it loud, teasing him – flirting. Asking him if he wanted to come to the party with us instead of some lame date with a college girl. Being real obnoxious. He got embarrassed, and that cracked us up. Also, we

331

were hoping he might take us all the way to the party, because we still had no idea where it was. So we kept nagging him, but he said no, he liked his girlfriend. I remember Janie getting really rude about that, saying something to the effect of "She's probably colder than ice. I can give you something she can't." That was the *wrong* thing to say. He stopped the car at Stone Canyon and Sunset and ordered us out. I started to, but Janie held me back, started ragging on him to take us to the house, and that just made him angrier. Janie was like that, she could be extremely pushy, had a real talent for getting on people's nerves. The nerd started shouting and shoved Janie and we got out and she flipped him off as he drove away.'

'Stone Canyon and Sunset. Close to the party.'

'*We* didn't know that. We were ignorant. And drunk. Back on the boulevard, we'd also boosted a bottle of Southern Comfort, had guzzled our way through most of it. I hated the stuff, to me it tasted like peaches and cough syrup. But Janie loved it. It was her favorite high. She said it was what Janis Joplin had been into and she was into Janis Joplin because she had some idea that her mom had been like Janis Joplin, back in the hippie days. That she'd named Janie after Janis.'

'Another fantasy,' I said.

She nodded. 'She needed them. Her mom abandoned her – ran away with a black guy when Janie was five or six, and Janie never saw her again. Maybe that's another reason Janie always made racist comments.'

Milo said, 'What'd the two of you do after you were dropped off?'

'Started walking up Stone Canyon and promptly got lost. There were no sidewalks, and the lighting was very bad. And no one was around to ask directions. All those incredible properties and not a soul in sight, none of the noises you hear in a real neighborhood. It was spooky. But we were having fun with it – an adventure. Once we saw a Bel Air Patrol car driving our way, so we hid behind some trees.'

She frowned. 'Complete idiocy. Thank God my boys aren't hearing this.'

'How'd you find the party?'

'We walked in circles for a while, finally ended up right where we started, back at Sunset. And that's when the second car picked us up. A Cadillac, turning onto Stone Canyon. The driver was a black guy, and I was sure Janie wouldn't want to get in – with her it was always "nigger" this, "nigger" that. But when the guy rolled down the window and shot us this big grin, and said, "You girls looking to party?" Janie was the first one in.'

'What do you remember about the driver?'

'Early twenties, tall, thin – for some reason when I think of him I always think of Jimi Hendrix. Not that he was Hendrix's spitting image, but there was a general resemblance. He had that rangy, mellow thing going on, loose and confident. Played his music really loud and moving his head in time.'

'A Cadillac,' said Milo.

'And a newer one but not a pimpmobile. Big conservative sedan, well taken care of, too. Shiny, fresh-smelling – sweet-smelling. Lilacs. Like it belonged to an old woman. I remember thinking that, wondering if he'd stolen it from an old woman. Because he sure didn't match the car, dressed the way he was in this ugly denim suit with rhinestones all over it, all these gold chains.'

'What color?'

'Something pale.'

Milo opened his briefcase, removed Willie Burns's mug shot, handed it across the desk.

Melinda Waters's eyes got big. 'That's him. *He's* the one who killed Janie?'

'He's someone we're looking for.'

'He's still out there?'

'Maybe.'

'Maybe? What does *that* mean?'

'It's been twenty years, and he was a heroin addict.'

'You're saying he'd have a poor life expectancy,' she said. 'But you're still looking for him . . . why *has* Janie's murder been reopened? What's the real reason?'

'I was the original detective on the case,' said Milo. 'I got transferred off. Now, I've been transferred back on.'

'Transferred back on by your department or you requested it yourself?' said Waters.

'Does it matter, ma'am?'

She smiled. 'It's personal, isn't it? You're trying to undo your own past.'

Milo smiled back, and Waters returned the mug shot. 'Wilbert Burns. So now I have a name.'

'He never introduced himself?'

'He called himself our new friend. I knew he was a junkie as well as a dealer. From how spacey he was – slurring his words. Driving *really* slow. His music was junkie music – slow jazz, this really draggy trumpet. Janie tried to change the station, but he put his hand on hers and she didn't try again.'

'How'd you know he was a dealer?' said Milo.

'He showed us his wares. Carried one of those men's purses and had it on the seat next to him. When we got in, he put it in his lap and after we were driving for a while, he zipped it open, and said, "How about a taste of something sweet, ladies?" Inside were envelopes of pills and little baggies full of white stuff – I couldn't tell you if it was coke or heroin. *That* stuff I stayed away from. For me it was just grass and alcohol, once in a while acid.'

'What about Janie?'

'Janie had no boundaries.'

'Did she sample Burns's wares?'

'Not in the car, but maybe later. Probably later. Because she and Burns got something going on right from the beginning. All three of us were in the front seat, Janie alongside Burns and me next to the door. The minute he started driving she started in – flipped her hair in his face, rested her hand on his leg, started moving it up.'

'How'd Burns react to that?'

'He loved it. Said, "Ooh, baby," stuff like that. Janie was giggling, both of them were laughing at nothing in particular.'

'Despite her racism,' I said.

'I couldn't believe it. I elbowed her a couple of times, as in, "What's going on?" But she ignored me. Burns drove to the party – he knew exactly where it was, but we had to park up the road because there were so many cars there.'

'Did he say anything about the party?' said Milo.

'He said he knew the people throwing it, that they were rich but cool, it was going to be the finest of the fine. Then, when we got there, he said something along the lines of, "Maybe the President'll show up." Because the house had huge pillars, like the White House. Janie thought that was hilarious. I was pretty put out by then, felt like Janie was shutting me out.'

'What happened next?'

'We went inside the house. It was vacant and rancid-smelling and pretty much trashed, with beer cans and bottles and Lord knows what else all over the place. Kids running around everywhere, no band, just loud tapes – a bunch of different stereos set up all over the place, really cacophonous, but no one seemed to care. Everyone was blasted, kids were walking around looking dazed, bumping into each other, girls were on their knees, going down on guys right in the middle of the dance floor, there'd be couples dancing and right next to them, other couples would be screwing, getting kicked, stepped on. Burns seemed to know a lot of people, got plenty of high fives as we walked through the crowd. Then this funny-looking, kind of dumpy girl showed up out of nowhere and latched on to him.'

'Funny-looking how?'

'Short, fat, zits. Odd – spaced-out. But he immediately got all kissy-kissy with her, and I could see Janie didn't like that.' Waters shook her head. 'She'd known the guy all of fifteen minutes, and she was jealous.'

'Janie do anything about that?'

'No, she just got this ticked-off look on her face. I could read it because I knew Janie. Burns didn't see it – or he didn't care. Threw one arm around the dumpy girl, the other around Janie, and led both of them off. That little purse of his bouncing on his shoulder.'

'And you?'

'I stayed behind. Someone handed me a beer and hands started groping me. Not delicately. It was dark, and whoever was doing it started to get rough, yanking at my clothes. I broke away, started walking around, looked for a quiet room to mellow out in, but there was none. Every inch of that place was party-time. Guys kept putting their hands all over me, once in a while someone would pull me hard onto the dance floor and rather than fight it, I'd just dance for a while, then make my escape. Then the lights went out and the house got even darker and I could barely see where I was stepping. The Southern Comfort in my system wasn't helping, either. I felt nauseous, dizzy, wanted to get out of there, looked some more for Janie, couldn't find her, and got angry at her for bailing on me. Finally, I told myself *forget* her and the next time someone pulled me onto a dance floor, I danced for a while. And when someone offered me a pill, I swallowed it. The next thing I remember is waking up on the floor of an upstairs bathroom, hearing shouts that the cops were going to roust the party and running out of there along with everyone else – it was like a stampede. Somehow I ended up in the back of someone's truck, bouncing along Sunset.'

'Whose truck?'

'A bunch of guys. Surfer types. They ended up at the beach, Santa Monica or Malibu, I couldn't tell you which. We partied some more, and I fell asleep on the sand. The next morning, I woke up and I was alone. Cold and wet and sick to my stomach. The sun was rising over the ocean and I suppose it was gorgeous but all I could think about was how lousy I felt. Then I thought about my father – stationed up at Mugu – and I started crying and got it into my head that I had to go see him. It took me four hitches to get up there and when I reached the base the sentry wouldn't let me through the gate. I started crying again. It had been a long time since I'd seen my dad. He'd remarried, and his new wife hated me. Or at least that's what my mother was always telling me.

Whatever the truth was, he'd pretty much stopped calling. I bawled like a baby, and the sentry made a call and told me my dad wasn't there, he'd shipped out to Turkey three days before. I just broke down and I guess the sentry felt sorry for me because he gave me all the money in his pocket – thirty-three dollars and forty-nine cents.' She smiled. 'That I remember precisely.'

Reaching under her glasses, she fingered the inside corners of her eyes. 'Finally, someone was being nice to me. I never thanked him, never knew his name. Walked back to PCH, stuck out my thumb, caught a ride with some Mexicans heading over to Ventura to pick cabbage, just kept thumbing my way up the coast. My first stop was Santa Cruz, and I stayed there a while because it was beautiful and there was this retro-hippie thing going on, plenty of free food and parks to sleep in. Eventually, I moved on to San Francisco, Crescent City, Oregon, Seattle, back down to Sacramento. The next ten years are kind of a blur. Finally, I got it together – you don't want to know the boring details.'

'Like I said, we want to maintain your privacy.'

Melinda Waters laughed. 'Thanks for the thought.'

twenty-six

Milo asked her a few more questions – more gently, unproductively – then we left her sitting at her desk looking dazed. As I drove out of the lot, the smoke from the Italian restaurant's chimney caught my eye.

'Want lunch?' I said.

'I guess . . . yeah, why not.'

'No fast food, though. Let's aim high. We deserve it.'

'For what?'

'Making some progress.'

'You think so?'

The taverna across the street was divided into four small, whitewashed rooms, each warmed by a beehive-shaped fireplace and topped by low ceilings striped with rough-hewn logs. We ordered beer, a mixed antipasto, spaghetti with capers and olives and garlic, and osso bucco from a lithe young woman who seemed genuinely happy to serve us.

When she left, Milo said, 'Progress.'

'We can place Janie with Willie Burns and Caroline Cossack the night of the murder. You don't have doubts she was the dumpy girl, do you?'

He shook his head.

I said, 'Melinda's story also supplies a possible motive: jealousy. Caroline had a thing for Burns, thought Janie was moving in on her territory.'

'The eternal triangle leading to *that*?'

'The eternal triangle combined with dope and psychopathology and a low-inhibition party scene and Janie's racism. No shortage of triggers. And something else fits: Janie's murder presented as a sadistic sex killing and we've been wondering why other victims haven't shown up. Because cold, sexual sadists don't quit. But if the murder resulted from a passion-of-the-moment flare-up, a sole victim would make sense.'

'Janie in the wrong place at the wrong time.'

'Melinda's description of Janie makes her the perfect victim: drugged-out, not too bright, prone to fantasy, a tendency to irritate people, a history of sexual abuse. Throw enough ingredients into the stew, toss in a few careless "niggers," and who knows.'

'What do you think about Janie's blasé reaction to the downtown rape?'

'Doesn't surprise me,' I said. 'People expect rape victims to react the way they do on TV. And sometimes that happens. But pseudocalm is pretty common. Protective numbness. Given Janie's victimization by her father, it makes perfect sense.'

'For her it woulda been more of the same,' he said. 'Poor kid.'

He picked at his food, slid his plate away. 'There's a discrepancy between Janie's description of the rape as Melinda remembers it and what Schwinn told me. According to Melinda, the rapist dropped Janie off a couple of miles from her home. Schwinn's informant told *him* Janie'd been dumped in an alley and found unconscious by some wino.'

'That could've been Janie prettying up the picture,' I said. 'Grasping for a shred of dignity.'

'Pathetic,' he said.

'Any idea who Schwinn's informant was?'

'Nope. He never gave me a single bit of insider info. I kept waiting for him to clue me in, to help me learn the ropes, but we just went from call to call and when the time came for paperwork, he went home. And now here he is, pulling strings from the grave . . . If Janie made up the part about walking home, maybe the young guy in a Jag was bogus, too. Her not wanting to admit he was a drooling, scabby hunchback in a jalopy? The alleged wino.'

'Could be. But if she was being truthful, the Jag story's interesting. A young guy with hot wheels checking into a fleabag hotel wouldn't be safe. Unless he had connections. As in Daddy owns the place. And Janie told Melinda the clerk seemed to know the guy. It might be interesting to know who held the deed on fleabag hotels twenty years ago.'

'You're thinking some real estate honcho. The Cossacks. Or Larner.' He told me about Playa del Sol, rubbed his face. 'I remember a few of the hotels down there. The scuzziest ones were on or near Main, between Third and Seventh. SRO flops, full of winos. The Exeter, the Columbus – there must've been a good half dozen, mostly propped up by Federal subsidies . . . so now I'm supposed to solve a twenty-year-old rape with no victim as well as a murder. Don't think so, Alex.'

'Just tossing out suggestions,' I said. 'Isn't that what you pay me for?'

He forced a smile. 'Sorry. I'm feeling hemmed in.

Unable to do my usual investigative thing because it puts me in the crosshairs.'

'Paris Bartlett and the call from Personnel.'

'And the level of the players. That dinner with Obey, I don't imagine they were convening to crochet samplers. Bacilla and Horne live for graft, and if Walt Obey's involved in something, it has lots of zeros attached to it. Broussard wasn't at the restaurant, but his hand's been in this right from the beginning. He's Obey's neighbor, and Obey was one of his biggest supporters. All that makes me a *flea*. And guess what: a rumor's circulating around the department about an HIV-positive detective about to retire soon. "Stay healthy," huh?'

'Oh my,' I said. 'Subtle.'

'Cop's subtlety. We train with nightsticks, not scalpels. Looks like I couldn't have picked a worse time to stir the ashes, Alex. The hell of it is I've accomplished nothing . . . you finished? Let's get back to the smog. This city's too damn pretty.'

During the drive back to Albuquerque, he was glum and unreachable. The taverna's food had been excellent, but I'd finished more of my plate than he had, and that was a first.

He spent the flight to L.A. dozing. When we were back in the Seville, he said, 'Finding Melinda was progress in terms of motive, means, and opportunity. But what the hell's all that worth when I have no idea where my suspects are? If I had to bet, my money would be on Willie Burns in some unmarked grave. The money folks behind Caroline would have seen him as a threat, and even if they never got to him, there was his heroin habit. Crazy Caroline, who could also be dead, or anywhere

342

from the Bahamas to Belize. Even if I found her, what could I prove? They'd bring in one of your colleagues, and she'd go right back to some plush-padded room.'

'Sounds bleak,' I said.

'Some therapist you are.'

'Reality therapy.'

'Reality is the curse of the sane.'

I took Sepulveda to Venice, got onto Motor Avenue going south, drove past Achievement House.

'Talk about subtle,' he said.

'It's a shortcut.'

'There are no shortcuts. Life is tedious and brutish . . . it can't hurt to look into those SROs. Something I can do without attracting attention. But don't expect anything. And don't get *yourself* in trouble thinking you can fight my battles.'

'Trouble, as in?'

'As in anything.'

Robin had left a message on my machine, sounding hurried and detached. The tour had moved on to Vancouver and she was staying at the Pacific Lodge Hotel. I called the number and connected to her room. A happy male voice answered.

'Sheridan,' I said.

'Yes?'

'It's Alex Delaware.'

'Oh. Hi. I'll go get Robin.'

'Where is she?'

'In the bathroom.'

'How's my dog?'

'Uh . . . great—'

343

'The reason I'm asking is because you seemed pretty in tune with him. Showing up prepared with a Milk-Bone. Very intuitive.'

'He – I like dogs.'

'Do you?' I said.

'Well, yeah.'

'Well, good for you.'

Silence. 'Let me tell Robin you're on the phone.'

'Gee, thanks,' I said, but he'd put down the receiver, and I was talking to dead air.

She came on the line a few moments later. 'Alex?'

'Hi,' I said.

'What's wrong?'

'With what?'

'Sheridan said you sounded upset.'

'Sheridan would know,' I said. 'Being a sensitive guy and all that.'

Silence. 'What's going on, Alex?'

'Nothing.'

'It's not nothing,' she said. 'Every time I call you're more . . .'

'Insensitive?' I said. 'As opposed to you-know-who?'

Longer silence. 'You can't be serious.'

'About what?'

'About *him*.' She laughed.

'Glad to amuse you.'

'Alex,' she said, 'if you only knew – I can't believe this. What's gotten into you?'

'Tough times bring out the best in me.'

'Why in the world would you even think that?' She laughed again, and that was probably what set me off.

'The guy shows up with a damned dog biscuit,' I said.

'Let me tell you, hon, men are pigs. Altruism like that always comes with strings—'

'You are being totally *ridiculous*—'

'Am I? Each time I call your room, he's right there—'

'Alex, this is *absurd*!'

'Okay, then. Sorry.' But there was nothing remorseful in my tone, and she knew it.

'What's gotten into you, Alex?'

I thought about that. Then a rush of anger clogged my throat, and out it came: 'I suppose I can be forgiven a bit of absurdity. The last time you left me didn't turn out so great.'

Silence.

'Oh . . . Alex.' Her voice broke on my name.

My jaw locked.

She said, 'I can't do this.'

Then she hung up.

I sat there, perversely satisfied, with a dead brain and a mouth full of bile. Then that sinking feeling set in: *Idiot, idiot!* I redialed her room. No answer. Tried the hotel operator again, was informed that Ms Castagna had gone out.

I pictured her running through the lobby, tear-streaked. What was the weather in Vancouver? Had she remembered her coat? Had Sheridan followed, ever ready with consolation?

'Sir?' said the operator. '*Would* you like her voice mail?'

'Uh . . . sure, why not.'

I was connected, listened to Robin's voice deliver a canned message. Waited for the beep.

Chose my words carefully, but ended up choking and letting the phone drop from my hand.

★ ★ ★

I moved to my office, drew the drapes, sat in gray-brown darkness, listened to the throbbing in my head.

A fine fix you've gotten yourself into, Alexander . . . the hell of it was Bert Harrison had warned me.

Bert was a wise man. Why hadn't I listened?

What to do . . . send flowers? No, that would insult Robin's intelligence, make matters worse.

Two tickets to Paris . . .

It took a long time before I was able to shove my feelings somewhere south of my ankles, turn suitably numb.

I stared at the wall, visualized myself as a speck of dirt, worked hard at disappearing.

I booted up the computer and downloaded Google, because that search engine could locate a hamburger joint on Pluto.

'Walter Obey' pulled up three hundred and some-odd hits, 90 percent of them pertaining to the billionaire, with a quarter of those repetitive. Most were newspaper and business journal articles, about evenly divided between coverage of Obey's philanthropic activities and his financial dealings.

Walter and Barbara Obey had contributed to the Philharmonic, the Music Center, Planned Parenthood, the Santa Monica Mountains Conservancy, the Humane Society, shelters for homeless youth, a slew of foundations raging battle against tragic diseases. The Sierra Club, too, which I found interesting for a developer.

I came up with no connection to organized sports nor to any link between any of the aborted plans to bring sports teams to L.A. In none of the articles was Obey's name mentioned alongside those of the Cossack brothers or the Larners. He and his wife socialized very little and lived an understated life – for billionaires. A single, albeit baronial, residence in Hancock Park, no live-in help, off-the-rack clothing, no expensive hobbies. Barbara drove a Volvo and volunteered at her church. If the press could be believed, both Obeys were as wholesome as milk.

One item, a year-old *Wall Street Journal* piece, did catch my eye: one of Obey's development companies, a privately held corporation named Advent Builders, had invested in a huge parcel of land south of the L.A. city limits – an unincorporated county area where the developer planned to build an entire community, complete with ethnically diverse, low-to-middle-income housing, public schools, well-landscaped commercial districts and industrial parks, 'comprehensive recreational facilities.'

Obey had taken ten years to accumulate fifteen thousand acres of contiguous lots and had spent millions to rid the earth of toxic waste left behind by a long-defunct county power depot. Unlike other empire-builders, he'd considered the environmental impact of his projects from the beginning, was out to crown his career with something culturally significant.

The new city was to be named Esperanza – Spanish for 'hope.'

I combined 'Esperanza' with each of the Cossack brothers' names and the Larners but came up with nothing. Tossing John G. Broussard into the mix proved no more fruitful. I tried 'Advent Properties' and 'Advent.' Still nothing on the Cossacks and the Larners, but a back-page construction journal article informed me that L.A.'s police chief had been hired as a security consultant to the Esperanza project. Broussard, hamstrung by city regulations, was working for free, but private shares in Advent had been gifted to the chief's wife and his only child, daughter Joelle, a corporate attorney with a white-shoe downtown firm.

Broussard hadn't shown up at the private dinner but Milo's hunch was right on: the chief's hand was in everything.

The bitter aftertaste of my bad behavior with Robin kept rising like vomitus as I worked hard at concentrating on Obey and Broussard and the others and wondering what it could possibly mean.

'Comprehensive recreational facilities' could mean playgrounds for kids, or it was a buzzword for bringing pro football back to the L.A. environs.

Billionaire with a big dream – I could see that being the crowning glory of Obey's long career. And it made good sense to place the top cop on your masthead.

But if the PR about Obey's righteous mien and the size of his personal fortune was accurate, why would he waste time with the Cossacks, who alienated their neighbors and couldn't seem to get any projects off the ground? And in the case of the Larners, the association would be even more hazardous – they were outright hustlers tainted by the Playa del Sol debacle.

Unless Obey's balance sheets weren't as glowing as the press believed, and he needed financial backup for his dream. Even billionaires could lose sight of assets and debits, and Obey had spent a decade buying up land and financing and detoxifying his holdings without a single spadeful of Esperanza dirt dug.

Big dreams often meant cataclysmic problems.

I switched to several financial databases and probed

for thorns in Obey's numerous gardens. At least seven separate corporations were listed under his leadership, including Advent. But only one outfit was publicly traded, a commercial leasing company named BWO Financing.

BWO. Probably stood for Barbara and Walt Obey. Homey. From everything I could tell, the company was doing great, with common stock trading at 95 percent of its high, preferred units paying consistent dividends, and solid ratings from Standard & Poor.

Still, Wall Street's top analysts had been known to be caught with their pin-striped trousers around their ankles, because, at root, they were dependent upon what companies told them. And because their interests lay in selling stock.

Was Obey's empire teetering and had he sought out the Cossacks and the Larners for support? Did the Cossacks and the Larners have enough to offer Obey?

Bacilla and Horne's involvement was puzzling. Obey's planned city was located outside city limits, so what use could a pair of councilmen be?

Unless plans had changed and the focus had shifted back to downtown.

Nothing really sat right. Then I thought of the cement that held it all together:

John G. Broussard's aid in covering up the Ingalls murder implied he'd had connections to the Cossacks and maybe the Larners. Walt Obey was one of the chief's major patrons. Maybe Broussard had put them all together, earned himself a big fat finder's fee in addition to the private stock assigned to his wife and daughter.

Had the chief concealed a substantial lump sum payment from public scrutiny? With Obey's multiple corporations as shield, concealing cash would've been easy enough.

Payoff. Payback. For all his power and status, John G. Broussard remained a civil servant whose salary and pension by themselves would relegate him to upper-middle-class status, at best. Playing with the big boys could mean so much more.

I imagined the deal: Walt Obey salvaging his dream, the Cossacks and the Larners offered a big-time social and economic leap upward, from strip malls and parking lots to the grandest of monuments.

For Chief Broussard and the councilmen, good old cash.

So much at stake.

And now Milo had the opportunity to blow it all to smithereens.

twenty-seven

'Interesting theory,' said Milo. 'I was wondering along the same lines, except that night Obey's body language was more grantor than grantee. Bacilla and Horne were kissing up to him big-time.'

I said, 'Bacilla and Horne would be supplicants any way you look at it because their political life depends on fat cats. And Obey's been alpha-dog with politicians for a long time. But you never had a chance to watch him interact with the Cossacks.'

'No,' he admitted.

We were at his kitchen table. I'd spent a miserable hour mulling how to mend things with Robin, had made another attempt to reach her at the hotel. Out. When I reached Milo he was on the way home from the Hall of Records with a briefcase full of photocopies. He'd combed through the property tax files and found fourteen fleabag hotels operating near Skid Row twenty years ago, but no ownership by the Cossacks or any of the other players.

'So much for that.' I scanned the tax roster he'd spread out between us. Then a name jumped out at me. A trio of Central Avenue hotels – the Excelsior, the Grande Royale, the Crossley – owned by Vance Coury and Associates.

'A kid by the name of Coury hung out with the Cossacks and Brad Larner back in high school,' I said. 'They all belonged to some club called the King's Men.'

'Coury,' he said. 'Never heard of him.'

He brought his laptop over from the laundry room office. A search yielded three hits on two men named Vance Coury. An eleven-year-old *Times* piece described a Vance Coury, sixty-one, of Westwood, as having been brought up by the city attorney on slumlord charges. Coury was described as 'the owner of several buildings in the downtown and Westlake districts who had failed repeatedly to correct numerous building and safety violations.' One year prior to his indictment, Coury had been convicted of similar charges and sentenced, by a creative judge, to live in one of his own buildings for two weeks. He'd rehabbed a single unit in two days and set up housekeeping under protection by an armed guard. But Coury's empathy quotient hadn't risen a notch: he'd done nothing to improve his tenants' living conditions, and the judge lost patience. A follow-up article three weeks later reported that Coury had avoided a felony trial by collapsing in his attorney's office and dying of a stroke. An accompanying headshot showed a rail-thin, silver-haired, silver-bearded man with the defiant/frightened eyes of one scrambling to remember his latest tall tale.

Vance Coury, Jr, appeared in a two-year-old Sunday *Daily News* item, having contributed the custom paint job to the winning entry in a California hot rod contest. Coury, forty-two, owned an auto body shop in Van Nuys specializing in 'ground-up restoration of classic and specialty vehicles,' and his outfit had sprayed forty-five coats on a chopped and blown 1938 Dodge Roadster known as the Purple People Eater.

'Another father and son duo,' said Milo.

'Father owns the hotel, son makes use of the premises,' I said. 'And son was a pal of the Cossacks. Meaning he might very well have been at that party. Which turns the prism a whole new way. What if it went down this way: Janie separated from Melinda and tagged along with Burns and Caroline. Burns gave her some dope, introduced her to some of his rich-kid pals. All of a sudden, Janie finds herself face to face with Vance Coury, the Prince Charming who tied her up and raped her and dumped her in an alley like garbage. She freaks out, there's an altercation, and Coury, maybe with a little help from his friends, spirits Janie away before she can cause a scene. They subdue her and bring her somewhere secluded, and Coury thinks, hmm, why not take advantage of the situation? We know he's into bondage, and what would be more arousing than helplessness? He does his thing, and this time the others join in. It gets out of hand, goes really bad. Now they need to dump the body. Because of his father's properties, Coury's familiar with downtown, and he picks a spot he knows is quiet and relatively deserted late at night: the Beaudry on-ramp. He takes a buddy or two along, which would explain taking the risk of leaving Janie out in the open. With one person as lookout and to help with the body, the danger would've been minimized.'

Milo stared at the tax roster and placed his finger on Coury's name. 'Boys being boys. The Cossack brothers themselves, not just Caroline.'

'Them, Coury, Brad Larner, maybe the other members of the King's Men – I think their names were Chapman and Hansen.'

'A high school club.'

'A party club,' I said. 'Noted for liquid refreshment, high jinks and other good fun. Janie's murder took place a few years after graduation, but that doesn't mean the fun stopped.'

'So where do Caroline and Burns fit into a gang-bang killing?'

'Both had reason to dislike Janie. So they could've participated. The fact that Caroline was stashed at Achievement House indicates her involvement. So does Burns's disappearance. A gang-bang killing also meshes with the absence of a sequel. It took the right combination to turn things bad: dope, a defiant victim, and the ultimate adolescent drug – group conformity.'

'Adolescent?' he said. 'All the males were in their twenties.'

'Arrested development.'

'Funny you should say that. When I saw the Cossacks' current house, that's exactly what went through my mind.'

He described the eyesore mansion, the cars, the history of neighbor complaints.

'It also matches something else you said early on,' he added. 'Women tend to be affiliative. Caroline wouldn't have had the drive or the strength to slice Janie up by herself, but once Janie was incapacitated, a few cuts and burns would've been easy enough.'

'But Caroline's involvement – and Willie Burns's – created a new level of risk for the boys: two weak links who couldn't be counted on to keep their mouths shut. Caroline because of her mental instability and Burns because he was a junkie with a tendency to flap his gums. What if Burns found himself in a desperate situation – poor cash flow and a strong heroin jones? What if he tried to scratch up some money by blackmailing the others? To a street guy like Burns, a bunch of rich white boys with a very nasty secret would've seemed perfect marks. That would explain Michael Larner's rage at Burns's disappearance. Burns had made himself a very viable threat to Larner's son, and now he was gone. Burns blackmailing would also explain his skipping on Boris Nemerov, even though he'd always been dependable before. Given all that, his paranoid rant about people being after him when he phoned Boris Nemerov makes perfect sense. Burns wasn't worried about going to jail. He'd been part of a brutal murder and had gotten on the wrong side of his coparticipants.'

Milo flipped his notepad open. 'Chapman and Hansen. Any first names?'

'All I read in the yearbook were initials, and I don't remember them.'

'High school,' he said. 'Oh, the glory days.'

'They *were* Garvey Cossack's glory days. He lied about being class treasurer.'

'Preparing for a career in finance . . . okay, let's go have a look at that yearbook.'

Within moments of our arrival, we'd filled out details on the other King's Men.

At eighteen, Vance Coury, Jr had been a good-looking, dark-haired boy with heavy, black eyebrows, a curled-lip smile that bordered on sneer, and a piercing stare. A certain type of girl would've thought him hot.

'Teenage Lothario,' I said. Just as Janie described. 'Despite what Melinda said, she wasn't always fantasizing. Ten to one his dad owned a Jag twenty years ago.'

As with the Cossacks and Brad Larner, Coury's

out-of-class interests had been limited: auto shop monitor and the King's Men.

L. Chapman turned out to be moon-faced Luke, a hulking, fair-haired boy with a vacant mien.

Nothing on his plate but the King's Men.

The last boy, Nicholas Dale Hansen, was a different story. A clean-cut, button-down youth with an ever-so-serious expression, 'Nick' Hansen had participated in the Junior Chamber of Commerce, Art Club, and the Boy Scouts. He'd also made honor roll for two semesters.

'The smart one in the group,' said Milo. 'Wonder if he was smart enough not to be there.'

'Or the brains behind the organization.'

We got hold of the *Who's Who* that had helped me locate the boys in the first place. No bios on anyone but Garvey Cossack, Jr.

'Coury's a Van Nuys fender-bender,' said Milo, 'so no big surprise there. And old Luke doesn't look like the brightest bulb in the chandelier. But personally, I'm disappointed in Nick Hansen. Maybe he didn't fulfill his promise.'

We left the library and sat out in front on a stone bench that ran along the reflecting pond flanking the entrance. I watched students come and go as Milo appropriated the identity of a Southwest Division Auto Theft detective and phoned DMV. It took some prodding to get the clerk to go back two decades, but when Milo hung up he'd filled two pages with scrawls: makes, models, owners, and addresses of record.

'Vance Coury, Sr, owned a Jaguar Mark 10 sedan, a Lincoln Continental, and a Camaro.'

'So Janie was right on,' I said. 'The Lincoln was probably the missus's wheels, and Vance, Jr drove the

Camaro. When he was out to impress girls, he took Daddy's car with the deep pile carpeting. Something that would set them at ease before he got them up in that room and pulled out the rope.'

'He's got himself a slew of wheels, now: eight registered vehicles, mostly classics, including a couple of vintage Ferraris.'

'You said the Cossacks had a Ferrari out in front of their house. Maybe the King's Men never went dormant, and Coury's bunking in.'

'Coury's home address is listed in Tarzana, but could be,' he said. 'And guess what: I was wrong about Nicholas Dale Hansen not living up to his capabilities. Drives a BMW 700 and lives in Beverly Hills on North Roxbury. Guess he just didn't want a bio.'

'Modest,' I said.

'Or he shuns the limelight,' he said. 'Because who knows what too much attention can do.'

'What about Luke Chapman?'

'Nothing on him. Never owned a car in California.'

'Meaning he hasn't lived in California for a while,' I said. 'Maybe the family moved out of state after high school. Or it's another disappearing act, voluntary or otherwise. If he was as dull as his picture implies, he would've been considered another weak link.'

'Snipping off loose ends,' he said.

'That makes me think of two other ends, both apparent accidents: Bowie Ingalls hitting that tree and Pierce Schwinn hitting that rock.'

'Oh, your imagination,' he said. 'So how'd the boys get the parents to stash Caroline?'

'She'd been the problem child for years. If she poisoned that dog, her parents probably had a sense the

357

problem was serious. If the boys came to them feigning horror at something terrible Caroline had done, they might very well have believed it.'

'The *boys*,' he said. 'Bunch of sleazes and that Boy Scout. *He's* the one who interests me.'

'Merit badge for murder,' I said. 'What a concept.'

Walking back to the Seville, he said, 'Something that smells of evidence, I'm starting to feel like a real-life detective, gee whiz. The question is where to take it. Can't exactly march into the boardroom at Cossack Development and accuse the brothers of being scumbag killers.'

'Can't confront John G. Broussard, either.'

'A working cop never mentions John G. Broussard in polite company. Did you see that piece in the paper about him this morning?'

'No.'

'The mayor approved him for a raise but the police commission has the authority and they say no way. Last few weeks, the *Times* has printed a few other less-than-complimentary comments about John G.'s management style.'

'Broussard's on the way out?' I said.

'Good chance. He must've finally annoyed the wrong people.' As we neared the parking structure, his cell-phone squawked and he slapped it to his ear. 'Hello – hey, how's it – what? *When?* Where are you? Okay, just stay right there – no, just stay put, I'm with Alex over at the U, we'll be there in ten.'

He hung up and sped up to a jog. 'That was Rick. Someone stole the Porsche.'

'Where?' I said, matching his pace.

'Right out of the doctors' lot at Cedars. You know how he loves that car . . . he sounded shook up. C'mon, let's go.'

I broke speed laws and made it to the Cedars-Sinai complex in fifteen minutes. Rick was waiting at the corner of Beverly Boulevard and George Burns Avenue wearing a long white coat over blue scrubs. Except for surgeon's fingers that never ceased flexing, he was motionless.

As I pulled to the curb, Milo bounded out of the Seville, rushed to Rick's side, and listened as Rick talked. At a casual glance, they appeared to be two middle-aged men exhibiting no obvious physical affection but the bond between them was obvious to me and I wondered if anyone else could see it. Wondered about something else, too: Hot Dog Heaven, where Paris Bartlett had accosted Milo, was only a block away, and the fast-food stand's picnic tables afforded a full frontal view of the hospital. Sometimes Milo dropped in at Cedars to have lunch with Rick, or just to say hi. Had he been watched, and if so, for how long?

Then I thought about the two cops gabbing in the ER cubicle. Supposedly unaware of Rick's presence in the next booth. But maybe the chat about the HIV detective forced to retire *had* been for his benefit.

Throw in Bartlett's little display, the call from LAPD Personnel, and a stolen car, and it added up to psychological warfare.

As Milo and Rick talked, I sat in the driver's seat and looked around. All I saw was a flood of anonymous faces and cars, the usual L.A. ratio of one pedestrian to five hundred vehicles.

Rick stopped talking, slumped a bit. Milo patted his back and eyed the Seville. Rick got in back and Milo returned to the front passenger seat.

'Hey, Alex,' said Rick.

'Sorry about the car.'

He grimaced. 'An alarm and a steering lock, and it's gone.'

Milo glanced back at him. His eyes were cold, his neck cords were taut, and his mandible jutted like that of a fighting cur, straining to enter the pit.

I said, 'When did it happen?'

Rick said, 'I got to work at five A.M., didn't come out until two P.M., so sometime in between.'

'He thinks he might've been followed,' said Milo, 'driving to work.'

'It was probably nothing,' said Rick. 'But that early, you don't expect too many cars on the street and there was a set of headlights behind me when I pulled out to San Vincente and it stayed with me until I got to Third Street.'

'And you have no idea exactly when that started?' said Milo.

Rick sighed. 'I told you, no. I had an emergency splenectomy at six. My focus was on getting psyched up.' Rick's voice was steady. His fingers kept flexing. 'I really don't think it was anything, Milo. Probably some other early bird.'

'How many other cars do you usually see when you hit the early shift, Rick?'

'Usually none. But sometimes one or two – as I said, I don't pay attention. If the Porsche hadn't been ripped off, if you hadn't asked me about being tailed, I'd never have given it a thought.'

'*Give* it a thought,' said Milo. 'We've both got to think.'

'About what?'

'Watching our backs. Maybe even a temporary change of address.'

'Oh, come on,' said Rick.

'I'm serious.'

Silence. Rick said, 'Well, first things first. I need a rental car. Alex, would you be so kind as to drive me over to—'

'*I'll* take you,' said Milo. 'Drop us off a block from our house, Alex.' To Rick: 'You wait while I check out the premises. I'll pick you up in the Taurus and drive you to Budget. No, let's use another company, just to play it safe. I want to minimize any links between us.'

'You *can't* be serious,' said Rick.

'Drive, Alex.'

'Minimize *links*?' said Rick.

'Sorry,' said Milo. 'Right now putting a layer of separation between you and me is the nicest thing I can do for you.'

twenty-eight

Alex dropped Rick and Milo around the corner and drove off. Milo left Rick waiting under a Brazilian floss tree and walked to his house with his eyes on high beam. The rental Taurus sat alone in the driveway, and he gave it a cursory once-over. Nothing weird. Slipping behind the car, he made his way up the driveway, unholstered his gun, and unlatched the back door, feeling foolish. The alarm buzzed, a positive sign. He disarmed the system, covered each room as if stalking a suspect. Playing Robocop in his own domicile. Jesus.

Nothing had been disturbed that he could see and the junk in the spare bedroom closet was stacked just as he'd left it: on top of the movable floorboards that concealed the safe. Still, the prickly heat of paranoia coursed up and down his back. He hadn't relaxed a bit by the time he got in the Taurus and drove back to Rick.

Rick said, 'Everything okay, I assume.'

'Seems to be.'

'Milo, the Porsche probably had nothing to do with anything.'

'Maybe.'

'You don't think so?'

'I don't know what to think.'

'Well, given that,' said Rick, 'let's not get overly dramatic. After I get a rental, I'm going back to work, and afterward I'm coming home.'

Milo started up the Taurus but kept it in park. Rick cleared his throat, the way he did when he got impatient.

Milo said, 'What'd you do this morning, work-wise?'

'Why?'

'How many surgeries did you perform?'

'Three—'

'Was I there in the OR, telling you which scalpel to use?'

'Listen,' said Rick. Then he went silent.

Milo tapped the steering wheel.

Rick said, 'Fine, I accede to your superior knowledge of the rotten side of life. But expertise doesn't mean infallibility, Milo. If someone wanted to intimidate you, why steal *my* car?'

Because that's the way they think.

Milo didn't answer.

Rick said, 'It was a car theft, plain and simple. You always told me if a pro wanted the Porsche, he could get it no matter what I did.'

'There are pros, and there are pros,' said Milo.

'Meaning what?'

'Meaning I don't know what really happened to the Porsche, but I do know that I want you away from my mess. So stop giving me a hard time even though you think I'm being melodramatic. Worse comes to worst, I was an idiot and you were inconvenienced. What kind of rental car do you want?'

Rick frowned. 'Doesn't matter.' He tapped the Taurus's dashboard. 'One of these will be fine.'

'Anything but one of these,' said Milo. 'I don't want you in something that could be confused with mine. How about an SUV? This city, that's like joining the ant swarm.'

'As if I care,' said Rick, folding his arms across his chest. 'Sure, an SUV. Maybe I'll go hiking.'

'Not a bad idea. Take some time away from the city.'

Rick's head whipped around. 'You're serious. You really want me gone.'

'I want you safe.'

'Forget it, big guy, just dismiss the thought. I've got a solid week of shift plus built-in overtime. We've got bills to pay.'

'Get real,' said Milo. 'When's the last time we worried about making the bills?'

'Not since the Porsche was paid up. But now I'll probably need a new car and that'll mean new monthlies and we were talking about taking some time off and going to Europe this summer, so I need to stockpile revenue.'

Milo didn't answer.

Rick said, 'You *were* serious about Europe? I've been organizing my entire schedule with an eye toward taking a month off.'

'I was serious.'

'Maybe we should travel right now.'

Milo shook his head.

'Why not?' said Rick. 'If you're right, why stick around and be a target?'

'The weather,' said Milo. 'If I bother to lay out bucks for Europe, I want sunny weather.'

'Now you're a meteorologist.' Rick took hold of Milo's arm. 'What if your anxiety doesn't level off? Am I supposed to go into long-term exile?'

'It's not a matter of anxiety. It's my finely honed sense of threat.'

'That stupid rumor those cops were talking about? I've been thinking about that. For all you know, there is an HIV-positive detective in your division. Someone deep in the closet. Or those cretins were just flapping their gums the way cops do. I know, I see them all the time when they bring in suspects. Standing around drinking coffee and gabbing while we sew the poor devils up.'

'Another West L.A. gay detective,' said Milo. 'Sure, that's likely.'

'Who says he's gay? And, what, only you can be a celebrity?'

'Yeah, that's me, a star. Rick, it's more than the rumor—'

'That old case, I know. Maybe it was shunted aside all these years precisely because no one *gives* a hoot. What if you've just built it up in your head, Milo? With Alex's help.'

'What's that supposed to mean?'

'It means that you and Alex have this bizarre chemistry. The two of you put your heads together, and strange ideas start to pour out.'

'I've found Alex to be right more often than he's wrong. And what's the murder book, a schoolboy prank?'

'It's possible.'

Milo was silent.

'Fine,' said Rick. 'Let's not talk about this anymore. Get me a rental.'

Milo drove Melrose west to Doheny then north to Santa Monica Boulevard. Past the clubs he and Rick no longer patronized.

Rick said, 'Where exactly are you going?'

'Beverly Hills. The Hertz office at the Beverly Hilton.'

'As a well-known companion of mine always says,

"Hoo-hah." Maybe I'll rent a Rolls.'

'Forget it, we've got bills to worry about.'

Rick stared at him and he stared back and they both broke into laughter. Milo knew it was temporary tension relief, more Band-Aid than cure. But that was fine.

Milo watched Rick drive away in the rental Volvo. The counter agent had been a good-looking blonde woman, and she'd taken one look at Rick, flirted outrageously, and upgraded him.

No meeting of the minds about where Rick would stay and for how long. Milo agreed to let it ride until tonight.

Alone, he drove downtown, to Skid Row. The fleabags that Vance Coury, Sr had owned twenty years ago had all been situated on a two-block stretch of Main Street. The chance that any personnel from that era remained was nil, but what did he have to lose?

The moment he drove by each of the hotels, the iota of optimism vanished. The spots where the Excelsior and the Crossley had stood were now parking lots, and the Grande Royale was the Shining Light Mission.

He made his way back to the Hall of Records and pulled property tax records on all three parcels. The parking lots were leased to a Nevada corporation, but the land was owned by Concourse Elegance, Inc., which traced to Concourse Auto Restoration on Van Nuys Boulevard. Vance Coury's shop. Junior had inherited the buildings, torn two of them down and converted to low-hassle, income-churning asphalt.

The Shining Light Mission was interesting, though. The Shining Light Foundation was a nonprofit run by the Reverends Fred and Glenda Stephenson – a pair Milo knew because back in his uniform days he'd transported bums to their soup kitchen on San Pedro. He'd found the couple to be saints who put in twenty-hour days serving the poor. Coury probably donated the third lot as part of some sort of tax deal, in order to end up with the other two, free and clear.

Feeling like Don Quixote's dumber brother, he moved on to death records. Sucked in his breath when he encountered unexpected success.

Luke Matthew Chapman had died in a drowning accident, twenty years ago, at the age of twenty-two.

Date of death: 14 December. Six months after Janie Ingalls's murder. Eight *days* prior to Caroline Cossack's final day at Achievement House and nine days prior to Boris Nemerov's execution.

He phoned the coroner's office, got hold of one of the few friendly voices at his disposal: a morgue assistant who'd come out of the closet after learning about Milo's travails. Milo was uncomfortable being viewed as inspirational, but the guy had come in handy from time to time.

Today, Darren asked no questions and went to pull the file. Milo wouldn't have been surprised to encounter another vanished folder, but a few minutes later he had the relevant data jotted down in his notepad:

Luke Chapman had parked his car on PCH and gone night-swimming at Zuma Beach. An illegal dip, because state sand was off-limits after dark and Chapman had had to scale a high link fence. Chapman's alcohol level was twice the legal limit, which made Milo wonder about his ability to climb the fence, but the coroner's theory was that 'this young, white, well-nourished male' had been caught in a riptide and lost coordination due to intoxication. Water in the lungs confirmed drowning. The corpse had washed up at the far end of Zuma, where public sand abutted Broad Beach. Multiple contusions and abrasions consistent with battery by surf and sand had been apparent. But no obvious signs of foul play.

No obvious signs unless you were prepared to interpret the bruises on Chapman's arms and legs and back as evidence of his having been forced down into the water. Knew Zuma had been one of the King's Men's party spots.

Milo recalled Chapman's vacant expression. The dumb kid in the group. Participating in Janie Ingalls's murder and sitting on the horror for months, but unable to get over it. Maybe he'd gotten loaded and blubbered the wrong thing to his buddies and made himself an extreme liability.

Bought himself the big blue kiss.

On the other hand, accidents happened . . .

Bowie Ingalls: man versus tree.

Pierce Schwinn: man versus rock.

Luke Chapman: man versus water.

What was left – fire? Suddenly Milo's head filled with images of Caroline Cossack and Wilbert Burns roasted alive. Bodies charred beyond recognition, the perfect obliteration of the past.

The King's Men. A nasty bunch of spoiled, rich party animals cleaning up after themselves and earning a nice, cushy twenty years.

More than cushy: Ferraris and chauffeurs, cribs in Holmby, dabbles in the film biz, private dinners with politicos and power brokers.

They'd gotten away with it.

These King's Men would've jumped at the chance to stomp Humpty Dumpty's skull.

The Cossack brothers, Specs Larner, Coury. And the

smart one – Nicholas Dale Hansen. What was *he* about?

He looked the guy up in the property files. Nothing. What did that mean, he was leasing the house on North Roxbury?

He found himself a quiet corner in the basement of the building, hidden between stacks of old plot maps, made sure no one was around and took the risk of an NCIC call using the ID of a West Valley DI named Korn – a punk he'd supervised two years ago, low on initiative, high on attitude.

Wasted risk: Nicholas Dale Hansen had no criminal history.

The only thing left to do was go home and play with his laptop. Or take a shortcut and ask Alex to do it – his friend, initially a computer Luddite, resistant to the whole notion of the Internet, had become quite the Web-surfing whiz.

He began the two-block walk to the city lot where he'd left the Taurus. Melting in with the afternoon pedestrian throng, dialing up his cell-phone like every other lemming on the street. Probably giving himself ear cancer or something, but those were the breaks. Faking normal felt good.

Alex picked up on the first ring, and Milo thought he sounded disappointed. Waiting for a call from Robin? What was up with *that*?

Milo asked him about running a search on Nicholas Hansen, and Alex said, 'Funny you should ask.'

'Oh yeah, I forgot,' said Milo. 'I'm dealing with Nostradamus.'

'No, just a guy with spare time,' said Alex. 'Hansen wasn't hard to find, at all. Guess what he does for a living?'

'He looked kinda corporate in high school, so some hoo-hah financial thing with a bad smell to it?'

'He's an artist. A painter. Quite a good one, if the images posted by the New York gallery that handles him are accurate.'

'An artist and he leases in Beverly Hills and drives a big Beemer?'

'A successful artist,' said Alex. 'His prices range from ten to thirty thousand a canvas.'

'And what, he churns them out?'

'Doesn't look like it. I phoned the gallery pretending to be an interested collector, and he's sold out. They described his style as post-modern old masters. Hansen mixes his own pigments, makes his own frames and brushes, lays down layer after layer of paint and glaze. It's a time-consuming process and the owner said Hansen finishes four, five pictures a year. She implied she'd love to have more.'

'Four, five a year at his top fee means a hundred and fifty, max,' said Milo. 'A year's lease on a house in the flats could be more than that by itself.'

'Plus galleries usually take around thirty percent,' said Alex, 'so, no, it doesn't add up.' He paused. 'I hope you don't mind, but I drove by his house. It's a nice one – big old Spanish thing that hasn't been made over. The BMW's in the driveway. Freshly polished. Dark green, almost the exact same shade as my Seville.'

Milo laughed. 'Do I mind? Would it make a difference? No, it's fine unless you knocked on the door and accused the bastard of murder. Which, *I'd* love to do. Because, guess what, the plot curdles.'

He told Alex about Luke Chapman's drowning death.

'Another accident,' said Alex. 'Normally, I'd say "ah,"

but you've been crankier than usual.'

'Say it. I'll give you Novocaine before I start drilling.'

Alex let out an obligatory chuckle. 'I also got a brief look at Hansen. Or someone who's living at the same address. While I was driving by, a man came out the front door, went to the BMW, and removed a sheet of wood from the trunk. Nicholas Hansen paints on mahogany.'

'An artist,' said Milo, 'with independent income. Ambling out to his driveway in comfy clothes, doing whatever the hell he pleases. Life's sure fair, ain't it?'

There were things Milo wanted to do after dark, so he thanked Alex, told him to stay out of trouble, he'd call in the morning.

'Anything else I can do for you, big guy?'

Milo quashed the impulse to say again, 'Stay out of trouble.' 'No, not right now.'

'Okay,' said Alex. He sounded disappointed. Milo wanted to ask about Robin, but he didn't.

Instead, he hung up, thinking about Janie Ingalls and how some lives were so short, so brutish, that it was a wonder God bothered.

He slogged through yet another rush-hour mess from downtown, wondering what to do with Rick and deciding that a nice hotel for a few days was the best solution. Rick would be profoundly unhappy, but he wouldn't scream. Rick never screamed, just tucked himself in psychologically and grew quiet and unreachable.

It wouldn't be fun, but in the end Rick would agree. All these years together, and they'd both learned to pick their battles.

★ ★ ★

371

He made it home by five o'clock.

Midway up his block, he stopped.

Something white was stationed in his driveway.

The Porsche.

He looked around, saw no strange cars on the block, gunned the Taurus, and swung it behind the pearly 928. From what he could tell the car was intact – no joyriding wounds or missing parts. More than intact – shiny and clean, as if it had been freshly washed. Rick kept it spotless, but Milo couldn't remember when he'd last scrubbed it down . . . last weekend. For most of the week, Rick had garaged the car, but the last two days he'd left it out to be ready when he hit the ER early. Two days' dirt would have shown itself easily on the white paint.

Someone had *detailed* the damn thing.

He surveyed the block, put his hand on his gun, got out cautiously, walked over to the Porsche and touched the car's convex flank.

Glossy. Washed and waxed.

A peek through the window added *freshly vacuumed* to the picture; he could see the tracks in the carpet.

Even the steering wheel lock had been put back. Then he saw something on the driver's seat.

A brown paper bag.

He gave the block another up-and-down, then kneeled down and examined the Porsche's underside. No ticking toys or tracers. Popping the trunk revealed an intact rear engine. He'd worked on the car himself, had rust-proofed the belly for all those cold-weather trips that had never materialized. He knew the Porsche's guts well. Nothing new.

He unlocked the driver's door, took a closer look at the

bag. The paper mouth was open, and the content was visible.

A blue binder. Not shiny leather like Alex's little gift. Your basic blue cloth.

The same kind of binder the department used to employ before the switch to plastic.

He took hold of the top of the bag with his fingertips and carried it inside the house. Sat down in the living room, heart racing, hands icy, because he knew exactly what would be inside. Knew also that, despite the certainty, he'd be shocked.

His jaw hurt and his back ached as he opened the book to Janie Ingalls's case file.

Very thin file. Milo's own notes on top, followed by the official death shots, and yes, Schwinn had lifted the photo out of this set. Body drawings with every wound delineated, autopsy summary. Not originals, nice clean photocopies.

Then, nothing else. No tox screens or lab tests, no investigative reports by the Metro boys who'd supposedly taken over. So either that had been a lie, or pages had been left out.

He flipped to the postmortem summary. No mention of semen – of anything much. This had to be the sketchiest autopsy synopsis he'd ever read. 'This white, adolescent, well-nourished female's wounds were accomplished by sharp, single-bladed . . .' Thanks a heap.

No sign of the toxicology screen he'd requested. He didn't need official confirmation; Melinda Waters had said Janie began the evening stoned.

No semen, no foreign blood types. Forget DNA.

But one detail in the autopsy summary did catch his

eye: ligature marks around Janie's ankles, wrists, and throat.

Same pattern of restraints as in the hotel.

Vance Coury spotting Janie and going for an encore.

This time, adding his buddies to the mix.

He reread the file. Nothing revelatory, but someone wanted to make sure Milo saw it.

He settled his head with vodka and grapefruit juice, checked the mail, punched the phone machine.

One message from Rick, who'd made it easy for him by taking on an extra shift.

'I won't be through until tomorrow morning, probably crash in the doctors' room, maybe go for a drive afterward. Take care of yourself . . . I love you.'

'Me too,' Milo muttered to the empty house. Even alone, he had trouble saying it.

twenty-nine

I opened the door for Milo at 9 A.M., doing my best impression of awake and human. Last night, I'd woken up every couple of hours, thinking the kind of thoughts that erode your soul.

Three calls to Robin had gone unanswered. Her hotel refused to say if she'd checked out – guest security. Next stop, Denver. I pictured her on the bus, Spike sleeping in her lap, gazing out the window.

Thinking of me, or anything but?

Milo handed me the blue binder. I thumbed through it and led him into my office.

'Your typing wasn't any better back then,' I said. 'Any theories about who delivered it?'

'Someone with a talent for grand theft auto.'

'Same messenger who sent me the deluxe version?'

'Could be.'

'Doesn't sound like Schwinn's secret girlfriend,' I said. 'Or maybe I'm being sexist; I suppose women can steal cars, too.'

'This was no amateur. I print-powdered the wheel and the door handles. *Nada*. Nothing on the book other than my paws. They put the crooklock back on. Picked it, didn't slice it.'

'Same question,' I said. 'A criminal pro, the department, or a rogue cop?'

'A rogue cop would mean Schwinn had a buddy back then or made a new one. I never saw him hang with anyone. The other detectives seemed to shun him.'

'Any idea why?'

'At first, I figured it was his charming personality, but maybe everyone knew about his bad behavior, could see he was ready for a fall. Everyone except me. I was a dumb-ass rookie caught up in my own paranoia. At the time I wondered if I'd been paired with him because I was seen as a pariah, too. Now, I'm sure of it.'

'Not that much of a pariah,' I said. 'They got rid of him and transferred you to West L.A.'

'Or I hadn't accrued enough time on the job to accumulate embarrassing information.'

'Or to develop street sources. Like the one who cued Schwinn right to Janie.'

He fingered the edge of the blue cloth binder. 'Another burnout cop . . . maybe. But why send this to me a week after the deluxe version?'

'More covering of the rear,' I said. 'Pacing himself. He couldn't be sure you'd be seduced. You started investigating and qualified for the next installment.'

'More installments coming?'

'Could be.'

He got up, circled the room, returned to the desk but remained on his feet. I'd kept the drapes drawn and a razor edge of light ran across his torso diagonally, a luminous wound.

I said, 'Here's yet another theory: the IA man who interrogated you along with Broussard – Poulsenn. Any idea what happened to him?'

'*Lester* Poulsenn,' he said. 'Been trying to recall his first name, and it just came to me. No, never heard of him again. Why?'

'Because the real target of renewing interest in the case could be Broussard. John G. built his career on an upright reputation, exposure of a cover-up would destroy him. Lester Poulsenn could have a good reason to resent Broussard. Think about it: a black man and a white man are partnered, but the black man is put in charge. Then the black man ascends to the top of the department ladder, and the white man's never heard from again. Was Poulsenn also drummed out due to bad behavior? Or maybe he wasn't good at keeping secrets. Either way, we could be talking about one disgruntled gentleman.'

'And Poulsenn would've known about *Schwinn's* resentment . . . yeah, it'd be interesting to know what happened to *his* career. I can't exactly waltz into Parker Center and stick my nose in the files . . .' He frowned, called DMV and identified himself as someone named Lt Horacio Batista. A few minutes later, he had statistics on three Lester Poulsenns living in California, but all were too young to be the man who'd played second fiddle to John G. Broussard.

'He could've moved out of state,' I said, 'meaning he's probably not our man. Or he's yet another disappearing act.'

He got to his feet again and paced; the light razor bounced. Returning to the book, he touched a blue cover. 'Installments – hey, folks, join the murder book club.'

We divided up the workload this way:

1.   I'd try to learn what I could about Lester Poulsenn,

check newspaper microfilms for twenty- to twenty-five-year-old stories about misbehaving cops and chase down whatever details I could find about the disposition of their cases. A long shot, because the department kept corruption stories quiet, just as it had with Pierce Schwinn. Unless, as in the Rampart scandal or the Hollywood Division burglary case of ten years ago, the stink got too strong to mask.

2. Milo would go off to do his thing, not telling me what or where or when.

The search on my computer revealed no Lester Poulsenns who fit the bill. I made another futile call to Vancouver, comforted myself with self-pity, and drove to the U.

It took three hours to go through five years of microfilm, and I came up with several instances of felonious police officers. A pair of West Valley detectives had offered their services as contract killers. Both were serving life sentences in protective isolation at the state penitentiary at Pelican Bay. A Glendale traffic officer had been arrested for having sex with a thirteen-year-old baby-sitter. Ten years of jail, this prince was out by now, but an alliance with Schwinn and a child molester seemed unlikely. A female Pasadena gang officer had slept with several minor-age gang members, and two Van Nuys uniforms had been caught burglarizing pawnshops on their patrol route. Convictions and incarceration for all. In each instance a hookup with Schwinn seemed improbable. I copied down all the names, anyway, punched Lester Poulsenn's name into the periodicals index and felt my pupils dilate as a single reference popped into view.

378

Twenty-year-old reference.

> Poulsenn, L.L. Veteran LAPD detective
> found murdered in Watts.

The *Sacramento Bee*. I located the spool, jammed it into the machine, twirled like mad until I came to the story. Associated Press wire service piece. The L.A. papers hadn't picked it up.

The *Bee* had run it in a side column at the back of the main section titled 'Elsewhere in the State.' Sandwiched between the account of a dead black rhinoceros at the San Diego Zoo and a Berkeley bank robbery.

The date was 5 January. Fourteen days after Caroline Cossack had checked out of – or had been taken from – Achievement House.

I did an instant photocopy on the machine, then read the text.

(AP) Los Angeles police are investigating the shooting death of one of their own, in what appears to be a homicide and attempted cover-up by arson. The body of Lester Louis Poulsenn, formerly a detective with the department's Internal Affairs Unit and recently appointed to the Metro Major Crimes Unit, was found inside a burning house in Watts. Poulsenn, 39, a thirteen-year LAPD veteran, was discovered by firefighters dispatched to put out a blaze at the private residence on West 156th Street. A police spokesman said Poulsenn had been shot twice in the head in what appeared to be an execution-style killing.

'This is a rough neighborhood, with lots of gang

activity,' said the source, who neither confirmed nor denied reports that Poulsenn had been in Watts on official business. The structure, a single-family dwelling that had been vacant for some time, was described as a total loss.

I kept spooling, in search of a follow-up.

Nothing. Which was crazy; nothing mobilizes a police department faster than a cop's murder. Yet local press coverage of Poulsenn's death had been suppressed, and no further official statements had been issued.

Recently transferred to Metro. Translation: Poulsenn had taken over the Ingalls case?

Twenty years ago, a pair of IA men had interrogated Milo. One had merited success, the other was dead seven months later.

A white man shot to death in a black neighborhood, just like Boris Nemerov. Dispatched execution-style, just like Boris Nemerov.

Arson cover-up. Milo had wondered out loud about fire. Beleaguered or not, he had perfect pitch.

I called him, got no answer at any of his numbers, thought about what to do.

Nice mild morning. Time to wash the car.

Two hours later, the Seville was as shiny as a '79 Seville could be, and I was hurtling over the Glen to the Valley. Mere cleanliness hadn't satisfied me. I'd waxed and hand-buffed the chesterfield-green paint, added detail spray, scrubbed the tires, the hubcaps, the beige vinyl top and matching upholstery, wiped down those crafty little simulated wood insets, vacuumed and shampooed the rugs. I bought the car fifteen years ago from the proverbial little old lady (a heavy-footed retired school-teacher from Burbank, not Pasadena) and had pampered it since. Still, 105,000 miles had taken its toll, and one day I'd be forced to decide between an engine rebuild or something new.

No decision at all. No more changes of heart.

Concourse Auto Restorers was one of the many car-oriented businesses lining Van Nuys Boulevard between Riverside and Oxnard. Modest setup – not much more than a double tin-roofed garage behind an open lot filled with chrome and lacquer. A sign above the garage, done up in red Day-Glo Gothic lettering, advertised 'CUSTOM PAINT, PLATING, AND BODY-OFF RESTORATION' above a cartoonish rendering of an equally red, priapic Ferrari coupe. I parked on the street and made my way among muscle cars, hot rods, and one very white stretch Mercedes with its roof hacked off and a blue tarp spread across its interior. Years ago the state had passed laws restricting outdoor spray painting, but the air above Concourse Auto was chemically ripe.

Midway up the lot, two men in greasy T-shirts and baggy cutoffs were inspecting the doors of a seventies Stutz Blackhawk done up in the same copper finish as a gourmet frypan. Both were young and husky and Hispanic, with shaved heads and mustaches. Face masks hung around their necks. Their arms and the backs of their necks were brocaded with tattoos. The inkwork was dusky blue, square-edged and crude – prison handiwork. They barely raised their eyes as I passed, but both were paying attention. My nod evoked squints.

'Vance Coury?' I said.

'In there,' said the heavier of the two, curling a thumb

toward the garage. His voice was high-pitched, and a teardrop tattoo dripped under one eye. That's supposed to mean you've murdered someone, but some people brag. This fellow had a hunched posture and flat eyes, and boasting didn't seem his style.

I moved on.

As I got closer to the garage, I saw that my first impression of a small lot had been wrong. A driveway ran to the left of the building, and it led to a rear half-acre of chain-linked dirt piled high with tires and fenders, bumpers and broken headlights and random garbage. Two spray booths were affixed to the rear outer wall of the garage, and a few intact cars were parked in the dirt, but most of the land was dumping ground.

I returned to the front of the structure. The garage door to the left was shut and bolted, a wall of corrugated iron. In the open right-hand bay sat a red, white, and blue Corvette Stingray. The 'Vette's windows were tinted amethyst, its nose had been lengthened a foot, a rear spoiler arced over the trunk, and twenty-inch, chrome-reversed wheels extended several inches wider than the body. Primer spots blemished the passenger side, and another shaved-head Latino crouched at one of them, hand-sanding. Yet another tattoo-boy sat at a workbench to the rear of the bay, arc-welding. The decor was raw walls, cement floor, bare bulbs, gasoline reek. Tacked to the wall beams were auto-parts calendars and foldouts of naked women with an emphasis upon luxuriant pubic hair and angles that bespoke an interest in amateur gynecology. A scattering of hard-core shots was dispersed among the collection; someone had a thing for skinny, crouching, supplicant blondes with dope-eyes performing oral sex.

The sander ignored me as I edged behind the 'Vette, avoided the sparks from the welding gun, and stepped into the sealed section of the garage. Half a black Porsche roadster occupied this bay – a racer sliced neatly in half so that the number 8 on the door had been bisected and turned into a 3. At the rear of the room, behind the truncated torso, a broad-shouldered man sat at a metal desk, phone nestled under his chin, fingers busy at a calculator.

Fortyish, he had long, thick silver hair slicked straight back and tucked behind his ears, incongruous too-black eyebrows, and an equally inky goatee. The bulb hanging above the desk greened an already olive complexion. Dark, brooding eyes were bottomed by pouches, his neck was creased and soft, and his face had long surrendered to flab. Remnants of the good-looking high school kid were hard to find, and I didn't want to stare. Because Vance Coury had his eyes on me, as he continued talking and calculating.

I walked over to the desk. Coury gave off a strong whiff of musky aftershave. His shirt was black silk crêpe with blousy sleeves rolled to the elbows and a high, stiff collar that nearly reached his earlobes. A gold chain flashed around his neck. A gold Rolex the size of a pizza banded a thick, hirsute wrist.

He studied me without acknowledging my presence. Stayed on the phone, listening, talking, listening some more, adjusting the instrument in the crook of his neck. Never ceasing the tapping of the calculator keys. The desk top was littered with papers. A half-empty bottle of Corona served as a paperweight.

I left him and strolled over to the demi-Porsche. The car retained no internal organs, was just half a shell. The edges had been smoothed and painted. Finished product; no one was intending to put this one back together again.

All the king's horses . . .

'Hey,' said a raspy voice behind me.

I turned. Coury said, 'What do you want?' Alert, yet disinterested. One hand rested on the calculator. The other was cupped and aimed at me, as if ready to collect something.

'I'm thinking of some custom work.'

'What kind of car?'

'Seville. Seventy-nine. Are you Mr Coury?'

He looked me over. 'Who referred you?'

'Read your name in an auto magazine,' I said. 'From what I could tell you seem to work on a lot of contest winners.'

'It happens,' he said. 'Seventy-nine Seville? A box. They built 'em on Chevy Two Nova chassis.'

'I know.'

'What do you want done to it?'

'I'm not sure.'

He smirked. 'Can't think of any contest you'd enter that in – unless it's one of those AIDS things.'

'AIDS things?'

'They're trying shows, now. To raise money for AIDS. Some little fruit came in, wanted me to cherry up his '45 BMW.'

'Take the job?' I said.

The cupped hand waved off the question. 'Seventy-nine Seville,' he said, as if offering a diagnosis. 'It's still gonna be a box unless we get radical. And then there's the engine. It sucks.'

'It's been good to me. No problems in fifteen years.'

'Any rust on the belly?'

'Nope. I take care of it.'

'Right,' he said.

I said, 'It's here, if you want to see it.'

He glanced down at the calculator. Punched numbers as I stood there. 'Where's here?'

'Out in front.'

He snickered. 'In front.' He stood to six-three. His upper body was massive, with meaty shoulders and a swelling gut, outsized for the narrow hips and long, stalky legs that supported it. Tight, black, plain-front slacks slimmed the legs further and accentuated the effect. On his feet were black crocodile boots with silver straps banding the shins. He came around the desk jangling. Walked right past me and out of the garage.

Out at the curb, he laughed.

'Tell you what, we wreck it, give you four hundred bucks, call it a day.'

I laughed back. 'Like I said, it's been good to me.'

'Then leave it the hell alone – what the hell would you want to do with this?'

'I was thinking about turning it into a convertible.'

'Figures,' he said. 'What, chain-saw the roof off?'

'Only car you can do that with is a Rolls Silver Cloud,' I said. 'Not enough tensile strength in any other chassis. I was figuring take the roof off, strengthen the frame, install an automatic soft-cover with a mohair liner, rechrome, and do a custom-color. You guys still doing lacquer?'

'Illegal,' he said. 'Listen, man, you want a convertible, go buy yourself one of those little Mazdas.'

'I want this car converted.'

He turned his back.

I said, 'Too complicated for you?'

He stopped. Caught his lower lip between his teeth and bit down. The pouches beneath his eyes rode up and obscured the bottom half of the irises. The two home-boys working on the Stutz looked our way.

Coury kept his lip between his teeth and rotated his jaw. 'Yeah, that's it,' he said. 'Too complicated.'

He left me standing there and walked back toward the lot. But he only made his way halfway through, paused by the Stutz. As I drove away he was watching.

thirty

Milo stared into his coffee cup, pretended the soil-
colored liquid was a bog and he was sinking.

If this was a normal case, he'd have gotten himself
backup. As much as he hated meetings and personalities
and all the other crap that went with teamwork, multiple
suspects demanded it.

An army of suspects on Janie. Six, with Luke Chapman
dead. And then there was after-burn: Walt Obey and
Germ Bacilla and Diamond Jim.

And the glue that held it all together: J.G. Broussard.

And now, yet another unknown: Alex's theory about a
rogue cop.

Milo'd spent some time thinking about that, trying
to come up with a possible name, but all he could
conjure was an abstraction. Some asshole doing
Pierce Schwinn's postmortem bidding, playing
games and yanking his strings. Someone with the gall to
rip off Rick's car and return it detailed, with a nice little
gift.

Vance Coury was in the car biz and wasn't that a
coincidence? But Coury sure wouldn't have delivered the
real murder book.

So maybe the use of the car meant someone was

pointing him *toward* Coury. Or was he really getting overly complicated now?

The anger that had percolated within him since the first murder book had surfaced kept rising in his gorge.

Coury. The bastard shaped up as a sadist and a rapist and a control freak. Maybe the dominant one in the group. If he and his rich buds were cornered, they'd be likely to ambush the enemy, cut his throat, and burn his body.

One army deserved another, and all *he* had was Alex.

He laughed silently. Or maybe he'd let out sound because the old lady in the second booth over looked up, startled, and stared at him with that antsy expression that takes hold of people when they confront the weird.

Milo smiled at her, and she retracted her head behind her newspaper.

He was back at DuPars in Farmers Market, trying to sort things out. Vance Coury had stayed in his head because it had been Coury who'd raped Janie the first time and maybe initiated the scene that led to Janie's murder.

Normally, he'd have investigated the hell out of the guy. But . . . then something hit him. Maybe there *was* a safe way to learn more.

He threw money on the table and left the coffee shop. The old woman's stare followed his path to the door.

The Shining Light Mission was five stories of brick-faced stucco painted corn yellow and sided by rusting gray fire escapes. No friezework, no moldings, not the slightest nod to design. It reminded Milo of one of those drawings little kids do when asked to render a building. One big rectangle specked with little window squares. The place even tilted. As a hotel, the Grande Royale had been anything but.

Old men with collapsed jaws and runny eyes years past self-torment loitered in front and every one of them greeted Milo with the excessive amiability of the habitual miscreant.

Knowing exactly what he was – no way could he be taken for anything else. As he entered the mission, he wondered if the cop aura would stick after he left the department. Which might be sooner rather than later; going up against the chief wasn't a formula for career longevity.

Even an unpopular chief who might be leaving soon himself. Milo had been scouring the papers for Broussard stories, and this morning he'd found yet another one in the *Times*. Pontification on the chief's rejected raise by two members of the police commission. Defying the mayor who'd appointed them, which meant they were serious.

'*Chief Broussard represents a long-entrenched police culture that contributes to intracommunity tension.*'

Politico-blab for 'Update your résumé, J.G.'

Broussard had come into office in the aftermath of the Rampart scandal, and the commission had offered no hint at new corruption. The chief's problem was his personality. Arrogance as he bucked the commission at every turn. In that sense, the chief still thought like a cop: Civilian meddling was the enemy. But Broussard's imperious nature had alienated the wrong people, well past the point where even pals like the mayor and Walt Obey could help him.

Then again, maybe Broussard didn't care about losing his job, because he had something waiting in the wings.

Converting his unpaid position as security consultant to Obey's Esperanza project into a nice, fat corporate gig that would guarantee him long-term status and bucks, keep the wife in Cadillacs and whatever else floated her canoe.

If so, what was Obey getting out of the deal?

The Cossacks' participation as refinancers fit perfectly. They owed Broussard big-time for the Ingalls cover-up, would go with the flow. Could Alex be right about Obey getting himself into a financial bind, needing the brothers as white knights?

Any way you turned it, Milo knew he was a flea. What the hell, safety and security were for wimps.

He entered the mission lobby. The vaulted space had been converted to a TV room where a dozen or so bums sat slumped on folding chairs, staring at a movie on big-screen. The scene featured actors and actresses in long hair and beards and camel-colored robes wandering through a desert that looked like Palm Springs. Despite the camels. Some biblical epic that asked you to buy the Hebrews as blond and blue-eyed. Milo shifted his attention to the reception desk – maybe the very desk where Vance Coury had obtained the key to his rape den. The counter was topped by several plastic, screw-top cookie jars, and the bookcase behind it was jammed with red-bound Bibles with crosses on their spines. Off to the left were two brown-painted elevator doors. A metal-railed staircase ran straight back and hooked sharply to the right.

The place smelled of soup. Why did so many places dedicated to salvation smell of soup?

An old black guy, more cleaned up than the others, got up from his chair and limped over. 'I'm Edgar. May I help you, sir?'

Big bass voice but a little bandy-legged fellow wearing pressed khakis, a blue-gray plaid shirt buttoned to the neck, and sneakers. Bald except for tufts of kinky white cotton above his ears. White-white dentures made for smiling. The total effect was clownlike, benign.

Milo said, 'Is Reverend Fred or Reverend Glenda in?'

'Reverend Fred's at the City of Orange Mission, but Reverend Glenda's upstairs. Who shall I say is calling?'

The guy had a refined way of enunciating, and his eyes were clear and intelligent. Milo could see him doing butler time at some country club, kissing up to rich folk using perfect grammar. Different skin color, and maybe he'd have been the one getting served.

'Milo Sturgis.'

'And this is about, Mr Sturgis?'

'Personal.'

The old man regarded him with compassion. 'One moment, Mr Sturgis.' He made his way slowly up the stairs and returned a few minutes later. 'Reverend Glenda's waiting for you, Mr Sturgis. Next floor up, second door to the right.'

Sitting behind a small oak desk in a small, nearly empty office fitted with an ancient radiator and masked by yellowed venetian blinds, Glenda Stephenson looked exactly as she had ten years ago. Fifty pounds overweight, way too much makeup, a teased-up meringue of brunette waves atop a broad, welcoming face. Same kind of clothes too: pink, dotted Swiss dress with a frothy collar. Every time Milo'd seen her she'd worn something frilly and inappropriate in that same soap-bar pink.

He didn't expect her to remember him but right away she said, 'Detective S! It's been so long! Why haven't you brought me anyone in so long?'

'Don't hang out much with the living these days, Rev,' said Milo. 'Been working Homicide for a long time.'

'Oh, dear,' said Glenda Stephenson. 'Well, how have you been with that?'

'It has its moments.'

'I'll just bet it does.'

'How's the soul-saving business, Reverend?'

Glenda grinned. 'There's never a lack of work.'

'I'll bet.'

'Sit down,' said Glenda Stephenson. 'Cup of coffee?'

Milo saw no urn or pot. Just an alms box on the desk, next to a neat stack of what looked to be government forms. Impulsively, he reached into his pocket, found a bill, dropped it in.

'Oh, that's not necessary,' said Glenda.

'I'm Catholic,' said Milo. 'Put me in a religious environment, and I have an urge to donate.'

Glenda giggled. Little girl's giggle. For some reason it wasn't as foolish coming out of that dinner-plate face as it should've been. 'Well, then come by often. There's never a lack of need, either. So . . . Edgar said this is personal?'

'In a way,' said Milo. 'Work and personal – what I mean is it needs to be kept confidential.'

Glenda sat forward, and her bosoms brushed the desk top. 'Of course. What's the matter, dear?'

'It's not about me,' said Milo. 'Not directly. But I am involved in a case that's . . . ticklish. A name came up, and I traced a connection to the mission. Vance Coury.'

Glenda sat back. Her chair creaked. 'The son or the father?'

'The son.'

'What has he done?'

'You don't sound surprised.'

In repose, Glenda's customary face was unlined – nothing filled wrinkles as well as fat. But now worry lines appeared at the periphery – etching the corners of her mouth, her eyes, her brow.

'Oh dear,' she said. 'Could this reflect in any way on the mission?'

'Not that I can see. I certainly wouldn't do anything to put you in a bad position, Reverend.'

'Oh, I know that, Milo. You were always the kindest. Taking time from your patrol to deliver sad souls. The way you held their arm, the way you . . . ministered to them.'

'I was trying to clean up the streets, and you were there. I'm afraid there's nothing pastoral in my makeup.'

'Oh, I think you're wrong,' said Glenda. 'I think you would've made a wonderful priest.'

Milo's face went hot. Blushing, for God's sake.

Glenda Stephenson said, 'Coury, the son . . . when Fred and I accepted the building, we had our reservations. Because you know we're grizzled old veterans of this neighborhood, knew darn well what his father had been like – everyone on Skid Row knew about his father.'

'Slumlord.'

'Slumlord and a mean man – never gave us a dime, and, Milo, we asked. That's why we were shocked when a few months after he died we received a letter from the son's lawyer letting us know he was donating the hotel to the mission. I'm afraid our immediate response was to harbor uncharitable thoughts.'

'As in, what's the catch,' said Milo.

'Exactly. The father . . . no, I won't speak ill of the dead, but suffice it to say that charity didn't appear to be his strong point. And then there were the people he employed. They'd always made the lives of our men difficult. And the son had kept them on.'

'What people?'

'Angry young men from East L.A.,' said Glenda.

'Which gang?' said Milo.

She shook her head. 'You hear talk. Eighteenth Street, the Mexican Mafia, Nuestra Familia. I really don't know. But whoever they were, when they showed up on the street, they intimidated our men. Swaggering by, driving by. Sometimes they'd get out and demand money, become threatening.'

'Physically?'

'Once in a while someone got punched or pushed. Mostly it was psychological intimidation – looks, threats, verbal bullying. I suppose they felt entitled – territorial. Mr Coury – the father – had used them as rent collectors. When the son offered us the building, the first request we made on him was that he ask his crew to stay away from the men. Because we thought he was going to hold on to the other hotels, and we didn't want to be geographically close to that kind of environment. His lawyer said there'd be no problem, Coury was going to tear the buildings down and pave them for parking lots. It ended up being a very smooth transition. Our lawyer talked to his lawyer, papers were signed, and that was it. Fred and I kept waiting for some ulterior motive but the way our lawyer explained it, the son was in an inheritance tax bind and the Grande Royale could be appraised in a manner that would serve his best interests.'

'Inflated appraisal?'

'No,' said Glenda. 'Fred and I wouldn't be party to that. In fact, we demanded to look at the most recent county assessments, and everything was in line. The Grande Royale was worth approximately twice what the other hotels were, so apparently it fit the son's tax needs. It wasn't the only thing he sold. Mr Coury, the father, had owned many properties. But the three hotels had been acquired as a package through some sort of government housing deal, so by donating the Royale, everything worked out.'

'Coury aiding the Lord's work,' said Milo.

'Funny, isn't it? The father acquired filthy lucre by oppressing the poor and now at least some of those profits have served to elevate the poor.'

'Happy ending, Reverend. Doesn't happen very often.'

'Oh, it does, Milo. You just have to know where to look.'

He talked to her a bit longer, stuffed more money in the alms box over her protests, and left.

Vance Coury had made good on his promise to keep the gang-bangers away from the Mission, and now that the two other hotels had been torn down for parking lots his need for rent collectors had disappeared.

But the gang thing intrigued Milo, and when he drove by the lots and took a look at the attendants, he saw shaved heads and skulking posture. Tattoos conspicuous enough to be visible from the curb.

thirty-one

What I'd seen of Vance Coury's demeanor synched with the profile of a domination rapist: surly, hyper-macho, eager not to please. The supercharged ambience in which he operated fit, too: big engines, flashy paint, the photos of submissive fellatrices tacked to the walls of the garage. The mutilated Porsche.

A corrupt father completed the picture: Coury had been raised to take what he wanted. Throw in some like-minded buddies, and Janie Ingalls had been a rabbit in a dog pit.

Junior hadn't been interested in my patronage. Did he really regard the Seville as a hunk of junk? Or did those parking lots pay the bills and the auto-customizing business was recreational? Or a front . . . all those gang boys.

I headed for the city and thought about the bisected Porsche. Evisceration on display. The joy of destruction. Maybe I was interpreting too much, but the few minutes I'd spent with Coury had left me wary and creeped-out, and I kept checking the rearview mirror well past Mulholland.

Back at home, I imagined the party scene twenty years ago: Janie's encounter with Coury, amid the noise and the dope, the flash of recognition – pleasure for Coury, horror for Janie.

He moves in and takes over. The King's Men join in.

Including a King's Man who seemed different from the others?

The images Nicholas Hansen's gallery had posted on its website were still-lifes. Lush, luminously tinted assemblages of fruit and flowers, rendered meticulously. Hansen's work seemed galaxies away from the ruined sculpture assembled on the Beaudry on-ramp – from any brutality. But art was no immunization against evil. Caravaggio had slain a man over a tennis game and Gauguin had slept with young Tahitian girls knowing he'd be infecting them with syphilis.

Still, Nick Hansen seemed to have taken a different path than the others, and deviance has always fascinated me.

It was nearly three, maybe past the New York gallery's closing time, but I phoned anyway, and got a young, female voice on the other end. The first time I'd contacted the gallery, I'd talked to an older woman and hadn't left my name, so here was a chance for some new dissembling.

I shifted into art-speak and presented myself as a collector of old masters drawings who'd run out of the sunlight-free space such treasures demanded and was considering switching to oils.

'Old masters oils?' said the young woman.

'A bit beyond my budget,' I said. 'But I *have* been impressed by some of the contemporary realism that's managed to assert itself among all the performance pieces. Nicholas Hansen, for example.'

'Oh, Nicholas's wonderful.'

'He's certainly not daunted by tradition,' I said. 'Could you tell me more about his background – is it rigidly academic?'

'Well,' she said, 'he did go to Yale. But we've always felt Nicholas transcends academic painting. There's something about his sensibilities. And the way he uses light.'

'Yes. Quite. I like his sense of composition.'

'That, too. He's simply first-rate. Unfortunately, we have no paintings by him in stock, at this time. If you could give me your name—'

'I always research an artist before I take the plunge. Would you happen to have some biographical information on Hansen that you could fax me?'

'Yes, of course,' she said. 'I'll get that right out to you. And about the academic aspect . . . Nicholas *is* well schooled, but please don't hold that against him. Despite his meticulousness and his way with paint as matter, there's a certain primal energy to his consciousness. You'd need to see the pictures in person to really appreciate that.'

'No doubt,' I said. 'There's nothing like in person.'

Five minutes later, my fax machine buzzed, disgorging Nicholas Hansen's curriculum vitae. Education, awards, group and individual exhibitions, corporate collections, museum shows.

The man had accomplished plenty in two decades, and unlike his old pal Garvey Cossack he hadn't recounted any of it in a pumped-up biography. No mention of high school at all; Nicholas Hansen's account of his education began with college: Columbia University, where he'd received a BA in anthropology, summers filled with painting fellowships, a Master of Fine Arts at Yale, and two years of postgraduate work at an atelier in Florence, Italy, learning classical painting technique. Among his museum shows were group spots at the Art Institute of Chicago and the Boston Museum of Fine Arts. Prominent names figured among those who collected his work.

An accomplished man. A polished man. Hard to fit that with Vance Coury's garage or the Cossacks' vulgar lifestyle. A gang-rape murder.

I went over the dates on Hansen's résumé. Saw something else that didn't fit.

Milo still wasn't answering any of his phones, so I tried to dispel my restlessness with a beer, then another. I carried the bottle down to the pond, thought about kicking back, decided to net leaves instead. For the next hour or so I pruned, raked, busied myself with mindless chores. I was just about to allow myself a moment of repose when the phone rang up in the house.

Robin? I ran up the stairs, grabbed the kitchen extension, heard Dr Bert Harrison's voice. 'Alex?'

'Bert. What's up?'

'It was nice to see you,' he said. 'After all this time. Just checking to see how you're doing.'

'Did I look that bad?'

'Oh, no, not bad, Alex. Perhaps a bit preoccupied. So . . .'

'Everything's rolling along.'

'Rolling along.'

'No, that's a lie, Bert. I screwed up with Robin.'

Silence.

I said, 'I should've followed your advice. Instead, I brought up the past.'

More dead air. 'I see . . .'

'She reacted just as you'd imagine. Maybe I wanted her to.'

'You're saying . . .'

'I really don't know what I'm saying, Bert. Listen, I appreciate your calling, but things are kind of . . . I don't feel like talking about it.'

'Forgive me,' he said.

Apologizing again.

'Nothing to forgive,' I said. 'You gave me good advice, I screwed up.'

'You made a mistake, son. Mistakes can be remedied.'

'Some.'

'Robin's a flexible woman.'

He'd met Robin twice. I said, 'Is that your natural optimism speaking?'

'No, it's an old man's intuition. Alex, I've made my share of mistakes, but after a few years one does get a sense for people. I'd hate to see you misled.'

'About Robin?'

'About anything,' he said. 'Another reason I'm calling is that I'm planning to travel. Perhaps for a while. Cambodia, Vietnam, some places I've been to, others I haven't.'

'Sounds great, Bert.'

'I didn't want you to try to reach me and not find me here.'

'I appreciate that.' Had I come across *that* needy?

'That sounds presumptuous, doesn't it?' he said. 'To think you'd call. But . . . just in case.'

'I appreciate your telling me, Bert.'

'Yes . . . well, then, good luck.'

'When are you leaving?' I said.

'Soon. As soon as final arrangements are complete.'

'Bon voyage,' I said. 'When you get back, give me a call. I'd love to hear about the trip.'

'Yes . . . may I offer one bit of advice, son?'

Please don't. 'Sure.'

'Try to season each day with a new perspective.'

'Okay,' I said.

'Bye, now, Alex.'

I placed the receiver back in its cradle. What had *that* been about? The more I thought about the conversation, the more it sounded like goodbye.

Bert going somewhere . . . he'd sounded sad. Those comments he'd made about senility. All the apologies.

Bert was a first-rate therapist, wise enough to know I hadn't wanted advice. But he offered a parting shot, anyway.

Try to season each day with a new perspective. Last words from an old friend facing deterioration? Taking a trip . . . a final journey?

There I was again, off on some worst-case tangent.

Keep it simple: the old man had always traveled, loved to travel. No reason to think his destination was anywhere but Southeast Asia . . .

The phone rang again. I switched it to speaker and Milo's voice, distant and flecked with static, filled the kitchen. 'Any new insights?'

'How about an actual fact?' I said. 'Nicholas Hansen couldn't have been involved in Janie's murder. Early in June he was finishing up his last year at Columbia. After he graduated, he went to Amsterdam and spent the summer at a life-drawing course at the Rijksmuseum.'

'That assumes he didn't come home for the weekend.'

'New York to L.A. for the weekend?'

'These were rich kids,' he said. 'Anything's possible,

but I just don't see it. Hansen's different from the other King's Men. His life took a whole different turn, and unless you can uncover some present-day dealings with Coury and the Cossacks and Brad Larner, my bet is he distanced himself from the group and maintained that distance.'

'So he's no use to us.'

'On the contrary. *He* might be able to provide insights.'

'We just drop in and say we want to chat about his old pals the sex-killers?'

'Any other promising leads at the moment?' I said.

He didn't answer.

I said, 'So what'd you do today?'

'Nosed around about Coury, Junior. His daddy was the nasty piece of work the papers made him out to be. Used gang-bangers to collect the rent. And looks like Junior's continued the relationship. The dubious citizens working his parking lots have that homeboy thing going on.'

'Funny about that.' I told him about my visit to the garage.

'Chopping the Seville as a cover story?' he said. 'Did it ever occur to you Coury didn't want to do the job 'cause he wasn't buying your story? Jesus, Alex—'

'Why wouldn't he buy it?' I said.

'Because maybe someone in the enemy camp knows we've been snooping around the Ingalls case. You got the goddamned murder book in the first place because someone knew we worked together. Alex, that was goddamned stupid.'

'Coury wasn't suspicious, just apathetic,' I said, with more confidence than I felt. 'My take is that he doesn't need the money.'

'Was he doing other chop jobs?'

'Yes,' I admitted.

'Meaning he works, but he just didn't want to work with *you*. Alex, no more improvisation.'

'Fine,' I said. 'Gang connections would have given Coury ready personnel for odd jobs. Like taking care of Luke Chapman, and possibly Willie Burns and Caroline Cossack. Maybe Lester Poulsenn, too. I located him – safely, all computer work – and guess what, he died less than two weeks after Caroline left Achievement House. Shot in the head in a house in Watts, then the house was burned down. He'd just been transferred from IA to Metro, meaning maybe he was working on Janie's case, right?'

'Burned to death,' he said. His voice was tight. 'What was he doing in Watts?'

'The paper didn't say. Sacramento paper, by the way. A detective got murdered in L.A. but the L.A. papers didn't print a word about it.'

'The article say where in Watts?'

I read off the address.

No answer.

'You still there?'

'Yeah . . . okay, meet me in Beverly Hills in an hour. Time for art appreciation.'

thirty-two

Nicholas Hansen's green BMW sat in the cobbled driveway of the house on North Roxbury Drive. The street was lined with struggling elms. A few trees had given up, and their black branches cast ragged shadows on the sparkling sidewalks. The street was quiet but for a Beverly Hills symphony: teams of gardeners pampering the greenery of mansions up the block.

Milo was parked in a new rental car – a gray Oldsmobile sedan – six houses north of Hansen's vanilla hacienda. By the time I'd switched off the engine he was at my window.

'New wheels,' I said.

'Variety's the spice.' His face was pallid and sweaty.

'Something else happen to make you switch?'

'Contacting Hansen is a risk and maybe not a smart one. If he's still in touch with the others, everything hits the fan. If he's not, there may be no real payoff.'

'But you're going ahead, anyway.'

He yanked out a handkerchief and sopped moisture from his brow. 'The alternative is doing nothing. And who says I'm smart?'

When we reached Hansen's property, he scowled and peered through a window of the BMW. 'Clean.

Meticulous.' As he stepped up to the door and stabbed the bell, he looked ready to tear something apart.

Nicholas Hansen answered wearing faded black sweats, white Nikes, and a distracted look. Brown and red paint stains on his fingers were the only clues to his occupation. He was tall and spare with an oddly fleshy face, looked closer to fifty than forty. Soft neck, basset eyes the color of river silt, grayish mouth stitched with wrinkles, a bald, blue-veined scalp ringed by a beige buzz. A middle-aged crisis stoop rounded his shoulders. I'd have guessed a burnt-out lawyer taking a day off.

Milo flashed the badge, and Hansen's muddy eyes came alive. But his voice was low and mumbly. 'Police? About what?'

I was standing behind Milo, but not so far that I couldn't smell the alcohol breeze Hansen had let forth.

Milo said, 'High school.' His voice was rough, and he didn't use Hansen's name, hadn't even offered a cop's patronizing 'sir.'

'High school?' Hansen blinked, and the paint-stained fingers of one hand capped his bald head, as if he'd been afflicted by a sudden migraine.

'The King's Men,' said Milo. Hansen dropped the hand and rubbed his fingers together, dislodging a fleck of paint, inspecting his nails. 'I really don't understand – I'm working.'

Milo said, 'This is important.' He'd kept the badge in Hansen's face, and the artist took a step backward.

'The King's Men?' said Hansen. 'That was a very long time ago.'

Milo filled the space Hansen had vacated. 'Those who forget the past are condemned to repeat it, and all that.'

Hansen's hand floundered some more, ended up on

the doorjamb. He shook his head. 'You've lost me, gentlemen.' His breath was ninety proof, and his nose was a relief map of busted capillaries.

'Be happy to clarify,' said Milo. He flicked his wrist, and sunlight bounced off the badge. 'I assume you don't want to talk out here in full view.'

Hansen shrank back some more. Milo was only an inch or so taller than Hansen, but he did something with his posture that increased the gap.

'I'm a painter, I'm in the middle of a painting,' Hansen insisted.

'I'm in the middle of a homicide investigation.'

Hansen's mouth slackened, revealing uneven, yellowed teeth. He shut his mouth quickly, looked at his watch, then over his shoulder.

'I'm a big art fan,' said Milo. 'Especially German Expressionism – all that anxiety.'

Hansen stared at him, stepped back farther. Milo remained in the dance, positioned himself inches from Hansen's worried eyes.

Hansen said, 'I hope this doesn't take long.'

The house was cool and dim, saturated with the geriatric reek of camphor. The chipped terracotta tiles of the entry hall floor continued up the steps of a narrow, brass-railed staircase. Thirteen-foot ceilings were crossed by carved oak beams. The wood was wormholed and aged nearly black. The walls were hand-troweled plaster two shades deeper than the external vanilla and dotted with empty niches. Smallish leaded windows, some with stained-glass insets picturing New Testament scenes, constricted the light. The colored panes projected rainbow dust beams. The furniture was heavy and dark and clumsy. No art on the walls. The place felt like some ill-attended church.

Nicholas Hansen motioned us to a sagging, fringed sofa upholstered in a scratchy tapestry fabric, sat down facing us in a bruised leather chair, and folded his hands in his lap.

'I really can't imagine what this could be about.'

'Let's start with the King's Men,' said Milo. 'You do remember them.'

Hansen gave his watch another glance. Cheap digital thing with a black plastic band.

'Busy day?' said Milo.

Hansen said, 'I may have to interrupt if my mother wakes up. She's dying of colon cancer, and the day nurse took the afternoon off.'

'Sorry,' said Milo, with as little sympathy as I'd ever heard him offer.

'She's eighty-seven,' said Hansen. 'Had me when she was forty-five. I always wondered how long I'd have her.' He plucked at a cuff of his sweatshirt. 'Yes, I remember the King's Men. Why would you connect me to them after all these years?'

'Your name came up in the course of our investigation.'

Hansen showed yellow teeth again. His eyes creased in concentration. 'My name came up in a murder investigation?'

'A very nasty murder.'

'Something recent?'

Milo crossed his legs. 'This will go more quickly if I ask the questions.'

Another man might've bristled. Hansen sat in place, like an obedient child. 'Yes, of course. I'm just – the King's Men was just a stupid high school thing.' Slight slur in his voice. His eyes shot to the ceiling beams. A pliable man. The addition of booze made Milo's job easier.

Milo pulled out his notepad. When he clicked his pen open, Hansen was startled but he remained in place.

'Let's start with the basics: you were a member of the King's Men.'

'I'd really like to know how you . . . never mind, let's do this quickly,' said Hansen. 'Yes, I was a member. For my last two years at Uni. I arrived as a junior. My father was an executive with Standard Oil, we moved around a lot, had lived on the East Coast. During my junior year, Father was transferred to L.A., and we ended up renting a house in Westwood. I was pretty disoriented. It's a disorienting time, anyway, right? I guess I was irritated at my parents for uprooting me. I'd always been obedient – an only child, overly adult. I guess when I got to Uni I figured I'd rebel, and the King's Men seemed a good way to do it.'

'Why?'

'Because they were a bunch of goof-offs,' said Hansen. 'Rich kids who did nothing but drink and dope. They got the school to recognize them as a legitimate service club because one of their fathers owned real estate and he let the school use his empty lots for fund-raisers – car washes, bake sales, that kind of thing. But the Men weren't about service, just partying.'

'A dad with real estate,' said Milo. 'Vance Coury.'

'Yes, Vance's father.'

Hansen's voice rose at the word 'father,' and Milo waited for him to say more. When Hansen didn't, he said, 'When's the last time you saw Vance Coury?'

'High school graduation,' said Hansen. 'I haven't been in touch with any of them. That's why this whole thing is rather odd.'

Another glance upward. Hansen had never boned up on the body language of deception.

'You haven't seen any of them since graduation?' said Milo. 'Not once?'

'By the time we graduated, I was moving in another direction. They were all staying here, and I'd been accepted at Columbia. My father wanted me to go to business school, but I finally accomplished a genuine rebellion and majored in anthropology. What I was really interested in was art, but that would've caused too much tumult. As is, Father was far from amused, but Mother was supportive.'

A third look at his watch, then a glance toward the stairs. Only child hoping for maternal reprieve.

Milo said, 'You didn't really answer the question. Have you seen any of the other King's Men since graduation?'

Hansen's muddy irises took yet another journey upward, and his mouth began to tremble. He tried to cover it with a smile. Crossed his legs, as if imitating Milo. The result was contortive, not casual.

'I never saw Vance or the Cossacks or Brad Larner. But there was another boy, Luke Chapman – though we're talking twenty years ago, for God's sake. Luke was . . . what is it you want to know, exactly?'

Milo's jaw tightened. His voice turned gentle and ominous. 'Luke was what?'

Hansen didn't answer.

Milo said, 'You do know he's dead.'

Hansen nodded. 'Very sad.'

'What were you going to say about him?'

'That he wasn't very bright.'

'When, after graduation, did you see him?'

'Look,' said Hansen. 'You need to understand the

context. He – Luke – was no genius. Honestly, he was
dull. Despite that, I'd always thought of him as the best of
them. That's why – does this have to do with Luke's
drowning?'

'When did you see Chapman?'

'Just once,' said Hansen.

'When?'

'My first year in grad school.'

'What month?'

'Winter break. December.'

'So just weeks before Chapman drowned.'

Hansen blanched and brought his eyes back to the
carved beams. He sank in his chair and looked small.
Incompetent liar. Painting had been a better choice than
the corporate thing. Milo slapped his pad shut, shot to
his feet, strode to Hansen and placed his hand on the
back of Hansen's chair. Hansen looked ready to faint.

'Tell us about it,' said Milo.

'You're saying Luke was murdered? All those years
ago . . . who do you suspect?'

'Tell us about the meeting with Chapman.'

'I – this is – ' Hansen shook his head. 'I could use a
drink – may I get you something, as well?'

'No, but feel free to fortify yourself.'

Hansen braced himself on the arms of his chair and
rose. Milo followed him across the tiled entry, across an
adjoining dining room and through double doors. When
the two of them returned, Hansen had both his hands
wrapped around a squat, cut-crystal tumbler half-filled
with whiskey. When he sat down, Milo resumed his
stance behind the chair. Hansen twisted and looked up at
him, drained most of the whiskey, rubbed the corners of
his eyes.

'Start with where.'

'Right here – in the house.' Hansen emptied the glass. 'Luke and I hadn't been in contact. High school was long out of my consciousness. They were *stupid* kids. Stupid *rich* kids, and the thought that I'd found them cool was laughable. I was an East Coast nerd scared witless about making yet another lifestyle switch, thrown into a whole new world. Tanned bodies, loud smiles, social castes . . . it was a sudden overdose of *California*. Luke and I had World History together. He was flunking – he was this big blond lunk who could barely read or spell. I felt sorry for him so I helped him – gave him free tutoring. He was dull, but not a bad kid. Built like a fridge, but he never went out for sports because he preferred drinking and smoking dope. That was the essence of the Kingers. They made a big point of not engaging in anything *but* partying and at that specific time in my life that kind of abandon seemed attractive. So when Luke invited me to join the group, I jumped at it. It was somewhere to belong. I had nothing else.'

'Were you welcomed by the others?'

'Not with open arms, but they weren't bad,' said Hansen. 'Tested me out. I had to prove myself by drinking them under the table. That I could do, but I never really felt comfortable with them and maybe they sensed it because, toward the end, they got . . . distant. Also, there was the economic thing. They'd figured I was rich – there'd been a rumor circulating that Father *owned* an oil company. When I told them the truth, they were clearly disappointed.'

Hansen passed the tumbler from hand to hand, stared at his knees. 'Listen to me, going on about myself.' He took a deep breath. 'That's the sum total: I hung out with them for the second half of my junior year and a bit into my senior year, then it tapered off. When I got into Columbia, that put them off. *They* were all planning to live off their parents' money in L.A. and keep partying.'

Milo said, 'So you were home on break and Luke Chapman just dropped in.'

'Yes, it was out of the blue,' said Hansen. 'I was spending my time holed up in my room drawing. Luke showed up unannounced, and Mother let him in.'

Hansen hefted the empty tumbler.

'What did he want?' said Milo.

Hansen stared at him.

'What was the topic, Nicholas?'

'He looked terrible,' said Hansen. 'Disheveled, unwashed – smelled like a barn. I didn't know what to make of it. Then he said, "Nick, man, you were the only one who ever helped me, and I need you to help me now." My first thought was he'd gotten some girl pregnant, needed guidance about where to get an abortion, something like that. I said, "What can I do for you." And that's when he broke down – just fell apart. Rocking and moaning and saying everything was fucked up.'

He held up the tumbler. 'I could use a refill?'

Milo turned to me. 'The bottle's on the counter. Nicholas and I will wait here.'

I entered the kitchen and poured two fingers from the bottle of Dalwhinnie single-malt on the counter. Taking in details as I made my way back: yellow walls, old white appliances, bare stainless-steel counters, empty dish drainers. I opened the refrigerator. Carton of milk, package of sweating bacon, something in a bowl that looked like calcified gruel. No food aromas, just that same mothball stink. The whiskey bottle had been three-quarters empty. Nicholas Hansen cared little for nutrition, was a solitary drinker.

Back in the living room, Milo was ignoring Hansen and flipping the pages of his notepad. Hansen sat paralytically still. I handed him the drink and he took it with both hands and gulped.

Milo said, 'Luke fell apart.'

'I asked him what was wrong but instead of telling me he pulled out a joint and started to light up. I grabbed it out of his hand, and said, "What do you think you're doing?" I guess I sounded irritated because he shrank back and said, "Oh, Nick, we really fucked up." And that's when he let it all out.'

Hansen finished the second Scotch.

Milo said, 'Go on.'

Hansen regarded the empty glass, seemed to be considering another shot, but placed the tumbler on a side table. 'He told me there'd been a party – a big one, some place in Bel Air, an empty house—'

'Whose house?'

'He didn't say and I didn't ask,' said Hansen. 'I didn't *want* to know.'

'Why not?' said Milo.

'Because I'd moved on, they were long gone from my consciousne—'

'What did Chapman tell you about the party?' said Milo.

Hansen was silent. Looked anywhere but at us.

We waited him out.

He said, 'Oh my.'

'Oh my, indeed,' said Milo.

Hansen snatched up the tumbler. 'I could use a—'

Milo said, 'No.'

413

'A girl got killed at the party. I really need another drink.'

'What was the girl's name?'

'*I don't know!*' Hansen's irises were wet – boggy mud.

'You don't know,' said Milo.

'All Luke said was there'd been a party and things had gotten wild and they'd been fooling around with a girl and things got even wilder and all of a sudden she was dead.'

'Fooling around.'

No answer.

'All of a sudden,' said Milo.

'That's how he put it,' said Hansen. Milo chuckled. Hansen recoiled, nearly dropped the tumbler.

'How was this *sudden* death brought about, Nick?'

Hansen bit his lip.

Milo barked, 'Come on.'

Hansen jumped in his chair and fumbled the glass again. 'Please – I don't know what happened – *Luke* didn't know what had happened. That was the point. He was confused – disoriented.'

'What did he tell you about the girl?'

'He said Vance tied her up, they were partying with her, then all of a sudden it was bloody. A bloody scene, like one of those movies we used to watch in high school – slasher movies. "Worse than that, Nick. It's much worse when it's real." I got sick to my stomach, said, "What the hell are you talking about?" Luke just babbled and blubbered and kept repeating that they'd fucked up.'

'Who?'

'All of them. The Kingers.'

'No name for the girl?'

'He said he'd never seen her before. She was someone

414

Vance knew, and Vance noticed her and picked her up. Literally. Slung her over his shoulder and carried her down to the basement. She was stoned.'

'In the basement of the party house.'

'That's where they . . . fooled with her.'

'Fooled with her,' said Milo.

'I'm trying to be accurate. That's how Luke put it.'

'Did Chapman take part in the rape?'

Hansen mumbled.

'What's that?' demanded Milo.

'He wasn't sure, but he thought he did. He was stoned, too. Everyone was. He didn't remember, kept saying the whole thing was like a nightmare.'

'Especially for the girl,' said Milo.

'I didn't want to believe him,' said Hansen. 'I'd come home from Yale for ten days. The last thing I needed was this dropping in my lap. I figured it had been a dream – some sort of drug hallucination. Back when I'd known Luke he was always on something.'

'You said he wanted help from you. What kind of help?'

'He wanted to know what to do. I was a twenty-two-year-old *kid*, for Christ's sake, what position was I in to give him advice?' Hansen's fingers tightened around the tumbler. 'He couldn't have picked a worse time to drop it on me. People were telling me I had talent, I was finally standing up to Father. The last thing I needed was to get sucked into some . . . horror. It was my *right* not to get sucked in. And I don't know why *you* feel you have a right to—'

'So you just dropped it,' said Milo. 'What'd you tell Chapman?'

'No,' said Hansen. 'That's wrong. I didn't drop it. Not

415

completely. I told Luke to go home and keep all of it to himself, and when I figured things out, I'd get back to him.'

'He listened to you?'

Hansen nodded. 'It was what . . . he wanted to hear. He thanked me. After he left, I kept telling myself it had been the drugs talking. I *wanted* to drop it. But something happened to me that year – a painting class I'd taken. The teacher was an Austrian expatriate, a Holocaust survivor. He'd told me horror stories of all the good citizens who'd claimed to know nothing about what was going on. What liars they were. How Vienna had cheered when Hitler took power and everyone had turned a blind eye to atrocities. I remembered something he'd said: "The Austrians have convinced themselves that Hitler was German and Beethoven was Austrian." That stuck with me. I didn't want to be like that. So I went over to the library and checked out the newspapers for the time period Luke said the murder had taken place. But there was *nothing*. Not an article, not a single *word* about any girl being murdered in Bel Air. So I decided Luke *had* been freaking out.'

Hansen's shoulders dropped. He allowed himself a weak smile. Trying to relax. Milo played the silence and Hansen tightened up again. 'So you're saying there really . . . ?'

'Did you ever call Chapman back? Like you said you would?'

'I had nothing to tell him.'

'So what'd you do next?'

'I went back to Yale.'

'Chapman ever try to reach you at Yale?'

'No.'

416

'When were you in L.A. next?'
'Not for years. The next summer I was in France.'
'Avoiding L.A.?'
'No,' said Hansen. 'Looking for other things.'
'Such as?'
'Painting opportunities.'
'When did you move back to L.A.?'
'Three years ago, when Mother became ill.'
'Where were you living before that?'
'New York, Connecticut, Europe. I try to spend as much time as I can in Europe. Umbria, the light—'
'What about Austria?' said Milo.
Hansen's face lost color.
'So you're here to take care of your mother.'
'That's the *only* reason. When she passes, I'll sell the house and find myself somewhere peaceful.'
'Meanwhile,' said Milo, 'you and your old buddies are neighbors—'
'They're not my bud—'
'—ever make you nervous? Your being a semipublic figure and having a bunch of murderers knowing you're back in town?'
'I'm not semipublic,' said Hansen. 'I'm not any kind of public. I *paint*. Finish one canvas and start another. I never truly believed anything *happened*.'
'What did you think when you learned about Chapman drowning?'
'That it was an accident or suicide.'
'Why suicide?'
'Because he'd seemed so upset.'
'Suicide out of remorse?' said Milo.
Hansen didn't answer.
'You believed Chapman had been hallucinating, but

you left town without trying to convince him there was nothing to worry about.'

'It wasn't my – what is it you *want* from me?'

'Details.'

'About what?'

'The murder.'

'I don't have any more details.'

'Why would Chapman feel remorse for something that never happened?'

'I don't know, I'm not a mind reader! This whole thing is insane. Not a word in the papers for twenty years, and all of a sudden someone cares?'

Milo consulted his pad. 'How'd you learn about Chapman's death?'

'Mother included it in her weekly letter.'

'How'd you feel about it?'

'What do you *think*? I felt *terrible*,' said Hansen. 'How *else* could I feel?'

'You felt terrible, then just forgot about it.'

Hansen rose out of his chair. Spittle whitened the corners of his lips.

'What was I *supposed* to do? Go to the police and repeat some far-fetched, stoned-out story? I was twenty-two, for Christ's sake.'

Milo flashed him a cold stare, and Hansen slumped back down. 'It's easy to judge.'

'Let's go over the details,' said Milo. 'The girl was raped in the basement. Where'd Chapman say they killed her?'

Hansen shot him a miserable look. 'He said there was a big property next door to the party house, an estate, no one living there. They brought her over there. He said she was unconscious. They took her into some wooded area

418

and started talking about how they needed to make sure she didn't turn them in. That's when it got . . .'

'Bloody.'

Hansen covered his face and exhaled noisily.

'Who's "they"?' said Milo.

'All of them,' Hansen said through his fingers. 'The Kingers.'

'Who exactly was there? Names.'

'Vance and Luke, Garvey and Bob Cossack, Brad Larner. All of them.'

'The Kingers,' said Milo. 'Guys you don't see anymore. Guys you're not worried about being your neighbors.'

Hansen's hands dropped. 'Should I be worried?'

'It does seem odd,' said Milo. 'For three years you've been living in L.A. but you've never run into them.'

'It's a big city,' said Hansen. 'Big as you want it to be.'

'You don't run in the same social circles?'

'I don't have *any* social circle. I rarely leave the house. Everything's delivered – groceries, laundry. Painting and taking Mother to the doctor, that's my world.'

I thought: *Prison.*

Milo said, 'Have you followed the others' lives?'

'I know the Cossacks are builders of some kind – you see their names on construction signs. That's it.'

'No idea what Vance Coury's been up to?'

'No.'

'Brad Larner?'

'No.'

Milo wrote something down. 'So . . . your buddies took the nameless girl to the property next door and things just *kind* of got bloody.'

'They weren't my buddies.'

'Who did the actual killing?'

419

'Luke didn't say.'

'What about the rape? Who initiated that?'

'He – my impression was they all joined in.'

'But Chapman wasn't sure if he participated or not.'

'Maybe he was lying. Or in denial, I don't know,' said Hansen. 'Luke wasn't cruel but – I can see him getting carried along. But without the others, he never would've done anything like that. He told me he'd felt . . . immobilized – as if his feet were stuck. That's the way he phrased it. "My feet were stuck, Nick. Like in quicksand." '

'Can you see the others doing something like that on their own?'

'I don't know . . . I used to think of them as clowns . . . maybe. All I'm saying is Luke was a big softie. A big Baby Huey type of guy.'

'And the others?'

'The others weren't soft.'

'So,' said Milo, 'the murder started out as a way to silence the girl.'

Hansen nodded.

'But it progressed to something else, Nicholas. If you'd seen the body, you'd know that. It was something you wouldn't want to paint.'

'Oh, Lord,' said Hansen.

'Did Luke Chapman make any mention at all of who initiated the murder?'

Hansen shook his head.

'How about taking a guess?' said Milo. 'From what you remember about the Kingers' personalities.'

'Vance,' said Hansen, without hesitation. 'He was the leader. The most aggressive. Vance was the one who picked her up. If I had to guess, I'd say Vance was the first to cut her.'

Milo slapped his pad shut. His head shot forward. 'Who said anything about cutting, Nicholas?'

Hansen turned white. 'You said it – you said it was ugly.'

'Chapman told you they'd cut her, didn't he?'

'Maybe – he could've.'

Milo stood and stomped his way slowly toward Hansen on echoing tiles, came to a halt inches from Hansen's terrified face. Hansen's hands rose protectively.

'What else are you holding back, Nicholas?'

'Nothing! I'm doing my best—'

'Do better,' said Milo.

'I'm *trying*.' Hansen's voice took on a whine. 'It's twenty years ago. You're making me remember things I repressed because they disgusted me. I didn't *want* to hear details then, and I don't want to now.'

'Because you like pretty things,' said Milo. 'The wonderful world of art.'

Hansen clapped his hands against his temples and looked away from Milo. Milo got down on one knee and spoke into Hansen's right ear.

'Tell me about the cutting.'

'That's it. He just said they started cutting her.' Hansen's shoulders rose and fell, and he began weeping.

Milo gave him a moment of peace. Then he said, 'After they cut her, what?'

'They burned her. They burned her with cigarettes. Luke said he could hear her skin sizzle . . . oh God – I really thought he was . . .'

'Making it up.'

Hansen sniffed, wiped his nose with his sleeve, let his head fall. The back of his neck was glossy and creased, like canned tallow.

421

Milo said, 'They burned her, then what?'

'That's all. That really *is* all. Luke said it was like it became a game – he had to *think* of it as a game in order not to freak out completely. He said he'd watched and tried to pretend she was one of those inflatable dolls and they were playing with her. He said it seemed to go on forever until someone – I think it was Vance, I can't swear to it, but probably Vance – said she was dead and they needed to get her out of there. They bundled her up in something, put her in the trunk of Vance's Jaguar, and dumped her somewhere near downtown.'

'Pretty detailed for a hallucination,' said Milo.

Hansen didn't respond.

'Especially,' pressed Milo, 'for a dull guy like Chapman. You ever know him to be that imaginative?'

Hansen remained mute.

'Where'd they take her, Nicholas?'

'I don't *know* where – why the hell wasn't it in the *papers*?' Hansen balled a hand into a fist and raised it chest high. Making a stab at assertiveness. Milo remained crouched but somehow increased his dominance. Hansen shook his head and looked away and cried some more.

'What'd they do afterward?'

'Had coffee,' said Hansen. 'Some place in Hollywood. Coffee and pie. Luke said he tried eating but threw up in the bathroom.'

'What kind of pie?'

'I didn't ask. Why wasn't there anything in the *papers*?'

'What would your theory be about that, Nicholas?'

'What do you mean?' said Hansen.

'Given what you know about your buddies, what's your theory?'

'I don't see what you're getting at.'

422

Milo got up, stretched, rolled his neck, walked slowly to a leaded window, turned his back on Hansen. 'Think about the world you inhabit, Nicholas. You're a successful artist. You get thirty, forty thousand dollars for a painting. Who buys your stuff?'

'Thirty thousand isn't big-time in the art world,' said Hansen. 'Not compared to—'

'It's a lot of money for a painting,' said Milo. 'Who buys your stuff?'

'Collectors, but I don't see what that has to—'

'Yeah, yeah, people of taste and all that. But at forty grand a pop not just any collectors.'

'People of means,' said Hansen.

Milo turned suddenly, grinning. 'People with money, Nicholas.' He cleared his throat.

Hansen's muddy eyes rounded. 'You're saying someone was bribed to keep it quiet? Something that horrible could be – then for God's sake why didn't it *stay* quiet? Why is it coming to light now?'

'Give me a theory about that, too.'

'I don't have one.'

'Think.'

'It's in someone's best interests to go public?' said Hansen. He sat up. 'Bigger money's come into play? Is that what you're getting at?'

Milo returned to the sofa, sat back comfortably, flipped his pad open.

'Bigger money,' said Hansen. 'Meaning I'm a total *ass* for talking to you. You caught me off guard and used me—' He brightened suddenly. 'But you screwed *up*. You were obligated to offer me the presence of an attorney, so anything I've told you is inadmissible—'

'You watch too much TV, Nicholas. We're *obligated* to

423

offer you a lawyer if we arrest you. Any reason we should arrest you, Nicholas?'

'No, no, of course not—'

Milo glanced at me. 'I suppose we could exercise the option. Obstruction of justice is a felony.' Back to Hansen: 'Charge like that, whether or not you got convicted, your life would change. But given that you've cooperated . . .'

Hansen's eyes sparked. He pawed at the scant hair above his ears. 'I need to be worried, don't I?'

'About what?'

'*Them.* Jesus, what have I done? I'm stuck here, can't *leave*, not with Mother—'

'With or without Mother, leaving would be a bad idea, Nicholas. If you've been straight – really told us everything – we'll do our best to keep you safe.'

'As if you give a damn.' Hansen got to his feet. 'Get out – leave me alone.'

Milo stayed seated. 'How about a look at your painting?'

'*What?*'

'I meant what I said,' said Milo. 'I do like art.'

'My studio's private space,' said Hansen. 'Get out!'

'Never show a fool an unfinished work?'

Hansen tottered. Laughed hollowly. 'You're no fool. You're a user. How do you live with yourself?'

Milo shrugged, and we headed for the door. He stopped a foot from the knob. 'By the way, the pictures on your gallery website are gorgeous. What is it the French call still-lifes – *nature morte*? Dead nature?'

'Now you're trying to diminish me.'

Milo reached for the door, and Hansen said, 'Fine, take a look. But I only have one painting in progress, and it needs work.'

★ ★ ★

We followed him up the brass-railed staircase to a long landing carpeted in defeated green shag. Three bedrooms on one end, a single, closed door off by itself on the north wing. A breakfast tray was set on the rug. A teapot and three plastic bowls: blood-colored jello, soft-boiled egg darkened to ochre, something brown and granular and crusted.

'Wait here,' said Hansen, 'I need to check on her.' He tiptoed to the door, cracked it open, looked inside, returned. 'Still sleeping. Okay, c'mon.'

His studio was the southernmost bedroom, a smallish space expanded by a ceiling raised to the rafters and a skylight that let in southern sun. The hardwood floors were painted white, as was his easel. White-lacquered flat file, white paint box and brush holders, glass jars filled with turpentine and thinner. Dots of color squeezed on a white porcelain palette fluttered in the milky atmosphere like exotic butterflies.

On the easel was an eleven-by-fourteen panel. Hansen had said his current painting needed work, but it looked finished to me. At the center of the composition was an exquisitely bellied, blue-and-white Ming vase, rendered so meticulously that I longed to touch the gloss. A jagged crack ran down the belly of the vase, and brimming over its lip were masses of flowers and vines, their brilliance accentuated – animated – by a burnt umber background that deepened to black at the edges.

Orchids and peonies and tulips and irises and blooms I couldn't identify. Hot colors, luminous striations, voluptuous petals, vaginal leaves, vermiform tendrils, all interspersed with ominous clots of sphagnum. The fissure implied incipient explosion. Flowers, what could

425

be prettier? Hansen's blooms, gorgeous and boastful and flame-vivid as they were, said something else.

Gleam and hue fraying and wilting at the edges. From the shadows, the black, inexorable progress of rot.

Conditioned air blew through a ceiling vent, flat, artificial, filtered clean, but a stink reached my nostrils: the painting gave off the moist, squalid seduction of decay.

Milo wiped his brow, and said, 'You don't use a model.'

Hansen said, 'It's all in my head.'

Milo stepped closer to the easel. 'You alternate paint and glaze?'

Hansen stared at him. 'Don't tell me you paint.'

'Can't draw a straight line.' Milo got even nearer to the board and squinted. 'Kind of a Flemish thing going on – or maybe someone with an appreciation of Flemish, like Severin Roesen. But you're better than Roesen.'

'Hardly,' said Hansen, unmoved by the compliment. 'I'm a lot less than I was before you barged into my life. You *have* diminished me. I've diminished myself. Will you really protect me?'

'I'll do my best if you cooperate.' Milo straightened. 'Did Luke Chapman mention anyone else being present at the murder? Any of the other partygoers?'

Hansen's fleshy face quivered. 'Not here. Please.'

'Last question,' said Milo.

'No. He mentioned no one else.' Hansen sat down at the easel and rolled up his sleeves. 'You'll protect me,' he said in a dead voice. He selected a sable brush and smoothed its bristles. 'I'm going back to work. There are some real problems to work out.'

426

thirty-three

When we were back on Roxbury Drive, Milo said, 'Believe his story?'

'I do.'

'So do I,' he said, as we walked to our cars. 'I also believe I'm a hypocrite.'

'What do you mean?'

'Playing Grand Inquisitor with Hansen. Making him feel like shit because he repressed twenty-year-old memories. I did the same damn thing, with less of an excuse.'

'What's his excuse?' I said.

'He's weak. Cut him open, you'll find a Silly Putty spine.'

'You sensed the weakness right away,' I said.

'You noticed that, huh? Yup, moved right in on ol' Nicky. Got a nose for weakness. Doesn't that make me pleasant company?'

When we reached the gray Olds, I said, 'I know you're going to tell me I'm laying more shrink stuff on you, but I don't believe your situation's comparable to Hansen's. He had access to firsthand information about the murder and kept it to himself for twenty years. In order to do

that, he convinced himself Chapman had been hallucinating, but those details – cigarette burns, the way they
moved Janie – say he knew better. Hansen engaged in two
decades of self-delusion, and who knows what it did to
his soul. You tried to do your job and were ordered off
the case.'

'Following orders?' He gazed up the block absently.

'Fine,' I said. 'Torment yourself.'

'Hansen paints, I don't,' he said. 'We all need our
hobbies . . . listen, thanks for your time, but I need to
sort things out, figure which way to go with this.'

'What about the main point we got from Hansen's
story?' I said.

'Which is . . .'

'What you were getting at with that final question in
the studio about anyone else being at the murder.
Chapman spilled his guts to Hansen but made no
mention of Caroline Cossack or Willie Burns. Meaning
they probably weren't there. Despite that, the Cossacks
stashed Caroline at Achievement House for six months
and had her tagged with a behavioral warning. Burns
returned to the streets, got busted for dope, took a big
risk by getting himself a job at Achievement House.
Maybe he skipped on Boris Nemerov because of what
he'd seen at the party. If he went to jail on the drug
beef, he'd be a sitting duck.'

'Burns as a witness.'

'Maybe he followed the King's Men because he figured
there'd be more doping and he could peddle more
merchandise. Caroline could've just been hanging with
him. Or she wanted to hang out with her brothers – the
odd little sister who'd always gotten shunted to the
background. The initial motive for Janie's murder was to

silence her. Luke Chapman may have died for the same reason. Caroline and Burns would've been extreme liabilities.'

'Victims, not murderers,' he said. 'And all the more likely to be dead.'

'Those two photos preceding Janie's death shot. A dead black guy and a mangled white female mental patient. Maybe whoever sent the book was trying to tell you about two other db's.'

'Except, as you pointed out, the dead black guy was in his forties, which would be Burns's age now, not twenty years ago.' He took hold of the door handle. 'I need to develop a few migraines over this. Ciao.'

'That's it?'

'What?' he said.

'You go your way, I go mine?' I said. 'Is there something you aren't telling me?'

His half-second hesitation belied his answer. 'I wish I *had* something not to tell, Alex – look, I appreciate your effort but we can go over theories till the Second Coming, and it won't move me any closer to solving Janie.'

'What will?'

'Like I said, I need to do some thinking.'

'Alone.'

'Sometimes,' he said, 'alone helps.'

I drove away wondering what he was keeping from me, peeved at being shut out. Thinking about what didn't await me at home turned irritation to dread, and before I knew it I was hunched over the wheel, driving too fast – going nowhere fast.

Nothing worse than a big house when you're alone. And I had no one to blame but myself.

I'd screwed things up, royally, despite Bert Harrison's wise counsel. Like most expert therapists, the old man wasn't one for offering unsolicited advice, but during my visit he'd made a point of warning me off the paranoia trail when it came to Robin.

'*Sounds like small things have been amplified . . . this is the girl for you.*' Had he sensed something – sniffed out nuances of my impending stupidity? Why the hell hadn't I listened to him?

A blast of honks jolted me. I'd been sitting at the green light at Walden and Sunset for who knew how long and the cute young woman in the VW Golf behind me thought that justified a snarl and a stiff finger.

I waved at her and sped off. She passed me, stopped talking on her cell-phone long enough to flip me off again, nearly collided with the curb as her VW struggled with the winding road.

I wished her well and returned to thoughts of Bert Harrison. The other opinions the old man voiced that day – outwardly casual remarks tossed out at the tail end of my visit.

Coincidence or the old therapist's trick of harnessing the power of the parting word? I'd used it myself hundreds of times.

Bert's parting shot had been to bring up Caroline Cossack. Out of context – well after we'd stopped discussing the Ingalls case.

'*That girl. So monstrous, if it's true.*'

'*You seem skeptical.*'

'*I do find it hard to believe that a young female would be capable of such savagery.*'

Then Bert had gone on to express doubts about Willie Burns as a lust murderer.

'*A junkie in the strict sense – heroin? Opiates are the great pacifiers . . . I've certainly never heard of a junkie acting out in such a sexually violent manner.*'

Now it looked as if Bert had been right on.

Was all that the intuition of an exceptionally insightful man?

Or did Bert *know*?

Had Schwinn continued to work the Ingalls case for years after leaving the department? Had he told *Bert* about what he'd unearthed?

Bert had admitted knowing Schwinn but claimed the relationship was casual. Chance meetings in theater lobbies.

What if it was anything *but* casual?

Schwinn had fought his way out of drug addiction, and perhaps he'd done so on his own. But that kind of progress would've been helped along by treatment, and Bert Harrison had trained in addiction treatment at the Federal hospital in Lexington.

Schwinn as Bert's patient.

Psychotherapy. Where all kinds of secrets tumbled out.

If any of that was true, Bert had lied to me. And *that* could explain all those apologies he'd tendered. His contrition – so puzzling at the time that I'd wondered about Bert's deteriorating mental state.

Bert had *encouraged* my suspicions: '*One regresses. Loses one's sense of propriety. Forgive me.*'

'*There's nothing to forgive—*'

I remembered how he'd wiped away tears.

'*Is everything okay, Bert?*'

'*Everything is as it should be.*'

Seeking forgiveness because he knew he had to lie to me? Protecting Schwinn because of patient confidentiality?

431

But Schwinn had been buried seven months ago and any privilege had died along with his body. Perhaps Bert held himself to higher standards.

Or maybe he was protecting a *living* patient.

In drug treatment – the kind of intensive treatment Bert would've prescribed for a long-term addict like Schwinn – family members were included. And Marge was all the family Schwinn had had left.

Bert shielding Marge. It made sense. I strained to recall anything in our conversation that pointed to that and came up with something quickly: Bert had deflected any suggestion Marge could've mailed the murder book.

Protecting her, or had *Bert* been the messenger? A doctor honoring his patient's last wishes.

What if Janie's murder had eaten at Schwinn – corroded his late-in-life serenity – to the point where he felt impelled to stir up the ashes? Because even though the department had booted him out, and outwardly he'd made major life changes, Pierce Schwinn had held on to a detective's bulldog sensibilities.

Janie wasn't only a cold case, she'd been Schwinn's *last* case. One massive overdose of unfinished business. Perhaps Schwinn had connected the unsolved murder with his breakdown.

Bert would have wanted to help him with that.

The more I thought about it, the better it fit. Schwinn came to trust Bert, showed Bert the murder book, eventually bequeathed the album to his psychiatrist. Knowing Bert would do the right thing.

Bert's involvement would also explain why the blue-bound horror had been mailed to me. He'd met Milo a couple of times, but he knew me much better and was well aware of my relationship with Milo. For Bert, my handing over the book to Milo would have been a certainty.

Fingerprints wiped clean. I could see the old man doing that.

What I *couldn't* see was him driving down to L.A., stealing Rick's Porsche, and returning the car with the original Ingalls file on the front seat. The GTA combined with the HIV detective rumor and that weird encounter with the man who called himself Paris Bartlett had Big Blue written all over it.

Someone in the department. Or once associated with the department. Maybe even the cop buddy I'd hypothesized, stepping in once the wheels had begun to turn.

Theories. . . Bert had just called to let me know he was leaving town. A few days ago, he'd mentioned nothing about travel plans.

Escaping *because* of my visit? Bert and I weren't everyday acquaintances, there'd be no reason for him to notify me of his itinerary. Unless he was trying to distance himself from the fallout.

Or call me off.

By the time I made it to the bridle path that leads to my property, my head ached with conjecture. I pulled up in front of my house . . . our house. The damn thing looked cold, white . . . foreign. I sat in the Seville with the engine running. Turned the car around and drove back toward the Glen.

You *could* go home again, but what was the point?

My nerves were exposed wire sizzling with impulse. Maybe a long, pretty drive would help cool them down.

Alone.

Milo was right about that.

thirty-four

Milo drove out of Beverly Hills, mulling over the interview with Nicholas Hansen.

The guy was pathetic, a momma's boy and a drunk, no big challenge browbeating him into spilling. But would Hansen change his story once he had time to stew, maybe call an attorney? Even if he did hold fast, his tale amounted to third-party hearsay.

Still Milo knew what he had to do: go home, transcribe his notes of the interview, making sure he got all the details down, then stash the transcription with all the other good stuff he kept to himself – the floor safe in his bedroom closet.

He took Palm Drive to Santa Monica, then the diagonal shortcut to Beverly, driving like a gangster's chauffeur – slower than usual, checking the scenery all around, scoping out the drivers sitting two, three, four car lengths behind the rented Olds. Taking a different route than usual – past La Cienega, then doubling back on Rosewood. As far as he could tell, everything clear.

One thing the Hansen interview *had* accomplished: Milo knew now that he couldn't let go of Janie.

All these years he'd coped with department bullshit and propped up his self-image with secret little pep talks, the psychobabble he'd never share with anyone. *You're different. Noble. Heroic, nonstereotypic gay warrior traversing a goddamn heterosexual universe.*

Rebel with a lost cause.

Maybe all that self-delusional swill was what had helped him conveniently forget Janie. But the moment Alex had shown him that death shot, his heartbeat and his sweat glands told him he'd lived nearly half his life as the worst kind of chump.

Conning himself.

Was that insight? If so, it sucked.

He laughed out loud because cursing lacked imagination. He and Hansen were two peas in the same cowardly, ass-covering pod. Alex, ever the shrink – ever the *friend* – had tried to spin it differently.

Thank you very much, Doctor, but that don't change the facts.

Yeah, old Nicholas was a moral mollusk, but meeting him had solidified things.

As he cruised through quiet West Hollywood streets, he formalized the next risky step: get closer to the murder by leaning on someone who'd actually been there. The choice of targets was: Brad Larner. Because twenty years after high school, Larner was low man among the King's Men, a loser who'd worked for Daddy, then regressed to lackeying for his buddies.

One of those walking-around guys. A jerk.

A follower. If Vance Coury and the Cossacks were sharks, Larner was a remora, ready to be plucked off the body corrupt.

Milo ached to get the bastard in a quiet little room. But Larner wasn't living at his own home, might very well be bunking with the Cossacks. The challenge was to snag him alone, away from the others.

A-hunting we will go.

Normally, even with his cop sensibilities, he might not have noticed the navy blue Saab heading his way down his own block. West Hollywood parking laws kept the streets fairly clear but permit parking was allowed and homeowners could grant guest passes, so it was by no means weird to see an unfamiliar vehicle stationed near the curb.

But today he'd mainlined adrenaline instead of vodka and was noticing everything. So when the blue Saab sped by him and he caught a half-second eyeful of the driver, he knew he'd have to confirm what his brain was telling him.

He lowered his speed, watched in his rearview as the Saab turned onto Rosewood and disappeared from view. Then he hooked a sharp U and went after it.

Thank God for the brand-new rental he'd picked up on the way home. The gray Dodge Polaris had sagging bumpers and poorly camouflaged dings all over its abused chassis. But with power to spare and windows tinted way past the legal limit, it was exactly what he needed. For this one, he'd forsaken Hertz and Avis and Budget and patronized a guy he knew who ran a yard full of clunkers on Sawtelle and Olympic, out past the 405 South. Budget wheels for the spiky-haircut-and-skinny-lapeled-black-suit types – *arriviste* thespians and screenwriters and would-be dot.com gajillionaires who thought it way cool to tool around L.A. in something outdated and ugly.

Milo stomped the gas, and the Polaris responded, laying down a nice little patch of vertebra-rattling speed. He followed the Saab's trajectory, making sure he didn't get too close when he spotted his quarry turning north on San Vicente. A medium-congestion traffic flow allowed him to settle five lengths behind the Saab and do a little creative swerving so he could keep his eye on the vehicle.

From what he could tell, just the one male at the wheel. Now it was time to confirm the rest of his first impression. The Saab continued past Melrose and Santa Monica, turned left on Sunset, and got stuck in a serious jam caused by orange CalTrans cones blocking off the right-hand lane.

Cones only, no work or workers in sight. The road agency was run by sadists and fools, but this time Milo blessed their mean little hearts as the congestion allowed him to jockey to the right, catch sight of the Saab's plates, copy them down. Traffic moved fifty feet. Milo cell-phoned DMV, lied – Lord, he was getting good at it – *liked* it.

The plates came back to a one-year-old Saab owned by Craig Eiffel Bosc, address on Huston Street in North Hollywood, no wants or warrants.

The chrome sludge oozed another few yards, and Milo did some more rude maneuvering and managed to close the gap between the Dodge and the Saab to three cars. Three more stop-and-gos and a smooth but slow flow resumed and he was alongside the Saab, passing on the right, hoping the Dodge wouldn't register in his quarry's memory and if it did, that the blackened glass would cover him.

Another half a second was all he needed – mission accomplished.

437

The face was one he'd seen before. Mr Smiley. The asshole who'd accosted him at the hot dog stand, claiming to be Paris Bartlett.

Craig Eiffel Bosc.

Eiffel/Paris. Cute.

Bosc/Bartlett stymied him for a moment, then he got it: two varieties of pears.

How imaginative. Sell it to the networks.

Bosc/Bartlett was moving his head in time to music, oblivious, and Milo sped up, got two cars *ahead* of the Saab, used the next red light to peer through the intervening Toyota with its two little chicklets also bopping – to some bass-heavy hip-hop thing. He tried to get another look at Craig Eiffel Bosc but caught only the girls' hyperactivity and the Toyota's windshield glare. The right lane opened up and he eased back into it, allowed the Toyota and the Saab to pass.

Glancing to the left without moving his head as Smiley Pear zipped by. Then catching up and keeping pace with the Saab just long enough to take a mental snapshot.

Smiley was in shirtsleeves – deep blue shirt – with his sky-colored tie loosened, one paw on the wheel, the other wrapped around a big fat cigar. The Saab's windows were untinted but shut, and the interior was clouded with smoke. Not thick enough, though, to obscure the smile on Craig Eiffel Bosc's struggling-actor-handsome countenance.

Such a happy fellow, toking tobacco and cruising and grooving in his zippy little Swedish car on a sunny, California day.

On top of the world.

We'll see about that.

★ ★ ★

Craig Bosc took Coldwater Canyon into the Valley. Medium traffic made the tail easy. Not that Bosc would be looking out for him. The guy was no motor-pro – a real ninny for showing himself in plain view on Milo's block. The cigar and his grin said he couldn't even imagine the tables turning.

At Ventura, the Saab turned right and drove into Studio City, where it pulled into the parking lot of a twenty-four-hour yuppie gym on the south side of the boulevard. Craig Bosc got out with a blue bag and half jogged to the front. One good arm push and he was through the door and gone.

Milo looked around for a vantage point. A seafood restaurant across Ventura offered a perfect view of the gym and the Saab. The surf-and-turf special sounded enticing – he was hungry.

Ravenous.

He indulged himself with an upgrade from the special: extra big lobster, Alaskan crab legs, sixteen-ounce top sirloin, baked potato with sour cream and chives, a mountain of fried zucchini. All that washed down with Cokes instead of beer, because he needed his wits.

He ate slowly, figuring Bosc would be in there for at least an hour, doing the old body-beautiful thing. By the time he'd asked for the check and was working on his third coffee refill, the Saab was still in plain view. He threw down money, hazarded a trip to the men's room, left the restaurant, and sat in the Dodge for another half hour before Bosc emerged with wet hair. Back in his street clothes – the blue shirt and black slacks – minus the tie.

Bosc bounced over to the Saab, disarmed the alarm,

439

but instead of getting in, stopped to check his reflection in the side window. Fluffing his hair. Undoing the shirt's second button. Milo watched the asshole show off that big smile for the glass audience – Bosc actually turned his head here and there. Appreciating his own damn face from multiple angles.

Then Bosc got in the Saab and did an L.A. thing: *drove* less than a block before pulling into another parking lot.

A bar. Little cedar-sided cube stuffed between a sushi bar and a bicycle shop. A painted sign above the cedar door labeled the place as *EXTRAS*. A banner to the right advertised the psychic benefits of happy hour.

Half a dozen cars in the lot. Not too many happy people?

But Craig Bosc was. Grinning as he parked next to a ten-year-old Datsun Z, got out, checked his teeth in the side mirror, rubbed them with his index finger, went inside.

EXTRAS. Milo'd never enjoyed the ambience, but he knew the bar by reputation. Watering hole for small-time actroids – pretty people who'd arrived in L.A. with a couple years of Stanislavski or summer stock or college theater under their belts, fueled by Oscar fantasies but settling, a thousand cattle calls later, for the occasional walk-ons and crowd scenes and nonunion commercials that comprised 99.9 percent of movie work.

Craig Eiffel Bosc, Master Thespian.

Time for a bad review.

Bosc stayed in the bar for another hour and a half and emerged alone, walking a little more slowly and tripping once. When the guy resumed driving west on Ventura, he'd slowed to ten miles under the limit and was doing that dividing line nudge that made it clear he was under the influence.

A 502 stop would offer the opportunity for a face-to-face with Bosc, but pulling the turkey over for a deuce was the last thing Milo wanted. Being off duty, the most he could pull off would be a citizen's arrest. That meant holding on to Bosc while calling a patrol car, then having the blues take over and losing any hope of private time with Mr Smiles.

So he continued tailing the Saab and hoped Bosc wouldn't attract law enforcement attention or run someone over.

Another short ride – two blocks to a strip mall near Coldwater, where Bosc went shopping for groceries at a Ralphs, deposited two paper bags in the Saab's trunk, made a five-minute stop at a mailbox rentals place, and returned to the car with a stack of envelopes under his arm.

Mail drop, same setup as the West Hollywood POB where he'd registered as Playa del Sol. The tail resumed, with Milo two lengths behind as Bosc turned right on Coldwater, traveled north past Moorpark and Riverside, then east on Huston.

Quiet street, apartments and small houses. That made it a tough follow-along, even with the quarry oblivious and slightly intoxicated. Milo waited at the corner of Coldwater and Huston and kept his eye on the Saab. The blue car traveled one block, then another, before hooking left.

Hoping Bosc didn't live in some security building with a subterranean garage, Milo waited half a minute, wheeled his way up a block and a half, parked, got out and continued on foot toward the spot where he'd estimated the Saab had come to rest.

Luck was with him. The blue car was out in the open, sitting in the driveway of a one-story, white stucco bungalow.

The house had a cement lawn and no fence. A couple of scraggly palms brushing the front façade were the only concessions to green. The driveway was twenty feet of cracked slab, barely long enough for a single vehicle, and it ended at the house's left side. No backyard. The bungalow sat on a fractional lot – a sliver that had escaped tear-down and development – and behind the tiny house, on the rear-neighboring property, loomed a four-story apartment complex.

The glamour of Hollywood.

Milo returned to the Dodge and drove twenty feet past the bungalow. Plenty of parked cars here, but he managed to find a spot between a van and a pickup that afforded him a clean, diagonal view. Bosc's gym-bar-shopping excursion had taken up most of the afternoon, and the sun was beginning to drop. Milo sat there, his 9mm resting on his hip, the weapon substantial and cool and comforting, and he felt better than he had in a long time.

Maybe Bosc was in for the evening, because by 5 P.M. he hadn't shown himself, and lights had gone on in the white bungalow's front rooms. Lacy curtains obscured the details, but the fabric was sheer enough for Milo to make out flashes of movement.

Bosc shifting from room to room. Then, at nine, a window on the right side of the house went cathode-blue. TV.

Quiet night for Master Thespian.

Milo climbed out of the Polaris, stretched the stiffness from his joints, made his way across the street.

He rang the bell, and Bosc didn't even bother to shout out a 'Who's there?', just opened it wide.

The actor had changed into khaki shorts and a tight black T-shirt that hugged his actorly physique. One hand gripped a bottle of Coors Light. The other held a cigarette.

Casual, loose, eyes bloodshot and droopy. Until Milo's face registered and Bosc's well-formed mouth dropped open.

The actor didn't react to the roust like an actor would – like any kind of civilian would. His legs spread slightly and he planted his feet, the beer bottle jabbed at Milo's chin and the cigarette's glowing tip headed for Milo's eyes.

Split-second reaction. Tight little martial arts ballet.

Milo was mildly surprised, but he'd come ready for anything and retracted his head. The vicious kick he aimed at Bosc's groin landed true, as did the chop to the back of Bosc's neck, and the guy went down, putting an end to any debate.

By the time Bosc had stopped writhing on the floor and the green had gone out of his complexion, his hands were cuffed behind him and he was panting and struggling to choke out words and Milo was kicking the door shut. He lifted Bosc by the scruff and dumped him on the black leather couch that took up most of the living room. The rest of the decor was a white beanbag chair, a huge digital TV, expensive stereo toys, and a chrome-framed poster of a wound red Lamborghini Countach.

443

Bosc sprawled on the sofa, moaning. His eyes rolled back and he retched and Milo stepped back from the expected projectile puke. But Bosc just dry heaved a couple of times, got his eyes back on track, looked up at Milo.

And smiled.

And laughed.

'Something funny, Craig?' said Milo.

Bosc's lips moved a bit, and he struggled to talk through the grin. Sweat globules as big as jelly beans beaded up his forehead and rolled down his sculpted nose. He flicked one away with his tongue. Laughed again. Spit at Milo's feet. Coughed and said, 'Oh yeah. You're in *big* trouble.'

thirty-five

I sped up Highway 33, sucking in the grass-sweet air of Ojai. Thinking about Bert Harrison living here for decades, light-years from L.A. For all that, the old man had been unable to avoid the worst the city had to offer.

As I approached the bank of shops that included O'Neill & Chapin, I eased up on the gas pedal. The stationery shop was still shuttered and a CLOSED sign was propped in the window of the Celestial Café. Midway through town, I turned onto the road that led up to Bert's property, drove a hundred feet from his driveway, and parked behind a copse of eucalyptus.

Bert's old station wagon was parked out in front, which told me nothing. Perhaps he'd left for his overseas trip and had been driven to the airport. Or his departure was imminent, and I'd enter to find him packing.

Third choice: he'd lied about the journey, wanting to discourage me from returning.

I admired Bert, wasn't eager to examine the possibilities. Returning to the Seville, I swung back onto the highway. Ready to tap the source, directly.

The entry to Mecca Ranch was latched but unlocked. I freed the arm, drove through, closed the gate behind me, and motored up under the gaze of circling hawks – maybe the same birds I'd seen the first time.

The corral floated into view, glazed by afternoon sun. Marge Schwinn stood in the center of the ring, wearing a faded denim shirt, tight jeans and riding boots, her back to me. Talking to a big stallion the color of bittersweet chocolate. Nuzzling the animal, stroking its mane. The sound of my tires crunching the gravel made her turn. By the time I was out of the Seville, she'd left the enclosure and was heading toward me.

'Well, hello there, Dr Delaware.'

I returned the greeting, smiling and keeping my voice light. The first time I'd met her, Milo hadn't introduced me by name or profession. Suddenly I felt good about the trip.

She pulled a blue bandana from her jeans pocket, wiped both hands, offered the right one for a firm, hard shake. 'What brings you up here?'

'Follow-up.'

She pocketed the bandana and grinned. 'Someone think I'm crazy?'

'No, ma'am, just a few questions.' I was looking into the sun and turned my head. Marge's face was well shaded, but she squinted, and her eyes receded into a mesh of wrinkles. The denim shirt was tailored tight. Her breasts were small and high. That same combination of girlish body and old woman's face.

'What kind of questions, Doctor?'

'For starts, have you thought of anything new since Detective Sturgis and I visited?'

'About . . . ?'

'Anything your husband might've said about that unsolved murder we discussed.'

'Nope,' she said. 'Nothing about that.' Her eyes drifted to the corral. 'I'd love to chat, but I'm kind of in the middle of things.'

'Just a few more things. Including a sensitive topic, I'm afraid.'

She clamped both hands on hard, lean hips. 'What topic?'

'Your husband's drug addiction. Did he overcome his habit by himself?'

She dug a heel into the dirt and ground it hard. 'Like I told you, by the time I met him, Pierce was past all that.'

'Did he have any help getting there?'

A simple question, but she said, 'What do you mean?' She'd maintained the squint, but her eyes weren't shut tight enough to conceal the movement behind the lids. Quick shift down to the ground, then a sidelong journey to the right.

Another bad liar. Thank God for honest people.

'Did Pierce have any drug treatment?' I said. 'Was he ever under the care of a doctor?'

'He really didn't talk about those days.'

'Not at all?'

'He was past it. I didn't want to rake things up.'

'Didn't want to upset him,' I said.

She glanced over at the corral again.

I said, 'How did Pierce sleep?'

'Pardon?'

'Was Pierce a sound sleeper or did he have trouble settling down at night?'

'He was pretty much a—' She frowned. 'These are strange questions, Dr Delaware. Pierce is gone, what difference does it make how he slept?'

'Just general follow-up,' I said. 'What I'm interested in

specifically is the week or so before the accident. Did he sleep well or was he restless?'

Her breath caught, and the hands on her hips whitened. 'What happened, *sir*, is what I told you: Pierce fell off Akhbar. Now he's gone and I'm the one has to live with that and I don't appreciate your raking all this up.'

'I'm sorry,' I said.

'You keep apologizing, but you don't stop asking.'

'Well,' I said, 'here's the thing. Maybe it was an accident, but you did ask for a drug scan on Akhbar. Paid the coroner quite a bit of money to do it.'

She took a step away from me, then another. Shook her head, plucked a piece of straw out of her hair. 'This is ridiculous.'

'Another thing,' I said. 'Detective Sturgis never introduced me by name, but you know who I am and what I do. I find that kind of curious.'

Her eyes widened and her chest heaved. 'He said you might do this.'

'Who did?'

No answer.

I said, 'Dr Harrison?'

She turned her back on me.

'Mrs Schwinn, don't you think we need to get to the bottom of things? Isn't that what Pierce would've wanted? Something was keeping him up at night, wasn't it? Unfinished business. Wasn't that the whole point of the murder book?'

'I don't know about any book.'

'Don't you?'

Her lips folded inward. She shook her head again, clenched her jaw, swiveled, and caught a faceful of sun. A tremor jogged through her upper body. Her legs were planted, and they absorbed the motion. She turned heel and half ran toward her house. But I followed her inside; she didn't try to stop me.

We sat in the exact same spots we'd occupied a few days ago: me on the living-room couch, she in the facing chair. The last time, Milo had done all the talking, as he usually does when I tag along, but now it was my game and, God help me, despite the anguish of the woman sitting across from me, I felt cruelly elated.

Marge Schwinn said, 'You guys are spooky. Mind readers.'

'We guys?'

'Head doctors.'

'Dr Harrison and I,' I said.

She didn't answer, and I went on: 'Dr Harrison warned you I might be back.'

'Dr Harrison does only good.'

I didn't argue.

She showed me her profile. 'Yes, he was the one who told me who you were – after I described you and that big detective, Sturgis. He said your being here might mean things would be different.'

'Different?'

'He said you were persistent. A good guesser.'

'You've known Dr Harrison for a while.'

'A while.' The living-room windows were open, and a whinny from out in the corral drifted in loud and clear. She muttered, 'Easy, baby.'

'Your relationship with Dr Harrison was professional,' I said.

'If you're asking was he my doctor, the answer is yes. He treated us both – Pierce and me. Separately, neither of us knew it at the time. With Pierce it was the drugs. With me it was . . . I was going through . . . a depression. A situational reaction, Dr Harrison called it. After my mother passed. She was ninety-three, and I'd been taking care of her for so long that being alone was . . . all the responsibility started bearing down on me. I tried to go it alone, then it got to be too much. I knew what Dr Harrison was, had always liked his smile. So one day I got up the courage to talk to him.'

The admission – the confession of weakness – clenched her jaws. I said, 'Was Dr Harrison the one who introduced you to Pierce?'

'I met Pierce at the end of . . . by the time I was better, able to take care of things again. I was still talking to Dr Harrison from time to time but was off the antidepressants, just like he said I'd be.'

She leaned forward suddenly. 'Do you really know Dr H? Well enough to understand what kind of man he is? When we first started talking, he used to come over every day to see how I was doing. *Every day.* One time I came down with the flu and couldn't do my chores and he did them for me. Everything – vacuumed the house, washed and dried the dishes, fed the horses, cleaned up the stables. He did that for four days running, even made trips into town for supplies. If I'd paid him by the hour, I'd be dead broke.'

I knew Bert was a good man and a master therapist, but her account astonished me. I pictured him tiny, aged, purple-clad, sweeping and hosing horse stalls, and wondered what I'd have done in the same situation. Knew damn well I'd have fallen far short of that degree of caring.

What I was doing right now had nothing to *do* with caring. Not for the living.

How much was owed to the dead?

I said, 'So you met Pierce when things had smoothed out.' Sounding wooden, formulaic. *Shrinky.*

She nodded. 'Dr H told me I should get back into my old routine – said my old habits had been good ones. Before Mama got terminal, I used to drive into Oxnard and shop at Randall's for feed. Old Lady Randall used to work the counter and she and Mama were old friends and I used to like going in there and talking to her, hearing the way things used to be. Then Mrs Randall took sick and her boys started working the counter and I had nothing to say to them. That and my energies were flagging so I switched to a mail-order feed outfit that delivered. When Dr Harrison said it would be good for me to get out, I started going to Randall's again. That's where I met Pierce.'

She smiled. 'Maybe it was all part of his plan – Dr Harrison's. Knowing Pierce and me both. Figuring there'd be some kind of chemistry there. He always said no, but maybe he was being modest like he always is. Whatever the truth, there *was* a chemistry. *Must've* been, 'cause the first time I saw Pierce he looked like nothing but an over-the-hill hippie and I'm an old Republican ranch girl, shook Ronald Reagan's hand, wouldn't normally be attracted to that type. But something about Pierce . . . he had a *nobility*. I know your detective friend probably told you stories about the way Pierce used to be, but he became a different man.'

I said, 'People change.'

'That's something I didn't learn till late in life. When Pierce finally got up the courage to ask me out for coffee, he was so shy about it, it was . . . almost cute.' She shrugged. 'Maybe we met at just the right time – the

451

planets moving perfectly or something.' Tiny smile. 'Or maybe Dr Harrison's a tricky one.'

'When did you tell Dr Harrison you were seeing Pierce?'

'Pretty soon after. He said, "I know. Pierce told me. He feels the same way about you, Margie." That's when he told me he'd known Pierce for some time. Had been doing volunteer psychiatry at Oxnard Doctors' Hospital – counseling sick and injured people, burnt people – after the Montecito Fire they put in a burn unit and he was their psychiatrist. Pierce wasn't any of those things, he came into the emergency room having terrible seizures from his addiction. Dr Harrison detoxified him, then took him on as a patient. He told me all this because Pierce asked him to. Pierce had strong feelings about me but was deeply ashamed of his past, depended on Dr Harrison to clear the air. I still remember the way Dr H phrased it. "He's a good man, Margie, but he'll understand if this is too much baggage for you to carry." I said, "These hands have been hauling hay for forty years, I can carry plenty." After that, Pierce's shyness mostly left him, and we got close.' Her eyes misted. 'I never thought I'd find anyone, and now he's gone.'

She fumbled for the bandana and spit out laughter. 'Look at me, what a *sissy*. And look at *you*: I thought you guys were supposed to make people feel *better*.'

I sat there as she cried silently and wiped her eyes and cried some more. A sudden shadow streaked the facing wall, then vanished. I turned in time to see a hawk shoot up into the blue and disappear. Foot stomping and snorting sounded from the corral.

'Red-tails,' she said. 'They're good for the vermin, but the horses never get used to them.'

I said, 'Mrs Schwinn, what did Pierce tell you about the unsolved case?'

'That it was an unsolved case.'

'What else?'

'Nothing else. He didn't even tell me the girl's name. Just that she was a girl who got torn up and it was his case and he'd failed to solve it. I tried to get him to open up, but he wouldn't. Like I said, Pierce always wanted to shelter me from his old life.'

'But he talked to Dr Harrison about the case.'

'You'd have to ask Dr Harrison about that.'

'Dr Harrison never spoke to you about it?'

'He just said . . .' She trailed off and twisted so that all I could see was the outline of her jaw.

'Mrs Schwinn?'

'The only reason it came up in the first place was because of Pierce's sleep. He'd started having dreams. Nightmares.' She turned suddenly and faced me. 'How'd you *know* about that? What was it, a *real* good guess?'

'Pierce was a good man, and good men don't take well to corruption.'

'I don't know about any corruption.' Her voice lacked conviction.

'When did the nightmares start?' I said.

'A few months before he died. Two, three months.'

'Anything happen to bring them on?'

'Not that I saw. I thought we were happy. Dr Harrison told me he'd thought so, too, but turns out Pierce had never stopped being plagued – that's the word he used. *Plagued.*'

'By the case.'

'By failure. Dr Harrison said Pierce had been forced to walk away from the case when they railroaded him off the department. He said Pierce had fixed it in his mind that giving up had been some kind of mortal sin. He'd been punishing himself for years – the drugs, abusing his body, living like a bum. Dr H thought he'd helped Pierce get past it, but he'd been wrong, the nightmares came back. Pierce just couldn't let go.'

She gave me a long, hard stare. 'Pierce broke rules for years, always wondered if he'd have to pay one day. He loved being a detective but hated the police department. Didn't trust anyone. Including your friend, Sturgis. When he got railroaded, he was sure Sturgis had something to do with it.'

'When I was here with Detective Sturgis, you said Pierce had spoken kindly of him. Was that true?'

'Not strictly,' she said. 'Pierce never breathed a word to me about Sturgis or anyone else from his old life. These are all things he told Dr Harrison, and I was trying to keep Dr Harrison out of all this. But yes, Pierce had changed his opinion about Sturgis. Followed Sturgis's career and saw he was a good detective. Found out Sturgis was homosexual and figured he had to have a *lot* of courage to stay in the department.'

'What else did Dr Harrison tell you about the case?'

'Just that walking away had stuck in Pierce's brain like a cancer. That's what the nightmares were all about.'

'Chronic nightmares?' I said.

'Chronic enough. Sometimes they'd hit Pierce three, four times a week, other times he'd be okay for a stretch. Then boom, all over again. You couldn't predict, and that made it worse, because I never knew what to expect when my head hit the pillow. Things got to a point where I was scared to go to bed, started waking up at night myself.' Her smile was crooked. 'Kind of funny. I'd be lying there all wound up, unable to sleep, and Pierce'd be snoring away and I'd tell myself it was finally over. Then the next night . . .'

'Did Pierce say anything during the nightmares?'

'Not a word, he just moved – thrashed. That's how I'd know a fit was coming on: the bed would start moving – thumping, like an earthquake, Pierce's feet kicking the mattress. Lying on his back, kicking with his heels – like he was marching somewhere. Then his hands would shoot up.' She stretched her arms toward the ceiling. 'Like he was being arrested. Then his hands would slam down fast, start slapping the bed and waving around wild, and soon he'd be grunting and *punching* the mattress *and* kicking – his feet never stopped. Then he'd arch his back and freeze – like he was paralyzed, like he was building up steam to explode, and you could see his teeth gnashing and his eyes would pop real wide. But they weren't looking at anything, he was somewhere else – some hell only he could see. He'd hold that frozen pose for maybe ten seconds, then let go and start punching *himself* – in the chest, on the stomach, on the face. Sometimes, the next morning, he'd be bruised. I tried to stop him from hurting himself, but it was impossible, his arms were like iron rods, it was all I could do to jump out of the bed to avoid getting hit myself. So I'd just stand there and wait for him to finish. Just before he was finished, he'd let out a howl – this loud howl that would wake up the horses. *They'd* start mewling, and sometimes the *coyotes* would chime in. *That* was something to hear – coyotes screaming from miles away. Ever hear that? When a pack of them goes at it? It's not like a dog barking, it's a thousand creatures gone crazy. Ululation's the name for it. They're supposed to do it only when they're killing or

JONATHAN KELLERMAN

mating, but Pierce's howling would get them going.'

She'd squeezed the bandana into a blue ball. Now she studied her fingers as they uncurled. 'Those coyotes were scared witless by the sound of Pierce's fear.'

She offered me a drink that I declined, got up and filled herself a glass of water from the kitchen tap. When she sat back down, I said, 'Did Pierce have any memory of the nightmares?'

'Nope. When the fit was over he'd just go back to sleep, and there'd be no mention of it. The first time that happened, I let it pass. The second time, I was shook up but still said nothing. The third time, I went to see Dr Harrison. He listened and didn't say much and that evening he came by, paid a visit to Pierce – alone, in Pierce's darkroom. After that, Pierce started seeing him for regular sessions again. About a week in, Dr H had me over to his house, and that's when he told me about Pierce struggling to live with failure.'

'So you and Pierce never talked about the case directly?'

'That's right.'

I said nothing.

She said, 'I know it's hard for you to understand, but that's what we were like. Close as two people can be, but there were sides to each of us that we didn't get into. I realize it's not fashionable to hold on to privacy anymore. Everyone talks about everything to everyone else. But that's phony, isn't it? Everyone's got secret parts of their mind. Pierce and I were just honest about admitting it. And Dr Harrison said if that's the way we really wanted it, that was our choice.'

So Bert had tried to edge husband and wife toward

456

more openness, and they'd resisted.

Marge Schwinn said, 'It was the same with Pierce's drug problem. He was too proud to expose himself to me, so he used Dr Harrison as a go-between. We were content with that. It kept things pleasant and positive between us.'

'Did you ever ask Dr Harrison about the unsolved murder?'

Strong headshake. 'I didn't want to know. I figured for it to plague Pierce it had to be really bad.'

'Did the nightmares ever clear up?'

'After Pierce started seeing Dr Harrison regularly again, they faded to maybe two, three times a month. Also, Pierce's photography hobby seemed to help, got him out of the house, got him some fresh air.'

'Was that Dr Harrison's idea?'

She smiled. 'Yes, he bought Pierce the camera, insisted on paying for it. He does that. Gives people things. There was a gal used to live in town, Marian Purveyance, ran the Celestial Café before Aimee Baker took charge of it. Marian came down with a muscle disease that wasted her away, and Dr Harrison was her main comfort. I used to visit Marian during her final days, and she told me Dr Harrison decided she needed a dog for companionship. But Marian was in no physical state to take care of a dog, so Dr Harrison found one for her – an old, half-lame retriever from the shelter that he kept at his house, fed, and bathed. He brought it over to Marian's for a few hours each day. That sweet old dog used to stretch out on Marian's bed, and Marian would lie there stroking it. Toward the end, Marian's fingers wouldn't work, and the dog must've known, because it rolled over right next to Marian and put its paw on Marian's hand so she'd have something to touch. Marian died with that old dog next to her, and a few weeks later the dog passed on.'

Her eyes were fierce. 'Do you get what I'm saying, young man? Dr Harrison *gives* people things. He gave Pierce that camera and gave me a bit of peace by letting me know the nightmares had nothing to do with me. Because I was wondering if they did. Maybe Pierce's being cooped up here with an old spinster after all those years on his own was having a bad effect on him. And – Lord forgive me – when I watched Pierce thrash around, I couldn't help wonder if he'd somehow backslid.'

'Into drug use.'

'I'm ashamed to admit it, but yes, that's exactly what I wondered. Because it was drug seizures that brought him into the hospital in the first place, and to my ignorant eye these looked like seizures. But Dr Harrison assured me they weren't. Said they were just bad nightmares. That it was Pierce's *old* life rearing its ugly old head. That I was nothing *but* good for Pierce and shouldn't ever think otherwise. That was a great relief.'

'So the nightmares thinned to two or three times a month.'

'That I could live with. When the thumping started, I'd just roll out of bed, go to the kitchen for a glass of water, walk outside to calm the horses, and when I'd return, Pierce'd be snoozing away. I'd hold his hand and warm it up – the nightmares always turned his hands icy. We'd lie there together and I'd listen to his breathing slow down and he'd let me hold him and warm him up and the night would pass.'

Another hawk's swoop striated the wall. She said, 'Those birds. They must *smell* something.'

'The nightmares thinned,' I said, 'but they returned the

last few days before Pierce's death.'

'Yes,' she said, nearly choking on the word. 'And this time I started getting worried because Pierce didn't look so good in the morning. He was worn-out, kind of clumsy, slurring his words. That's why I blame myself for letting him take Akhbar. He was in no shape to ride, I shouldn't have allowed him to go off by himself. Maybe that time he did have some kind of seizure.'

'Why'd you test Akhbar for drugs?'

'That was just me being stupid. What I *really* wanted to do was have *Pierce* tested. Because despite what Dr Harrison had said when the nightmares came back, I let myself lose faith in Pierce, again. But after he died, I couldn't bring myself to come out and admit my suspicions. Not to Dr H or the coroner or anyone else, so instead I laid them on poor Akhbar. Figuring maybe once the subject of drugs came up, someone would catch on and test Pierce, too, and I'd know, once and for all.'

'They did test Pierce,' I said. 'It's standard procedure. The drug screen came back negative.'

'I know that, now. Dr Harrison told me. It was an accident, plain and simple. Though sometimes I still can't help thinking Pierce shouldn't have been riding alone. Because he *wasn't* looking good.'

'Any idea why that last week was rough for him?'

'No – and I don't want to know. I need to put all this behind me, and this isn't helping, so could we please stop?'

I thanked her and stood. 'How far from here did the accident occur?'

'Just a ways up the road.'

'I'd like to see the spot.'

'What for?'

459

'To get a feel for what happened.'

Her gaze was level. 'Do you know something you haven't told me?'

'No,' I said. 'Thanks for your time.'

'Don't thank me, it wasn't a favor.' She leaped up, walked past me to the door.

I said, 'The spot—'

'Get back on 33 heading east and take the second turnoff to the left. It's a dirt path that leads up a hill, then starts swooping down toward the arroyo. That's where it happened. Pierce and Akhbar tumbled from the rocks that look down into the arroyo and ended up at the bottom. It's a place Pierce and I rode together from time to time. When we did, I used to lead.'

'About Pierce's photography.'

'No,' she said. 'Please. No more questions. I showed you Pierce's darkroom and his pictures and everything else the first time you were here.'

'I was going to say he was talented, but one thing struck me. There were no people or animals in his shots.'

'Is that supposed to be some big psychological thing?'

'No, I just found it curious.'

'Did you? Well, I didn't. Didn't bother me one bit. Those pictures were beautiful.' She reached around me and shoved the door open. 'And when I asked Pierce about it, he had a very good answer. Said, "Margie, I'm trying to picture a perfect world." '

thirty-six

S he stood by the Seville, waiting for me to leave.

I turned the ignition key, and said, 'Did Dr Harrison mention taking a vacation?'

'Him, a vacation? He never leaves. Why?'

'He told me he might be doing some traveling.'

'Well, he's certainly entitled to travel if he wants. Why don't you ask him? You're going there right now, aren't you? To check up on my story.'

'I'm going to talk to him about the unsolved case.'

'Whatever,' she said. 'Doesn't bother me being checked up on, because I'm not hiding anything. That's the thing about not letting yourself get involved in hopeless things. Less to worry about. The shame about my Pierce was he never really learned that.'

The turnoff she'd described led to an oak-shielded path barely wide enough for a golf cart. Branches scraped the Seville's flanks. I backed out, left the car on the side of the road, and hiked.

The spot where Pierce Schwinn had died was half a mile in, a dry gully scooped out of a granite ledge and backed by mountainside. A sere corridor that would fill during rainy seasons and transform to a green, rushing stream. Now, it was bleached the color of old bones and littered with silt, rocks and boulders, leathery leaves, snarls of wind-snapped branches. The largest rocks tended toward ragged and knife-edged and glinted in the sun. Up against them, a man's head wouldn't fare well.

I walked to the edge and stared down into the arroyo and listened to the silence, wondering what had caused a well-trained horse to lose its footing.

Contemplation and the warmth of the day lulled me into something just short of torpor. Then something behind me skittered and my heart jumped and the tip of my shoe curled over into open space and I had to jump back to avoid pitching over.

I regained my bearings in time to see a sand-colored lizard scurry into the brush. Stepping back from the ledge, I cleared my head before turning and walking away. By the time I reached the car, my breathing had nearly returned to normal.

I drove back to the center of Ojai, cruised to Signal Street, past the fieldstone-lined drainage ditch, and parked in the same eucalyptus grove, where I peered through blue shaggy leaves at Bert Harrison's house. Thinking about what I'd say to Bert if I found him. Thinking about Pierce Schwinn's nightmares, the demons that had come back to haunt him during the days before his death.

Bert knew why. Bert had known all along.

No movement from the old man's house. The station wagon was parked right where it had been. After a quarter-hour I decided it was time to make my way to the front door and deal with whatever I found, or didn't.

Just as I got out of the Seville, the door squeaked open

and Bert stepped out onto his front porch in full purple regalia, cradling a large brown paper shopping bag in one arm. I grabbed the Seville's door before it clicked shut, hurried back behind the trees, and followed the old man's descent down the wooden staircase.

He loaded the bag on the station wagon's passenger seat, got behind the wheel, stalled a couple of times, finally fired the engine. Backing away from the house with excruciating slowness, he took a long time to complete a three-way turn. Battling with the wheel – manual steering. A small man, face intent, hands planted at 10 o'clock–2 o'clock, just the way they teach you in Driver's Ed. Sitting so low his head was barely visible above the door.

Crouching low, I waited until he drove past. The old Chevy's tired suspension wasn't up to the semipaved road, and it creaked and whined as it bounced by. Bert stared straight ahead, didn't notice me or the Seville. I waited till he'd passed from view, then jumped in my own chariot. Power steering gave me an edge, and I caught up in time to spot the wagon lurching east on 33.

I sat at the intersection as the Chevy diminished to a dust mote on the horizon. The empty road made following too risky. I was still wondering what to do when a pickup truck loaded with bags of fertilizer came to a rolling stop behind me. Two Hispanic men in cowboy hats – farmworkers. I motioned them around and they passed me and turned left. Interposing themselves between Bert and me.

I set out behind the truck, lagging a good ways behind.

A few miles later, at the 33–150 intersection, the truck kept going south and Bert managed a torturous, over-cautious right onto 150. I stayed with him but increased my distance, barely able to keep the wagon in sight.

He drove another couple of miles, past private camp-grounds and a trailer park and signs announcing the impending arrival of Lake Casitas. The public reservoir doubled as a recreational facility. For all I knew the paper bag was filled with breadcrumbs, and Bert was planning to feed the ducks.

But he veered off the road well before the lake, swinging north at a corner that housed a single-pump filling station and a one-room bait shop and grocery.

Another unmarked trail, this one dotted thinly with unpainted cabins, set well back from the road. A hand-painted sign at one of the first properties advertised homemade berry cobbler and firewood; after that, no messages. The underbrush grew thick here, nurtured by a shade canopy of ancient oaks and pittosporum and sycamores so twisted they seemed to writhe. Bert bounced along for another two miles, oblivious to my presence, before slowing, and turning left.

Keeping my eye on the spot where he'd disappeared, I pulled over and waited for two minutes, then followed.

He'd gone up a gravel drive that continued for two hundred feet, then angled to the left and vanished behind an unruly hedge of agave – the same spiky plants that fronted his own house. No building in sight. Once again, I parked and continued on foot, hoping the wagon's destination was measured in yards, not miles. Staying off the gravel for quiet's sake, and walking on the bordering greenery.

I spotted the Chevy another hundred feet up, stationed haphazardly in the dirt lot of a tin-roofed, green-boarded house. Larger than a cabin, maybe three rooms, with a sagging front porch and a stovepipe chimney. I edged closer, found myself a vantage point behind the continuing agave wall. The house was nestled by forest but sat on a dry-dirt clearing, probably a firebreak. Diminishing sunlight spattered the metal roof. A poorly shaped apricot tree grew near the front door, ungainly and ragged, but its branches were gravid with fruit.

I stayed there for nearly half an hour before Bert reemerged.

Pushing a man in a wheelchair. I recalled the chair in his living room.

Keeping it for a friend, he'd said.

Dr Harrison gives.

Despite the mildness of the afternoon, the man was wrapped in a blanket and wore a wide-brimmed straw hat. Bert pushed him slowly, and his head lolled. Bert stopped and said something to him. If the man heard, he gave no indication. Bert locked the chair, went over to the apricot tree, picked two apricots. He handed one to the man, who reached for it very slowly. Both of them ate. Bert held his hand to the man's mouth and the man spit the pit into his palm. Bert examined the seed, placed it in his pocket.

Bert finished his own apricot, pocketed that pit, too.

He stood there, looking up at the sky. The man in the wheelchair didn't budge.

Bert unlocked the chair, pushed it a few feet farther. Angled the chair and allowed me to catch a glimpse of the passenger's face.

Huge mirrored sunglasses below the straw hat dominated the upper half. The bottom was a cloud of gray beard. In between was skin the color of grilled eggplant.

I stepped out of the trees, made no attempt to muffle

the crunch of my footsteps on gravel.

Bert turned abruptly. Locked eyes with me. Nodded. Resigned.

I came closer. The man in the wheelchair said, 'Who's that?' in a low, raspy voice.

Bert said, 'The fellow I told you about.'

thirty-seven

Craig Bosc lay prone on his living-room carpet, smiling again. Plastic tie-cuffs from Milo's cop kit bound his ankles together, and another set linked to the metal cuffs around his wrists secured him to a stout sofa leg.

Not a hog-tie, Milo had pointed out, just a nice submissive position. Letting the guy know that any resistance would result in something more painful.

Bosc offered no comment. Hadn't uttered a word since telling Milo he was in big trouble.

Now his eyes were closed, and he kept the smile pasted on his face. Maybe acting, but not a drop of sweat on his movie star face. One of those psychopaths with a low arousal rate? Despite Milo's having the upper hand, Bosc looked too damn smug, and Milo felt moisture running down his own armpits.

He began searching the house. Bosc opened his eyes and laughed as Milo walked around the kitchen opening cabinets and drawers, checking Bosc's bachelor fridge – beer, wine, piña colada mix, three jars of salsa, an open can of chili-con-whatever. As Milo checked the freezer, Bosc chuckled again, but when Milo turned to look at him, the guy's eyes were shut tight and his body had gone loose and he might've been napping.

467

Nothing hidden behind the ice trays. Milo moved to the bedroom, found a closet full of designer duds, too many garments for the space, everything crammed together on cheap wire hangers, some stuff crumpled on the floor among two dozen pairs of shoes. On the top shelf were three tennis rackets, a hockey stick, an old deflated basketball, and a fuzzy, blackened leather thing that had once been a football. Joe Jock's sentimental memories.

A pair of thirty-pound Ivanko dumbbells sat in the corner, next to a sixty-inch TV, VCR-DVD combo. A mock-walnut video case held action thrillers and a few run-of-the-mill porno tapes in lurid boxes: busty blondes playing orifice-bingo.

Bosc's three-drawer dresser offered up rumpled underwear and socks and T-shirts and gym shorts. It wasn't till Milo hit the bottom drawer that things got interesting.

Buried beneath a collection of GAP sweatshirts were three guns: a 9mm identical to Milo's department issue, a sleek black Glock complete with German instructions, and a silver derringer in a black leather carrying case. All three loaded. Additional ammo was stored at the rear of the drawer.

Next to the guns was a small cache that added up to Bosc's personal history.

A North Hollywood High yearbook, fifteen years old, revealed that Craig Eiffel Bosc had played tight end for the varsity football squad, pitched relief for the baseball team, and served as a basketball point guard. Three letters. Bosc's grad shot showed him to be clean-cut and gorgeous, flashing that same cocky smile.

Next came a black leatheroid scrapbook with stick-on letters that spelled out **SIR CRAIG** on the cover. Inside were plastic-sheathed pages that made Milo flash to the murder book.

But nothing bloody here. The first page held a certificate from Valley College attesting that Bosc had earned a two-year associate degree in communications. From North Hollywood High to Valley. Both were within a bicycle ride to Bosc's house. Valley Boy hadn't moved around much.

Next came Bosc's honorable discharge from the Coast Guard; he'd been stationed at Avalon, on Catalina Island. Probably earned himself a nice golden tan while discharging his duty in scuba gear.

At the back of the album were five pages of Polaroids showing Bosc screwing a variety of women, all young and blonde and buxom, the emphasis upon close-up insertion and Bosc's grinning face as he kneaded breasts and pinched nipples and rear-ended his companions. The girls all wore sleepy expressions. None seemed to be playing for the camera.

Stoned cuties caught unawares. All appeared to be in their early to midtwenties, with big bleached hair and out-of-fashion do's that made Milo think *small-town cocktail waitress*. A few plain ones, one or two real lookers, for the most part an average-looking bunch. Not up to the level of the babes in the porno videos, but the same general type. Another indication Bosc had a limited range.

Milo searched for the hidden camera, figuring it would be focused on the bed, and found it quickly. Little pencil-lens gizmo concealed in the VCR box. Sophisticated bit of apparatus; it stood out among the general shoddiness of Bosc's apartment and made Milo wonder. Also stashed in the box were several tightly rolled joints and half a dozen tabs of Ecstasy.

Kiss the girls and make them stoned. Naughty, naughty.

He returned to the scrapbook, flipped to the next page. Wasn't really surprised at what he found, but still, the confirmation was unsettling and sweat gushed from every pore.

Certificate of Bosc's graduation from the L.A. Police Academy ten years ago. Then a group shot and an individual photo of Bosc in his probationer's uniform. Clean-cut, made-for-TV cop; that same obnoxious grin.

The subsequent paperwork recounted Bosc's LAPD progress. A couple years of North Hollywood patrol before promotion to Detective-I and transfer to Valley Auto Theft, where he'd spent three years as an investigator and left as a D-II.

Cars. Fast-track promotion for a hot-wire cowboy. Bastard probably had a collection of master keys to every known make and model hidden somewhere. With that kind of know-how and equipment, boosting Rick's Porsche and returning it vacuumed and wiped clean of prints would've been a sleepwalk for Detective Bosc.

After car-time, the guy had been moved downtown to Parker Center Records, then Administration.

Then a year with Internal Affairs.

Finally: a kick up to D-III and his current assignment.

Administrative Staff at Chief Broussard's office.

The bastard was an executive aide to John G.

Milo disconnected the pencil camera, brought it and the homemade pornos and the dope back to the living room. Bosc was still working on maintaining his mellow but Milo's footsteps opened his eyes and when he saw what

Milo was showing him, he flinched.

Then he recovered. Smiled. 'Gee, you must be a detective.'

Milo held an E-tab under Bosc's nose. 'Bad boy, Craig.'

'I'm supposed to be worried?'

'Pocketful of felonies, Georgie Porgie.'

'Another country heard from,' said Bosc.

'You think John G.'s gonna protect you? Something tells me the chief doesn't know about your film career.'

Bosc's eyes got hard and cold, offering a glimpse of the meanness that lurked beneath the pretty-boy façade.

He said, 'What I think is you're fucked.' Laughter. 'In the ass. Then again . . .'

Milo hefted the camera and the drugs.

Bosc said, 'You think you're seeing something, but you're not. None of that exists.' He shook his head and chuckled. 'You are *so* fucked.'

Milo laughed along with him. Stepped forward. Placed his foot on one of Bosc's shins and bore down.

Bosc cried out in agony. Tears filled his eyes as he struggled to twist away.

Milo lifted his shoe.

'You asshole-fuck,' Bosc panted. 'You stupid faggot fuck.'

'S'cuse me, Craig-o.'

'Go ahead,' said Bosc, catching his breath. 'You're only digging your own grave.'

Milo was silent.

Bosc's smile returned. 'You just don't get it, do you? This is L-fucking-A. It's not what you do, it's who you know.'

'Connections,' said Milo. 'Got yourself an agent yet?'

'If you had a brain, you'd be an ape,' said Bosc. 'You gain access to my premises with a clear B&E/kidnap combo, then add assault. We're talking major felony, prison time to the next millennium. You think any of that shit you're holding's going to stand up evidentiary-wise? I'll say you planted it.'

Milo fanned the photos. 'It's not my dick in these.'

'That's for sure,' said Bosc. 'Yours would be half the size and packed in fudge.'

Milo smiled.

'You're out of it, man,' said Bosc. 'Have been from the beginning, always will be. No matter how many 187s you close. No good deed goes unpunished, man. The longer you keep me here, the more screwed you are, and so is your shrink buddy.'

'What does he have to do with it?'

Bosc smiled and closed his eyes again, and for a moment Milo thought the guy would revert to silence. But a few seconds later, Bosc said, 'It's a game. You and the shrink are pawns.'

'Whose game?'

'Kings and bishops.'

'John G. and Walter Obey and the Cossack brothers?'

Bosc's eyes opened. Cold again. Colder. 'Stick your head up your ass and get yourself a clue. Now let me go, and maybe I'll help you out.' Snapping out the order.

Milo placed the contraband on a table. Paced the room, as if considering compliance.

Suddenly, he hurried back to Bosc's side, kneeled down next to Bosc, placed the tip of his finger on Bosc's shin. Precisely on the spot where his shoe had dug in.

Bosc began to sweat.

'Chess analogy,' said Milo. 'How erudite, Bobby

472

Fischer. Now tell me why you ripped off my car and put on that show at the hot dog stand and rented a post-office box under Playa del Sol and were snooping around my house today.'

'All in a day's work,' said Bosc.

'At John G.'s request?'

Bosc didn't answer.

Milo pulled out his gun and pressed the barrel into the soft, tan flesh under Bosc's chin.

'Details,' he demanded.

Bosc's lips jammed shut.

Milo retracted the weapon. As Bosc laughed, Milo said, 'Your problem, Craig, is you think you're a knight, but you're a shit-eating pawn.' He rapped the butt of the gun against Bosc's shin, hard enough to evoke an audible crack.

He waited for Bosc to stop crying, then raised the gun again.

Bosc's panicked eyes followed the weapon's ascent, and he scrunched his eyes and sobbed out loud.

Milo said, 'Craig, Craig,' and began to lower the weapon.

Bosc yelled, 'Please, please, no!' Began jabbering.

Within minutes, Milo had what he wanted.

Good old Pavlovian conditioning. Would Alex be proud?

thirty-eight

Bert Harrison placed a hand on the shoulder of the man in the wheelchair. The man rolled his head and hummed. I saw my image doubled in his mirrored lenses. A pair of grim strangers.

I said, 'My name's Alex Delaware, Mr Burns.'

Willie Burns smiled and rolled his head again. Orienting to my voice the way a blind man does. The skin between his white beard and the huge lenses was cracked and scored, stretched tight over sharp bones. His hands were long and thin, purplish brown, the knuckles lumped arthritically, the nails long and yellowed and seamed. Across his legs was a soft, white blanket. Not much bulk beneath the fabric.

'Pleased to meet you,' he said. To Bert: 'Am I, Doc?'

'He won't hurt you, Bill. He will want to know things.'

'Things,' said Burns. 'Once upon a time.' He hummed some more. High-pitched voice, off-key but somehow sweet.

I said, 'Bert, I'm sorry I had to follow you—'

'As you said, you had to.'

'It was—'

'Alex,' he said, quieting me with a soft palm against my cheek. 'When I found out you were involved, I thought this might happen.'

'Found out? You sent me the murder book.'

Bert shook his head.

'You didn't?' I said. 'Then who?'

'I don't know, son. Pierce sent it to someone but never told me who. He never told me about the book, at all, until the week before he died. Then one day, he brought it to my house and showed it to me. I had no idea he'd gone that far.'

'Collecting mementoes.'

'Collecting nightmares,' said Bert. 'As he turned the pages, he cried.'

Willie Burns stared sightlessly at the treetops, humming.

'Where'd Schwinn get the photos, Bert?'

'Some were his own cases, others he stole from old police files. He'd been a thief for quite some time. His characterization, not mine. He shoplifted habitually, took jewelry and money and drugs from crime scenes, consorted with criminals and prostitutes.'

'He told you all this.'

'Over a very long period.'

'Confessing,' I said.

'I'm no priest, but he wanted salvation.'

'Did he get it?'

Bert shrugged. 'Last time I checked there were no Hail Marys in the psychiatric repertoire. I did my best.' He glanced at Willie Burns. 'How are you feeling today, Bill?'

'I'm feeling real good,' said Burns. 'Considering.' He shifted his face to the left. 'Nice breeze coming in from the hills, can you hear it? That plunking of the leaves, like a nice little mandolin. Like one of those boats in Venice.'

I listened. Saw no movement among the trees, heard nothing.

Bert said, 'Yes, it is pretty.'

Willie Burns said, 'You know, it's getting kinda thirsty out here. Maybe I could have something to drink, please?'

Bert said, 'Of course.'

I wheeled Burns back into the green board house. The front room was barely furnished – one couch along the window and two bright green folding chairs. Pole lamps guarded two corners. Framed magazine prints – garden scenes painted in Giverny colors – hung askew on plaster-board walls. Between the chairs, a wide pathway had been left for the chair, and the rubber wheels had left gray tracks that led to a door at the rear. No knob, just a kickplate.

Push door. Wheelchair-friendly.

The kitchen was an arbitrary space to the right: pine cabinets, sheet-metal counters, a two-burner stove upon which sat a copper-bottomed pot. Bert took a Diet Lemon Snapple from a bulbous, white refrigerator, wres-tled with the lid, finally got it loose, and handed the bottle to Willie Burns. Burns gripped the bottle with both hands and drank down half, Adam's apple rising and falling with each gulp. Then he placed the glass against his face, rolled it back and forth along his skin, and let out a long breath.

'Thanks, Dr H.'

'My pleasure, Bill.' Bert looked at me. 'You might as well sit.'

I took one of the folding chairs. The house smelled of hickory chips and roasted garlic. A string of dried cloves hung above the stove, along with a necklace of dried chilies. I spotted other niceties: jars of dried beans, lentils, pasta. A hand-painted bread box. Gourmet touches in the vest-pocket galley.

I said, 'So you have no idea how the murder book got to me?'

Bert shook his head. 'I never knew you had anything to do with it until Marge told me you and Milo had been to visit and talked to her about an unsolved murder.' He began to lower himself onto the second folding chair, but straightened and stood. 'Let's get some air. You'll be okay for a few minutes, Bill?'

Burns said, 'More than okay.'

'We'll be right outside.'

'Enjoy the view.'

We walked into the shade of the surrounding trees.

Bert said, 'You need to know this: Bill doesn't have much longer. Nerve damage, brittle diabetes, serious circulation problems, hypertension. There's a limit to how much care I can give him, and he won't go to a hospital. The truth is no one can really help him. Too many systems down.'

He stopped and smoothed a purple lapel. 'He's a very old man at forty-three.'

'How long have you been taking care of him?' I said.

'A long time.'

'Nearly twenty years, I'd guess.'

He didn't answer. We walked some more, in slow, aimless circles. No sound issued from the forest. Not a trace of the music Willie Burns had heard.

'How'd you meet him?' I said.

'At a hospital in Oxnard.'

'Same place you met Schwinn.'

His eyes widened.

I said, 'I was just over at Marge's place.'

'Ah.' Once a shrink . . . 'Well, that's true,' he said. 'But Pierce's being there wasn't really a coincidence. He'd been tracking Bill for a while. Not very successfully. And not very consistently, because his amphetamine habit had rendered him pretty much incapacitated. Occasionally, he'd grow lucid, convince himself he was still a detective, make a stab at investigating, then he'd binge and drop out of sight. Somehow, over the years – through his criminal contacts – he managed to figure out that Bill had come up the coast. He knew Bill would need medical care and eventually, he pinpointed the hospital, though not until well after Bill had been discharged. But he began hanging around, checking himself in for spurious reasons. They had him tagged as an addicted hypochondriac.'

'He was trying to get access to Burns's records.'

Bert nodded. 'The hospital staff thought he was just another down-at-the-heels junkie out to steal drugs. As it turns out, he was really ill. An on-call neurologist who didn't know him ordered some testing and found a low-level seizure disorder – petit mal, mostly, some temporal symptoms, all due to drug toxicity. They prescribed anticonvulsants with mixed results, admitted him for short-term care several times, but I was never on duty during those periods. One day, he had a grand mal seizure out in the parking lot and they brought him into the ER and I *was* on call. One thing led to another.'

'Willie Burns needed medical care because he was burned in a house fire.'

Bert sighed. 'You're as skillful as ever, Alex.'

'A house on 156th Street in Watts. A neighborhood where a black man would be comfortable hiding out. Where a white face would stand out. A white police detective named Lester Poulsenn was assigned to guard

Burns and Caroline Cossack and one night he was shot and the house was torched as cover. A high-ranking cop murdered but LAPD kept it quiet. Interesting, don't you think, Bert?'

He remained silent. I went on, 'It's a safe bet Poulsenn got ambushed by the people sent to get rid of Caroline and Willie. People who'd pulled off an ambush before and murdered a bail bondsman named Boris Nemerov. Burns's bondsman. Did he tell you about that?'

Nod. 'It came out in therapy. Bill felt guilty about causing Nemerov's death. He would have liked to come forward, to come clean about what he saw, but that would have put him in mortal danger.'

'What's his version of the ambush?'

'He phoned Nemerov for help because Nemerov had always been kind to him. He and Nemerov arranged a meeting, but Nemerov was followed and murdered and stuffed in the trunk of his car. Bill was hiding nearby, saw it all. Knew Nemerov's death would be blamed on him.'

'Why was Burns offered a police guard in the first place?'

'He had contacts in the police department. He'd worked as an informant.'

'But after Poulsenn's and Nemerov's murders the department let him dangle.'

'Contacts, Alex. Not friends.'

'The house was set on fire, but Burns and Caroline got away. How severe were their injuries?'

'She wasn't hurt, his were severe. He neglected the wounds, didn't seek care until months later. His feet had been scorched almost down to the tendons, multiple infections set in, at the time of admission the wounds were suppurating, gangrenous, flesh falling off the bone.

Both feet were amputated immediately, but sepsis had spread up into the long bones and additional amputation was necessary. You could actually smell it, Alex. Like barbecue, the marrow had been *cooked*. We had some marvelous surgeons, and they managed to preserve half of one femur, a third of another, created skin flaps and grafted them. But Bill's lungs had also been burned, as had his trachea and his esophagus. He formed fibroid scars internally and removing the damaged tissue required additional multiple surgeries. We're talking years, Alex. He bore the agony in silence. I used to sit by the whirlpool as the skin sloughed off. Not a whimper. How he tolerated the pain I'll never know.'

'Was it the fire that blinded him?'

'No, that was the diabetes. He'd been ill for a while, had never been diagnosed. Made matters worse by indulging an addict's sweet tooth.'

'And the nerve damage? Heroin?'

'A bad batch of heroin. He scored it the day of the fire. Slipped away from Poulsenn and walked down the block to meet his supplier. That's how they traced him – something else he feels guilty for.'

'How'd he escape on burnt feet?'

'They stole a car. The girl drove. They managed to get out of the city, found themselves on Highway 1, hid out in a remote canyon in the hills above Malibu. At night, she sneaked into residential neighborhoods and scrounged in garbage cans. She tried to take care of him but his feet got worse and the pain caused him to shoot up that last hit of heroin. He lost consciousness, stayed that way for two days. Somehow she cared for him. At the end, she was trying to feed him grass and leaves. Gave him water from a nearby creek that added an intestinal parasite to his miseries. When I saw him in the burn ward, he weighed ninety-eight pounds. All that, and he'd withdrawn cold turkey. His survival's nothing short of a miracle.'

'So you became his doctor,' I said. 'And Schwinn's. And eventually, the two of them connected. Was that by design?'

'I listened to Bill's story, then Pierce's, finally put it all together. Of course, I never told either of them about the other – Pierce still thought of himself as a detective. Looking for Bill. Eventually – after much work – I got Bill's permission and confronted Pierce. It wasn't easy but . . . eventually they both came to understand that their lives were intertwined.'

Matchmaking. Just as he'd done with Schwinn and Marge. The grand physician. *Giving.*

'You waited until it was clear Burns had nothing to fear from Schwinn,' I said. 'Meaning you learned the details of Janie Ingalls's murder. But all of you agreed not to pursue it. You became part of the cover-up. That's why you offered me all those apologies.'

'Alex,' he said. 'Some decisions are . . . these are shattered lives. I couldn't see any other way . . .'

'Schwinn changed things,' I said. 'Changed his mind about keeping the secret. Any idea why he grew agitated about the murder during the weeks before his death? Why he sent out the murder book?'

'I've asked myself all that so many times, and the best I can come up with is the poor man felt he was going to die and had an urge to make peace.'

'Was he sick?'

'Nothing I could diagnose, but he came to me and complained about feeling weak. Shaky, out of focus. A month before his death, he began experiencing crushing headaches. The obvious possibility was a brain tumor, and I sent him up to the Sansum Clinic for an MRI. Negative, but the consulting neurologist did find some abnormal EEG patterns. But you know EEGs – so crude, hard to interpret. And his bloodwork was normal. I wondered about some late-term amphetamine sequelae. He'd been drug-free for years, but perhaps the self-abuse had taken its toll. Then, a week before the night terrors began, he blacked out.'

'Did Marge know about any of this?'

'Pierce insisted on keeping everything from her. Even hid his headache medication in a locked box in his darkroom. I tried to convince him to communicate with her more openly, but he was adamant. Their entire relationship was like that, Alex. Each of them talked to me, and I translated. In that sense, she was the perfect woman for him – stubborn, independent, fiercely private. He could be a profoundly *unmovable* man. Part of what made him a good detective, I suppose.'

'Do you think the night terrors were neurological, or unfinished business come back to haunt him?'

'Maybe both,' he said. 'Nothing unusual was found at his autopsy, but that means nothing. I've seen postmortem brain tissue that looks like Swiss cheese and turns out the patient was functioning perfectly. Then you come across perfectly healthy cerebral cortexes in people who fall apart neurologically. At the core, we humans defy logic. Isn't that why we both became doctors of the soul?'

'Is that what we are?'

'We are, son – Alex, I am sorry for concealing things from you. At the time I believed it was the right thing to do. But that girl . . . the killer's still out there.' Tears filled his eyes. 'One sets out to heal and ends up being complicit.'

I placed a hand on his narrow, soft shoulder.

He smiled. 'Therapeutic touch?'

'Friendship,' I said.

'The purchase of friendship,' he said. 'Cynics coined the term to demean what we do. Sometimes I wonder about the direction my own life has taken . . .'

We strolled toward the gravel pathway.

I said, 'What kind of relationship did Schwinn and Burns develop?'

'Once I knew Pierce could be trusted, I brought him out here. They began talking. Relating. Pierce ended up helping Bill. He'd come out from time to time, clean the house, wheel Bill around.'

'And now Pierce is gone, Burns remains as the last living witness to the Ingalls murder.'

Bert stared at the earth and kept walking.

I said, 'You call him Bill. What's his new surname?'

'Is that important?'

'It's going to come out eventually, Bert.'

'Is it?' he said, lacing his hands behind his back. He steered me toward the open space at the front of the house. 'Yes, I suppose it is. Alex, I know you need to talk to him, but as I told you, he has very little time left, and like most ex-addicts, his self-assessment is brutal.'

'I'll be mindful of that.'

'I know you will.'

'When we spoke earlier,' I said, 'you made a point of mentioning that heroin addicts were unlikely to be violent. You were trying to steer me away from Burns's trail. Caroline Cossack's, as well, by pointing out to me that females were unlikely to be involved in that kind of sexual

483

homicide. All true, but how'd they end up witnessing the murder?'

'Bill came upon the scene once the poor girl was dead, saw what had been done to her.'

'Was Caroline with him?'

He hesitated. 'Yes. They were together at the party. She was allowed to be at the party *because* he was supervising her.'

'Supervising?'

'Keeping an eye on her. Her brothers paid him for that.'

'Drug pusher baby-sitting the strange little sister?' I said.

Bert nodded.

I said, 'So she tagged along with Burns, followed her brothers and their pals to the neighboring estate, came upon the kill spot. The killers saw them, had to be worried they'd unravel. Caroline, because her psychiatric history made her unreliable, Burns because he was a junkie. But instead of eliminating Caroline, they hospitalized her. Probably because even though the Cossacks had participated in murder, they couldn't quite bring themselves to murder their sister. They *would've* killed Burns, but he disappeared into the ghetto, and being rich white kids, they had no easy way to find him. Burns was scared, tried to make a big score, took too many risks and got arrested, made quick bail thanks to LAPD connections and Boris Nemerov's goodwill, and vanished again. But then, a few months later, he surfaced – got himself a job at Achievement House so he could see Caroline. The boys found out and decided the big step had to be taken. But before they could arrange the hit, Burns was gone again. He and Caroline managed to remain in contact. Eventually, he got her out of Achievement House, and the two of them hid out in Watts. How am I doing so far?'

'A-plus, Alex. As always.'

'But something doesn't make sense, Bert. Why would Burns put himself in terrible jeopardy by wangling a job at Achievement House? Why in the world would he risk his life?'

Bert smiled. 'Irrational, wasn't it? That's what I mean about human beings being hard to categorize.'

'Why'd he do it, Bert?'

'Very simple, Alex. He loved her. Still does.'

'Present tense?' I said. 'They're still together? Where is she?'

'They're very much together. And you've met her.'

He brought me back into the house. The front room was empty and the push door remained shut. Bert held it open, and I stepped into a corn yellow bedroom not much bigger than a closet.

Tiny bathroom off to one side. In the sleeping area were two single beds placed side by side, each made up with thin, white spreads. A stuffed bear sat atop a low dresser painted hospital green. The wheelchair was positioned at the foot of the nearer bed, and the man who called himself Bill remained seated, the nearly empty Snapple bottle in one hand, the other grasped by the pudgy, white fingers of a heavyset woman wearing an oversize, royal blue T-shirt and gray sweatpants.

Her downturned eyes were aimed at the bedspread, and my appearance didn't cause them to shift. She had a pasty, acne-scarred face – raw bread dough, pocked by airholes – and her flat nose nearly touched her upper lip.

Faded brown hair striped with silver was tied back in a stub of a ponytail.

Aimee, the cook at the Celestial Café. She'd prepared my crêpes, doubled my portion without charging me extra, remained virtually mute.

Just as I'd finished my meal, Bert had come in. Nice coincidence; now I knew it had been anything but.

Marian Purveyance had owned the café until Aimee Baker took over.

He gives people things.

I said, 'Didn't know you were a restaurateur, Dr Harrison.'

Bert flushed nearly as purple as his jumpsuit. 'I used to fancy myself an investor, bought up a few local properties.'

'Including the land this house stands on,' I said. 'You even transplanted agaves.'

He kicked one foot with the other. 'That was years ago. You'd be amazed at the appreciation.'

'If you ever sold anything.'

'Well . . . the time has to be right.'

'Sure,' I said, and I found myself throwing my arms around the old man.

Aimee turned, and said, 'You're nice.'

Bill said, 'Which one you talking about, baby?'

'Both,' she said. 'Everyone's nice. The whole world is nice.'

thirty-nine

Detective III Craig Bosc whimpered. Vomit flecked his well-formed lips.

Milo said, 'I'll be right back. Don't think of leaving, lad.'

Bosc watched with panic as Milo collected the home-made videos and the dope and left. Milo brought the stash out to the rental Polaris, locked them in the trunk, and moved the car directly in front of Bosc's house. When he returned, the former auto cop hadn't budged.

He undid the leg restraint and hauled Bosc to his feet. Pressed his gun in the small of Bosc's back, making sure not to grow overconfident of his own dominance. Bosc was a fool, and he'd lost more than a bit of self-confidence, but he was also an athlete, young and strong and desperate. When he took hold of Bosc's arm he felt iron musculature.

'Now what?' said Bosc.

'Now, we take a ride.'

Bosc's body grew limp and Milo had to struggle to maintain his grip. Maybe a ploy . . . no, Bosc was really frightened. He'd passed wind and the stench filled the room and Milo eased him back on the couch, let him sit.

487

Putting on the stone face, but he felt ashamed. What had he sunk to?

'Come on,' Bosc pleaded. 'I told you everything. Just let it be.'

'What do you take me for, Craig?'

'I take you for smart. You're supposed to be smart,' said Bosc.

'Exactly.'

'You can't be serious, this is crazy.' Genuine terror enflamed Bosc's eyes. Imagining the worst, because he, himself, was sorely lacking in the conscience department, and if the tables were turned . . .

The truth was Milo hadn't come up with a clear idea of what to do with the idiot. But that was no reason to allay Bosc's fears.

In a creepy, regretful voice, he said, 'There's really no choice, Craig.'

'Jesus,' said Bosc. 'We're both on the same team. Look: we're both . . . outsiders.'

'That so?'

'You know what I mean, man. You're on the outside because . . . you know. And I don't judge you for that, live and let live. Even when other guys put you down, I stood up for you. Said, look at the dude's solve rate, who the fuck cares what he does when he's – I kept telling them it's the job that counts. And you *do* your job, man. I *respect* that. There's been talk of promoting you, you've got a future, man, so don't blow it, no way you can get away with this. Why would you want to get *involved* in shit like this?'

'You've involved me,' said Milo.

'Come on, what did I really *do*? Followed a few orders and played some head games? Okay, it was wrong,

sucked, granted, sorry, but no big deal, it was all just to –
even that whole HIV rumor shit, man. And that wasn't
my idea. I was against that. But all of it was just to – you
know.'

'To get me focused.'

'Exact—'

'Well, I'm nice and focused now, Craig. Get up.' Milo
backed up the command with a wave of the 9mm.
Wondering what he'd do if Bosc complied because walking the guy outside to the rental car, even that short
distance, would be risky in full daylight. Even in L.A.,
where a block was likely to be as devoid of people as one
of Schwinn's nature photos.

'Please,' said Bosc. 'Don't do this, we're both—'

'Outsiders, yeah, yeah. How are *you* an outsider,
Craig?'

'I'm artistic. Into different stuff than the typical
morons in the department.'

'Cinematography?' said Milo.

'Drama – acting. I was in a rock video a few years back.
The Zombie Nannies. Played a highway patrol chippie.
Before that, I did a nonunion commercial for the transit
authority. And art – paintings. I like art, man. Your
typical department moron is into riding Harleys and
pumping iron and drinking beer, I'm hitting the museums. I dig classical music – went to Austria couple of
summers ago, to the Salzburg festival. Mozart,
Beethoven, all that good stuff. You see what I'm trying to
say? It's *because* I understand the art community that I get
where *you're* coming from.'

'I'm an artist.'

'In a sense you are. Without the people in your
community, art would go dead. It would be a fucked

489

world, man – come on, don't *do* this. This is stupid, we're both worthwhile, we both have lots to live for.'

'Do we?'

'Sure,' said Bosc, voice smoothing at the nuance of calm in Milo's reply. 'Just think about it: there's lots of good stuff waiting for both of us.'

'Why,' said Milo, 'do I think you've taken a hostage negotiation course?'

Bosc smiled uneasily. 'You're dissing *me*, but I'm being *real* with *you*. Fine, I can dig that. I dissed you, played with your head, you're entitled. But focus on this: at this very moment I'm being realer than anyone you'll ever meet.'

Milo approached the sofa from one side, took hold of Bosc's T-shirt. 'Get up, or I'll shoot you in the kneecap.'

Bosc's smile dropped like a stone down a glacier hole. 'You take me out there, and I scream—'

'Then you'll die screaming.'

He yanked and Bosc stumbled to his feet and Milo marched him toward the door.

Bosc said, 'I give you credit, man, switching wheels the way you did. I thought I knew all the tricks, but you were too quick for me, I give you credit, give you full credit. Only there's something you *don't* know.'

'There's plenty I don't know, Craig,' said Milo. Figuring the guy was bargaining for time – another negotiation trick. If only he knew he was expending needless energy. Because eventually, he'd be let loose. What choice did Milo have? The question was where and when. And Bosc would reward the largesse with instant hatred and an overpowering bloodlust for revenge. Given Bosc's position in the department, he'd be very likely to do serious damage, and Milo knew he was screwed.

In big trouble, just as Bosc had gloated. But what choice had there been? Continue flopping around as others yanked the strings, Mr Meat Puppet?

He shoved Bosc toward the door. Bosc said, 'No, I mean something you should know right *now*. Specifically. For your own sake.'

'What's that?'

'You've gotta let me go, first.'

'Right.'

'I mean it, man. At this point, I've got nothing to lose, so you can do what the fuck you want to me and I'm not gonna tell you. Because why would I squander my last chip? Come on, make it easy for both of us and I'll tell you and save your friend's ass and we'll both forget any of this happened and be square.'

'My friend,' said Milo. Thinking: *Rick?* Jesus, it had been *Rick* Bosc tailed initially, *Rick's* car Bosc boosted. All these years he'd managed to keep Rick out of this world, and now . . .

He jammed the gun hard into the small of Bosc's back. Bosc gasped, but kept his voice cool. 'Your shrink friend Delaware. *You* switched cars, but he didn't. Still driving round in that green Caddy. I put a satellite tracer on it days ago, know exactly where the dude goes. It feeds into a computer, and I get the data, I know where the feed is. And let me tell you, man, he's been a traveling fool. Did he tell you he was gonna improvise?'

'Where'd he go?'

Long silence.

Milo poked even harder. Used his other hand to clamp the back of Bosc's neck.

'Uh-uh, no way,' Bosc gasped. 'You can fucking blow out my spine, do whatever bad stuff you want, but I'm not giving up my trump card. And something else. And this is the main issue: I'm not the only one knows where the dude is. Other people know, by now. Or they will, real soon. The bad guys. 'Cause the plan was to tell them, leave them one of those anonymous phone calls. We fucking set up your *buddy*, man. Not to hurt him, necessarily, just to use him, to get everyone together. Converging, you know? It was supposed to be perfectly timed, you were supposed to be in on it, too. That's what I was doing at your place today. I was gonna have another try at tagging your car, then you'd be called, too. To motivate you. But you weren't home, so I figured I'd try you later.'

'Bullshit,' said Milo. 'You were settled in for the night, work was the last thing on your mind.'

'Bullshit yourself, I'm a night owl, fucking Batman-Dracula, come alive when the sun goes down. The plan was perfect, only *you* screwed it by being too smart and switching cars, and now Delaware's out in the cold, man, and if you want to help him, there's only one thing you can do and you better do it quick.'

Milo twirled Bosc around, clamped Bosc's gullet at arm's length, aimed the gun at Bosc's groin.

'Go ahead,' said Bosc. 'Do your thing. I'm gonna hold on to my dignity.'

Staring back defiantly.

Sincere.

If the word could be applied to the bastard.

forty

Bert said, 'Yes, Aimee, the world is nice. Now how about you and I go over to the café, see if we can bake up something.'

Aimee smiled, kissed Bill on the forehead, and padded out of the room without a glance at me. Bert said, 'We'll be back in a short while. I'll bring you a sugarless brioche, Bill. Alex, what can I get you?'

'I'm fine.'

'I'll get you something. You may be hungry later.'

I sat on the bed, opposite the wheelchair. 'Good to meet you, Mr . . .'

'We're the Bakers, now,' said Bill. 'It was as good a name as any, and it made Aimee smile. Because one thing she could always do was cook and bake.'

'Bill Baker.'

He grinned and rolled his head. 'Sounds like a rich white man, huh? Bill Baker, attorney. Bill Baker, businessman.'

'It does have a ring to it,' I said.

'It does, indeed.' He grew serious. 'Before we start, I need you to know something. My Aimee, she's like a kid. Always been different, always been scorned. I used to

493

scorn her, like everyone else. Back when I was pushing dope and her brothers used to buy product from me. I liked selling to them because it was a nice change of pace for a South Central junkie. I'd meet them up in the hills above Bel Air, and it was so gorgeous, nothing like my usual transaction locales. I used to call it the scenic route. Make some quick money and get a tour of the way the other side lives.'

The same hills where Bowie Ingalls had died in a single-car encounter with a tree. The boys agreeing to meet *him* in a familiar spot.

I said, 'Did you have lots of clients on the Westside?'

'Enough. Anyway, that's how I met Aimee. Once in a while, the boys would bring her along. When their parents were in Europe or somewhere, which was a lot of the time, those parents were always gone. When they did bring her, they'd leave her in the car and make cruel comments. Embarrassed to be seen with her. To be related to her. I went along with the program. Back then, I had not an atom of compassion in my soul, was hollow, cold, manipulative, thinking only of me, me, me, and not very much of myself, at that. 'Cause if I'd really thought a lot about myself, I wouldn't have done the things I did.'

He raised his arms with effort. Compressed his face and pressed his palms together.

'I was a very bad person, sir. I can't say that I'm a good person now, and I don't give myself any credit for changing, because it was life that changed me.' A slow smile split his head. 'How much sin can a blind man with no feet get into? I'd like to think I wouldn't be bad, even with eyes and legs. But I can never be sure. I don't really feel sure of myself, here.' One hand lowered laboriously and touched his belly.

He laughed. 'Eye for an eye, leg for a leg. I ruined lots of lives, and now I'm paying for it. Almost ruined Aimee's life, too. Gave her dope – big dose of LSD, blotter acid. Her brothers' idea, but I didn't have to be talked into it. We forced her to swallow it, big joke, hahaha. She hollered and fussed and cried, and I stood around laughing with them.'

He drew a hand over sightless eyes.

'Poor little thing, hallucinated for four straight days. I think it might've changed her nervous system. Slowed her down even further, made her life even more difficult, and believe me, life had never been easy for that girl. Next time I saw her was her fourth day of freaking out. Garvey and Bobo wanted to score some mushrooms, and I was the candy man and I met them up in the hills the way we always did and there she was, sitting in the back of the car, but not still, like usual. She was rocking and moaning and crying her little eyes out. Garvey and Bobo just laughed, said she'd been tripping heavy since we blotted her, tried to plunge her hand in boiling water, had almost jumped out of a second-story window, they'd finally tied her down to the bed, she hadn't had a bath or eaten. Laughing about it, but they were worried because their parents were coming home and even though their parents didn't like her, they wouldn't have approved. So I brought her down with barbiturates.'

'Her parents didn't like her?' I said.

'Not one bit. She was different, looked it, acted it, and they were a nouveau riche family that made a big thing of looking good all the time. Country club and all that. Those boys were bad to the core, but they dressed well and combed their hair and used the right aftershave, and that made everyone happy. Aimee didn't know how to do

495

any of that, couldn't be taught to fake it. She was less than a dog in that family, sir, and Garvey and Bobo took advantage of it. Did stuff and blamed it on her.'

'What kind of stuff?' I said.

'Anything that could get 'em in trouble – stealing money, peddling dope on the secondary market to other rich kids, setting fires for fun. They killed a dog, once. Bobo did. Neighbor's dog. Said it barked too much, annoyed him, so he tossed some poison meat at it, and after it died, he and Garvey had Caroline walk by the dog's gate a bunch of times when they were sure the neighbor was watching. So the neighbor would assume. Stuff like that. They bragged to me about it, thought it was funny. They talked about her like she was dirt. I don't know why I started feeling sorry for her 'cause really I was no better than them, but somehow I did. Something about her . . . I just felt sorry for her, can't explain it.'

'Obviously you weren't like them.'

'Kind of you to say so, but I know what I was.' He removed the mirrored sunglasses, revealed sunken black discs split by comma-shaped slits, scratched the bridge of his nose, replaced the glasses.

'You felt sorry for her and started baby-sitting her,' I said.

'No, I did it for the money,' he said. 'Told the boys I'd hang with her when the parents were out of town if they'd pay me. They laughed, and said, "You could turn her out, you should pay us, bro," figuring I wanted to do sexual things to her or maybe I was going to pimp her. And that was agreeable to them. I started coming by the house in my old Mercury Cougar and taking her places.'

'She just went along?'

'She was happy to be getting out. And she was like that – easygoing.'

'She wasn't in school?'

'Not since fifth grade. Severe learning problems, she was supposed to be tutored but never really was. She still can't really read much or do numbers. All she can do is cook and bake, but man, does she do that good, that's her God-given talent.'

'Where'd you take her?' I said.

'Everywhere. The zoo, the beach, parks, she'd keep me company when I did deals. Sometimes we'd just ride around and listen to music. I'd be high, but I never gave her anything again – not after I saw what that blotter did to her. Mostly, I'd talk – trying to teach her stuff. About street signs, the weather, animals. Life. She knew nothing, I never met anyone who knew less about the world. I was no intellectual, just a stupid junkie-pusher, but I had plenty to teach her, which tells you how pathetic her situation was.'

He craned his neck. 'Could I trouble you for another Diet Snapple, sir? Always thirsty. Sugar-diabetes.'

I brought him another open bottle, and he finished it within seconds and handed me the empty. 'Thank you much. The thing you should know is I never did anything sexual to her. Not once, never. Not that I get any credit for that. I was a junkie, and you being a doctor knows what that does to your sex urge. Then the diabetes took over, and the plumbing went south, so I haven't been much for sex in a long time. Still, I'd like to think it wouldn't have made a difference. Respecting her, you know? Not taking advantage of her.'

'Sounds like you respected her from the beginning.'

'I'd like to think so. You sound just like Dr H. Trying

to tell me something good about myself . . . anyway, that's the story with my Aimee. I like that name for her, chose it for her. Her family gave her the old name and they treated her like dirt so she deserved a new beginning. Aimee means friend in French and I've always wanted to go to France, and that's what she's been to me, my only real friend. Outside of Dr H.'

He managed to place his hands on the wheels of the chair, rolled back an inch, and smiled. As if the merest movement was pleasure. 'I'm going to die soon, and it's nice knowing Dr Harrison will be here to take care of my Aimee.'

'He will.'

The smile dissipated. 'Course, he's old . . .'

'Have you and he made plans?'

'It hasn't come to that, yet,' said Bill. 'We better do it soon . . . I've chewed your ear off, and you don't want to know about my personal problems. You're here to find out what happened to the Ingalls girl.'

'Yes,' I said.

'Poor Janie,' he said. 'I can see her face as clear as day, right here.' Tapping a mirrored lens. 'Didn't know her, but I'd seen her around, thumbing on Sunset. She and this friend she was always with, this good-looking blonde. I figured the two of them were hooking, because the only girls still thumbing were hookers and runaways looking to be hookers. Turns out they were just careless girls. The night I found them, I was driving to the party, ready to do some heavy business, saw them standing around on Sunset all confused. Not on the Strip, Bel Air, 'cross the street from the U. They were just a walk from the party but had no idea. So I gave 'em a lift. I still think about that. What if I hadn't?'

'You brought them to the party, then what?'

He smiled. 'Move it right along? Yeah, I brought 'em, tried to get 'em high. Janie smoked some weed, dropped some pills, drank, the blonde one just drank. We hung around together a little, it was a lunatic scene, rich kids and crashers, everyone high and horny, doing their thing in that big, old, empty house. Then Aimee showed up. Attaching to me like she always did. She was there in the first place because I'd agreed to watch her. The parents were off in India, or some place. Had just bought a bigger house, and the boys decided to give themselves a little goodbye bash. Anyway, Janie and her friend – I think her name was Melissa, something like that – were getting into the scene.'

'Melinda Waters,' I said.

He cocked his head, like a guard dog on alert. 'So you know plenty.'

'I don't know how it happened.'

'How it happened is Janie got noticed. By one of the brothers' buddies, a mean kid. You know his name, too?'

'Vance Coury.'

'That's the one,' he said. 'Sweet piece of work, he wasn't any older than the others, but he had this seasoned bad guy's way about him. He noticed Janie, and that's the reason she died. Because he'd had her, before, wanted her again.'

'Had her how?' I said.

'He picked her up when she was thumbing. Took her to some hotel his old man owned downtown, tied her up, did her, whatever. He bragged about it.'

'To you?'

'To all of us. The brothers were with him, coupla other buddies, too. They'd come over to me to score,

499

when Coury spotted Janie. She was off dancing, by herself, tank top half-off, pretty much in dreamland. Coury spots her and gives out this big grin, this big wolfy grin, and says, "Look at that, the slut." And the other boys check out Janie and nod, 'cause they know who she is, heard the story before, but Coury tells it again, anyway. How easy it was, like it was some safari and he'd bagged big game. Then he tells me not only did he do the slut but so did his old man. And the other guys crack up and tell me their daddies did her, too. Seems Janie's own dad was a lowlife scum who'd been selling her since she was twelve.'

Fighting revulsion, I said, 'The other guys' daddies. Do you remember which ones?'

'The brothers, for sure – Garvey and Bobo's old man, and this other creep, this nasty nerd named Brad something-or-other. He piped up and said his daddy'd had her, too. Laughing about it. Proud.'

'Brad Larner.'

'Never knew his last name. Skinny, pale nerd. Mean mouth.'

'Any other buddies in the group, that night?'

'One other, this big doofus, this surfer type . . . Luke. Luke the Nuke was my name for him cause he always looked bombed, would eat anything I sold him.'

'Luke Chapman,' I said. 'Had his father had sex with Janie?'

He thought. 'I don't recall his saying so . . . no, I don't think so, 'cause when the others were going on about it, he looked a little uneasy.'

Multigenerational rape. Michael Larner's assault on Allison Gwynn had been more than a passing fancy. Garvey Cossack, Sr had harbored similar tastes and I was willing to bet Slumlord Coury played in that league, too.

Like father, like . . .

Bowie Ingalls had primed his only child by abusing her, then trafficking in her flesh. I thought about Milo's description of Janie's nearly empty room. A place she didn't, wouldn't think of as home.

Ingalls had been evil and calculating but stupid. Showing up at the meeting with his blackmail targets, drunk and overconfident.

I said, 'What happened when they finished bragging?'

'Coury made some crack about "Honor thy father." Went after Janie – just grabbed her and threw her over his shoulder. The others followed.'

'She resist?'

'Not much. Like I said, she was pretty much out of it. I took Aimee and got out of there. Not because I was a good man. But all that talk about ganging up on a girl, taking sloppy seconds from their daddies, made me feel . . . uncomfortable. Also, Aimee had to go to the bathroom, had been pulling at my arm for a while, complaining she needed to go. But finding a bathroom wasn't so easy in that place, every toilet was being used for getting high or having sex or throwing up or doing what a toilet's for. So, I took her out of the house, over to the backyard, all the way in back, to the bushes and trees, told her to go in there, I'd keep watch.'

He shrugged. The movement caused him pain, and he winced. 'I know it sounds crude, but we'd done that before, Aimee and me. I'd be driving her somewhere far from the city – we used to like to go up into the mountains, out in the San Gabriels or over in the West Valley near Thousand Oaks, or up on Mullholland

Highway or Rambla Pacifica, top of Malibu. Anywhere we could find empty space and just enjoy the quiet. And no matter how many times I'd tell her to go to the bathroom *before* we set out, wouldn't you believe she'd have to go where there was no facilities?'

Big smile. 'Like a kid. So I was used to leading her into the bushes and keeping watch and that's what I did out in the backyard and when we were heading back to the house, we heard voices over the wall – her brother's voice, Garvey, whooping and laughing. Then the others. They were outside, too, going to the next-door property. I knew that because they'd taken me there, it was this huge place, acres, this estate, the owner was some rich European who was never there and most of the time the house was empty. They used to go there to party because no one would bother them. They had a way of getting in, this side gate, up toward the back with a bolt that was easy to wiggle loose and once you were back there you were so far from the house no one could spot you.'

'Party spot.'

'I partied with them, there,' he said. 'Like I said, I was the candy man. Anyway, Aimee wanted to tag along and go over there, like she always did – anything those boys did she thought was cool. No matter how they treated her, she'd want to be with them. I tried to talk her out of it, brought her back inside the party house and sat down and tried to groove on some music. 'Cause while Aimee was in the bushes, I'd shot up, was feeling mellow. But when I opened my eyes, she was gone, and I knew where she'd gone and I was responsible for her so I went after her. And found her. Looking. From behind some trees, into a clearing. She was shaking really bad, teeth chattering, and when I saw what she was looking at, I dug why.'

'How much time had passed since Coury had made a move for Janie?' I said.

'Hard to say. It felt like a long time, but I was going in and out – weaving, you know? Ever been on opiates?'

'When I was a kid I split myself open and they gave me Demerol to stitch me up.'

'Like it?'

'I liked it fine,' I said. 'Everything slowed down and pain turned into a warm glow.'

'So you know.' He rolled his head. 'It's like the best kiss. The sweetest kiss, straight from God's lips. All these years, even knowing what it did to my life, I *still* think about it . . . about the *idea* of doing it. And Lord help me, sometimes I pray that when I do die and if by some miracle I end up upstairs, there'll be this big syringe waiting for me.'

'What was Aimee looking at?'

'Janie.' His voice cracked on the name, and he rocked gently in his wheelchair. 'Oh, Lord, it was bad. Someone was holding a flashlight on her – Luke the Nuke – and the others were standing around, staring. They had her spread out on the ground, with her legs apart, and her head was nothing but blood and she was all cut up and burned and dead cigarettes and blood was all over the ground.'

'Did you see a weapon?'

'Coury and Bobo Cossack were holding knives. Big hunting knives, like you'd get in an army surplus store. Garvey had the pack of cigarettes – Kools. Trying to be hip.'

'What about Brad Larner?'

'He was just standing and staring. And the other one, this big dumb-looking dude, was behind him, freaked out, dead scared, you could see it all over his face. The others were more . . . frozen. Like they'd done something and now it was sinking in. Then Coury said, "We need to get the bitch outta here," and he told Brad to go to his car, get out these blankets he kept there. Then Aimee started retching out loud, and they all turned toward us, and Garvey said, "Oh, shit, you fucking moron!" and I grabbed Aimee and tried to get the hell out of there. But Garvey had got hold of her arm and wouldn't let go and I just wanted to be as far from there as I could so I left her with him and ran as fast as I could and got in my car and drove the hell out of there. I drove like a maniac, it's a miracle no cop pulled me over. Went over to the Marina, then east on Washington, sped all the way east to La Brea, then south into the ghetto.'

He smiled. 'Into the high-crime neighborhood. Watts. That's when I finally felt safe.'

'Then what?'

'Then nothing. I kept a low profile, ran out of money and smack, did what I knew how to do, and got busted.'

'You never thought about reporting the murder?'

'Sure,' he said. 'Rich kids from Bel Air and a black junkie felon tells the cops he just happened to see a white girl get carved up? Cops used to stop me for driving while black, run my license and reg, pull me out, have me do the spread for no reason. Even in my old Mercury Cougar, which was a piece of junk, appropriate for a black junkie felon.'

'That night,' I said, 'you had better wheels. Late-model white Cadillac.'

'You know that?' he said. 'You already know stuff?' Something new crept into his voice – an aftertone of menace. Hint of the man he'd once been. 'You having me go through the motions?'

'You're the first eyewitness we've found. I know about the Caddy because we located Melinda Waters, and she mentioned it. But she split from the party before the murder.'

His head rolled slowly, and he canted it away from me. 'The Caddy was a borrowed car. I maintained the Merc the way a junkie would and finally it broke down and I sold it for dope money. Next day I realized that without wheels I was nothing – good old junkie planning. I planned on boosting some wheels but hadn't gotten around to it, too stoned. So that night, I borrowed from a friend.'

'Nice car like that,' I said, 'must've been a good friend.'

'I had a few. And don't ask me who.'

'Was it the same friend who helped you escape?'

The mirrored shades tilted toward me. 'Some things I can't say.'

'It'll all going to come out,' I said.

'Maybe,' he said. 'If it happens by itself, it's not my responsibility. But some things I can't say.' He turned his head sharply toward the front of the house.

'Something's wrong,' he said. 'Aimee's coming, but that's not her usual walk.'

I heard nothing. Then: a faintest crunch – footsteps on gravel. Footsteps stopping and starting, as if someone was stumbling. But for the panic on his face, it would've floated right past me.

I left him and stepped into the front room, parted the drapes on a small, cloudy window, and looked out at the filmy, amber light of impending dusk.

Up the drive, maybe a hundred feet from the house,

two men were walking Aimee and Bert toward us. Aimee and Bert's hands were up in the air as they marched forward reluctantly. Bert looked terrified. Aimee's pasty face was expressionless. She stopped suddenly and her escort prodded her with something and she winced and resumed walking.

Crunch.

One of the men was large and beefy, the other a head shorter and wiry. Both were Hispanic and wore cowboy hats. I'd seen them half an hour ago – in the pickup loaded with fertilizer that had interposed itself between Bert's car and mine, then dropped away at the 33–150 intersection.

Lucky break, I'd thought at the time, enabling me to use the truck for cover as I tailed Bert.

Bill called out, 'What's happening?'

I rushed back to him. 'Two cowboys have them at gunpoint.'

'Under the bed,' he said, waving his arms helplessly. 'Get it. Now.'

Barking the order. Sounding like anything but a junkie.

forty-one

The computer gizmo that read out the trace on Alex was right in Craig Bosc's Saab, hooked up to the dash, a cute little thing with a bright blue screen and a printer. It sputtered to life after Bosc punched a few keys.

Nineties guy, everything he needed, close at hand.

Milo hadn't found any printouts in Bosc's house, meaning Bosc had left those at his office. Or at someone else's.

As Bosc kept typing, the screen filled with readout – columns of numbers in a code that Bosc explained with no prodding. Bosc pushed another key, and the columns were replaced with what looked like blueprints. Vectors and loci, computerized map lines, everything loading at warp speed.

Bosc was sitting in the Saab's passenger seat. Hands free to work, but Milo had rebound his ankles, first, kept the gun at the back of Bosc's neck.

Promising to let him go when he'd done his bit for humanity.

Bosc thanked him as if he was Santa Claus with a bag full of goodies. The guy stank of fear, but you'd never know it from looking at him. Smiling, smiling, smiling.

Gabbing technotalk as he worked.

Killing time and filling space; keep those psych tactics going.

His fingers rested. 'That's it, amigo. Look at the capital X, and you've got him.'

Milo studied the map. 'That's the best you can do?'

'That's pretty damn good,' said Bosc, offended. 'Within a hundred-yard radius.'

'Print it.'

His pocket filled with paper, Milo yanked Bosc out of the Saab and walked him to the rear of the car.

'Okay, Milo, we're just gonna forget this happened, right?'

'Right.'

'Could I have my legs back, please, Milo.'

The easy, repetitive use of his name filled Milo's head with enraged buzzing. He looked up and down the street, now graying. During the time Bosc had played with the computer, a single car had driven by. Young woman in a yellow Fiero, blond and big-haired enough to be one of Bosc's unwitting home movie costars. But she sped by fast, went two blocks, disappeared, never returned.

Now the street was empty again. Thank God for L.A. alienation.

Milo popped the Saab's trunk, gave Bosc a swift, hard kick behind one knee and as Bosc collapsed predictably, shoved him inside, slammed the lid and walked away to the muffled drumbeat of Bosc thumping and screaming.

All that noise, someone would find him soon enough.

★ ★ ★

He hurried to the Polaris, checked the gas gauge, fired up, sped toward the 101 freeway, driving like a typical SoCal idiot: way too fast, steering with one hand, the other gripping his mobile phone as if it was a life preserver.

forty-two

A husky voice from outside the cabin bellowed, 'Every-one out, hands up.' A second later: 'No fucking around or we kill the retard and the old guy.'

I crouched closer to the window. 'We're coming out. I have to get him in the chair.'

'*Do* it.'

I returned to the bedroom, clamped my hands around the grips of Bill's wheelchair. I'd put a bright white stocking cap on his bald head and had covered him with two soft blankets, despite the heat.

Or maybe it wasn't that hot. I was sweat-drenched but he, the diabetic, remained freakishly dry.

A moment before, he'd prayed silently, lips quivering, hands hooked in the blankets.

He said, 'My, my, my' as I wheeled him forward. When we reached the door, the footrests of his chair nudged it open, and we stepped out into an amethyst twilight.

The pair of cowboys holding Aimee and Bert were twenty or so yards up the gravel drive, off center, closer to the western edge of the pathway, where the forest began. The sky was slate, and the foliage had deepened to olive drab. Flesh tones remained vivid; I saw the fear on Bert's face.

The bigger cowboy was positioned slightly in front of his partner. The pickup's driver. Midforties, five-eleven, with a potbelly that strained his ice-blue shirt, thick thighs that turned his blue jeans into sausage casing, a complexion the color of dirty copper, and a bristling, graying mustache. His hat was broad-brimmed, brown felt.

Bored demeanor, but even at this distance I could see the edgy movement around his eyes. He towered over Bert, held the old man by the scruff.

Just behind him, to the right, the smaller intruder maintained a grip on Aimee, clutching her sweatshirt from behind, stretching the fabric over the rolls and bulges of her torso. Younger, five-five, midtwenties, he wore a baggy black T-shirt and saggy black jeans too urban for his straw headpiece. The hat looked cheap, a hurried addition. He had a round face bottomed by a wispy goatee. Dull, distracted eyes. A mass of tattoos ran up his arms.

One of the car restorers at Vance Coury's garage.

The sun didn't move, but Bert Harrison's complexion grayed.

Aimee said, 'Billy, what's happening?' She made a move toward the chair but the small cowboy cuffed the back of her head. She flapped her arms clumsily. He said, 'Cool it, retard.'

'Bill—'

Bill said, 'Everything's cool, babe, we'll work it out.'

'Sure we will,' said the big cowboy, in the husky voice that had brought us out. A pack of cigarettes swelled one of the pockets of his shirt. Western shirt, with a contrasting white yoke, pearl buttons, still box-creased. He and his pal had dressed for the occasion. He said, 'Get the fuck over here, Willy.'

511

'Over where?' said Bill.

'Over here, Stevie Wonder.' Glancing at me: 'You –
asshole – wheel him over here real slow – take your hands
off the fucking chair, and I'll blow your fucking head off.'

'Then what?' said Bill.

'Then we take y'all somewhere.'

'Where?'

'Shut the fuck up.' To the smaller man: 'We'll load 'em
in back with the shit. Under them tarps, like I showed
you.'

Small said, 'Why don't we just do 'em here?' in a nasal
voice.

The big man's chest swelled. Taking a deep breath.
'That's the plan, *mijo*.'

'What about the wheelchair?'

Big laughed. 'You can have the chair, okay? Give it to
that kid of yours to play with.' To me: 'Wheel him.'

'Where's the truck?' I said.

'Shut up and wheel him.'

'*Is* there a truck?' I said. 'Or are we just taking a little
walk?' Stalling, because that's what you did in situations
like that. Because what was there to lose?

The big man yanked Bert's hair, and Bert's face
creased with pain.

'I'll just do this old *payaso* right here, you keep talking.
Blow out his eyes and make you fuck the sockets.'

I rolled the wheelchair forward. The tires caught in the
gravel, kicked up rocks that pinged the spokes. I pretended to be stuck. My hands stayed wrapped around the
grips.

Big maintained his hold on Bert and watched me
closely. His companion's attention span wasn't as good,
and I saw him glance off into the darkening trees.

512

'Bill?' said Aimee.

'*Bill?*' mimicked Big. 'That's what you call yourself now, Willie?'

'He's Bill Baker,' I said. 'Who do you think he is?'

Big's eyes slitted. 'Was I talking to *you*, asshole? Shut the fuck up and get the fuck over here.'

'Hey,' said Bill, cheerfully. 'What do you know? I thought I recognized that voice. Ignacio Vargas. Long time, Nacho. Hey, man.'

Recognition didn't trouble the big man. He smirked. 'Long time no see, nigger.'

'Real long time, Nacho. Doc, I used to sell this *vaquero* product. He was smart, never tasted, just distributed to his homeboys. Hey, Nacho, didn't you go off somewhere for a vacation – Lompoc? Or did you make it to Quentin?'

'Nigger,' said Vargas, 'before I went away I tried to party with you and the retard over at that house in Niggertown, but you got away. Now, here we are, after all those years. One a those . . . reunions. Who said you don't get a second chance?'

His mouth opened, displaying rows of broken, brown teeth.

Two decades of sanctuary, and I'd brought the enemy to the gates.

'You know what they say, amigo,' said Bill. 'If you don't succeed at first – but, hey, let the old guy go. He's just a doctor happens to treat me, got a bad heart, gonna kick soon, anyway, why bother?'

Bert had been staring at the gravel. Now his eyes climbed very gradually. Came to rest on me. Dispirited.

Bill said, 'Let her go, too. She can't hurt anybody.'

Bert shifted his weight and Nacho Vargas cuffed him

513

again. 'No squirming around, Grampa. Yeah, I think I heard that one, before. If you don't succeed at first, make sure you kill the fucker dead the second time, then go out for a good meal. Come on, Whitebread, keep moving, then when I tell you to stop, let go the wheel and *slowly* put your hands up then get down on the ground and put your hands behind your head and eat dirt.'

I edged the chair another foot forward. Got stuck again. Freed the wheels.

Bill said, 'Nacho was intelligent-o, selling but never using. I could've learned from you, Nacho.'

'You couldn'ta learned nothing. You were stupid.'

I closed the space between us and Vargas to ten yards.

'I don't see any truck,' I said.

'There's a fucking *truck*,' said Small.

Vargas shot a disgusted look intended for his partner, but kept his eyes on me. He began tapping his boot impatiently. Shiny, needle-toed black boots that had never known stirrups; the jeans looked fresh, too. Big shopping spree.

A one-day costume, because you could never really wash out the blood.

Bill said, 'Nacho, my man, be smart: I got nothing to look forward to, put me out of my misery, but leave the old guy and Aimee and everyone else alone. Take me off in that truck of yours and do what you want with—'

'Like I need your fucking permission,' said Vargas.

Bill's head rolled. 'No you don't, no one's saying you do, it's just why not be smart, like I said, he's got a heart condition—'

'Maybe I should have him run around in circles till he drops dead. Save on bullets.' Vargas laughed, kept his gun hand behind Bert, lifted the other arm and jacked Bert

514

up effortlessly. The old man's toes barely grazed the gravel. He'd gone deathly pale. A rag doll.

Vargas said, 'Hey, this is like playing puppet.' His gun hand shifted upward, too. Just an inch or so.

'Nacho, man—'

'Yeah, sure, we'll let everyone go. Maybe we'll let you go, too. Hey, that's a good idea – let's all go out and have a beer.' He snorted. 'She ain't the only retard.' The boot tapped faster. 'C'mon, c'mon, move it.'

I closed the gap to twenty feet, fifteen, exerted downward pressure that tipped the chair slightly, got stuck again.

'What the fu – you playing with me, Whitebread?'

'Sorry,' I said, in a tremulous voice. 'You told me to keep my hands – just a sec.'

Before Vargas could reply, Bert sagged in his grip, cried out in pain, clutched his chest. Vargas laughed, too clever to be taken in by an obvious ruse, but Bert kept thrashing, gave his head a hard shake, and the sudden movement tugged Vargas's arm down and Bert struggled to twist away. As Vargas tried to contain him, his gun hand rose and the weapon was visible. Sleek, black automatic. Aimed at the sky. Behind him, Small was cursing, his attention directed at the struggle. Aimee stared, too, not resisting.

The moment Bert had shown distress, I'd pushed the chair faster, got within five feet of Vargas. Stopped. Vargas continued to grope for Bert. I gave a low grunt.

Bill groped under the folds of the top blanket and pulled out the shotgun.

Old but clean Mossberg Mariner Eight-Shot Mini Combo with pistol grip and speed-feed. Extreme saw-off, barely any barrel left. I'd found it under the bed, where he'd said it would be, stored in a black canvas case coated with dust bunnies. Lying next to two rifles in similar housing and half a dozen boxes of ammo.

'Use the big shells,' he said. I'd loaded the weapon.

Then handed it over to a stiff-fingered blind man.

Vargas got a firm grip on Bert, but Bert saw the shotgun, turned, and bit down on Vargas's arm, and when Vargas bellowed and let go of him, he dropped to the ground and rolled away.

I muttered, 'Now,' and Bill yanked the trigger.

The explosion boxed my ears, and the recoil shoved the wheelchair into my groin as Bill's head snapped backward and connected with my midriff.

Nacho Vargas was blown away as if caught in a personalized tornado. The bottom half of his face turned to smoky, bloody dust, and a giant, ruby-pink orchid blossomed where his gullet and chest had once been. As he fell, white-flecked red broth shot out through his back, spattering Aimee and the small cowboy, who looked stunned. I threw myself at him, swung one fist upward, connected under his nose, got hold of his groin with my other hand and twisted hard.

The whole thing had taken five seconds.

The small man went down, landed on his back, cried out in pain. His black T-shirt was grimed with what looked like steak tartare and bone bits and gobbets of something gray-pink and spongy I knew to be lung tissue. His gun – shiny and silver – remained entwined in his fingers, and I stomped his hand and kicked the weapon loose. The gun rolled away and I dived for it, slid into gore and skidded and went facedown into the gravel, feeling the buzz of impact, then searing pain along one half of my face, both elbows and knees.

516

I'd fallen atop the weapon, felt it biting into my chest. Now the damned thing would go off and blow a hole through me. What a dignified demise.

I rolled away, grabbed the gun, sprang to my feet, hurried back to the small man. He lay there, immobile, and I felt under his filth-encrusted jaw, got a slow steady pulse. The hand I'd stomped looked like a dead crab, and when I lifted his eyelids all I saw was white.

A few feet away, what had once been Nacho Vargas was an exhibit for the forensic pathology texts.

Aimee said, 'Careful.' Talking to Bill, not me. She was behind the chair now, had removed his watch cap, was stroking his head.

Bert was on his feet, tottering, holding Vargas's weapon with two hands. Staring at it with revulsion. His color made me unsure if the chest pains had been a total ruse.

I kept the silver gun trained on the unconscious man, heartbeat racing way beyond optimal, muscles pumped, head boiling.

Up close, he looked barely twenty.

Give it to that kid of yours to play with.

A young man with one kid, maybe a new father. Would he have helped Vargas dispatch all of us, then gone home and played with Junior?

He moaned, and my fingers tightened around the trigger. Another moan, but he didn't move. I trained the gun on him, had to work at releasing the pressure in my fingers. Slowing my breathing, struggling to think clearly, sort things out.

The clearing around the house deepened to a sickening, syrupy gray. Bill sat there in the chair, the shotgun across his lap. Aimee and Bert stood by, silently. The small man didn't move. Silence settled around us. From somewhere off in the forest, a bird peeped.

A plan: I'd tie up the unconscious man, put him and the wheelchair in the trunk of the Seville, drive us all to some safe place – I'd figure out where along the way. No, first I'd call Milo from the house – I had to get them all in the house – the bloody gravel, the corpse with its yield of shredded body parts, would be dealt with later.

'Do you have any rope?' I asked Bill.

His mirrored glasses were off, and Aimee was dabbing at the gray hollows with a corner of the top blanket. Unmindful of the porridge that splotched her clothing and her face.

He said, 'No. Sorry.'

'Nothing to tie him with?'

'Sorry . . . the other one's alive?'

'Out cold but alive. I thought with that arsenal—'

'The arsenal was my . . . baggage . . . never really thought I'd use it . . .'

The shotgun had been clean, freshly oiled.

He must've read my mind, said, 'I taught my Aimee how to take care of it.'

Aimee recited: 'Ream the barrel, wipe it down, oil it up.'

'But no rope,' said Bill. 'Ain't that a hoot. Maybe we can shred some clothing.' Tired. One hand caressed the truncated shotgun.

Aimee mumbled.

'What's that, sugar?'

'There is rope. Kind of.'

'There is?' he said.

'Twine. I use it for my rolled roast.'

'Not strong enough, baby.'

'Oh,' she said. 'It holds in the roast.'

'Bert, come here and keep a close aim on him,' I said, pocketing the silver gun and pulling the small man to his feet. He was 130 pounds tops, but deadweight and the noradrenaline cool-down made dragging him to the house an ordeal.

I got him to the door, looked back. No one had followed. Nighttime turned the others to statuary.

'Inside,' I said. 'Let's take a look at that twine.'

forty-three

Bill was right about the cooking twine. Too flimsy. I used it anyway, sitting the small man in a chair in the front room and using both rolls to create a macramé mummy. He looked out of it, hopefully for a while. My heart started racing again.

I searched the small kitchen, found a crushed, nearly empty roll of duct tape beneath the sink, unspooled enough to run two tight bands around his body and the chair, at nipple and waist levels. What was left I used to bind his ankles together. He offered no resistance . . . how old was his kid?

I said, 'Where's the phone?'

Bert shuffled over to a corner, bent behind another chair, retrieved an old black dial phone, and handed it to me. He hadn't said a word since the shooting.

I lifted the receiver. No dial tone. 'Dead.'

Bert took the phone, jabbed the receiver button, dialed O. Shook his head.

'Do you generally have phone problems?'

'No, sir,' said Bill. 'Not that we use it much. Maybe—' He frowned. 'I know that smell.'

'What smell?' I said.

The concussion came from behind, from the rear of

the house. The impact of something striking wood, followed by a loud sucking *swoosh!* Then the xylophone glissando of broken glass.

Bill turned toward the sound. Bert and I stared. Only Aimee seemed unconcerned.

Suddenly daylight – a false orange daylight – brightened the bedroom, followed by a rush of heat and the cellophane-snap of flames.

Fire licked the curtains, a zipper of it, running up to the ceiling and down to the floor.

I ran for the bedroom door, slammed it shut over the spreading inferno. Smoke seeped from under the panel. The odor hit: metallic, acrid, the chemical bitterness of a flash storm ripping open a polluted sky.

The smoke from beneath the door fattened from wisp to wormy coil to clouds, relentless and oily, white to gray to black. Within seconds, I could barely make out the forms of the other people.

The room grew furnace-hot.

The second firebomb hit. Again, from behind. Someone was stationed out back, in the forest, where the phone wires ran.

I grabbed hold of Bill's chair, waved frantically to Bert and Aimee's smoke-obscured silhouettes.

'Get out!' Knowing that what I was sending them to was unlikely to be safety. But the alternative was roasting alive.

No answer, and now I couldn't see them at all. I rolled Bill toward the front door. From behind came roaring protest. The door collapsed and flames shot forward as I shoved the wheelchair. Groping the air for Aimee and Bill. Screaming with clogged lungs: 'Someone's out there! Stay low—'

521

My words were choked off by convulsive coughing. I made it to the door, reached for the knob, and the hot metal broiled my hand.

Handicapped push door, idiot. I shouldered it hard, shoved Bill's chair, lurched outside, eyes burning, retching, coughing.

Running into the darkness and aiming the chair to the left as a bullet impacted against a front window.

Smoke billowed out of the house, a smothering curtain of it. Good cover, but poisonous. I ran as far from the gravel drive as possible, into the underbrush that formed at the house's eastern border. Racing with the chair, struggling to manipulate the contraption over rocks and vines, getting caught in the underbrush. Unable to free the chair.

Jammed. I lifted Bill out of the chair, slung him over my shoulder, and ran, adrenaline-stoked again, but his weight bore down and I could barely breathe and after ten steps I was on the verge of collapse.

My legs buckled. I visualized them as iron rods, forced them straight, lost my breath completely, stopped, shifted the load, panted and coughed. Feeling the dangle of Bill's ruined legs knocking against my thighs, the dry skin of one palm against the back of my neck as he held on tight.

He said something – I felt it rather than heard it – and I resumed carrying him into the forest. Pulled off ten more steps, counted each one, twenty, thirty, stopped again to force air into my lungs.

I looked back at the house. None of the Halloween glare of fire, just smoke, funnels of it, so dark it bled easily into the night sky.

Then the spot where the little green house had stood

was suddenly engulfed by a crimson ball haloed in lime green.

The kerosene stink of a stale campground. Something igniting – the kitchen stove. The explosion threw me to the earth. Bill landed on top of me.

No sign of Aimee or Bert.

I stared back at the house, wondering if the fire would spread to the forest. Not good for the forest, but maybe good for us if it attracted attention.

Nothing but silence. No spread; the firebreak serving its purpose.

I rolled Bill off me and propped myself up on my elbows. His glasses had come loose. His mouth moved soundlessly.

I said, 'You okay?'

'I – yeah. Where's . . .'

'Let's keep moving.'

'Where is she?'

'She's fine, Bill, come on.'

'I need to—'

I got hold of his shoulder.

'Leave me here,' he said. 'Let me go, I've had enough.'

I began lifting him.

'Please,' he said.

My burned hand began to throb. Everything throbbed.

A raspy voice behind me said, 'Dead end, Mr Cadillac.'

forty-four

Vance Coury's silver hair caught moonlight. A black leather headband held it in place. The musk of his aftershave managed to seep through the scorched air.

He shone the flashlight in my face, shifted the beam to Bill, lowered it and held it at an angle that brightened the forest floor. As the white spots cleared from my eyes, I made out the rectangle in his right hand. Columnar snout. Machine pistol.

He said, 'Up.' Businesslike. Tying up loose ends.

He wore light-colored, grease-stained mechanics overalls – outfitted for messy work. Something flashed around his neck – probably the same gold chain I'd seen at the garage.

I got to my feet. My head still rang from the explosion.

'Walk.' He motioned to his right, back to the clearing.

'What about him?' I said.

'Oh, yeah, him.' He leveled the pistol downward, peppered Bill's frame with a burst that nearly cut the blind man in two.

The fragments of Bill's corpse bucked and flopped and were still.

Coury said, 'Any more questions?'

He marched me out of the forest. A pile of cinders, snarls of electrical conduit, random stacks of bricks, and twisted metal chairs were the remnants of the little green house. That and something contorted and charred, lashed and duct-taped to a chair.

'Playing with matches,' I said. 'Bet you liked that as a kid.'

'Walk.'

I stepped onto the gravel path. Keeping my head straight but moving my eyes back and forth. Nacho Vargas's corpse remained where it had fallen. No sign of Aimee or Bert.

A cloud of musk hit my nostrils, sickly sweet as a Sacher torte. Coury, walking close behind me.

'Where we going?' I said.

'Walk.'

'Walk where?'

'Shut up.'

'Where are we going?'

Silence.

Ten steps later, I tried again. 'Where we going?'

He said, 'You are *really* stupid.'

'Think so?' I said, reaching into my pocket and pulling out the short man's silver gun and wheeling fast.

Inertia caused him to pitch forward, and we nearly collided. He tried to step back, free the machine pistol, but couldn't get enough room to maneuver. Stumbled.

He hadn't bothered to pat me down. Overconfident rich kid who'd never grown up. All those years of getting away with bad stuff.

The little silver gun shot forward, as if of its own accord. Coury's goatee spread as his mouth opened in surprise.

I focused on his tonsils, shot three times, hit with every bullet.

I took his machine pistol and pocketed the silver gun, scurried off the gravel, found refuge behind a sycamore. Waited.

Nothing.

Stepping on greenery to muffle my footsteps, I inched forward, heading toward the road. Wondering who and what awaited me there.

I'd been overconfident, too, thinking Vargas and the small man had made up the entire army. Too important a job for a pair of thugs.

Coury had been a precise man who specialized in deconstructing high-priced machines and reconstituting them as works of art.

A good planner.

Send in the B team while the A team waits. Sacrifice the B team and attack from the rear.

Another ambush.

Coury had come himself to take care of Bill. Bill was a living witness, and eliminating him was the primary goal. The same went for Aimee. Had he taken care of her – and Bert – first? I hadn't heard gunfire as I carried Bill away, but the firebombs and the kerosene blast had filled my head with noise.

I walked five steps, stopped, repeated the pattern. The mouth of the gravel drive came into view.

Choice point, none of the options good.

I found nothing.

Just the Seville, all four tires slashed flat, hood open, distributor cap gone. Tire tracks – two sets, both deep and heavily treaded – said the pickup and another working vehicle had departed.

The nearest house was a quarter-mile up the road. I could barely make out yellow windows.

I was bloodstained and bloodied, one side of my face scraped raw, and my burnt hand hurt like hell. One look and the residents would probably bolt their doors and call the police.

Which was fine with me.

I almost made it before the rumble sounded.

Big engine, heading my way from Highway 150. Loud enough – close enough – for visibility, but no headlights.

I ran into the bushes, crouched behind a flurry of ferns, watched as the black Suburban sped past and slowed fifty feet before the entrance to Bill and Aimee's property.

It came to a halt. Rolled forward, twenty feet, stopped again.

A man got out. Big, very big.

Then another, slightly smaller but not by much. He gave some kind of hand signal, and the two of them pulled out weapons and hurried toward the entrance.

Anyone at the wheel? The Suburban's tinted windows augmented the night and made it impossible to tell. Now I knew that a run for the neighbors' house would be risky and wrong: Coury's shooting of Bill resonated in my head. Coury had pulled the trigger, but I'd been the angel of death, couldn't justify extending the combat to more innocents.

I crouched and waited. Tried to read my watch, but the crystal was shattered and the hands had been snapped off.

527

I counted off seconds. Had reached three thousand two hundred when the pair of big men returned.

'Shit,' said the shorter one. 'Goddammit.'

I stood, and said, 'Milo, don't shoot me.'

forty-five

Aimee and Bert sat in the third row of the Suburban. Aimee clutched Bert's sleeve. Bert's eyes lacked focus.

I got in next to Milo, in the second row.

At the wheel was Stevie the Samoan, the bounty hunter Georgie Nemerov called Yokuzuna. Next to him sat Red Yaakov, crew-cut head nearly brushing the roof.

'How'd you find us?' I said.

'The Seville car got tagged, and I got hold of the tagger.'

'Tagged?'

'Satellite locating device.'

'One of Coury's car gadgets?'

His hand on my shoulder was eloquent: *We'll talk later.*

Stevie drove to Highway 150 and pulled over just short of the 33 intersection, into a tree-shaded turnaround where three vehicles sat. Toward the rear, half-hidden by the night, was the pickup truck, front end facing the road, still loaded with fertilizer. A few feet away was a dark Lexus sedan. Another black SUV – a Chevy Tahoe – blocked both other vehicles.

Stevie dimmed his lights, and two men stepped from

behind the Tahoe. A muscular, shaved-head Hispanic wearing a black muscle T-shirt, baggy black cargo pants and a big leather chest holster, and Georgie Nemerov in a sport coat, open-necked white shirt, rumpled slacks.

The muscular man's T-shirt read: BAIL ENFORCEMENT AGENT in big white letters. He and Nemerov approached the Suburban. Milo lowered his window, and Nemerov peered in, saw me, raised an eyebrow.

'Where's Coury?'

Milo said, 'With his ancestors.'

Nemerov tongued the inside of his cheek. 'You couldn't save him for me?'

'It was over by the time we got there, Georgie.'

Nemerov's eyebrow arched higher as he turned to me. 'I'm impressed, Doc. Want a job? The hours are long and the pay sucks.'

'Yeah,' said Yaakov, 'but de people you got to meet are deezgusting.'

Stevie laughed. Nemerov's smile widened reluctantly. 'I guess results are what counts.'

'Was there anyone else?' I said. 'Besides Coury?'

'Sure,' said Nemerov. 'Two other party animals.'

'Brad Larner,' said Milo. 'That Lexus is his. He and Coury arrived in it, Larner was driving. He was parked near the house, waiting for Coury, when we spotted him behind the truck. Dr Harrison and Caroline were tied up in the truck bed. Another guy was at the wheel.'

'Who?'

Nemerov said, 'Paragon of virtue named Emmet Cortez. I wrote a few tickets for him before he went away on manslaughter. Worked in the auto industry.'

'Painting hot rods,' I said.

'Chroming wheels.' Nemerov's grin was sudden,

mirthless, icy. 'Now he's in that big garage in the sky.'

'Rendered inorganic,' said Stevie.

'Steel organic,' said Yaakov. 'Long as deyr someting left, he steel organic, right, Georgie.'

'You're being technical,' said Stevie.

'Let's change the subject,' said Nemerov.

forty-six

'Pancakes,' said Milo.

It was 10 A.M., the next morning, and we were at a coffee shop on Wilshire near Crescent Heights, a place where old people and gaunt young men pretending to write screenplays congregated. One half-mile west of the Cossack brothers' offices, but that hadn't been what drew us there.

We'd both been up all night, had returned to L.A. at 6 A.M., stopped at my house to shower and shave.

'Don't wanna wake Rick,' he'd explained.

'Isn't Rick up by now?'

'Why complicate things?'

He'd emerged from the guest bathroom, toweling his head and squinting. Wearing last night's clothes but looking frighteningly chipper. 'Breakfast,' he proclaimed. 'I know the place, they make these big, monster flappers with crunchy peanut butter and chocolate chips.'

'That's kid food,' I said.

'Maturity is highly overrated. I used to go there all the time. Believe me, Alex, this is what you need.'

'Used to go there?'

'Back when I wasn't watching my figure. Our endocrine systems are shot so we need sugar – my maternal grandfather ate pancakes every day, washed them down with three cups of coffee sweeter than cola, and he lived till ninety-eight. Woulda gone on a few more years, but he tumbled down a flight of stairs while ogling a woman.' He pushed an errant thatch of black hair out of his face. 'Unlikely to be my fate, but there are always variants.'

'You're uncommonly optimistic,' I said.

'Pancakes,' he said. 'C'mon, let's get going.'

I changed into fresh clothing, thinking about Aimee and Bert, all the unanswered questions.

Thinking about Robin. She'd called last night, from Denver, left a message at 11 P.M. I phoned back at 6:30, figuring to leave a message at her hotel, but the tour had moved on to Albuquerque.

Now, here we were, facing two stacks of peanut butter hotcakes the size of frypans. Breakfast that smelled eerily of Thai food. I corroded my gut with coffee, watched him douse his stack with maple syrup and begin sawing into it, then took hold of the syrup pitcher in my unburnt hand. The ER doctor at Oxnard Hospital had pronounced the burn 'first-degree plus. A little deeper and you would've made second.' As if I'd missed a goal. He'd administered salve and a bandage, swabbed my face with Neosporin, wrote me a scrip for antibiotics, and told me to avoid getting myself dirty.

Everyone at the hospital knew Bert Harrison. He and Aimee were given a private room near the emergency admissions desk, where they stayed for two hours. Milo and I had waited. Finally, Bert came out, and said, 'We're going to be here for a while. Go home.'

'You're sure?' I said.

'Very sure.' He pressed my hand between both of his, gave a hard squeeze, returned to the room.

Georgie Nemerov and his crew drove us to the spot at the entrance to Ojai where Milo had left his rental Dodge, then disappeared.

Milo had joined up with the bounty hunters, formulated a plan.

Lots of questions . . .

I tipped the pitcher, followed the syrup's drizzle, watched it pool and spread, picked up my fork. Milo's cell-phone chirped. He clicked in, said, 'Yeah?' Listened for a while, hung up, stuffed his face with a wad of pancake. Melted chocolate frosted his lips.

I said, 'Who was that?'

'Georgie.'

'What's up?'

He cut loose another triangle of hotcake, chewed, swallowed, drank coffee. 'Seems there was an accident late last night. Eighty-third Street off Sepulveda, rental Buick hit a utility pole at high speed. Driver and occupant rendered inorganic.'

'Driver and occupant.'

'Two db's,' he said. 'You know what high-speed impact does to the human body.'

'Garvey and Bobo?' I said.

'That's the working hypothesis. Pending verification of dental records.'

'Eighty-third off Sepulveda. On the way to the airport?'

'Funny you should mention that, they did find tickets in the wreck. Pair of first-class passages to Zurich, hotel reservations at some place called the Bal du Lac. Sounds pretty, no?'

'Lovely,' I said. 'Maybe a ski vacation.'

'Could be – is there snow there, right now?'

'Don't know,' I said. 'It's probably raining in Paris.'

534

He motioned for a coffee refill, got a new pot, poured, and drank slowly.

'Just the two of them?' I said.

'Seems that way.'

'Odd, don't you think? They've got a full-time chauffeur and choose to drive themselves to the airport? Own a fleet of wheels and use a rental car.'

He shrugged.

'Also,' I went on, 'what would they be doing on a side street in Inglewood? That far south, you're heading for the airport, you stay on Sepulveda.'

He yawned, stretched, emptied his coffee cup. 'Want anything else?'

'Is it on the news, yet?'

'Nope.'

'But Georgie knows.'

No answer.

'Georgie has the inside track,' I said. 'Being a bail bondsman and all that.'

'That must be it,' he said. He brushed crumbs from his shirtfront.

I said, 'You've got syrup on your chin.'

'Thanks, Mom.' He threw money on the table and got up. 'How 'bout we take a little digestive stroll.'

'East on Wilshire,' I said. 'Up to Museum Row.'

'You are nailing those hypotheses, Professor. Time for Vegas.'

We walked to the pink granite building where the Cossack brothers had once played executive. Milo studied the façade for a long time, finally entered the lobby, stared down the guard, left, and returned to the front steps where I'd been waiting, pretending to feel civilized.

'Happy?' I said, as we headed back to the coffee shop. 'Ecstatic.'

We retraced our walk to the coffee shop, got into Milo's rental of the day – a black Mustang convertible – drove through the Miracle Mile and across La Brea and into the clean, open stretch of Wilshire that marked Hancock Park's northern border.

Milo steered with one finger. No sleep for two days but beyond alert. I had to fight to keep my eyes open. The Seville had been towed to a shop in Carpenteria. I'd phone in later today, get a report. Meanwhile, I'd drive Robin's truck. If I could stand the sweet smell of her permeating the cab.

He turned on Rossmore, drove south to Fifth Street, hooked back to Irving, and pulled over to the curb, six houses north of Sixth. On the other side was Chief Broussard's city-financed mansion. An immaculate white Cadillac sat in the driveway. A single plainclothesman stood guard, looking bored.

Milo stared at the house, same hostility as when he'd eye-zapped the guard in the Cossacks' lobby. Before I could ask what was up, he U-turned, headed south, then west to Muirfield, where he cruised slowly to the end of the block and stopped at a property concealed behind high stone walls.

'Walt Obey's place,' he said, before I could ask.

Stone walls. Just like the Loetz estate that neighbored the party house. The kill spot. Build walls, and you could get away with plenty.

Janie Ingalls abused by two generations of men. A closed-circuit camera atop one gatepost rotated.

Milo said, 'Say cheese.' Waved. Jammed the Mustang into DRIVE and sped away.

★ ★ ★

He dropped me back home, and I slept until 5 P.M., woke in time to turn on the news. The Cossack brothers' deaths missed the network affiliate broadcasts but were featured an hour later on a local station's six o'clock spot.

The facts were just as Georgie Nemerov had reported: single-car accident, probably due to excessive speed. Thirty seconds of bio identified Garvey and Bobo as 'wealthy Westside developers' who'd built 'some controversial projects.' No identifying photos. No suspicion of foul play.

Another death occurred that night, but it never hit the L.A. news because it went down ninety miles north.

Santa Barbara News-Press item, forwarded to me by e-mail, with no accompanying message. The sender: sloppyslooth@sturgis.com. That was a new one.

The facts were straightforward: the body of a sixty-eight-year-old real estate executive named Michael Larner had been found two hours ago, slumped in the front seat of his BMW. The car had been driven into a wooded area just north of the Cabrillo exit off the 101, on the outskirts of Santa Barbara. A recently fired handgun sat in Larner's lap. He'd died of 'an apparent single wound to the head, consistent with self-infliction.'

Larner had come to Santa Barbara to identify the body of his son, Bradley, forty-two, the recent victim of a heart attack, who'd also – irony of ironies – succumbed in a car. Bradley's vehicle, a Lexus, had been discovered just a few miles away, on a quiet street on the north end of Montecito. The grieving father had left the morgue just after noon, and investigators had come up with no accounting of his whereabouts during the three hours leading up to his suicide.

A homeless man had discovered the body.

'I was going in there to take a nap,' reported the vagrant, identified as Langdon Bottinger, fifty-two. 'Knew something was wrong right away. Nice car like that, pushed up against a tree. I looked inside and knocked on the windows. But he was dead. I was in Vietnam, I know dead when I see it.'

forty-seven

After dropping Alex off, Milo turned on the Mustang's radio and dialed to KLOS. Classic rock. Van Halen doing 'Jump.'

Kicky little thing, the 'Stang. Something with a little zip.

'Used to be owned by Tom Cruise's gardener,' the multipierced girl at the alternative rental yard had told him. Night owl; she worked the midnight-to-eight shift.

'Great,' said Milo, pocketing the keys. 'Maybe it'll help on auditions.'

The girl nodded, knowingly. 'You go out for character roles?'

'Nah,' said Milo, heading for the car. 'Not enough character.'

He returned to John G. Broussard's digs on Irving, sat and watched for hours. The chief's wife emerged at 1:03 P.M., escorted to the driveway by a lady cop who held open the driver's door of the white Caddy. Mrs B drove toward Wilshire and was gone.

Leaving John G. alone in the house? Milo was fairly certain Broussard wasn't in the office; he'd phoned the chief's headquarters, impersonated a honcho from Walt

Obey's office, was told very politely that the chief wouldn't be in today.

No surprise, there. Yet another anti-Broussard piece had run in the morning *Times*. The Police Protective League griping about poor morale, dumping it all in Broussard's lap. Commentary by some law prof, psycho-analyzing Broussard. The clear implication was that the chief's temperament was a poor fit for modern-day policing. Whatever the hell that meant.

Add all that to the events of last night – and Craig Bosc's report to the chief – and Broussard had to know the walls were closing in.

John G. had always been the most cautious of men. So what was he doing now? Upstairs in his bedroom closet, picking out a cool suit from a rack of dozens? It was almost as if he didn't care.

Maybe he didn't.

Milo kept watching the Tudor digs, stretched his legs, ready for the long haul. But five minutes later a dark green sedan – an unmarked Ford, blackwalls, pure LAPD – backed out of the driveway.

Solitary driver. A tall man, rigid at the wheel. The unmistakable outline of the chief's noble profile.

Broussard turned south, just like his wife had. Stopped at Wilshire and sat there for a long time, with his left-turn signal blinking – what a good example – waited for the traffic to thin before swinging smoothly onto the boulevard.

Heading east. So maybe he *was* going to work. Tough-ing it out, show the bastards.

One way to find out.

Broussard stuck precisely to the speed limit, gliding in

the center lane, signaling his right turn on Western well within DMV parameters. He drove south, past Washington Boulevard, picked up the 10 East and engineered a textbook entry into the afternoon flow.

Freeway traffic was moderately heavy but steady, perfect tail situation, and Milo had no trouble keeping an eye on the Ford as it passed through the downtown interchange, stayed on the 10, and exited at Soto, in East L.A.

The coroner's office?

And Broussard did drive to the clean, cream morgue building on the west end of the County Hospital complex, but instead of turning in to park among the vans and the cop cars, he kept going, continued for another two miles. Made a perfect stop at a narrow street called San Elias, turned right, and did a 20 mph cruise through a residential neighborhood of tiny bungalows packaged by chain link.

Three blocks up San Elias, then the street dead-ended and the green Ford pulled over.

The terminus was marked by twenty-foot-high iron double gates, rich with flourishes and topped by Gothic arches. Above the peaks, the iron had been bent into lettering. Milo was a block away, couldn't make out what they spelled.

John G. Broussard parked the Ford, got out, locked it, tugged his suit jacket in place.

Not dressed for the office – the chief never showed up at Parker Center out of uniform. Lint-free, all those razor-presses, his chest festooned with ribbons. During ceremonial occasions, he wore his hat.

Thinking he was a fucking general or something, said the scoffers.

Today Broussard wore a navy suit tailored snugly to his

trim physique, a TV blue shirt, and a gold tie so bright that it gleamed like jewelry from a block away. Perfect posture accentuated the chief's height as he walked to the big iron gates with a martial stride. As if presiding at some ceremony. Broussard paused, turned a handle, stepped through.

Milo waited five minutes before getting out. Looked over his shoulder several times as he covered the block on foot. Feeling antsy, despite himself. Something about Broussard . . .

When he was halfway to the gates, he made out the lettering.

Sacred Peace Memorial Park

The cemetery was bisected by a long straight pathway of decomposed granite, pink-beige against a bordering hedge of variegated boxwood. Hollywood junipers formed high green walls on three sides, too bright under a sickly gray sky. No orange trees in sight, but Milo could swear he smelled orange blossoms.

Twenty feet in, he came upon a statue of Jesus, benevolent and smiling, then a small limestone building marked OFFICE and fringed with beds of multicolored pansies. A wheelbarrow blocked half the path. An old Mexican man in khaki work clothes and a pith helmet stooped in front of the flowers. He turned briefly to look at Milo, touched the brim of the helmet, returned to weeding.

Milo circumvented the wheelbarrow, spotted the first row of gravestones, kept going.

Old-fashioned markers, upright, carved of stone, a few of them tilting, a handful decorated by sprigs of desiccated flowers. Milo's parents had been buried in a very different ambience, huge place, not far from Indianapolis, a suburban city of the dead bordered by industrial parks and shopping malls. Mock-colonial buildings with all the authenticity of Disneyland, endless rolling green turf fit for a championship golf course. The markers in his parents' cemetery were brass plaques embedded flat in the bluegrass, invisible until you got close. Even in death Bernard and Martha Sturgis had been loath to offend . . .

This place was flat and tiny and treeless except for the bordering junipers. Two naked acres, if that. Full up with gravestones, too – an old place. Nowhere to hide, and finding Broussard was easy enough.

The chief was standing off in a corner in the lower left quadrant of the cemetery. Second-to-last row, a snug, shady place. His back was to Milo as he faced a marker, big, dark hands laced behind his ramrod back.

Milo walked toward him, making no effort to squelch the sound of his footsteps. Broussard didn't turn.

When Milo got to the gravesite, the chief said, 'What took you so long?'

The stone that had occupied Broussard was charcoal granite edged with salmon pink and carved beautifully with a border of daisies.

Jane Marie Ingalls
MAY SHE FIND PEACE IN ETERNITY

Entry and exit dates spelled out a sixteen-year-three-month life span. A tiny smiling teddy bear had been chiseled above Janie's name.

A gray-blue juniper berry had lodged in the bevel that created the bear's left button eye. John G. Broussard stooped and plucked it out and placed it in a pocket of his jacket. The suit was double-breasted, blue with a maroon chalk stripe. Suppressed waist, high side vents, working buttonholes on the sleeves. *Look, Ma, I'm custom-made.* Milo remembered Broussard's terrific threads and poreless skin during the interrogation twenty years ago.

The thousandth time he'd thought about that day.

Up close, the chief hadn't changed much. The graying hair, a bit of crease at the corner of his lips, but his complexion glowed with health, and his huge hands looked strong enough to crack walnuts.

Milo said, 'You come here a lot?'

'When I invest in something, I like to keep an eye on it.'

'Invest?'

'I bought the marker, Detective. Her father didn't care. She was going to end up in a potter's field.'

'Guilt offering,' said Milo.

Broussard remained still. Then he said, 'Detective Sturgis, I'm going to examine you for listening devices, so relax.'

'Sure,' said Milo, stifling the 'Yes, sir' on the tip of his tongue. No matter how hard he tried, Broussard made him feel small. He drew himself up as the chief turned, faced him, did an expert pat-down.

That figured. An ex-IA man would have experience with wires.

Finished, Broussard dropped his hands and maintained eye contact. 'So what is it you want to tell me?'

'I was hoping you'd have things to tell me.'

Broussard's lips didn't move, but a glint of amusement brightened his eyes. 'You'd like some sort of confessional statement?'

'If that's what's on your mind,' said Milo.

'What's on your mind, Detective?'

'I know about Willie Burns.'

'Do you?'

'The tax rolls say the place where he hid out on 156th – where your partner Poulsenn got nailed – was owned by your wife's mother. The night Willie took Janie Ingalls to the party he was driving a borrowed car. Brand-new white Cadillac, beautifully maintained. Your wife likes those, has owned six Caddies in the last twenty years, all white. Including the one she's driving at this very moment.'

Broussard stooped and brushed dust off Janie Ingalls's headstone.

'Burns was family,' said Milo.

'Was?' said Broussard.

'Very much *was*. It went down last night. Just like you choreographed.'

Broussard straightened. 'There are limits to protection. Even for family.'

'What was he, a cousin?'

'Nephew,' said the chief. 'Son of my wife's eldest brother. His siblings were all respectable. Everyone in the family went to college or learned a trade. Willie was the youngest. Something went wrong.'

'Sometimes it works out that way,' said Milo.

'Now you're sounding like that shrink friend of yours.'

'It rubs off.'

'Does it?' said Broussard.

'Yeah. Hanging around with the right people is good

545

for the soul. Vice versa, too. Musta been a burden, you playing by the rules, taking all that racist crap, climbing the ranks, meanwhile Willie's going on his merry way shooting and selling smack. Lots of potential for bad PR. But you did your best to help him, anyway. That's why he never served much jail time. You hooked him up with Boris Nemerov, probably went his cash bonds. And at first he came through for Nemerov, kept you looking good.'

Broussard remained impassive.

Milo said, 'Musta been a strain, associating with a known felon.'

'I never broke the law.'

Milo's turn to keep quiet.

Broussard said, 'There's always flexibility in the law, Detective. Yes, I carried him. My wife adored him – remembered him as a cute little kid. To the family he was *still* the cute little kid. I was the only one seemed to realize he'd metamorphosed into a reprobate junkie. Maybe I should've seen it sooner. Or let him deal with the consequences earlier.'

The chief's posture relaxed a bit. Bastard was actually slumping.

Milo said, 'Then Willie got himself in a whole new level of trouble. Witnessed a very nasty 187 and got paranoid and told you they were going to pin it on him.'

'Not paranoia,' said Broussard. 'Reasonable apprehensiveness.' He gave a cold smile. 'Black junkie with a felony record versus rich white boys? No one intended to bring Willie to trial. The plan was to float rumors, plant evidence, have Willie OD somewhere, call in an anonymous tip, and close the case.'

'So Willie skipped on Boris, but you paid Boris off.

Then you got Poulsenn assigned to the case, to cover it and control it, and meanwhile he could guard Willie and his girlfriend.'

'That was temporary. We were regrouping, assessing contingencies.'

'None of which included going after the real killers,' said Milo, surprised at the fury in his own voice. 'Maybe Schwinn and I wouldn't have solved it. On the other hand, maybe we *would've* pulled it off. We'll never know, will we? 'Cause you stepped in and sabotaged the whole goddamned thing. And don't tell me that was just because of Willie. Someone put the fix in for those rich kids. Someone you had to listen to.'

Broussard swiveled and faced him. 'You've got it all figured out.'

'I don't. That's why I'm here. Who was the fixer? Walt Obey? Janie was pimped by that piece of shit who called himself her father and used by two generations of rich scrotes, and who's richer than old Walt? Is that what doomed the investigation, John? Kindly, churchgoing Uncle Walt worried about having his nasty habits aired?'

Broussard's ebony face remained still. He stared past Milo. Let out a low, grumbling laugh.

'Happy to entertain, John,' said Milo. His hands were shaking, and he rolled them into fists.

'I'm going to educate you, Detective, about matters you don't understand. I've spent a lot of time in the company of rich folk, and it's true what they say. The rich *are* different. Life's little bumps get smoothed out for them, no one has the temerity to deny them anything. More often than not, their kids become monsters. Malignant entitlement. But there are exceptions, and Mr Obey's one of them. He's exactly what he claims to be:

religious, straightforward, ethical, good father, faithful husband. Mr Obey grew rich through hard work and vision and luck – he'd be the first to emphasize the luck component, because he's also a humble man. So understand this: he had nothing to do with any cover-up. You mention the name Janie Ingalls, and he'll stare at you blankly.'

'Maybe I'll try that,' said Milo.

Broussard's jaw set. 'Stay away from that gentleman.'

'Is that an official order, Chief?'

'It's sound advice, Detective.'

'Then who?' said Milo. 'Who the hell fixed it?'

Broussard ran a finger under his collar. Full sun had brought the sweat out on his brow, and his skin glistened like a desert highway.

'It wasn't like that,' he said finally. 'No one ordered the Ingalls investigation stopped, per se. The directive – and it was a departmental directive, straight from the top, the *very* top – was to effect damage control on Pierce Schwinn's many years of felonious conduct. Because Schwinn was spinning out of control, heavily addicted to amphetamines, taking extreme risks. He was a ticking time bomb, and the department decided to defuse him. You just happened to get the wrong partner. It could've been worse for you. You were spared because you were a rookie and had never been observed participating in Schwinn's transgressions. Except for one instance, when you *were* observed picking up a known prostitute in your on-duty car and chauffering her and Schwinn around. But I chose to overlook that, Detective. I had you transferred to greener pastures rather than drummed out in disgrace.'

'Is this the dramatic moment where I'm supposed to

thank you?' Milo cupped a hand to his ear. 'Where's the goddamn drumroll?'

Broussard's mouth curled downward in disgust. 'Suit yourself and be dense.'

'I didn't need your largesse, John. When I picked that hooker up I had no idea what was going to happen, figured her for an informant.'

Broussard smiled. 'I believe you, Detective. I had a pretty good notion that you wouldn't participate in any backseat calisthenics with a woman.'

Milo's face grew hot.

Broussard said, 'Don't get all indignant on me. I won't pretend to understand what you are, but it doesn't bother me. Life's too short for intolerance. I know what it's like to be on the outside, and I've given up on the whole idea of changing the way people feel. Let bigots feel any way they want to, as long as they don't misbehave.'

'You're a paragon of tolerance.'

'Not tolerance, constructive apathy. I don't care about your amusements – don't care about you, period, as long as you do your job.'

'When doing the job suits your interests,' said Milo.

Broussard didn't reply.

'You're an outsider, huh?' said Milo. 'For an outsider, you scampered up the ladder pretty quickly.'

'Hard work and persistence,' said Broussard, sounding as if he'd recited it a million times before. 'And good luck. Plus a good deal of yassuh-mastah posterior-kissing.' He unbuttoned his collar and loosened his tie. Aiming for casual, just one of the guys. His bearing said otherwise. 'Back when I worked patrol, I used to tape pictures in my locker. Photographs of men I admired. Frederick Douglass, George Washington Carver, Ralph

Bunche. One day I opened my locker and the pictures were ripped to shreds and the walls were decorated with "*Die, Nigger!*" and other genial messages. I pasted every one of those photos together, and if you go into my office today, you'll see them hanging behind my desk.'

'I'll have to take that on faith,' said Milo. 'Don't expect to be invited to your office anytime soon. Unlike that other worthy soul, Craig Bosc. I'm disappointed in you, John. Choosing a lowlife like that to run your errands.'

Broussard worked his lips. 'Craig has his talents. He went too far this time.'

'What was the idiot's assignment? Spook me into focusing on the Ingalls case, the old reverse psychology? Just in case sending Delaware the murder book wasn't enough to kick me in gear?'

'The *idiot's* directive,' said Broussard, 'was to aim you at the case and keep you focused. I thought you'd be interested, but for a while things seemed to be lagging. It *has* been twenty years.'

'So you steal my partner's car, float HIV-retirement rumors, have Bosc hit on me and make sure I get aimed at a POB that directs me to the Larners. Then you trail Dr Delaware and set Coury on his trail. He could've died last night, you manipulative sonofabitch.'

'He didn't,' said Broussard. 'And I don't deal in theoreticals. As I said, Craig grew overzealous. End of story.'

Milo cursed, caught his breath, bent, and caressed the top of Janie's grave. Broussard's shoulders tensed, as if the gesture was insulting.

'You buy a gravestone and think you're absolved, John. This poor little girl molders for two decades, and you've allowed yourself to grow righteous. Schwinn sent you the book, and you made me part of the chain letter via Dr Delaware. Why? It sure wasn't the search for justice.'

The chief's face returned to wooden. Milo visualized him wiping the murder book clean of prints, contemplating the 'contingencies,' finally deciding to forward the death shots to someone sure to pass them along. Using Alex to spook him, throw him off, wanting him to have to fight to regain his bearings, convince himself it was a noble quest.

And if Milo hadn't bitten, Broussard would've found another way. There'd never been any real choice.

'You've got a reputation,' said Broussard. 'As a contrarian. I thought it was wise to harness that.'

He shrugged, and the easy gesture turned Milo feverish. He locked his hands together, struggled not to hit Broussard, finally found his voice. 'Why'd you want the case solved now?'

'Times change.'

'What *changed* were your personal circumstances.' Milo jabbed a finger at the gravestone. 'You never gave a shit about Janie or the truth. Nailing Coury and the others became important because it was in your best interest, and boy, did you succeed. Bunch of dead guys in Ojai, couple more in S.B., the Cossacks bite it in Inglewood, and there's no reason to connect any of them. Now you're free to go about your merry way with Walt Obey's build-a-city game. That's what it's all about, isn't it, John? The old man's money. Fucking Esperanza.'

Broussard stiffened.

'Esperanza, what horseshit,' said Milo. 'It means "hope" and you're hoping it'll make you filthy-rich because you know you're a failure as chief, gonna have to leave the department soon under less-than-amiable circumstances, and Uncle Walt just happened to come up with an offer that'll make your pension seem like chump change. What's the deal, John? Chief of security for an entire city, maybe augmented by some bullshit corporate vice-presidency? Hell, Obey's probably tossing in preferred shares of the project that could shoot you into a whole new fiscal galaxy. Augmenting what he's already gifted to your wife and daughter. Man of color as co-owner of a *city* – ain't old Walt *liberal*. Everything was looking rosy until some nasty competition cropped up. Because Obey's grand scheme includes comprehensive recreational facilities aka finally bringing the NFL back to L.A. The old man pulls that off and Esperanza land values skyrocket and you're lunching at the country club and pretending the stiffs over there like you. But the Cossacks had other ideas. Wanted to rejuvenate the Coliseum, or some other downtown venue. Had Germ Bacilla and Diamond Jim Horne on their side, brought those two clowns to dinner at that stupid restaurant they own, did the whole private-room thing with Uncle Walt. Trying to convince Uncle Walt to cash in his chips and go along with them. Once upon Uncle Walt mighta blown off bullshit like that, but maybe this time he was willing to *listen*. The fact that he showed up at Sangre de Leon and didn't invite *you* says he was open-minded, and that had to spook you, John. Because even though the Cossacks had never pulled off anything close to that scope, this time they'd lined up decent financing and City Council support. And most important, Obey's losing steam. Because he's getting old and his wife's sick – really sick. Ain't that a hoot, John? You've come this far, and it could all come crumbling down.'

Broussard's eyes turned to cracks in asphalt. His lower

jaw jutted forward, and Milo knew the chief was struggling not to hit *him*.

'You don't know what you're talking about, Detective.'

'John,' he said, 'I watched a portable dialysis van pull up early this morning on Muirfield. Mrs O's seriously not well. Old Barbara needs a machine to survive. Hubby's initiative is being sapped.'

Broussard's hand flew to the knot of his tie. He tugged it down farther, stared off into nowhere.

Milo said, 'Obey's owned the land for years, so even with his mortgages he can sell at a huge profit. He woulda tossed you a consolation prize, but basically you'd have been a controversial ex-chief forced out and looking around for a gig. Maybe some drugstore chain would hire you to oversee security.'

Broussard didn't answer.

'All those years of posterior-kissing,' said Milo. 'All that upright behavior.'

'What,' said Broussard, very softly, 'do you want?'

Milo ignored the question. 'You shrug off that twenty-year-old directive to shaft Schwinn as the reason the case got sidelined, but that's crap. Handing Janie's case to Lester Poulsenn was a dodge. An IA spook, like you, what the hell would Poulsenn know about a sex homicide?'

'Les worked homicide. Wilshire Division.'

'For how long?'

'Two years.'

Milo applauded silently. 'A whole twenty-four months chasing gang-bang shootings, and suddenly he's the one-man squad on a nasty 187 like Janie. His main gig was guarding Willie and Caroline in Watts because your family loved Willie.'

553

Broussard said, 'I walked on eggshells with that . . . with Willie. The family always pushed for him. I bought my wife a spanking new Sedan de Ville and she lent it to him. An IA man's car at the scene of a murder.'

A trace of whine had crept into the chief's voice. Suspect's defensiveness. The bastard's discomfort flooded Milo with joy. He said, 'What'd you tell the family when Willie disappeared?'

'That he'd burned up in the house. I wanted to put an end to it.' Broussard cocked his head to the right. Two rows over. 'Far as they're concerned, he's here. We had a quiet family ceremony.'

'Who's in the coffin?'

'I burned papers in my office, put the ashes in an urn and we buried it.'

'I believe you,' said Milo. 'I believe you'd do that.'

'As far as I knew, Willie really was dead. Lester died in that fire and the Russian got ambushed and I knew it all had to do with Willie, so why wouldn't Willie be dead? Then he calls me a week later, sounding half-dead, telling me he's burnt and sick, send him money. I hung up on him. I'd had enough. I figured he'd last, what – a few months? He had a serious addiction.'

'So you made him dead.'

'He did that to himself.'

'No, John, Vance Coury did that to him last night. Sliced him in half with a MAC 10. I buried him with my own hands – hey, if you want, I'll retrieve what's left of him, you can dig up that urn, and we'll make everything right.'

Broussard shook his head, very slowly. 'I thought you were smart, but you're stupid.'

Milo said, 'We're a good team, you and me, John.

Between the two of us, we get everything tied up nice and neat. So who pushed Schwinn off that horse? Did you do it yourself or send a messenger, like old Craig? My guess is a messenger because a black face in Ojai would be conspicuous.'

'No one pushed him. He had an epileptic seizure and fell down a gully. Took the horse with him.'

'You were there?'

'Craig was there.'

'Ah,' said Milo. Thinking: Alex would laugh. If he'd reached the stage where he could laugh.

'Believe what you want,' said Broussard. 'That's what happened.'

'What I believe is Schwinn's sending you the book loosened your bowels. All these years you thought the guy was just a speed-freak burnout, and he turns out to have a long memory. And pictures.'

Broussard's smile was patronizing. 'Think logically: a few moments ago you constructed an elaborate theory about my desire to eliminate competition. If that's true, why would Schwinn's reactivating the Ingalls murder bother me? On the contrary, if the Cossacks could be implicated—'

'Except that Schwinn knew you'd put the original fix in. Once he was out of the way, you figured out a way to make everything work for you. You're nothing if not adaptable, John.'

Broussard sighed. 'Now you're being obstinate. As I told you, the directive was related to Schwinn's—'

'So what, John? If Walt Obey's half as righteous as you claim, he likes you because you've convinced him you're a choirboy. Schwinn comes forward, makes noises, sullies your rep, it's a threat to your executive wet dream. So he had to go, too. It's like bowling, isn't it? Human tenpins. Set 'em up, knock 'em down.'

'No,' said Broussard. 'I sent Craig to talk to Schwinn. To find out exactly what he knew. Why would I kill him? He could've been useful to me. Without him, I turned to you.'

'A seizure.'

Broussard nodded. 'Craig was driving to Schwinn's ranch, saw Schwinn ride his horse out the gates and followed along. There was a – there was contact, and Craig introduced himself and Schwinn got hostile. He'd wanted me to respond personally, not send a delegate. The man was presumptuous. Craig tried to reason with him. To get the facts of the case. Schwinn denied he'd had anything to do with the book, then he started to rave about DNA – finding semen samples, solving everything overnight.'

'Except there were no samples,' said Milo. 'Everything had been destroyed. Schwinn would've loved hearing that.'

'He was irrational, tried to charge Craig on horseback, but the horse wouldn't cooperate. Craig did his best to calm Schwinn down, but Schwinn started to dismount and suddenly his eyes rolled back in his head and he began salivating and convulsing. The horse must've panicked and lost its footing. It tumbled into the gully, Schwinn had one foot caught in the stirrup, got dragged, his head collided with a rock. Craig ran to help him, but it was too late.'

'So Craig left the scene.'

Broussard didn't answer.

'Terrific story,' said Milo. 'Forget building cities, John. Write a screenplay.'

'Maybe I will,' said Broussard. 'One day, when it's no longer raw.'

'When what isn't?'

'The pain. None of this has been easy for me.'

Broussard's left cheek ticked. He sighed. Injured nobility.

Milo hit him.

forty-eight

The blow connected square with the chief's nose and knocked him flat on his rear.

Broussard sat in the dust fronting Janie's grave, blood streaming from his nostrils, striping his Italian shirt, the beautiful golden tie, crimson deepening to rust as it met the pinstripe of his custom-made lapel.

He said, 'It's good I already have a broad nose.'

Smiling. Taking hold of the silk foulard in his breast pocket and wiping away the blood.

Making no attempt to get to his feet.

'You're immature, Detective. That's your problem, always has been. Reducing everything to black and white, the way a child does. Maybe it's tied in with your other problem. Generally arrested development.'

'Maturity's highly overrated,' said Milo. 'Mature people act like you.'

'I survive,' said Broussard. 'My grandfather never learned to read. My father went to college, then to music school, learned classical trombone but couldn't get a job so he worked his whole life as a porter at the Ambassador Hotel. Your problem can be concealed. You were born with unlimited opportunities, so spare me the pious lectures about morality. And don't even think about hitting me again. If you raise your hand to me, I'll shoot you and make up a plausible story to justify it.'

He patted his left hip, revealed the bulge under the pinstripe. Just a few subtle inches afforded by great tailoring.

'You could shoot me anyway,' said Milo. 'Sometime when I'm not expecting it.'

'I could, but I won't,' said Broussard. 'Unless you make it necessary.' He pressed silk to his nose. Blood continued to flow. 'If you act reasonably, I won't even send you the cleaning bill.'

'Meaning?'

'Meaning you've gotten it all out of your system and are prepared to return to work under new circumstances.'

'Such as?'

'We forget about this, you're promoted to lieutenant. Assigned to a division of your choosing.'

'Why would I want to push paper?' said Milo.

'No paper, you'll be a lieutenant detective,' said Broussard. 'Continue to work cases – challenging cases, but you pull a lieutenant's salary, enjoy a lieutenant's prestige.'

'That's not the way it works in the department.'

'I'm still the chief.' Broussard got to his feet, pretended to accidentally spread a flap of his double-breasted jacket, offered a full view of the 9mm nestled in a tooled-leather holster the color of fine brandy.

'You toss me a bone, and I go away,' said Milo.

'Why not?' said Broussard. 'Everything's been done that needs to be done. You solved the case, the bad guys are out of the picture, we all move on. What's the alternative, ruining both our lives? Because the worse you hurt me, the more pain you bring on yourself. I don't care how righteous you think you are, that's the way the world works. Think about Nixon and Clinton and all those other paragons of virtue. They got libraries, and all the people around them went down hard.'

Broussard stepped closer. Milo could smell his citrus aftershave and his sweat and the coppery tang of the blood that had finally begun to dry above his mouth.

'I've kept records,' said Milo. 'A paper trail hidden where even you'll never find it. Something happens to me—'

'Oh, please, look who's talking about screenplays,' said Broussard. 'You want to throw around threats? Think about Dr Silverman. Dr Delaware. Dr Harrison.' Broussard laughed. 'Sounds like a medical convention. You can be damaged beyond your wildest dreams. And to what end? What's the point?'

He flashed a smile. Winner's smile. A cold, damp wave of futility washed over Milo. Sapped; the blow to Broussard's nose had taken more out of him than it had out of its recipient.

Winners and losers – the patterns were probably set in place back in nursery school.

He said, 'What about Bosc?'

'Craig has resigned from the department with substantial compensation, effective one week ago. He'll never go near you – that I can promise you.'

'He does, he's a dead man.'

'He realizes that. He's relocating to another city. Another state.' Broussard wiped away blood, checked his handkerchief, found a clean corner and made sure it showed when he tucked the silk square back in his breast pocket. Buttoning his shirt and knotting his tie, he advanced even closer to Milo.

Breathing slowly, evenly. The bastard had sweet breath, minty-fresh. No more sweat on his ebony face. His nose had started to swell, looked a little off kilter, but nothing you'd notice once he got cleaned up.

'So,' he said.

'Lieutenant,' said Milo.

'Fast-track promotion, Detective Sturgis, once you choose your division. You can take some vacation time or jump right into work. Think of it as mutually constructive adaptation.'

Milo stared into the flat, black eyes. Hating Broussard and admiring him. *O great guru of self-deception, teach me to live as you do . . .*

He said, 'Fuck your promotion. I'll drop everything, but I don't want anything from you.'

'How noble,' said Broussard. 'As if you had a choice.'

He turned and walked away.

Milo remained by the grave, let his eyes wander over Janie's stone. Goddamn teddy bear.

Knowing there was nothing he could do. If he wanted to stay in the department, he'd take the offer and why the hell not, because anyone who mattered was dead and he was tired, so tired, and what *was* the alternative?

Making a choice. Not sure of what it would do to him – to his soul.

Someone else might have convinced himself that was courage.

Someone else wouldn't feel this way.

561

forty-nine

Bert Harrison's call came at 9 A.M. I'd been sleeping and tried to push the fatigue out of my voice, but Bert knew he'd woken me up.

'Sorry, Alex. I'll call back—'

'No,' I said. 'How're you doing?'

'*I'm* fine,' he said. 'Aimee is . . . she'll eventually come to grips with the loss. We'd begun dealing with it, because Bill didn't have long, and I was trying to prepare her. Despite that, of course, the shock was traumatic. For her sake, I'm emphasizing the quickness of it. His feeling no pain.'

'I can back you up on that. It was instantaneous.'

'You saw it . . . you must be—'

'I'm fine, Bert.'

'Alex, I should've been honest with you all along. You deserved better from me.'

'You had your obligations,' I said. 'Patient-doctor confidentiality—'

'No, I—'

'It's all right, Bert.'

He laughed. 'Listen to us, Alex. Alphonse, Gaston, Alphonse Gaston . . . you're really okay, son?'

'I really am.'

562

'Because you bore the brunt of it as I stood by like a—'

'It's over,' I said, firmly.

'Yes,' he said. Several seconds passed. 'I need to tell you this, Alex: you're such a *good* young man. I find myself calling you "son" from time to time, because if I'd . . . oh, this is silly, I just called to see how you were getting on and to let you know we're coping. The human spirit and all that.'

'Indomitable,' I said.

'What's the alternative?'

Milo had come by last night, and we'd talked through sunrise. I'd been thinking a lot about alternatives. 'Thanks for calling, Bert. Let's get together. When things settle down.'

'Yes. Absolutely. We must.'

He sounded old and weak and I wanted to help him, and I said, 'Soon you'll be getting back to your instruments.'

'Pardon – oh, yes, definitely. As a matter of fact, I did get on-line early this morning. Came upon an old Portuguese *gitarra* on eBay that looks intriguing, if it can be restored. Tuned differently than a guitar, but you might be able to get some sound out of it. If I get it at the right price, I'll let you know and you can come up here and we'll make music.'

'Sounds like a plan,' I said. Happy to have any.

fifty

The next few days degraded to a blur of solitude and missed opportunity. I took a long time to muster the energy to call Robin, never found her in.

She didn't call back, not once, and I wondered if we'd descended to a new level.

I tried not to think about Janie Ingalls or any of the others, did a pretty decent job of cutting myself off, knew it was unlikely Allison Gwynn had read about Michael Larner's death in the *Santa Barbara News-Press* and that I should tell her. I couldn't dredge up the initiative for that, either.

I buried myself in housecleaning, yardwork, clumsy jogs, TV hypnosis, obligatory, tasteless meals, perusals of the morning paper – not a word of print about the bloody night in Ojai, the Larners, the Cossacks. Continued sniping at John G. Broussard by politicians and pundits was the only link to what had been my reality since receiving the murder book.

On an uncommonly mild Tuesday, I took an afternoon run and came back to find Robin sitting in the living room.

She had on a black T-shirt, black leather jeans, and the pair of lizard-skin boots I'd given her two birthdays ago.

Her hair was long and loose, and she was made up and lipsticked and looked like a beautiful stranger.

When I went over to kiss her, I kept the bruised side of my face out of view. She offered me her lips but kept them closed. Her hand rested briefly on the back of my neck, then dropped off.

I sat down beside her. 'Tour over early?'

'I took a day off,' she said. 'Flew in from Omaha.'

'How's it going?'

She didn't answer. I took her hand. Her fingers were cool and limp as they brushed against my burnt palm.

'Before we get into anything,' she said, 'I'm going to tell you about Sheridan. He knew to bring a Milk-Bone because he'd met Spike before, has dogs of his own.'

'Robin, I'm—'

'Please, Alex. Just listen.'

I let go of her hand, sat back.

'Sheridan comes on strong,' she said, 'and his job puts him in close proximity to me, so I suppose I can understand your suspicions. But just for the record, he's a born-again Christian, married, has four kids under the age of six. He brings his entire family on tour with him, it's kind of a running joke with the rest of the crew. His wife's name is Bonnie, and she used to be a backup singer before she and Sheridan found religion. Both of them are what you'd expect from new converts: way too joyful, zealous, upright, quoting scripture. It's annoying, but everyone puts up with it because Sheridan's a nice person, and he's about the best tour coordinator in the business. When he does try to influence me it's in the form of not-so-subtle little asides about accepting Christ into my life, not sleazy little ploys to get in my pants. And yes, I know religious observance doesn't necessarily prevent bad behavior, but this guy means it. He's never come within a mile of anything remotely sexual. Most of the time when he's in my room, Bonnie's right there with him.'

'I'm sorry,' I said.

'I wasn't after an apology, Alex. I just wanted to tell you in person. So you wouldn't torture yourself.'

'Thank you.'

'What happened to your hand and your face?'

'Long story.'

'The same story,' she said.

'I suppose.'

'That's the other thing. The other reason I came by. Our situation. It's not simple, is it?'

'I missed you,' I said.

'I missed you, too. Still do. But . . .'

'There has to be a "but." '

'Don't be angry.'

'I'm not. I'm sad.'

'I am, too. If I didn't care about you, I'd have spared myself seeing you. Still, I'm not staying, Alex. A car is coming by to take me back to the airport and I'm rejoining the tour and remaining till the end. Which may stretch longer. We've been doing great, raising a bundle for the cause. There's been talk of a European extension.'

'Paris?' I said.

She began to cry.

I would've liked to join in, but there was no juice left in me.

We held hands for the rest of the hour, not moving from the couch except for the time when I got her a wad of tissues to wipe her eyes.

When the taxi arrived, she said, 'This isn't over. Let's see how it plays out.'

'Sure.'

I walked her to the door, stood on the terrace, and waved.

Three days later, I phoned Allison Gwynn's office and told her about Larner.

She said, 'Oh, my – it's going to take me some time to integrate this . . . I'm glad you told me. It was good of you to tell me.'

'I thought I should.'

'Are *you* okay?'

'I'm fine.'

'If *you* ever need someone to talk to . . .'

'I'll bear that in mind.'

'Do that,' she said. 'I mean it.'

Flesh and Blood

Jonathan Kellerman

Sometimes home is the last place you want to go . . .

When Alex Delaware first sees Lauren Teague she is a sullen teenager with all the usual problems; bad grades at school, moody, uncommunicative with her parents – which is why they think she needs to see a psychologist. But after only a few sessions, as Alex begins to gain her trust, Lauren abruptly terminates her therapy.

Years later, Lauren's mother is pleading for help once again. Lauren has vanished – and she thinks Alex can find her. He reluctantly agrees to try, but as he starts to investigate Lauren's troubled past he is drawn into the shadowy worlds of fringe psychological experimentation and LA's seedy sex industry. Sensing that Lauren's dark family secrets may hold the key to her disappearance, Alex disregards the advice of his trusted friend, LAPD detective Milo Sturgis, not to get involved. And as his quest for the truth becomes an obsession, he is prepared to risk his relationship with long-time lover Robin Castagna, and even puts his own life at risk . . .

Jonathan Kellerman's LA is evil, seductive, erotic and unforgiving, and FLESH AND BLOOD, with its ingenious plot, unforgettable characters and terrifying climax, is suspense fiction at its finest:

'Kellerman's speciality is getting quietly but persistently inside his hero's head . . . This is thoughtful and intelligent stuff, a sparse, precision-paced professional thriller that is slick, quick and a pleasure to read' *Mirror*

'An alert eye for detail . . . Engrossing' *New York Times*

'A very clever mystery with a whammy of a finale' *The Scotsman*

0 7472 6500 3

headline

The Forgotten

Faye Kellerman

When the past comes back . . .

A place of worship is vandalised, daubed swastikas testifying to a hatred that, for a time at least, defies understanding.

But the Deckers, Rina and her detective husband Peter, soon realise the violence done to their synagogue can be traced to one deeply disturbed adolescent, Ernesto Golding. Born into privilege but obsessed by the past, he is eventually charged, his case closed. But Peter Decker still worries that others were involved. And six months later Ernesto is found murdered.

Suddenly Decker and his family are plunged into a ghastly world, of damaged youth, ruthless parents, and of secrets, their roots in the horrors of the last generation, that seem to demand ultimate retribution . . .

Praise for Faye Kellerman

'Seamlessly weaves themes of religious belief and familial respect into a multilayered thriller . . . finely realized' *Publishers Weekly*

'Irresistibly plotted' *Financial Times*

'The most gripping of recent crime fiction' *Sunday Telegraph*

'Very exciting' *Mail on Sunday*

0 7472 5924 0

headline

You can buy any of these bestselling novels by **Jonathan** and **Faye Kellerman** from your bookshop or *direct from the publisher*.